Praise for *Th*

'An engaging sto   rs, sacrifi
                    und

I loved every minute of *The Return* – a truly won
novel, so beautifully written and with an engrossing plot'
Jill Mansell, bestselling author of *Should I Tell You?*

'Draws you in with a deeply held secret so
that just when you think it should all be over, it's
really just beginning – an enticing slant on wartime life'
Mandy Robotham, bestselling author of *The Resistance Girl*

'Set during WWII, Anita Frank weaves a beautiful and
poignant love story that tugged at my heartstrings'
Jenny Quintana, author of *The Hiding Place*

'An engrossing story of loss, betrayal and love on the farming home
front during WWII ... that immerses the reader in the struggles of
women in wartime and the traumas of the men who returned'
Carolyn Kirby, author of *The Conviction of Cora Burns*

'Beautiful, atmospheric writing and masterful storytelling'
Jenny Ashcroft, author of *Under The Golden Sun*

'A more modern take on *Far from the Madding Crowd*'
Historical Novel Society, Editors' Choice

'Utterly gripping. It wrapped me in its spell
from the first page to the last'
Iona Grey, author of *The Glittering Hour*

'A beautiful tale of love, loss and survival'
Fíona Scarlett, author of *Boys Don't Cry*

'A gripping, achingly romantic wartime drama'
Samantha King, author of *The Secret Keeper's Daughter*

Anita Frank was born in Shropshire and studied English and American History at the University of East Anglia. She lives in Berkshire with her husband and three children and is now a full-time carer for her disabled son. Her debut novel *The Lost Ones* was shortlisted for the Goldsboro Books Glass Bell Award and the Historical Writers' Association Debut Crown Award. *The Return* is her second novel.

Also by Anita Frank

The Lost Ones

The Return

Anita Frank

ONE PLACE. MANY STORIES

HQ
An imprint of HarperCollins*Publishers* Ltd
1 London Bridge Street
London SE1 9GF

www.harpercollins.co.uk

HarperCollins*Publishers*
1st Floor, Watermarque Building, Ringsend Road
Dublin 4, Ireland

This paperback edition 2022

1
First published in Great Britain by
HQ, an imprint of HarperCollins*Publishers* Ltd 2021

Copyright © Anita Frank 2021

Anita Frank asserts the moral right to be identified
as the author of this work. A catalogue record for this
book is available from the British Library.

ISBN: 9780008341299

For Mum and Dad

With all my love

PART ONE

CHAPTER ONE

Gwen

8th May 1945

It is Tom who hears them first.

She has been watching him run up and down the grassy margins at the edge of the field, his arms flung wide, the tops of his wellies flapping against his skinny calves. Although she cannot hear over the deafening putter of the tractor, she can easily imagine the nasal drone he is making as he swoops and dives, mimicking the Spitfires that sometimes fly over the farm.

She eases down the left-hand brake as she approaches the end of the row. As she feeds the steering wheel through her hands, bouncing on the Fordson's scooped steel seat, she notices him pull up. He stands rigid, his narrow chest rising and falling, his blond head cocked to one side, a shallow furrow in his brow.

Bringing the vehicle about, she twists around to check on Nora who is standing on the running board of the seed drill being pulled behind. The Land Girl sweeps her hand through the heaped grain in the trough before her, then lifts her head and grins. She offers Gwen a thumbs up, reassurance that the seed is falling evenly. Gwen nods in acknowledgement and allows her gaze to stray back to her son, who remains stationary by the hedgerow. Dark fumes belch from the exhaust stack as she lightly presses her foot to the throttle.

From the corner of her eye, she sees Tom turn. He starts to run across the harrowed soil, waving his arms, shouting, though she is unable to make out his words. Struck by a sense of unease, she slows the tractor until it chugs to a standstill, its coarse engine idling. Behind her, Nora raises a hand to shield her eyes from the sun, as she too begins to track the boy's advance.

At last, he reaches them, breathless and excited. He keeps back, wary of the tractor, warned of its dangers from an early age. 'Mummy!' he shouts over the grumbling motor. 'What is it? What's that noise?'

Gwen frowns. The Fordson is drowning out all other sounds. She is reluctant to pull the switch and kill the engine, knowing what a pig it will be to crank up again, but she has little choice. The tractor falls silent, the engine clicking as it cools.

There is barely a breath of wind. In the woods behind, crows complain like old men with tobacco-tempered voices. And then she hears it.

The sound rolls faintly up the valley. Nora's hand flies to her mouth. Gwen's heart stutters.

'What is it, Mummy?'

Nora jumps down from the seed drill. She stares over the fields to the village in the distance, the source of the celebratory clamour.

'Mummy?' Tom whines, fidgeting from foot to foot.

'Bells, Tom,' Gwen says at last. She clears her throat which is strangely tight. 'The bells . . . in the church. Church bells.'

She climbs down from the tractor and walks over to where

Nora and Tom now stand side by side. The church steeple is just visible above the folds of land below them. They listen to the pealing bells, awed into silence by the joyous sound.

'I've never heard church bells before,' Tom chirps up at last.

'No . . . no you won't have.' Gwen's hand strays to smooth his hair.

'It's over . . .' Nora spins towards them, her features illuminated by her exploding smile. 'Bloody hell, Gwen, that's it! They've done it! It's over!' She throws back her head and whoops, her shout echoing across the field. The crows erupt from the woods behind them, flapping skywards, past the ghostly half-moon that still graces the clear morning sky.

'Tommy boy! The war is over!' Nora grabs Tom under his armpits. Screeching, she whirls him round and around until he is flying like one of his beloved Spitfires. He giggles with delight, a smile splitting his cheeks, but it fails to mask the hint of uncertainty that lurks behind it.

Gwen does not engage with their joyful exuberance. Instead, she drifts forward, the significance of the tumbling bells weighing heavily on her thoughts.

The war is over.

'Oh, Gwen!'

She gasps as Nora wraps her in an unexpected embrace, rocking her from side to side and squeezing her so tightly she can barely breathe. Released, she stumbles.

'Our boys will be coming home at last!' Nora cries. She whips back to Tom. 'Tom, your daddy is coming home!'

Tom jumps up and down, matching Nora's ecstatic cheers with his own, but Gwen can tell he doesn't fully understand. How can he? Nora is fuelling his excitement for a man he has

5

never met, a man who, for him, fails to exist beyond the grey-and-white photograph that sits on the mantelpiece at home. How can he possibly comprehend his father's return?

And she alone knows he has no need to, because Jack Ellison won't be coming home.

He promised her.

He promised her faithfully he wouldn't.

CHAPTER TWO

Jack

June 1939

'Jack.'

The sudden weight of a hand on his shoulder startles Jack awake. His eyes flare as he recoils from the touch, his arm rising defensively, his boots scrabbling against the rough boards beneath him. He flails like an upturned beetle struggling to right itself.

'Easy, lad, easy, you're all right, now. You're safe.'

The familiar voice penetrates Jack's blind panic. The tightness in his chest eases and the blood coursing through his veins slows to a placid flow as his ragged breaths taper. He blinks. Striations of sunlight score his vision like lines in an exercise book. His fragmented memory pulls together until he is at last able to fix himself in time and place. Pain races up his stiff limbs as he shifts himself upright, his legs bent before him. He winces, licking his chapped lips.

'Ben,' he says at last, acknowledging the grinning face of the man squatting before him.

'Aye, you daft beggar. Wakey, wakey, rise and shine.'

'Jesus, but I hurt,' he groans, stretching his cramped limbs.

'Aye, well, it can't be said that a coal wagon is the most deluxe of travelling compartments . . . but it is the most discreet.' Ben bobs up to standing. His white collarless shirt is grubby and covered with smuts, while his trousers are as black as the coal he has spent the night shovelling into the train's furnace.

'And for that I'm grateful,' Jack says, taking the hand offered him. He winces again as he is hauled to his feet. He tightens his grip. 'For that I will always be grateful.'

Ben's boyish grin fades. He nods, grave now. Jack releases him and, keen to alleviate their solemnity, he runs his palm over his stubbled jaw.

'Do I look like shite?'

Ben snorts. 'Jesus, man, you always look like shite.'

Jack smiles in spite of himself. As he lowers his hand, he catches sight of his swollen knuckles, red raw and ingrained now with the coal dust that coats the wagon's floorboards and floats in the air around them, sparkling like black diamonds in the slanting beams of sunlight. He spots something else. His stomach clenches at the sight of a rusty blemish.

With trembling hands, he unties his neckerchief and pulls it free. He spits on its edge, then works at the coppery speckles until his skin is clean though bruised. When he finally stops, he realises Ben is studying him. Heat floods his cheeks as he stuffs the neckerchief into his trouser pocket.

'What are you going to do, Jack?'

The quiet question unsettles him. He draws his hand over his mouth and turns towards the slumped heap of coal that occupies the end of the wagon.

'I don't know.'

'Well this is the end of the line, I'm afraid. We've just

pulled onto a siding to let an express pass, but we'll be heading back up north as soon as it clears. You'd best get off here, while you can.'

'Right.' Gathering himself, he leans down to pick up his jacket, folded into a paltry pillow. Ben crosses to the wagon's broad door. It shunts stiffly on its runners as he opens it just enough for Jack to slip through.

'Where are we? Do you know?' Jack asks, shrugging on his coat before reaching for the small knapsack hastily packed the night before.

'Berkshire somewhere.' Ben peers out into the brightening light of the new day. 'As far away from home as I could get you.' He shoves his hands into his pockets and leans on the doorframe.

'Berkshire. A bit different to Tyneside then.'

Jack crosses the floor to stand shoulder to shoulder with his friend. They grin at each other, pretending this is little more than a merry jaunt, a boys' own adventure. He looks out at the grass-banked siding, studded with poppies and clumps of towering foxglove. His fingers wrap around the edge of the door, but he makes no move to leave. A surge of fear holds him in place. He wants nothing more than to anchor himself to Ben and be tethered to his unstinting loyalty. But he knows he cannot. He knows he must leave, yet he continues to linger in the warmth of his friend's mournful smile.

They both start as a train's whistle screams through the still morning air. The carriage shudders as the express whips past, the noise so great neither of them attempts to speak. The tracks rattle, then sing in its wake. Ben nudges him with his shoulder, his voice gentle with regret.

'You must go now, Jack. While you can, lad.'

'Aye.' Jack holds out his hand and when Ben grips it, he places his other hand on top.

'You've been a friend when I needed one, Ben. I won't forget it.'

He jumps down from the wagon, landing both feet on the ballast. He straightens his legs and brushes off the coal dust clinging to his trousers.

'Are you sure you're doing the right thing now, Jack?'

Jack stifles a bitter laugh. 'How am I supposed to answer that?' The stones crump as he grinds them under the scuffed toe of his boot, summoning the courage to look up. 'I don't know what else to do, Ben.'

Ben nods, then releases a resigned sigh.

'Your mam . . .'

Jack snorts. 'Won't even notice I've gone . . . at least not until rent's due or she needs money for booze. She probably won't even notice Jenny . . .' He shakes his head as his voice fails him. His next words escape as little more than a whisper. 'I can't go back, Ben . . . I can't risk it.'

'Aye . . . I reckon you're right . . .'

'I never meant . . .'

'No one can blame you, lad.'

Jack says nothing. Guilt tightens his throat like a drawstring purse. He merely nods to cover his mounting grief and adjusts the weight of the knapsack on his shoulder.

With a groan and a shriek, the train shunts forwards. Ben braces himself in the doorway.

'We're off,' he calls out.

Jack backs away.

'Take care of yourself, Jack,' Ben calls again, rocking to the train's building movement. 'Try and let me know how you're getting on.' The wheels protest as they grate against the tracks. Ben raises his voice again. 'Be sure to look me up when you get back, you hear?'

Jack raises his hand. He watches as Ben recedes into the distance. Only when he is out of sight does he allow his chin to sink to his chest. He turns and picks his way across the shingle.

They both know he won't be going back.

CHAPTER THREE

Gwen

8th May 1945

They all ride the Fordson back when it is time to get the cows in for milking. Tom sits astride Gwen's lap, his hands resting on the steering wheel, giggling as the engine's vibrations shudder through his small frame, while Nora clings on the back. Gwen can just about hear her high-pitched singing above the steady throb of the tractor.

She slows as they reach the field with the herd in. The cows have already gathered at the gate, eager to be relieved of their swollen udders. Nora waits until the tractor comes to a standstill before jumping down.

'See you back at the farm!' she hollers, returning Tom's salute. Gwen shifts the tractor's gear stick and rolls the vehicle forward as Nora undoes the gate.

Back in the farmyard, Gwen kills the engine and sets the handbrake as Tom scrambles from her lap and calls for Kip. A sheepdog appears from the open-fronted implement shed and races towards them, its bushy tail beating time as Tom collapses to his knees to welcome the ebullient creature into his embrace, squealing in delighted protest as it laps his face. She pauses for a moment to watch them, fondness softening features she fears have become stern before their time. Calling for the boy to come, she carries on across the yard, but the shrill *tring* of a bicycle bell stays her progress. A woman with pewter-coloured hair cycles in past the five-bar gate that sags open from the lane.

'Did you hear?' she asks as she stops just short of Gwen, planting her sturdy lace-up shoes in a manner that hints at a no-nonsense demeanour.

'The bells . . . I heard the bells,' Gwen says.

'It's over. Thank God. In Europe at least.' The bike chain ticks between them as they walk together towards the shallow steps that rise from the yard to the path running along the back of the house. 'They say Japan won't last long now.'

Gwen nods, then calls Tom again. The older woman rests the bicycle against the retaining wall, before removing a bundled apron from the wicker basket on its front. She opens it up with care.

'Look, spotted these on my way here. I'll make some soup if you can spare me a drop of cream for it.'

Gwen grins at the welcome sight of fieldcap mushrooms nestled in the scoop of cotton. 'Well, I won't tell if you don't, Muriel.'

'Let's just hope the end of the war means the end of rationing too,' Muriel mutters, bundling up the fruits of her foraging. 'Where's Nora?'

'Bringing in the cattle,' Gwen says, leading the way up the steps.

'I bet she's pleased. She'll be released from service, I suppose.'

'Not immediately, I wouldn't have thought. The country still needs feeding, and I can't manage without her.'

'No . . . I'm sure she'll have to stay for a while yet,' the woman concedes, though she doesn't look best pleased by the prospect.

As they reach the back door, Gwen calls again for Tom. Her voice contains a warning note this time that brings him to his feet.

'Gwen . . .' Muriel's sudden gravitas causes Gwen to pause, her hand resting on the latch. 'Have you heard from Jack?'

'No.'

'But you haven't heard anything to suggest . . .'

'No.' This time the word comes wearily, battle-worn and fearful.

'Gwen . . . what are you going to do?'

'Nothing.'

'But . . .'

'I'm going to do nothing, Muriel, because there is nothing to be done. Jack won't be coming back.' She opens the door into the farmhouse kitchen.

Muriel huffs, her grey brows pitching upwards. 'Certain of that, are you?' She brushes past Gwen to deposit the parcel of mushrooms on the table. 'Because I'll tell you now . . . I'm not.'

'He won't come back, Muriel.'

The old woman turns to face her.

'Perhaps he won't, but tell me this: what are you going to do if he does?'

CHAPTER FOUR

Jack

June 1939

He walks on in the burgeoning morning light, a foreigner in a strange land. He is used to gunmetal seas stretching, ever restless, to the horizon, not the patchwork of fields that peacefully flow before him now.

Even the air is different, he notes. It is light, pure, trailing scents of flowers and grass rather than the smog and miasma of poverty that his lungs have become hardened to over the years. The scream of factory whistles has been replaced with trilling bird song, while the lowing of cows in the meadow supplants the bellow of a ship's horn. The unaffected sounds serve to lift his leaden spirits as he tramps on.

Before long, his hunger begins to bite. He swings the knapsack off his shoulder and places it on the road before him so he can rifle through its meagre contents – a change of shirt, folded trousers, spare socks and pants. More precious is his leather roll of woodworking tools, his collection of fine chisels and bevelled gouges. In truth, it was the first thing he grabbed; the only item he could not leave behind.

Tucked into the bottom corner, he finds the apple he purloined from the basin on the drainer as he fled through the back door. He puts the knapsack back together and rises from his haunches before shouldering it once again. As he starts to walk, he sinks his teeth into the apple's crisp flesh. His mouth fizzes under its sting – a cooking apple, he realises immediately. Its sourness makes him flinch, but he is parched and therefore grateful for its harsh juice. He eats it down to the core.

He has no idea where he is or where he is going. He left his home with no other thought than to run – to flee while he still could. It seemed a good enough plan at the time. As he draws in a deep lungful of air, he reminds himself it is still a good plan. He knows all too well what would have happened if he had stayed; what would happen if he ever went back.

He finds himself on the outskirts of a village almost before he realises it. The fields give way to banked verdant verges bearing a plumage of bracken and topped with trees. Through laden canopies that whisper at his arrival, he spies glimpses of red brick and grey flint. The lane he is on tunnels downwards and, as he rounds the corner, the village blooms before him, houses spreading down into the broad-bottomed valley before rising up to populate the foothills in the distance. His pulse quickens.

It is still early and for the most part all is quiet. An upstairs window in a quaint terraced row rises on its sash as he walks past. The noise catches his attention and he notices a shadow fall back from the windowpane. Somewhere, a dog begins to bark, another soon joining it. He shifts his knapsack to his other shoulder and walks on, ignoring the grit biting through the worn soles of his boots.

The lane winds its way further into the village. A humped

bridge takes him across a single-gauge train track and along it he sees a small station, its solitary platform deserted. He carries on and soon a row of shops appears, flanking the road: a butcher's with its blinds drawn low and the canopy rolled back against its red-brick wall; a drapery with a handwritten advert for dressmaking lessons for 2/6d a week displayed in its window; a sweetshop; a hardware store; a greengrocer's and general provision.

Soon the main street curves around a grey stone church surrounded by a neatly kept graveyard that sides onto a meadow. Beyond it he discovers two more shops: a tobacconist, and a bakery that exudes the delicious smell of warm bread, though it has yet to open. His stomach gripes, but he walks on.

A pub with a heavy thatched roof and a pretty garden appears where the village gives way to the incline of the hill. The black-glossed door of its public bar is firmly shut, but Jack can almost taste the bitterness of hops. As he pauses to catch his breath, he looks up at the hill that awaits him, before turning back to view the tranquil scene below.

The village might look idyllic, but to him it lacks the familiarity of home, and he struggles to see any raw beauty beneath its primly kept exterior. He misses the cacophony of early morning Newcastle, the ding-ding of the trams, the clanking of cranes in the shipyards, the clatter of train wagons laden with coal. But most of all he misses the magnificence of giant hulls looming above the terraced streets, like Gulliver's ship arriving in Lilliput, bringing the promise of adventure and riches.

For the first time, he begins to question the wisdom of his decision to run. In the murky streets of his hometown, there was always somewhere to hide. He could merge with the shadows, blend with the crowds. As he looks down on the sleepy streets before him, all quiet and pristine, he realises how conspicuous he is – a noteworthy outsider – and as such, he is vulnerable and exposed.

A tabby cat sneaks out from a gap in the pub's garden wall and begins to slink across the lane. It stops, regards him dismissively, then carries on its way, disappearing into the long grass opposite. The cat has told him all he needs to know. There is no refuge to be found in such a place as this. He adjusts his knapsack which is beginning to chafe and starts to climb the hill.

The muscles in his legs are straining by the time he reaches the brow. The sun has shrugged off its modest shift of gauzy clouds and shines brightly now and Jack is beginning to sweat. He removes his jacket and slings it over his shoulder. As the vista opens, he is relieved to see the sprawl of a large town in the distance, a dark blot on the picturesque landscape. His unguided steps, it would seem, have not been in vain – he is heading the right way for obscurity. He finds he walks a little quicker as he tackles the winding road before him.

He hears the ring of hooves before he sees any evidence of a horse. Slowing his pace, he watches the approaching bend expectantly, the clipped sound growing louder and louder. Sure enough, the animal appears – a chestnut beauty, its short coat gleaming like a freshly hatched conker. The horse tosses its head at the sight of him, the metal bit jangling in its mouth, its dark eyes rolling with suspicion.

'Easy, Arthur,' the young woman on its back chides, leaning forward to reassure the capricious creature with a pat on its neck. She smiles down at Jack. 'Morning.'

Jack mumbles his reply. The young woman's jodhpur-clad

legs curve round the horse's sides and he sees her knee-high riding boots are splattered with dried mud. He backs into the verge, allowing her to pass. The horse's undulating rear disappears around the bend in the road, but the phantom echo of its hooves lingers.

He steps back into the lane, the corner of his mouth tugging upwards, though he is unable to say why.

The drone of a motor vehicle is faint at first, but as it draws closer, he detects the whine of a flogged engine and the sharp grating of crunched gears. A Bedford delivery van painted cardinal red hurtles around the corner towards him. Jack stumbles back into the blackthorn hedge, its barbs biting through his shirt, as the van races past him at such speed he is buffeted by its downdraught. He shouts in anger as he scrambles to his feet, but it has already disappeared, leaving him to choke on the cloud of purple fumes that trails in its wake.

In the next moment, he hears the screech of brakes.

A horse begins to scream.

CHAPTER FIVE

Gwen

8th May 1945

'We should go to the pub this evening.'

Gwen makes no attempt to respond to Nora's comment. She sits on the squat milking stool, her shoulders hunched, and gently grasps the cow's teats. Her hands begin to move rhythmically, up and down; jets of warm milk squirt into the empty pail before her.

'It's a momentous day, Gwen . . .' Nora perseveres, appearing at the rear of the cow, a half-full pail in her hand. 'Come on . . . we can't miss it. Let's go to the pub. I bet the whole village will be there.'

Gwen shakes her head. 'Tom . . .'

'Will be fine.' Nora rests her hand on the cow's dun-coloured rump. 'One late night isn't going to hurt. He'll remember this day for the rest of his life.'

'I don't know . . .'

'Even Muriel's going . . .'

Gwen closes her eyes. She has no desire to join in the celebrations. She is quite content to remain at the farm with a hot cocoa, listening to the wireless. She wants to avoid her neighbours, not join them. The teats fall dry under her gentle ministrations.

'You go . . .' she says, arching her back to ease the ache in her shoulders.

'I want you to come with me. You never get out and you'll regret missing this, I know you will.' Gwen knows full well she will have no such regrets and Nora clearly sees that conviction housed in her expression, for she hastily adds, 'Today is history in the making. You owe Tom the opportunity of this experience if nothing else.'

Gwen lets out a gusty sigh. Nora knows full well she would sacrifice anything for Tom, and it *is* impossible to ignore the importance of the day. His entire life has been lived in war. Today he has at least a partial taste of peace.

'All right.' Her concession rings hollow off the brick walls of the milking parlour. She smooths her palm over the cow's flank as she rises, stooping to pick up the pail, the weight of it pulling her arm. 'I'll come. But I can't promise I'll stay long. As soon as Tom—'

Nora cuts her off with a squeal. 'Say no more! We'll have some fun tonight, Mrs Ellison!' She dances up the aisle to the scales hanging on the wall. Hooking up the pail, she gathers up the pencil that swings from a grubby length of string attached to the open ledger on the neighbouring shelf. When the scale needle settles, she licks the lead and records the result. 'I promise you we'll make it a night to remember,' she continues, lifting the pail clear and turning to upend it into the cooler behind her. 'Mr Hitler is kaput, and we are out of the woods at last!'

Gwen forces a smile as she takes her place at the scales. How can she possibly explain to Nora that peace now threatens everything she has held dear for the past six years?

War hasn't endangered Gwen. War has kept her safe.

CHAPTER SIX

Jack

June 1939

Jack shucks off his knapsack and starts running.

The thin soles of his boots hammer down on the tarmacadam as his arms pump at his side. The horse's screams are accompanied by a tattoo of panicked hooves. He skims the bend at full pelt and skids to a stop.

The rider is on the ground, but her one boot remains trapped in its stirrup and her frantic mount is dragging her across the lane. She begs it to stand still, her voice shaking with fear and pain as she strains to free herself. Startled by Jack's sudden appearance, the horse throws back its head and whinnies in alarm. Its eyes roll until all Jack can see are its bloodshot whites as it wheels around, reins swinging loose on its barrel chest. The girl cries out as she is flung back against the road.

'Easy, chap, easy . . .' Jack's tone is soothing as he opens his arms, trying to envelop the horse in his aura of calm. He takes a tentative step forward, issuing gentle reassurances to the terrified creature. 'Keep still now, miss. I've nearly got him.'

'I'm not going anywhere,' she assures him through clenched teeth.

The horse stamps and snorts and backs away. Jack inches closer until finally he is able to grab the loose rein and though the horse throws back its head, he manages to slip his fingers under the bridle and steady him at last.

'Here now, let me help,' he says, holding the horse fast while reaching for the stirrup leather. With a groan, the girl finally succeeds in freeing her boot. It thuds onto the ground. She lies back in the dirt, breathing hard.

'Thank you.' She props herself up on her elbows, wincing.

'Are you hurt? I mean, stupid question, but . . .'

'I'm all right, I think. It could have been a lot worse. Bloody van!'

'Aye, he nearly knocked us flying and all.'

She is pale, deathly so. The glitter he witnessed earlier in her eyes has vanished like fairy dust. Now they are leaden and dull.

'Here, let me help you up . . .' He releases the bridle, but as he moves towards her the horse skittishly sidesteps, its hooves coming too close to the stricken rider for comfort. Jack goes for the reins, but the horse lunges at him with bared teeth and as he recoils it bolts, cantering down the road, the empty stirrups jiggling against its flanks as it disappears around the corner. The girl calls after him, but her voice breaks and fades with the horse's ringing hooves.

'Miss?' Jack drops into a crouch beside her. 'Miss?'

'Just . . . a minute . . .' She squeezes her eyes shut and pants in sharp bursts, battling against the pain. A bruise is already forming on the side of her face.

'I should go and get some help,' Jack says.

'Don't worry . . . it's not my first tumble.' She manages to sit up, emitting little gasps as she moves.

'Steady now,' Jack says.

'Can you help me stand?'

'Aye . . .'

He is acutely aware the hand he offers her is ingrained with filth, coal dust and worse, but he notices the hand she gives him is also far from perfect. Her fingernails are bitten short and he feels the scratch of callouses against his palm. As he rises from his haunches, he brings her with him, slowly, with care, until they are both on their feet. She lets out an involuntary cry.

'What is it?'

'My foot . . .' But it is down the lane that she looks. 'I must find Arthur.' She tries again to take her weight, but her ankle buckles. She clamps down on her cry, as if ashamed to be making a fuss.

'Miss, you can't go wandering around the countryside on that. We need to get you seen to.'

The colour is leaching out of her and Jack is unable to stifle his concern.

'I'll go home. I only live a short distance.'

'Let me help you.'

'No, really, I'll be fine . . . I've troubled you enough . . .' She casts another anxious glance in the direction of the departed horse. 'I shouldn't even be here . . .' she says miserably, looking away.

'Miss, you won't get far without some help. It's no bother.'

Her reluctance is evident, but in the end she relents. A single tear spills down her cheek as she tries to manoeuvre herself round, but she quickly wipes it away and Jack passes no comment. She takes his offered arm and begins to hop beside him, but it is soon evident he is providing insufficient support.

'Here, let me . . .' he hesitates, conscious of not offending or frightening her in any way. 'Three-legged race, like,' his lips quirk, 'you can lean on me properly then. You need to avoid putting pressure on that foot.'

She cautiously considers his proposal. 'All right,' she concedes at last. 'Yes, thank you.' He feels her tense as he slips his arm behind her waist, but a moment later she rests her arm across his shoulders.

'I live just ten minutes or so . . .' she gestures vaguely in the direction he had been going before the van appeared.

'Right. You ready?'

They move awkwardly at first. She grits her teeth and tries not to rely on him, but as her lips twitch with pain her reticence begins to slip until finally, through necessity, she loads him with her weight. They proceed more easily then, a synchronicity to their movements, and suddenly Jack is transported back to the Gateshead Fair and Jenny, doubled over, binding their ankles while he protests, giggling wildly as he tries to down his luke-warm beer before the race begins. Unexpected emotion clogs his throat. He lifts his face into the breeze and it stings his eyes. He pushes all thoughts of Jenny away and his molten heart becomes steel once again.

'This is very kind of you,' she manages after a while.

'Nee bother, miss.'

'Gwen.' She glances his way. 'My name is Gwen.'

'Jack.'

'Not from round here, Jack?'

A smile darts across his face, but quickly fades. 'Nee, lass.'

He fears she is about to ask him more, but as the road dips away from them, she lets out a cry of relief.

'There, there it is! Not far now.'

Just before them, set back from the lane, is a white rendered farmhouse, a yard to its side bordered by buildings, with fenced meadows beyond that back onto woodland.

By the time they reach the gateway, he is practically carrying her. She whimpers with every step.

A dog appears from the open-fronted building on the left, prick-eared and sharp-eyed. It races towards them, head low, its tail beating from side to side.

'All right, Kip,' Gwen mutters as it begins to dance around them, barking.

A man emerges from the same building, rubbing his oil-slickened hands on a piece of rag. His face flares with concern.

'Gwen?' He tosses the rag to one side.

Jack notices Gwen's breathing has become shallow. With inordinate effort, she steps clear of his grasp to address the man now running towards them.

'I got thrown, Dad,' she murmurs. Her lips turn the colour of chalk.

Jack catches her as she falls.

CHAPTER SEVEN

Jack

June 1939

'Into the house with her!'

The man Jack now knows to be Gwen's father runs before him, hastening up the steps from the yard to the back of the house, shouting, '*Muriel*,' before berating the dog that spins around his ankles, barking with excitement. Jack follows in his wake, Gwen's head lolling lifelessly against his shoulder. She is light in his arms and he realises she is little more than a scrap of a girl; he doubts she is yet twenty.

'Where the hell did it happen?'

'Just up the lane a bit, in the bends . . .'

'What the devil was she doing up there?'

The farmer's face creases with confusion, but he instantly dismisses the rhetorical question and urges Jack to hurry while quickening his own pace. By the time Jack reaches the top step, he has disappeared into the house. The back door hangs open and Jack turns his body to angle both himself and Gwen through its frame. He blinks, adjusting to the gloom of the kitchen he has entered, its low ceiling striped with tar-blackened beams that dispel the morning light.

He pauses, unsure where to go. The dog whines at him from the rush mat on the threshold. Faint voices carry back from the front of the house, their rapid modulation betraying increasing anxiety. Jack bounces Gwen into a more secure grip then advances towards them. Mounting the step into the doorway before him, he finds himself in a long narrow strip of hall beside a staircase.

'Hallo?' he calls. Gwen stirs in his arms.

The farmer and a middle-aged woman emerge from a doorway to the right, where the hall broadens out at the foot of the stairs. The woman clutches a duster, which she shoves into the front pocket of her floral housecoat, visibly paling at the sight before her. She pushes past the farmer.

'Can you manage her upstairs?'

'Just show me where,' Jack says.

'Shall I go for the doctor, Muriel?'

'Let's have a look at her first, Jim. No point fetching him if she's only fainted. Can you hear me, Gwen, love? This way,' she says to Jack, starting up the stairs. 'Did she hit her head?'

'I don't know.' Jack treads carefully in her wake, ensuring his balance with each step, aware the girl's father is following close behind. 'She'd fallen by the time I got to her, but her foot was caught in the stirrup. She was awake, like, but getting dragged about a bit by the horse. It was a delivery van going like the clappers that scared the poor creature, I reckon.'

'A delivery van?' Her father makes no effort to contain his fury. 'Did you catch the company? More's the bloody pity,' he spits as Jack shakes his head. 'I'd give them a piece of my mind, I tell you.'

They reach the landing.

'In here.' Muriel leads him into a good-sized room dominated by a brass bedstead with a light blue blouse hanging off its bottom post. She bustles forward to remove a splayed book from the crumpled pillow, before straightening the eiderdown and stepping back to make way for Jack.

He places Gwen gently upon the bed, sliding his arms out from underneath her, his focus lingering longer than it perhaps should. He is relieved when she mumbles drowsily, the tip of her tongue tracing the swell of her bottom lip.

'Dad . . .'

'I'm here, love.' The farmer's voice softens as he nudges Jack aside.

His eyes still on the girl, Jack backs away. He bumps into a dressing table set before the window, causing the array of perfume bottles clustered on its top to wobble and chink. He whips around to steady them, his large hands oafish against the delicate glass. He is momentarily distracted by the framed photograph of a woman with a little girl on her lap. The child bears such a strong resemblance to Gwen that he knows at once it is her. The woman in the photograph, though, is not the same woman who is clucking over her now, exclaiming at the sight of her swollen cheek, as she meticulously searches her scalp for injury. Gwen weakly protests at the fuss being made.

'I'm fine – the shock of it all just made me lightheaded. Where is Arthur?' She struggles to rise, but Muriel pushes her back down.

'Never mind that bloody horse, Gwen!' Her father paces the

room, his agitation ill-masked. 'I'd put a bullet in him if he were here. I've told you before – he's too damn skittish for my liking.'

'It wasn't his fault, Dad,' Gwen says. She cries out as Muriel eases off her boots.

'If he was steadier, he wouldn't have thrown you. No, I'll not have you ride him any longer – I'll see him in the knacker's yard before I see you on him again.'

'Hush now, Jim, for goodness' sake, that sort of talk isn't helping at all.'

Jack spies the wedding ring on Muriel's finger and wonders if she is a replacement for the woman in the picture. She peels back Gwen's sock to reveal an engorged foot already turning a nasty shade of purple. Gwen's father grimaces.

'Could it be broken?' he asks.

Gwen breathes in sharply as Muriel begins a careful examination. 'I don't think so, or at least nothing major – she's pulled it every which way though. But, Gwen, I do want to have a proper look at you, if you've been dragged about like this young man says you have.'

'It was nothing . . .' Gwen mutters.

'All the same, I'd rather give you the once-over. Come on now.' Muriel helps her to sit up.

'I should—' Jack starts, colour rising to his cheeks, but the farmer cuts him off.

'You come with me, lad.'

He wants to steal a final look, curious to see if she will make any attempt to watch him go, to catch his eye, perhaps say thank you. But Muriel is talking to her again, blocking her from his view, and he is disappointed that the opportunity has been snatched away. Instead, he follows her father from the room and though he longs to glance back at her, he resists the temptation to do so.

Just as he is pulling the door to, she calls out.

'Don't leave yet, will you?'

He is unable to suppress his smile.

CHAPTER EIGHT

Gwen

8th May 1945

'Right, that's me done,' Muriel says, putting away the last of the washed-up dishes from the evening meal. 'You'd best get a move on.'

Gwen looks up from the day's post spread across the tabletop before her, an assortment of bills and directives as well as an advice leaflet from the WarAg. There is nothing from Jack and for that she is grateful. She casts her mind back, trying to remember when she last received a letter from him, but she cannot say with any certainty. She would have to check the drawer in her desk, for she has not been so heartless as to throw his correspondence away. In truth she was unsure what to do with his letters, but on the basis that Tom might, at some point, start asking awkward questions, it seemed wise in the end to keep them. She hopes that day is a long way off. She needs to compose her own defence before then.

She folds the bill in her hand. 'Yes, I must.' She gathers up the post and pushes back her chair.

'I'll see you in the Hare and Hounds then, whenever you're ready,' Muriel says, bundling the apron in her hands.

Gwen nods distractedly. 'Yes . . . yes, I'll be along as soon as I've got Tom sorted.'

They hear Nora moving around in the room above, already preparing for her evening out.

'Gwen . . .' Muriel's gnarled knuckles crenellate on the back of the chair before her. 'People are bound to say something . . . they're bound to ask about Jack. You need to be ready for them.'

Gwen's grip tightens on the letters in her hand. She stares down at the tabletop. 'Yes. Yes, I know. I'll think of something.'

Muriel purses her lips and Gwen looks away, fearing she is about to be pressed for more. She can almost sense Muriel's internal battle, but in the end whatever arguments she had been aligning are stood down and the door clacks shut behind her. Gwen does not sense a victory, merely a temporary cessation of fire.

She steps up from the kitchen into the narrow strip of hallway alongside the stairs. She hears Tom in the front room as she lets herself into the small office immediately to her right.

Though the room is compact its large window overlooking the yard serves to alleviate its cramped conditions. Her father's roll-top desk stands against the side wall. The oak is sun-faded and in need of a polish, but Muriel knows better than to interfere in here, so whilst other furniture in the house gleams from her weekly attentions, the desk adopts a tarnished air of neglect.

The concertina top rattles as Gwen rolls it up. She places the day's post on the pile of correspondence inside, next to a bottle of Royal Blue ink and a box of paperclips. She is about to close the desk again when the stack of small red diaries tucked away in one of the cubbyholes at the back catches her eye, evoking an unexpected pang, which she attributes in part to the peculiar events of the day.

Fuelled by a maudlin whimsy, she reaches for the top book. The cherry red cloth is rough to the touch; *1939* gleams in its upper right-hand corner, the numbers embossed in gold. She brings the diary to her face and inhales the lingering scent of Woodbines before opening it up, cupping it reverentially in her hands, folding back the pages with her thumbs, as one might break bread.

The double-page spread is unevenly divided into seven, three days on the left, four on the right, Saturday and Sunday cramped together in a mean distribution of leisure – though it is immediately apparent from the pencilled entries that there are no weekends of idleness to be found on a farm. Animals know nothing of a day of rest.

The corners of her mouth tug with fondness as she scans her father's neat, brief entries:

Wind from the south. Mangles lifted. Tups sold.
Tried to rain all day but stayed dry. Harrowed Top Field.
Two calves, both healthy.

As she flicks through the diary, randomly stilling its whispering pages, the tension in her shoulders begins to ease and the weight that has been bearing down on her since hearing the clamorous church bells finally lifts. She can almost hear her father, summing up the day in his gruff but gentle voice. It is as if he is in the room with her and the comfort she takes from that foolish thought is so great that the pages flutter once again.

Fine, bright intervals. Strong N Wind.
Finished planting kale. Cultivated Mere Field.
Finished carting muck.

And then her eyes scan to the opposite page and one word leaps out at her:

Wedding

The word has been scored into the paper, just as the date has been carved into her heart. It has left an indelible scar on both. In the uncharacteristic slapdash scrawl, she feels her father's unforgiving anger. The seven letters which should have encapsulated his happiness and pride instead betray his disgust and disappointment, and she feels their cut so acutely she catches her breath. She slams the diary shut and tosses it back into the desk. Her eyes sting as she hastily instigates the rolled slats' unravelling descent. As the top clatters shut, she takes a steadying breath and blinks away her tears.

Closing the door on her father's contemptuous ghost, she allows the comforting sounds of Tom at play to carry her forward to the sitting room. The door is ajar and she pauses outside, listening. His childish prattle is balm to her troubled soul.

'Come on, Tom, we'd best get you ready to go out.'

The boy scrabbles to his feet, the die-cast car that Ted gave him for his birthday clutched in his hand. The toy continues to leave Gwen with a sense of disquiet she is at a loss to explain. She had chided her neighbour for giving such an extravagant gift to a child who is too young to understand its value or treat it with the care it deserves. Already, it bears evidence of Tom's careless play, its fragile epidermis of bright colour chipped away, exposing the drab metal beneath. But Ted had dismissed her reproof, his weathered face brightening at the sight of the boy's unbridled delight as he ripped away the gaudy wrapping paper to reveal the treasure beneath. Perhaps her discomfort stemmed from the fact the car had made her own gifts – home-made trinkets and hand-knitted jumpers – seem so paltry in comparison. Or perhaps it stemmed from something else entirely.

Pushing the unsettling thoughts from her mind, she holds out her hand but Tom runs past her and up the stairs, each tread protesting his rambunctious ascent.

She follows more sedately, her hand on the bannister, her steps soft on the threadbare runner. By the time she reaches the landing, Tom has disappeared into his bedroom. Nora's door is closed, but she can still hear the girl singing a popular jazz song, her voice husky and rich.

Tom has already stripped off his jumper and shirt and stands waiting for her in his vest. Gwen dampens a flannel with water from the jug on his washstand. He grumbles as she rubs about his face and neck, before drying him off on the towel that hangs over the rail.

She takes a clean shirt from the drawer of the tallboy and feeds his arms into the sleeves, then perches on the end of the bed to button it for him, Tom standing to attention at her knees.

'Tom . . .' she begins carefully, 'tonight . . . people will be very happy . . . very excited . . .'

'Because the war's over.'

'Yes, yes . . . it's wonderful.' She struggles with a button.

'Some people might ask about Daddy, Tom. They might say things – like Nora did – about Daddy coming home.' Her mind is racing as her tongue twists around the lies she must weave. Tom gazes at her with clear blue innocence. 'Tom . . . Even though the war is over . . . there is no guarantee Daddy will come back. I don't want you to get your hopes up . . .'

'But why not? If the war is over, why can't he come home?'

'The war isn't over for everyone, Tom, not yet. We don't know exactly where Daddy is right now . . . And a lot can happen . . .'

'But . . . he will come back . . . if he can? He will want to see me, won't he?'

'Oh Tom, of course, he would want to see you.' She cups his cheek in her palm. Sensing his sudden vulnerability, she pulls him against her, closing her eyes as she breathes in the scent of his hair, soft against her cheek.

'I hope my daddy comes home.'

Muffled against her chest, his little wish pierces her heart, and as he pulls free from her embrace, Gwen hates herself a little more.

In her own room, she sheds her work clothes and sloshes water into the bowl from the ewer. She rubs her face with a moistened flannel, roughly wiping away the day's dirt ingrained in her pores, before running it around her neck and under her arms. It is so much harder to cleanse herself of the guilt evoked by Tom's wish. She wipes until her skin is red, then throws the flannel back into the water, where it sinks below the surface. She thinks of Muriel's words of warning, of her father's disappointment and now of Tom's hopes, and her stomach roils. She is unsure whether she has the strength to face her neighbours. The thought of their well-meant enquiries terrifies her.

She has no choice, she tells herself. To not go would merely be delaying the inevitable – inescapable questions are bound to come, sooner or later – but she must go prepared. Forewarned is forearmed after all.

She slides a cotton slip over her head, then wrenches open the wardrobe door. The swan-necked coat hangers scrape against the metal pole as she rifles through her sparse selection of clothes. She deliberates over a navy dress. She bought it long before the war, but Nora – who has proven herself to be surprisingly skilled with the Singer – has modified it, nipping in the waist, bringing up the hem, until it is almost in fashion. It will do, she decides.

Once she has zipped herself in, she stands before the wardrobe's mirrored door and smooths down the fabric. The evening rays straining through the window catch the gold band on her left finger. Transfixed, she raises her hand to study it, as if strangely startled by its existence, doubtful of her own eyes. But there it is – dull now, and forever binding.

Before she knows what she is doing, she has gripped it between her right thumb and forefinger and she is twisting it round, dragging it forward, suddenly desperate to be free of it, if only for a moment. Alone in her room she might escape its judgement, its condemnation, be free of its bondage, but no matter how hard she pulls, it jams against her knuckle. She tries to suppress a rising sense of panic as she works it round and round, but it stubbornly digs into her flesh. It will not budge. It is stuck, trapped against her joint; it has become an irremovable part of her.

She snatches her fingers away. Her breaths are coming quickly now, provoking a terrifying tightness in her chest. She collapses onto the end of her bed, knocked off her feet by the dawning realisation that the men are coming home and there is no longer any way to avoid the mess she has made of her life. The future that stretches before her appears mined with horrors and she cannot see a clear path through.

It takes a concerted effort to calm herself. She closes her eyes and slows her breaths. When she finally looks again at her hands, she notices that her wedding band continues to shine, even though it is now cast in shadow.

She gets to her feet and this time when she checks her reflection, she does not allow her focus to stray, she does not allow herself to panic. She rationalises that her hands are simply too warm. The wedding ring will come off. As soon as she is cold again.

CHAPTER NINE

Jack

June 1939

'She's in good care, Muriel was a nurse before she got married.' The farmer holds out his hand to Jack. 'Jim Hughes, pleased to make your acquaintance, young man. I'm very grateful to you, for coming to Gwen's assistance like that.'

Conscious of his bruised knuckles, Jack angles them to conceal the worst of the damage as he shakes the farmer's hand. 'Jack Ellison. I'm just glad I was able to help the lass, sir.'

'Good lad, good lad.' Jim claps him on the back. 'Cup of tea for your trouble?'

'I wouldn't say no.'

In the kitchen, Jim lifts the kettle from the range and gestures for Jack to take a seat at the table. As Jack draws out the nearest chair, he takes in the neatly arranged crockery on the dresser, the coats hanging from the hooks by the back door and the stoneware bottle of scour treatment standing on the windowsill, its torn paper label bearing a pencil sketch of a calf.

'It's a good job you happened by when you did,' Jim says, placing the kettle on the hotplate of the range. He glances at Jack as he crosses the kitchen to retrieve two mugs from the cupboard. 'You're up and about early. Where were you heading?'

Jack rests his hands awkwardly on the tabletop, lacing his fingers, but at the sight of his bloated knuckles, he slips them free and hides them on his lap. 'The town down the valley.'

'Helvedon?'

He nods, careful not to meet the farmer's curious gaze.

'And what takes you there?'

'Work.' The word lodges in Jack's throat. He clears it with a cough, muttering an apology before reiterating his intentions.

'Work?' Jim wriggles the lid off a dented tea caddy. 'You got something lined up?'

'No. Just . . . looking . . .'

'You're looking a long way from home.'

Jim's softly delivered words come to bear. Jack keeps his eyes trained on the table. 'Aye.'

'And where is home, exactly? Up north somewhere, I'm guessing,' Jim says, spooning tea leaves into a brown teapot.

Jack hesitates. 'Sunderland.' He feels a sudden heat in his cheeks.

'That right? So, what brings you all the way down here?' Jack notes a change in Jim's voice. There is an artificial levity that fails to conceal the first hints of suspicion. Jack catches himself glancing at the door, subconsciously calculating the distance from where he sits . . . from where Jim stands.

'I worked in the shipyard, a riveter . . .' His flustered thoughts trip over themselves. 'But . . . it's not much of a life, you know? And life is tough up there anyway. I decided a change of scene might do me good. If not now, then when? I didn't want to be one of those old men down my local, who prop up the bar with their regrets.' He pauses. 'And if there is a war coming, I don't want to get trapped in the yards. I'd rather find another way to do my bit.'

The kettle begins to whistle; Jim moves to pull it free from the range. Jack says nothing more, just watches as the farmer pours the boiling water into the pot, curlicues of steam rising from its top.

'It's a big change,' the farmer says, using a teaspoon to swirl the leaves. 'Must be hard to leave your family behind.'

'I have no family to speak of,' Jack replies, not missing a beat. Beneath the table, his hands become fists.

'So, what do you hope to do down here?'

'Anything. Anything that pays.' Jack meets Jim's eye for the first time. 'I'm fit, keen, hard-working. I can turn my hand to most things . . . I do a bit of woodwork too, I like that . . .' he admits, lowering his gaze.

Jim nods. He pours the tea through a strainer into one of the mugs and, without asking, adds milk from a small jug near the sink and two teaspoons of sugar. He sets it before Jack. Somewhere outside, a cockerel crows.

'Do you have other family?' Jack asks at last. He is reluctant to pick up his tea, fearful that now there is nothing to distract him, the farmer might at last notice his battered hands.

Jim leans against the drainer, nursing his own mug. 'No, no it's only Gwen and me. Her mother died when she was just a girl. There hasn't been anyone else.'

'Oh, I thought . . .' Jack trails off, embarrassed that his tongue has run away with him. Jim takes his meaning and laughs.

'What, Muriel? God, no! I'd be lost without her, she's practically raised Gwen as her own, but no, no. Her own husband passed away nearly twelve months ago now. Stan was gassed in the war and never really recovered. Hit her hard at the time, but she's doing well now. Speak of the devil . . .' he says, as the woman's voice carries his name lightly into the room. He places the mug down on the table and asks Jack to excuse him. Jack listens to the stairs' creak.

Alone, he lifts his hands from his lap and wraps them around the mug. The tea is still too hot and as he blows across its top, his breath rippling its surface, he is vaguely aware of the shuffling steps on the easing boards above him. The gingham curtain at the open window flutters on an invasive breeze sweetly scented by the jasmine growing so vibrantly outside that the white, star-shaped flowers press against the glass.

Jack thinks of the place he has left behind, the grotty back-to-backs within spitting distance of the yards, their alleys the playground of children with sunken cheeks and dead eyes and hand-me-down clothes. He thinks of his own kitchen with its nicotine-stained ceiling and the chipped saucer on the table overflowing with fag ash and the concertinaed butts left by his mother and her gentleman callers.

Looking around the homely clutter of the farm kitchen, with its cosy muddle of possessions, he realises that he has always yearned for a home like this and perhaps, he tortures himself, he might have achieved it – or something similar. But in one of those shabby back alleys that he knows so well, where rats fight with seagulls for the scraps scattered on cobbles slick with urine and spilt liquor, he threw away any chance he had of making a better life for himself. He threw away his chance of having any life at all.

The tea is cooler now and he gulps it down. Pushing back his chair, he carries his mug to the sink and rinses it under the tap before placing it upside down on the drainer. He glances up at the ceiling. All is still.

He hovers, cocking his ear to the hallway door. Detecting no signs of life, he carefully replaces his chair under the table and, with a wistful backward glance, he lifts the latch on the door and steps out into the fresh morning air.

CHAPTER TEN

Gwen

8th May 1945

The three of them walk down the lane, the evening sun warm on their backs, the scent from the flower-laden hawthorn hedges sickly sweet in the air. Tom skips between them, imbued with Nora's mounting excitement. Gwen's lack of enthusiasm for the outing appears to go unnoticed.

The pub garden rolls out to greet them as they reach the outskirts of the village and Gwen sees at once that Nora's prediction is right. Villagers spill from the pub's open doorway, covering the lawn in convivial clusters, their incessant chatter like the hubbub of a boiling pot.

Tom races forward to reach the picket gate first. He plunges through but pulls up abruptly, daunted by the throng before him. She is not surprised when he falls back, his sticky fingers finding hers, his hesitancy mirroring her own.

'What a turn-out!' Nora crows, nudging past them, showing none of their reticence. 'I should think the entire village is here. Come on, you two, let's get a drink.'

Gwen envies the Land Girl her easy confidence as she barges

through the crowd, raising a hand and hallo-ing to familiar faces who call out in greeting. Gwen follows demurely in her wake, tugging Tom with her as she ducks beneath the door's blackened lintel.

Inside the pub is a crush. They can barely move; every inch of quarry-tiled floor is occupied and a yellow smog of tobacco smoke hovers amongst the thick beams that line the ceiling, the horse brasses tacked to their sides barely visible. The clamour is deafening and Gwen's ears ring, as beads of sweat begin to decorate her brow. The atmosphere is stifling.

'This is the most life I've seen in this place in four years,' Nora shouts back to Gwen. 'I'll get the drinks in.'

She is clearly in her element. A displaced Londoner, she is used to the dazzling lights of the city and the chaotic revelry of a Piccadilly pub. She has been a fish out of water in the placid shallows that Gwen has been content to bask in all her life, safe and familiar. Since her arrival, Nora has been like a salmon battling the current, determined to swim upstream to where wild torrents replace the still calms, and frenetic activity awaits. Gwen watches her now at the bar as she throws back her head and laughs at some raucous comment made by one of the local farm labourers, uncaring of the bold hand that snakes around her waist, or the press of the other lad standing beside her.

Gwen looks away. All she wants is to escape outside with half a pint, and maybe sit on the stone wall and smoke a celebratory cigarette.

Instead, as the crowd shifts and friends and neighbours mill past her, she finds herself pawed. She fields hands on her shoulders and arms around her waist as she is seized by those eager to share their goodwill and embrace her in celebration.

She does her best to reflect their bon viveur. *Such a wonderful day; oh, we just had to come, couldn't miss this for the world; yes, it's such a relief; thank goodness for Mr Churchill; our boys have been so brave; I don't know what it'll mean for rationing; I should think Nora will stay for a while yet, goodness knows I couldn't do without her.*

And then finally it comes, with the inevitability of thunder on a clammy day.

'You must be looking forward to getting your Jack back! Won't be long now, I'm sure, and all our boys will come marching home.'

Mrs Hamer, the baker's wife, grins up at her, the wrinkles in her face softening with pleasure. She looks down at Tom. 'Are you looking forward to your daddy coming home, young man?'

The direct address provokes a display of shyness and Tom buries his face into Gwen's navy dress. She fights to maintain the equilibrium of her smile as she glances towards the bar to see if Nora might be about to rescue them, but the Land Girl is now embroiled with a cluster of lads from the Young Farmers, all drawn to her effervescence like moths to a flame.

'Have you heard anything from him?' Mrs Hamer persists. 'My Joe telephoned – would you believe it? Mrs Morgan ran round from the post office to fetch me. But then, he's stationed over here so it's easier for him, I suppose.'

'No, no I haven't heard . . .' Gwen says at last. She leans forward, lowering her voice as if she does not want Tom to hear. 'The truth is, Mrs Hamer, I haven't heard anything for such a long while that . . .' She contrives an expression of dismay. Mrs Hamer is central to village life. She is loose-lipped – well-meaning perhaps, but a gossip nonetheless – and Gwen sees how

47

she can turn the unfortunate conversation to her advantage. The baker's wife clutches her glass of sherry to her chest.

'Oh, but my dear, you mustn't think like that. If something had happened you would have heard.'

'Would I? I'm not even sure where Jack is. He was never one for writing – just the occasional letter, you know. They've been few and far between and over the past few months . . .' She shrugs at her handiwork – truth gift-wrapped in lies.

'Oh, Gwen, love, you mustn't give up hope.' Mrs Hamer grips her arm. 'I'll pray for his safe return.'

Gwen hears her name being hollered from the bar and making her apologies she manages to extricate herself from Mrs Hamer's company. Nora is stretching over a sea of shoulders, Gwen's half pint in her hand. Gwen takes it as the beer's creamy top oozes down the side of the glass. She brings it straight to her lips to draw off the excess, while Nora weaves her way through the throng to join her, breathless and giggling.

'Blimey, what a crush. Everyone's in such good spirits though. Cheers!' She crashes her glass rather unnecessarily against Gwen's, jolting more liquid over its rim.

'Oh, did you get a drink for Tom?' Gwen asks. 'Tom, do you want a lemonade as a special treat?' She looks down to her side, but the space that Tom had occupied is empty. 'Where's Tom?'

'I thought he was with you?' Nora says, licking froth from her top lip.

'He was, just a minute ago.' Gwen searches at Tom height through the forest of legs around her, but there is no sign of her boy. She calls his name, but it is lost in the general buzz of conversation. 'Where is he?' A lump of panic lodges in her chest.

'Don't worry, he can't have gone far. You look here and I'll go and have a look in the snug.'

Gwen begins to push her way through the main bar, her stomach knotting. The rational part of her knows he must be here somewhere, tucked into a corner, perhaps playing with other children from the village, but then it dawns on her that since their arrival she has seen no other children. They have all been left at home. She is the only mother irresponsible enough to drag her son out after bedtime to enjoy the frivolities of the victory celebration. She curses herself for allowing Nora to sway her. Setting her glass down on a table, she continues to work her way through the crowd, asking all those she knows if they have seen Tom. Their blank expressions elevate her fears. She thinks it is the stinging smoke that brings tears to her eyes, but she cannot be sure.

The back door of the bar hangs open offering a tantalising glimpse of golden light, and it suddenly strikes her that the inviting glimmer of evening sun might have enticed Tom into the garden – a quiet place of respite from the overwhelming noise. She begins to make her way towards the door and when she finds herself snagged by the hands of well-meaning neighbours, she pauses only long enough to ask, 'Have you seen Tom?' before moving on, blood pulsing through her veins.

When she at last escapes outside, the deafening babble drops away and all she can hear is the faint hum of the bumblebees on the flowering heathers that border the path before her.

The rear garden is empty. Faint snatches of conversation carry from the front lawn where villagers continue to mingle, but here, behind the pub, there is no one to be seen. Her only company is a speckled thrush that flutters onto the wall, from where it observes her with a curious tilt of its head.

'Gwen.'

She wheels around. A cry escapes her as Tom comes running towards her, a big grin plastered across his face, unaware of her terror which dissipates as she scoops him up in her arms, his feet flying clear of the ground.

'Oh, Tom! You scared me half to death, I didn't know where you'd gone!' She looks past his shoulder at the man standing behind him and smiles. 'Thank you, Ted. He was with me one minute and gone the next. I was worried sick.'

'I caught him going off for a little walk, so I thought I'd best bring him back.' The man smiles, jangling the change in his trouser pockets. He is tall and broadly built, and his leathery skin is walnut brown from the sun. 'I think he found it a bit loud inside, didn't you, Tom?'

The boy slides free from Gwen's grasp, his feet landing on the path. He looks back at his rescuer and grins, brazen with familiarity – fondness even. Gwen ruffles his hair, her relief subsiding.

'I know how you feel, Tom.'

'Ah, it's a bit much, isn't it?' Ted says.

'Uncle Ted says he'll buy me a lemonade if you say I can have one, Mummy,' Tom wheedles, leaning against her legs.

'Did he now?' She is forced to shield her eyes from the sinking sun to look at their neighbour.

He offers her a sheepish smile. 'Well, I had to give him a reason to come back with me – didn't I, Tom? He'd have been halfway home else.'

Gwen laughs. Ted has been a constant in her life for as long as she can remember. She was only five when he took over the rundown farm next to theirs. He was a young newlywed of twenty-three, green behind the ears but hardworking and ambitious and he soon earnt her father's respect.

She can still remember him carrying her on his shoulders at harvest time, as he and her father helped each other bring in their corn. She remembers too his grief when tuberculosis claimed his wife and their little boy Henry in 1928, and how he had comforted her and her father when the same greedy disease had drowned her own mother later that year. And four years ago, it was Ted who pulled her away from her father's cooling corpse when they found him folded over the grain sacks in the barn, his heart having given up the ghost. He had pressed a glass of brandy into her hand as she sat sobbing at the kitchen table waiting for the doctor to arrive, and to this day she is unsure whether it was her father's sudden demise or her own unfettered grief that had moved him to tears.

In those terrible weeks that followed, Ted had single-handedly saved her home and livelihood. He would arrive in the yard at dawn to milk her herd before dividing the rest of his day working both farms, running himself into the ground to ensure neither was neglected, safeguarding Gwen's inheritance until she recovered and was able to manage alone.

Without Ted's sterling efforts, the WarAg would have seized the farm, she knows that for certain, the land and its produce being too precious to squander for the sake of family ties and grief. But through his endeavours, Ted had succeeded in holding them at bay until she was back on her feet, and when she was, he encouraged her to apply for a Land Girl so she could continue to farm the land to its full potential. The few meals she has offered him in return seem paltry payment for his self-sacrifice and kindness, but he is always grateful for them, and his place at her table every Sunday has become a given. Gwen always envisaged her father being Tom's role model, but since his death Ted has become the closest thing Tom has to a dependable man in his life.

'Oh! Thank God, you've found him!' Nora bursts through the doorway. 'Hello, Ted,' she throws him a cursory glance, before turning her attention on Tom. 'You're a rotter running off like that, worrying everyone silly.'

'I'm going to have a lemonade now,' Tom says, unperturbed.

'Well, I'm about to go to the bar, so come with me and I'll get it for you.' Nora holds out her hand and Tom takes it without hesitation.

'Here, Nora . . .' Ted pulls some coins from his pocket. 'I promised I'd buy him one.'

'Right, Tom, it's on Uncle Ted. Let's go and get you that lemonade. Do you two want anything?' she asks as an afterthought, but both Gwen and Ted shake their heads, so she disappears inside with Tom.

Gwen watches them go. She folds her arms across her chest as the light breeze begins to pick up, cooler now with only the sun's dying rays to warm it.

'I didn't know whether you would come or not,' she says.

'Ah well, special occasion and all that,' Ted replies, returning his hands to his pockets. 'I didn't know whether you'd be here. I did call round on my way down and saw that the house was all shut up.'

'Oh, you know Nora . . . never one to miss a party.' Gwen's wry tone elicits a smile.

Voices continue to sigh on the wind. The thrush flies from

its perch on the wall as far as the oak tree in the field behind. It launches into its evening song.

'So . . .' Ted says, suddenly appearing ill at ease. To Gwen's surprise, he avoids her direct gaze, half-turning instead to observe the swell of their fields in the distance, seamed together by snowdrifts of hawthorn and verdant field maple, dulled by the fading light. 'They'll all be coming home, I suppose . . . the men.'

'Yes.'

His voice drops. 'Your Jack among them.' It is a while before he adds, 'You must be pleased about that.' He shifts his gaze towards her.

With no voice to answer, all Gwen can do is look away.

CHAPTER ELEVEN

Jack

June 1939

They are all outside, grave-faced, when he finally reappears with Gwen's horse. It walks behind him, its head hung low, a picture of placid submission, but Jack's smarting shoulder bears testimony to the resistance the ill-tempered creature put up, though his shirt hides the reddened skin where it bit him. Only the smear of dried mud on the seat of his trousers hints at the trouble he's had.

'We thought you'd done a runner, lad!' Jim calls out, ambling down the steps towards him, his hands deep in his trouser pockets.

'You found Arthur!' Gwen cries. With her injured foot heavily bandaged, she is standing stork-like, her shoulder resting on the back wall of the farmhouse. At the sound of her voice, the horse throws back his head and whinnies, snatching Jack's hand up, and though he knows her resulting smile is not for him, he cannot help but relish its warmth. 'I can't believe you went and found him!'

'Well, I didn't want you to be worrying, like,' Jack mumbles, shifting the position of his retrieved knapsack on his shoulder before reaching up to pat the horse's neck. It shakes its head, chomping on its bit.

'You even ran up his stirrups,' Gwen observes with surprise.

Jack looks at his feet to hide the rush of blood to his cheeks. 'I can untack him for you, if you like.'

'Oh, I'll come and do that . . .' She pushes herself from the wall but winces as weight hits her bad foot.

'Stay where you are, Gwen, you need to keep off that injury, remember?' Jim stops her with a raised hand. 'Bring him this way, Jack.'

Jack clicks the horse into motion. He avoids looking at Gwen as he leads Arthur past her, but he feels her eyes upon him. He follows the farmer up the length of the yard to the brick-built stable block on the right. The doors hang wide and Jack leads the horse inside, his eyes taking a moment to adjust to the gloom. Jim opens the swing gate of the loosebox before him and, with a tip of his head, gestures for the horse to be brought in. Jack drops his knapsack on the cobbles, then walks the horse inside, his boots sinking into the thick bed of straw. Jim follows him in, closing the gate behind them.

Without waiting to be asked, Jack pushes back the side flap of the saddle and releases the buckle on the girth strap which he drops beneath the horse's belly. He drags the saddle towards him, resting it across his forearm, gathering up the girth as it reaches the horse's back, folding it over the dipped leather seat, before balancing the saddle upon the wooden divide of the loosebox. As he does so, he notices a curry brush resting on the top, and with Jim still busy unbuckling the horse's bridle, he sets about sweeping it over the horse's side in firm, steady strokes.

Jim glances back at him. 'You know horses, then?'

'My grandad was a miner. I used to spend quite a bit of time up at the pits helping out with the ponies when I was a wee lad.'

'A miner, eh? Not tempted to go mining yourself?'

'No, a life underground is no life. He never wanted that for me.'

'Was your dad a miner too?'

'Aye, though I never knew him. He died in the war when I was little more than a bairn.'

'That must have been hard.' Jim lifts the bridle clear. The straw rustles as the horse steps forward to reach the contents of the hay rack hanging from the wall.

'My mam moved to the city to get factory work during the war . . . better paid.' Jack considers revealing the detrimental results of her having to surrender that same job when the men came home, but decides against it. Instead, he carries on sweeping the brush over the horse's flank, liberating its short coat from the dust and sweat of its morning's adventures.

'And you ended up working the shipyards?'

'Aye . . . handy, you know.'

'But not handy enough to keep you there.'

Jack's strokes falter, but he soon regains his rhythm. 'Well, I got to thinking there might be more to life than hammering rivets . . . and it's dangerous work, you know. A lot of men get injured.'

'Is that what happened to your hand?'

Jack meets Jim's eye over the horse's scooped back. For a moment, they say nothing. It is Jack who looks away first. He applies more vigour to his brush work.

'Aye . . .' he says quietly, ducking under the horse's neck to tend to its other side, '. . . something like that.'

He is aware of Jim watching him for a moment before slipping the bolt on the loosebox door. The farmer slides the saddle from the wooden divide and leaves Jack to his currying while he puts the tack away in a small room just inside the stable door. Jack murmurs to the horse as he continues to brush him down. He feels a pang of regret when the task is complete.

Jim reappears as Jack is closing up the loosebox. He stops in the shafts of sunlight slanting into the stables through the open doorway.

'All done,' Jack says. He offers the farmer an awkward smile before retrieving his knapsack from the cobbles.

'You're on your way again?'

'Aye. Thank you for the tea.'

Jim grunts, turning his face to the light. He rubs his chin. 'Helvedon, you say?'

Jack shifts his weight. 'Aye.'

'But you've nothing lined up?'

'I'm happy to take my chances. I'm not fussy, I'll take what's offered.'

Jim grunts again. He pulls a grubby handkerchief from his pocket and wipes his nose, before tucking it away. He turns to Jack. 'Look, I can offer you work for the rest of the summer. I could do with a hand for the harvest . . . that'd take us into September, October maybe. I can't promise anything beyond that, we'll have to see what happens and I don't just mean how you do. There's all this talk of war and it seems we're heading that way, so I don't know how things will be long term, but . . . well, if you take to it and there is a war, you might be glad to find yourself working on the land. Farming is a reserved occupation.'

Jack traces the smooth curve of a cobble with the tip of his boot, before steadily meeting Jim's eye. 'If there is a war, I intend to fight for my country . . . just like my dad did.'

Jim nods. 'That's fair enough, lad.' Jack becomes the subject of Jim's quiet contemplation. He knows he is being measured and assessed and he tenses under the scrutiny. He is almost relieved when the farmer finally clears his throat. 'Well, look, the offer stands – if you want work for the time being, I'm happy to take you on. I warn you though, farming is not for the faint-hearted. It's hard graft.'

'Hard work never killed anyone,' Jack says quickly, his grandfather's words springing to mind, 'though worrying about it killed a fair few.'

Jim snorts, then chuckles. 'Ah, that's about right.' He skewers Jack with his pale blue stare. 'So how about it?'

'I don't know much about farming.'

'You willing to learn?'

'I am.' Jack steadies his breath. 'I am.'

'I can't put you up in the house, but I've had men stay in the tack room here before now,' Jim tips his head towards the door he's just come through. 'There's a camp bed and stove . . .'

'It'll do me fine.'

'Wages will reflect your bed and board – you'll take all your meals with us up at the house. I'm a fair employer, I'm not looking to diddle you in any way.'

'I don't doubt it.'

Jim's firm mouth finally relents with a smile. He claps his broad hands together in satisfaction. 'Right then.'

Jack wipes his palm on his trouser leg to rid himself of the grease from the horse's coat, then he holds his hand out to the man before him.

'I'm grateful to you.'

Jim's grip is strong and though his bruised flesh protests, Jack is careful not to show his discomfort. The farmer's subtle application of pressure conveys all he needs to know.

'Don't give me cause to regret it, lad,' Jim says, his voice gruff.

'I won't, sir.'

'Good.' Jim releases his hand with a final warning squeeze. 'Well, we'd better show you around, hadn't we?'

They walk the farm with the dog at their heels, all one hundred and twenty acres of arable and pasture. Jack crosses fields of dairy cows, ruddy brown with white dapples on their rumps, their heads lifting in curiosity. He is walked through a field of sheep, the bleats of frolicking lambs drifting on the breeze. They lean over five-bar gates to study cropped hayfields backed by woods of beech and fir, and they walk along tramlines through barley, the hairs on the heads slicing their skin, before crossing a lane to enter acres of chest-high corn, waiting to be burnished gold by the sun, until at last they return via a farm track to the paddock behind the yard, where two Clydesdales graze peaceably as chickens strut between them, pecking at ground bearing the indented smiles of the horses' hooves.

Back in the yard itself, Jim shows him the milking parlour, then – bypassing the stables and the tack room – the barn with its clay-tiled pitched roof and beside it the rickyard where already four hayricks stand, protected from the rain by their thatched conical hats. Finally, they arrive at the open-fronted shed where the implements – the plough share, the harrow, the potato riddle and seed drill – are neatly stored amongst yellow dandelions and tangled mayweed.

When they are done, Jim rubs his hands together and calls for a cup of tea. They walk back to the house, taking the steps up to the rear path, but before they reach the door, Jim spots Muriel digging potatoes from the vegetable patch before them. Clapping Jack on the back, he tells him to go on in, while he has a quick word with his housekeeper.

Jack feels like an intruder as he lets himself into the kitchen, despite the fact he has been given licence to do so. The room remains dim. The late-morning sun strikes the front of the house rather than the back, and the small window above the sink does not permit sufficient light to brighten the large low-ceilinged room, so the corners play host to shadows.

He leaves the door ajar for Jim and hovers just inside, glancing around him, the ticking of the wall clock the only sound. He rubs his chin, wondering at the unexpected turn of events, and wondering further whether this deviation from his plan is prudent. His intention had been to become a nondescript labourer in some large town – anonymous, insignificant. He is aware he will stand out here, on a farm on the outskirts of a village where gossip is sure to be abundant.

And yet, he has no desire to move on, even though he knows it would be wiser – safer – to do so. Something dormant had stirred deep inside him as he exchanged his first words with Gwen, and a peculiar peace had soothed his troubled soul as he traversed the land with Jim. He struggles to understand it, and certainly cannot explain it, this deep-seated knowledge that somehow the axis of his world has changed and his forward course has forever been altered. He has never believed in fate and yet now, standing in this kitchen, his eyes straining against the wan light, he feels he has stepped onto an inevitable path, one he could not have avoided even if he had tried. It is as if the terrible events of the past twenty-four hours have led him here – though for what purpose, he cannot even begin to fathom.

A noise from beyond the kitchen catches his attention and his thoughts spring to Gwen. He takes a careful step forward over the flagstone floor. The door to the hall hangs open and he hears again a rustle of movement, followed by the creak of a chair and a soft sigh. His heart stutters as he steps up into the hall, aware the sounds come from the room to his immediate right.

'Oh, you startled me!' Gwen cries, catching sight of him in the doorway as she sits before an open roll-top desk. She laughs, mocking her own skittishness as she swiftly folds the piece of paper she had been writing on, pushing it into the pocket of her skirt as she struggles to her feet. She lists to one side, the result of favouring her good foot.

'Your dad said to come on in for a cup of tea, like.' Embarrassed at having interrupted her, Jack lowers his eyes to his boots and in doing so realises he has trodden mud into the faded rug that lies upon the floorboards. 'Oh God . . . I'm so sorry, I should have taken my boots off at the door . . .'

'Oh, don't worry.' She hobbles forward, apparently welcoming the distraction. 'It happens all the time, Dad's forever traipsing in muck, it drives Muriel mad.' She gabbles breathlessly, pinpricks of colour warming her cheeks. She falls silent with an embarrassed smile. 'Let's go back through to the kitchen and I'll pop the kettle on,' she says at last, calmer now.

He stands aside to let her lead the way on her hop-cum-hobble, but when they are in the kitchen he pulls out a chair for her and, ignoring all protests, insists on filling the kettle himself. Muriel and Jim come in just as he is setting it upon the range.

'Ah, good man, that's it, let's get the kettle on,' Jim says, rubbing his broad hands together. Muriel says nothing but issues a tight-lipped stare at Jack as she slams a trug of earth-encrusted new potatoes upon the table. 'I've been showing Jack the farm. He's going to stay on for a while, help us out over the summer.'

'Really?' Gwen leans forward. Jack is wary of looking her way. He is intensely aware of Muriel's narrow-eyed inspection.

'Well, I've been toying with the idea of applying to the Women's Land Army now they've reinstated it, but to be honest, I'm feeling outnumbered as it is what with you and Muriel. I quite like the idea of Jack evening up the numbers. You know, Gwen, we've got more crops in than ever before. It's been worrying me for some time that you and I are not going to manage this year's harvest on our own. Bringing in the hay almost proved too much for us. Another pair of hands at this time of year wouldn't go amiss.'

Muriel scowls as she rinses her hands under the tap.

'Jim, you make the tea.' She turns to Jack. 'You can come and help me with your bedding,' she says, her voice sharp, her manner cool as she folds the towel over the back of a chair and bustles from the kitchen. Jack mumbles his assent and follows, heartened by the encouraging smile Gwen throws his way.

Muriel leads him upstairs to the landing. Gwen's bedroom door stands ajar and he cannot resist glancing in as he walks past, glimpsing the bottom of her bed and the jam jar of cow parsley on the windowsill.

Muriel yanks open the double doors of the laundry press and begins to search through the shelves of neatly ironed bedding, putting to one side items she deems suitable. She bends down to pull a rolled mattress cinched with two belts from underneath the bottom shelf. She thrusts it into Jack's arms. It is light and insubstantial and he knows at once it will provide little comfort, but he wisely passes no comment. She follows it up with a feather pillow, which he manages to catch in his fingers while wrestling with the mattress.

'I'll bring the bedding,' she says, drawing down the items she has set aside.

She pushes past him, making no attempt to hide her disapproval though Jack is at a loss to understand what he has done to deserve it.

As they descend the stairs, Jim and Gwen's voices flow towards them with the comforting burble of a mountain stream. The conversation lulls as they enter the kitchen. Gwen begins to rise, offering to help, but Muriel tells her to sit down and chastises her for being foolish.

'You'll never make it across the yard on that foot,' she says, continuing towards the back door. 'Nor should you try.'

The dog jumps around them as they step outside, excited by the scent of fresh linen and the prospect of fresh blood. Muriel snaps at him to settle down, cussing him under her breath. Juggling his load, Jack frees a hand to ruffle the fur on the dog's head. In the woods behind the farm, a cuckoo hails itself.

Muriel wastes no time in striding up the yard to the stable block. She is muttering something, but Jack is unable to determine her words – it crosses his mind that this might be for the best. The dog noses the air as it detects a scent more enticing than their own, and immediately hares off towards the imple-ment shed, its tail down, its head low to the ground as it begins ferreting through the weeds, weaving between the equipment.

The horse inside the stable block senses their approach and snickers as they reach the red-painted doors now weathered to lobster pink and flaking like sunburnt skin.

They cross the cobbles to the door on the left, the latch clacking under Muriel's hand. In spite of the warmth outside, the small room is cool to the point of chilly and Jack is relieved that there is indeed a little cast-iron stove tucked into the far corner, its black flue running up the wall and disappearing through the raftered roof above. The room smells of leather, saddle oil, and yeasty horse nuts. The back wall is studded with wooden prongs that support an array of saddles and bridles, while below sit stacked pails and sacks of oats, their rolled tops weighted down with large stones. Strands of straw sink between the cobbles, and the only window is draped with a filigree of cobwebs, which scoop across its corners like white silk, while its crumbling wooden sill is littered with the desiccated corpses of bluebottles. Beneath the window is an upturned apple crate, clearly intended to serve as a side table to the wooden camp bed shoved against the outside wall.

'You can unroll the mattress onto that,' Muriel says, her manner curt as her eyes roam the room, though she makes no comment on its condition or suitability.

Wordlessly, Jack does as he is bid, releasing the coiled mat-tress from its binds. He attempts to flatten it against the slatted frame but, despite his best efforts, its ends curl like stale bread.

While he battles with the mattress, Muriel brushes the dust from an old Bentwood chair that stands at the side of the room.

She sets the bedlinen upon it and selects a sheet. Elbowing Jack aside, she shakes it free from its crisp folds and flutters it over the mattress, moving briskly around the frame to tuck it in at each corner with two sharp swipes of her flattened hand.

'I can do that . . .' Jack offers, but she merely huffs. He feels the scald of her resentment and, unsure how to appease her, he remains silent. Instead, he tries to win favour by using his initiative. He tucks the feather pillow into the folded case he spies sitting on top of the linen pile. Muriel's eyebrows lift, as she takes another sheet to the bed.

'How long do you intend to stay?' she bites out at last.

Careful to ensure he is not in her way he places the pillow at the head of the bed. 'I don't know. For as long as they'll have me, I suppose.'

She pulls a face as she unfolds a coarse woollen blanket and lays it upon the folded-down top sheet. Jack thanks her quietly as she finishes smoothing it in place.

'There's logs for the stove in the store up by the house. Dinner is at six. You know where the privy is?'

Jack has already spotted the outdoor convenience, set away from the house at the end of the garden, a fair trek in the dark.

'When you come back to the house, I'll give you some candles and a box of matches. There's probably a spare paraffin lantern you can have too,' she says, reading his mind. She brushes down the front of her housecoat, as if reluctant to take the grubbiness of the tack room back with her. She turns to leave but, with her hand on the door, she pauses. She twists round to face him. 'They are good people. Kind. Trusting. Don't you take advantage of that.'

Having delivered her message in no uncertain terms, she leaves him to settle in.

CHAPTER TWELVE

Jack

June 1939

He is not to be trusted yet with the milking.

'We'll break you in gently,' Jim had told him the night before. 'I'll get you started on some general chores after you've had your breakfast. I'll make sure you're up in time to enjoy a good feed.'

True to his word, the farmer taps on the tack room window around seven the next morning, after he has driven the milked herd back to pasture. Jack is already waiting. The sound of cattle shuffling towards the parlour had woken him just after dawn. Stiff from the unrelenting camp bed, he had pulled on his trousers and buttoned his shirt, before heading from the stables to avail himself of the privy, taking the ewer with him. On his way back, he had filled the chipped jug at the cast iron pump that stands at the edge of the yard, the pump handle creaking with every lift and thrust.

Back in the tack room, he used the water to wash, then to shave. He had procured a mirror from Muriel the evening before, having plucked up the courage to enquire after one when she had emerged from the cellar and unceremoniously handed him the ewer and bowl. She had tutted and muttered under her breath before disappearing back through the door tucked under the stairs, returning a short time later with a small mirror of mottled glass. She wiped away the sticky string of cobweb clinging to its wooden frame.

'That'll have to do,' she said, her expression sour.

'It'll do well, thank you,' Jack had assured her, but she proved immune to his gratitude and with a huff had inched past him to retrieve her coat from the hook in the kitchen, leaving the house without so much as a backward glance.

The housekeeper is already in situ when he enters the kitchen now with Jim. She is standing at the range before a frying pan lined with bacon and glances up at them as they come in. Offering no greeting, she cracks the egg in her hand against the rim of a second pan of spitting fat, which hisses angrily as the egg slumps in.

Jack pays no heed to the housekeeper's lack of welcome, instead he stumbles over his greeting to Gwen, who is sitting at the side of the table, her bandaged foot resting on a chair. She waves away his concerned enquiries.

'It's fine . . . absolutely fine. It doesn't even hurt much. I wish you'd have let me help with the milking, Dad. It would have been no trouble – I'd have been sitting down anyway, for goodness' sake!'

'Sitting down to milk, but then you have to carry the pail to the scales and the cooler, then walk back to do the next cow . . . and what if one of my feisty ladies takes a hoof to you? No, you'll do as Muriel says and keep that leg up until the swelling's gone down.'

'I hate being idle.' She stretches across the table to pour ha'penny-coloured tea into the waiting mugs.

'Then you can help with my accounts. God knows I could do with some assistance in that department.'

After breakfast, Jim instructs Jack on how to clean out the parlour so it is ready for the afternoon's milking. Once he has convinced the farmer he can manage alone, he sets about shovelling dung from the shallow gutters that run behind the stalls, loading it into the barrow before wheeling it out across the yard and down the far side of the buildings. He guides its wobbling wheel along the wooden plank set against the pungent midden and upends it at the top.

When the milking parlour is clear of muck, he fills large buckets from the outside pump, working the heavy handle until water whooshes from its wrought-iron mouth. Taking a bucket in each hand he staggers back, the muscles in his neck standing proud as he strains under their combined weight. He sluices the floor one bucket at a time, sweeping through the swilled water with a hard-bristled broom until he fancies the stone practically gleams.

'He's giving you all the glamorous jobs, I see,' Gwen says as Jack ushers the last of the lying water out into the yard. She stands just beyond the door, her swollen foot cocked behind her, while she rests upon an upturned broom, its head – covered with a towel – tucked in her armpit.

'Impromptu crutch,' she explains with a wry smile. 'Muriel's idea.'

Jack finds her grin infectious. 'Very fetching.'

'How are you finding it?'

'It's proper graft . . . but I don't mind that.'

'Well, there's a pot of tea made up at the house. Dad usually comes in for one about now.'

'Fair enough, I'll just finish up here.'

She smiles and hobbles around. He returns inside to put away the broom and the buckets. When he comes to leave, he expects to see Gwen by the back door, but instead she has carried on past the house and is heading towards the gate and the stand from where the milk lorry collects the full churns each morning. He pauses in the doorway of the milking parlour watching her. There is something determined about the set of her shoulders as she labours her way down the yard with more speed than he has seen her use since her accident – with more speed than he thinks is wise. She is hurrying, that is clear, but her purpose is not.

She stops at the gatepost and wriggles a brick clear from the top, slipping something into the gap before swiftly replacing it. As she turns back, she catches sight of him watching her. Though she is too far away for him to clearly see her expression, Jack detects a tell-tale stiffening in her stance.

She drops her chin to her chest then resumes her return to the house.

Jim has Jack labouring for the rest of the day. The morning is spent cutting thistles from a fallow field that is to be cultivated, pressed into action by the local War Agricultural Executive Committee.

'If this war comes, the WarAg will make us plough up every damn acre we have, because it'll be crops the country will be crying out for, not meat. They'll be wanting every inch of land working as hard as it can if the country is to feed itself and not rely on imports – and you can't say it's doing that if it's just fattening up a few lambs for the Sunday roast. I can see us having to plough up every meadow before next year, if Chamberlain can't work things out with that bloody German,' Jim says, whipping his thistling hook through the spiky clumps before them with a dexterity and skill that Jack envies – his own wielding of the unfamiliar blade is decidedly cack-handed. 'Can't believe it's the same bloody lot as last time,' the farmer grumbles.

When the thistles have been thwarted they change tools, and Jim shows him how to cut back the spurting hedge that now encroaches upon the field, earning himself the chuntering disapproval of an evicted wren who flits to a nearby hazel to berate them.

By the time they break for lunch, Jack's palms are sore with fluid-filled blisters, his skin chafed by the billhook's wooden handle, but he makes no complaint. Instead, he helps the farmer gather the rubbish into a heap. Jim sets it alight with a match and it crackles and pops as the fire takes hold. He roots around for a long stick and when he finds one that pleases him, he unwraps the Spam sandwiches that Muriel has cut for them, and skewers one on the end to toast over the building flames. When it is cooked to his satisfaction, he pulls it free, juggling it like a hot potato as he offers it to Jack, amused by his dubious expression. The bread is a little charred, Jack finds, as he takes his first tentative bite, but the overall effect is surprisingly tasty and soon he is enjoying the hot sandwich with gusto, grinning sheepishly at the farmer's teasing taunts of 'doubting Thomas'.

Jim leaves him alone just before four, charging him with completing the task while he returns to the farm for the afternoon milking. Jack works consistently, pausing every so often to wipe the sweat from his forehead with the back of his arm, squinting up into the blue sky at a bird of prey he is unable to identify. As it wheels above him, he marvels at the unfamiliar peace of nature – the soft rush of rippling leaves, the warbling bird song, the thrum of bees crawling over the speckled petals of bramble blossom. For a moment, he is captivated by the fluttering dance of a butterfly, so blue it is as if a fragment of sky has fallen to earth to play upon the gentle breeze. For the first time since leaving Newcastle something settles inside him, filling the emptiness in the pit of his stomach, and the ever-present pain in his chest that has threatened to consume him recedes a fraction.

But it proves a false respite. Jenny requires no invitation to invade his thoughts, because she is already there, lingering in the dark recesses of his mind, a ghost he can sense if not see. Just as he is beginning to take succour in the new marvels that surround him, her spirit, unbidden, whispers into his consciousness and he finds himself thinking how she would have delighted in this bucolic scene. His vision blurs as an image of her tipping her freckled face to the sun burns itself into his mind's eye. In an instant, with a flood of anguish and remorse, his quiet contentment is destroyed. He is grateful then that he is alone. As the sun becomes lost behind a cavalcade of cloud the raptor plummets upon its prey, and sobs wrack Jack's body as he weeps for all that is lost and for acts that can never be undone.

Just after five, he gathers his things. His outpouring of grief has proven cathartic; his tension has ebbed, his anxieties – for the time being at least – have been ameliorated. The labour has also served to cleanse his soul, and as he leaves the small field, he pauses to survey the neat hedgerow and the thistle-free pasture. He savours his sense of satisfaction over his endeavours, manifested in the scratched and blistered hands he splays before him.

He takes a wrong turn on the way back to the farm and for a while is lost amongst banked narrow lanes bordered by fields which all the look the same. It is with some relief that he finally sees the white-rendered farmhouse rising like a beacon in the distance, and eventually he succeeds in guiding himself to it.

He does not go straight in. First, he washes up at the pump, splashing his face with handfuls of icy water, hoping to remove all evidence of his tears. He dries himself on the rolled sleeve of his shirt, then uses his wet hands to smooth down his errant hair.

Gwen is hobbling around the table laying cutlery while complaining to her father about paperwork as he enters through the back door. It is Muriel's early afternoon and she has already returned home, leaving Gwen to dish up the pie she has left in the warming oven. Jack offers to take the cutlery from her and as she relinquishes the task, their eyes meet and the knowledge of what he accidentally witnessed that morning comes between them. Her gaze slides from his, slick with guilt. Her secrecy fuels his curiosity, but he has no right to question her, so he remains silent as he sets out the places, and for that she appears grateful. Whatever she might be up to, it is clear they will not speak of it.

After they have eaten, Jim invites Jack to join them in the sitting room, just as he had the evening before. Gwen uses the broom crutch to make her way through the house, collapsing into an armchair by the unlit fire with a gusty sigh, before resting the swollen foot on a leather pouffe.

Jim retrieves the evening paper from the letterbox in the

front door, the brass plate rattling as it is released. He sits across from Gwen, methodically reading every article, and when he has finished and the paper rests in his lap, Jack leans forwards in his chair and asks if he might see it. The newspaper is passed between them like a baton in a relay race – but only Jack is aware of its importance. His mouth is dry as he scans each page, alert for the words that will catch his eye and reel him in. He is immune to the other headlines that vie for his attention – there is only one story that interests him and he knows it might not be boldly splashed across a page, but lurking in some innocuous corner, so he is thorough in his task.

'Looking for news of home?' Jim asks, pushing himself up to retrieve his packet of cigarettes from the mantel.

'Aye, something like that,' Jack admits quietly, heady with a bemusing cocktail of shame and relief as he finally closes the paper, his fears allayed for another day.

Just before nine, Jim turns on the wireless to catch the BBC News. They sit in companionable silence as an elegant voice reveals developments that appear to be the next steps in the inevitable march to war. Gwen loses herself in thoughts that lie beyond the window, her fingers limp on the novel in her lap.

Later, while there is still enough light in the sky, Jack accompanies Jim outside to complete the day's chores. They round up the chickens and shut them in the coop safe from roaming foxes, then check on the horses placidly cropping grass in the paddock. Jim sends Kip to his straw bed in the corner of the implement shed and, at last, they head back to the house for a final cup of cocoa that Gwen has promised to make in their absence.

'You must find us as dull as ditchwater after a life in the city,' she says, gently blowing across the top of her steaming mug, but Jack is quick with his contradictions.

When he finally bids them goodnight there is only moonlight to guide him across the uneven yard. He lets himself into the tack room and fumbles for the matches to light the candle, which is stuck upon a saucer with a dried puddle of wax. In its feeble glow, he strips off his clothes and slips his aching body between the bedsheets. The ticking-covered mattress surrenders without resistance to his weight. His head sinks into the feather pillow and he lies listening to some small creature skitter along the back wall. He permits himself a single thought of Jenny, then stretches over to blow out the candle. Its smoky trail fades into the darkness like a will o' the wisp. He closes his eyes and, as he finally allows his weariness to possess him, he is surprised to discover his greatest sensation is peace.

CHAPTER THIRTEEN

Gwen

8th May 1945

Tom is getting tired and Gwen herself is exhausted from the intricate dance she has been performing all night, as she sidesteps questions about Jack, nimbly skirting the subject with ambiguous answers and a few downright lies. Her head throbs from trying to keep track of all the half-truths she's told and who she's told them to, ever mindful that local gossip might further spin the tales she's spun.

It all puts her in mind of an incident from her youth, when she was caught trying to sneak out to a dance she had been forbidden to attend. She had facilitated her escape with an assortment of convoluted fibs that proved hard to keep track of. Her father had eventually fathomed out what she was up to and intercepted her en route, dragging her back home, banishing her to her room. She had flung herself upon her bed and sobbed at the unfairness of it all. 'If you're going to lie,' Muriel had told her, having mustered a little sympathy for her suffering, 'make up one simple tale and stick to it. Embellishments will prove your downfall.'

Muriel's wise advice had fallen on deaf ears and now, years later, Gwen fears she has, once again, tried too hard and said too much.

Tom's head is heavy on her arm. They are crammed into the bowed window seat of the lounge bar with Muriel, while Ted has taken one of the chairs on the opposite side of the table. Gwen gently tips Tom towards her housekeeper, then shuffles along the cushioned velveteen seat pocked with cigarette burns.

'I'm going to find Nora, I think we ought to be heading off.'

The public bar is as busy as it ever was. The quarry-tiled floor beneath her feet is tacky with spilt beer and a wiry terrier is lapping up a puddle from beneath a bar stool. Gwen spots Nora in the far corner, playing to a crowded table of young men sporting drink-flushed faces, and she knows at once that the Land Girl will not be coming home. She is laughing loudly, her throaty rasp inviting and sensuous as she sits on the lap of the youngest Adler boy whose family farms across the valley, uncaring that the skirt of her dress has ridden up to expose more thigh than is decent. Gwen suddenly feels much older than her twenty-five years, and she is on the brink of abandoning her fruitless mission when Nora spies her through the fog of cigarette smoke.

'Gwen! There you are! Come and join us. Move along, boys, let the lady take a seat.'

'No, no really, I can't sit down . . .' Gwen stutters, halting the noisy seat shuffle. 'Tom's tuckered out, so I'm going to take him home. I just wondered whether you were ready?'

Nora rifles through the many cigarette boxes discarded amongst the drained glasses on the table until she finds one that isn't empty. Helping herself, she calls for a light.

'I thought I might stay on a bit longer yet.' She leans across the table to cup the flaming match offered by one of her eager lotharios. She draws in and sits back, wriggling herself into a better position to address Gwen. 'You don't mind, do you?' Tendrils of smoke carry her words.

'Of course not.' Gwen smiles stiffly. She stopped trying to influence Nora's behaviour a long time ago. 'Stay as long as you like.'

Nora gets to her feet. She whips the cigarette from her mouth and holds it away as she kisses Gwen's cheek. 'Thanks, darling.' She tips her lips to Gwen's ear. 'Don't wait up.' She winks before plonking herself back down on young Adler's lap. His arm belts her waist, securing her in position as she effortlessly insinuates herself back into the raucous conversation. Gwen decides to leave them to it.

By the time she rejoins her table, Tom is barely able to keep his eyes open. She curses herself for not having had the foresight to bring her bicycle – at least then she could have wheeled him home – but now she must either cajole him into walking or carry him.

'Will you be all right?' Muriel asks, concern edging her voice as she chivvies the exhausted boy off the seat.

'We'll be fine,' Gwen assures him, taking Tom's hand, but doubt settles in as he rests his full weight against her.

'Here, I'm heading off myself, I'll come with you.' Ted tips back the dregs of his beer.

'You don't have to . . .'

'No, no I need to be getting back.'

It is dusk as they duck under the lintel. The air has grown chilly and Gwen's skin protests at its cool caress. She regrets not bringing a coat for Tom at least, but he is too tired to moan about the cold. He drags himself along beside her, his hand loose in hers. The change in air causes Ted to start coughing. He tries to contain it as he roots for his cigarettes. He is still spluttering as he lights one but manages to draw the smoke deep into his lungs. It seems to work. He offers the pack to Gwen, but she shakes her head.

They have not long left the pub garden when Tom begins to whine.

'Come here, lad, let's be having you.' Ted tosses away his cigarette and swings the boy onto his back. Tom links his hands around the farmer's neck and rests his cheek against his shoulder blade.

'Are you sure . . .?' Gwen asks.

'Yes, he's fine.'

'Well, if he starts to get heavy, I can take him.'

'Gwen, he's as light as a feather.'

They walk in silence, easy in each other's company. Ted begins to pant as he reaches the top of the hill, the village falling away behind them, but he rebuffs Gwen's renewed offer to take the boy. The wind susurrates through the trees and somewhere to their left a fox bark disturbs the hush, eerie in the dimming light, as threads of pink straddle the violet horizon – promise of a good day to come.

The white render of the farmhouse takes on an ethereal hue in the twilight. The windows stare blankly down on them and Gwen wishes now she had drawn the curtains before they left. As their steps dwindle to a standstill, she reaches for Tom.

'I'll carry him up for you,' Ted offers.

'Oh no, you've carried him far enough,' Gwen says, guiding

the sleeping boy into her arms. His eyelids flicker momentarily, but the realisation he is safely in his mother's grasp lulls him back into slumber.

'I don't mind. I like to help.'

Gwen detects an uncharacteristic gravitas in Ted's words. She hesitates. 'I know.'

The breeze pushes a strand of hair across her cheek. She juggles Tom's weight, freeing up a hand so she can tuck it behind her ear.

As they stand in the gathering darkness, the silence between them grows heavy with words unspoken. Tom shifts in Gwen's arms, mumbling sleepily as he slides his thumb into his mouth.

'I'd better get him in . . .'

Bidding Ted goodnight, she starts through the gateway. She turns back on an afterthought. Ted has not moved.

'Come for dinner tomorrow? Nora snared two rabbits today – Muriel is promising a stew of sorts.'

'Thank you. I will.'

'Goodnight, then.'

She does not look around again as she continues up to the house, but as she reaches the steps she hears his cough, faint on the wind, and knows that he is still there, watching her safely in.

CHAPTER FOURTEEN

Jack

June 1939

A gentle tapping at the window rouses him. He has been awake for much of the night, haunted by the memory of his fist pummelling flesh. For the past week, his nightmares have pursued him into consciousness and he cannot outrun them pacing the tack room's cobbled floor.

For the first time, he appreciates why the war-destroyed men his mother favoured would wake up screaming in the night. As a boy, he would bolt up in bed, wide-eyed and petrified, his heart thudding in the dark, and then through the paper-thin walls he would hear his mother soothing them, as one might calm a baby, until their sobs subsided. In the morning, dues paid, they would shuffle down the stairs, unable to meet his eye as he watched them leave – always via the back door to the yard, where they could slip out without being seen. His mother, still in her grubby nightgown, would tap a cigarette from the box on the table and tell him how it was her bit of kindness, comforting fellows such as these.

'They've seen things, done things, Jack, that stay with a man, play on his mind. War casts long shadows . . . especially at night.'

He failed then to appreciate the damage inflicted upon those tortured souls, but since the night he fled, he has come to understand the extent of their suffering, for now he too is haunted by things he can never unsee, by things he cannot undo. His sense of disconnect from the man he was to the man he has – over the course of one night – become is profound. He always feared it was in him, that seed of violence. He could almost feel its insidious roots penetrating every aspect of his being, leaching the goodness from his soul, waiting for that moment when it would finally break through his epidermis and unfurl in all its dark glory to dominate his landscape and blight his future with its deadly shade.

The tapping comes again. He rolls over on the unforgiving camp bed and squints up at the window from under heavy eyelids.

Gwen stands outside, her arm raised across her. She grins and points to her wristwatch, then beckons him. Jack feels for his own watch, laid out on the apple crate, and seeing the hour he curses and throws back the covers. He glances again at the window, relieved to see that Gwen has withdrawn, affording him some privacy as he pulls on his trousers and snatches his shirt from the back of the chair.

She is leaning against the stable wall, fondling Kip's ears when he finally emerges.

'Your foot back to working order I take it?' he says.

'It's good enough and I can't bear the thought of another day trapped in the office. I persuaded Dad last night to let me resume my duties. I have a present for you.' She holds out a folded white coat that matches her own. He takes it, bewildered. 'Today we make a dairy farmer out of you. Come on, I'm going to teach you to milk a cow.'

The lane is deserted as they go to collect the herd. The rising sun streaks the horizon with gold and stains the clustering clouds pink, while a fine mist hovers low over the fields, like the exhaled breath of a land stirring to life. The morning chorus is already playing at full volume.

The cows jog up the field when Gwen calls, their great hulks rippling. She holds the gate wide and they lumber through, steam billowing from their nostrils.

'Watch out, they'll happily trample you if you stand in their way,' she warns and Jack drops back to the grass verge that glistens with dew.

The cows lead the way back to the farm, their bony hips rising and falling under thinly stretched hides, their purple-veined udders swelling between their hind legs. Kip saunters left to right behind them, occasionally falling back to investigate an enticing scent in the hedgerow, before sprinting to catch up.

'You've been doing this forever, I suppose . . .' Jack says, when the silence between them becomes strained. 'Helping your dad?'

Gwen calls Kip away from something decomposing in the undergrowth. 'Not at first. It was after Mum died that I started taking a real interest. I think . . .' She looks off into the distance as she collects her thoughts. 'I think when she died I became terrified that Dad would die too, and then what would happen to me? So, I'd follow him around to keep an eye on him – make sure he was all right.'

She smiles. 'I drove Muriel mad. She'd leave me for five minutes stewing apple on the range and come back to find the apple burnt dry, the back door flung open and me nowhere in sight. Dad would send me back in with a flea in my ear, but it didn't make any difference. I used to take off from school too. As soon as morning break came, I'd sneak over the playground wall and make my way home.' Her laugh rings with impish delight. 'When he was at his wits' end, Dad offered me a deal: he'd let me help with anything he was doing, as long as I'd spent all day in school getting my education. That seemed fair enough.'

'So, is there anything you don't do?'

'No.' She laughs. 'He gave me a pony for my fifth birthday, a cow for my eighth and a pig for my tenth. I was milking by nine, ploughing by thirteen, and I had my own business raising geese for Christmas by fourteen. I can't dress a goose,' she declares with an air of triumph, having inadvertently stumbled on the answer to his question. 'I always left that to Muriel, in return for a cut of the profits.'

'Very enterprising.'

'I love it,' she confides with unashamed candour, 'this life. It's hard work, relentless . . . but there is nothing better than being outside, working the farm. I don't think I was ever cut out for anything else. The school room was an alien environment for me. There was nothing worth learning there, not when nature could teach me everything I needed to know. I belong to the land. It's part of me and I'm part of it.'

'I envy you that. That sense of belonging. I don't think I've ever felt that.'

'Not at home? Where you're from?'

'No. I mean, obviously the city's familiar, but it's a dirty, noisy, bustling place – I never relished being there – and perhaps it can afford opportunities, but it never really afforded me any. I worked the shipyards out of necessity, not passion. It was a job, a wage. I never felt any affinity with it, not like what you feel. I can tell, listening to you talk like that – you talk from in here.' Jack pats his chest with a furled fist. 'From the heart, like.'

'Yes . . . you're right. My heart is here, in this, in all I do. Whenever I clear a ditch, or plough a furrow, sow a field, pleach a hedge . . . I'm putting a little bit of me into it. Sometimes I don't know where I stop and the farm begins.'

'There's poetry in that.'

'Yes . . . yes, I think there is.'

As instinctive as Gwen's connection is with the land, so is the herd's sense of direction. They lead the way down the narrow country lane and when the farm gate appears, they turn into it, bellowing their arrival as they amble up the yard to the holding pen at the side of the milking parlour.

'Never underestimate the intelligence of a cow,' Gwen grins, as Jack exclaims his surprise. She swings the gate shut behind them. 'They can outsmart the best of us if they choose.'

Gwen shoos the first few cattle inside. They trudge into their preferred stalls and wait to be relieved of their bloated udders. Gwen hands Jack a bucket of soapy water and a rag.

'They need to be cleaned up before they're milked,' she explains, and shows him how to wash the mud and muck from the teats and milk sacs.

Jack feels the pressure of her supervision as she stands over him; he is profoundly relieved when he completes the task to her evident satisfaction. She fetches a galvanised pail and a three-legged milking stool, then calls for his attention as she settles herself down. Leaning her head into the cow's soft flank, she takes a firm grip of its teats and begins to work them, pulling them gently until jets of milk rattle into the empty pail beneath.

She continues for a couple of minutes then stands aside, urging Jack to take her place. He squats down on the stool, all gangly limbs, like a giant who has blundered into the wrong fairy tale. Leaning forward, he puts his forehead against the stretched plane of hide and instinctively apologises for what he is about to do, eliciting a poorly suppressed smile from Gwen. Abashed, he reaches under the cow and closes his fingers around two teats, hot beneath his cold hands. He tugs down, just as Gwen had done, but nothing happens. He tries again and the cow stamps her back hoof against the stone floor of the stall. When he tries a third time to no avail, the poor creature looks round to glare at him.

'You need to gently squeeze at the same time as you pull,' Gwen says, 'that's what a calf does, you see . . .' She leans over him, her body lightly pressed against his as she covers his hands with her own. 'Like this . . .' She applies pressure to his fingers until they move under hers. The milk spurts into the pail with a satisfying *whisst – whisst* as she picks up the rhythm. 'You try,' she encourages, her breath warm on his stubbled cheek as she relaxes her grip, though her hands continue to rest on his as he works the cow's teats alone. When the milk flows steadily into the pail she draws back. Jack tries to focus on the task in hand, yet he can't help feeling bereft as she moves away.

She rewards him with a smile that lifts his soul when he finally drains the udder dry. She shows him how to weigh and log the cow's yield in the milk ledger, before tipping the warm milk into the cooler; then she starts him on the next cow, and when she is confident he can be left to work alone, she sets about her own milking.

Jack insists on tackling the final beast.

'Oh, I'm not sure . . . Meredith can be a bit of a handful . . .' Gwen warns, but he dismisses her concerns.

'You watch, I'm an old hand at this now,' he says, settling himself down on the milking stool, the pail chinking against the stone as he places it ready.

'Well, if you're sure . . .' Gwen says, resting against the side of the stall.

'Aye, you're making a fuss, lass.' Jack grins as he starts working the teats. His confidence grows as the milk flows freely. He is unperturbed by the back hoof that paws the stone with building impatience, nor does he notice Gwen's wary expression.

'There you are . . . no problems at all . . .' he crows as the milk begins to wane.

The cow's tail hitches and Gwen recoils. He looks around in time to see a cascade of liquid muck flow from the cow's rear, spattering onto the stone, splashing his trouser leg. The smell is ripe. Cursing, he springs up just as the ill-tempered cow delivers a well-aimed kick to the bucket, sending it clattering onto its side, a river of creamy milk mingling with the steaming slurry to form a sickening mire.

Forgetting himself, Jack throws up his arms swearing like the docker he is, damning the animal before him to hell and back. It is some minutes before he notices Gwen is doubled over. As he falls silent, she throws back her head. Her raucous guffaw rips through the milking parlour and the tears streaming down her cheeks charm his furious scowl into a fool's grin.

She is still teasing him as they roll the final churns down to the milk stand at the farm gate, ready for collection by the local creamery. Jack grunts as he lifts them up onto the platform, the metal casings grating as he nestles them together.

'All done,' he says.

They turn back for the yard, but just after Jack has passed through the gate, Gwen drops down to a crouch.

'Laces,' she declares, as she begins to redo them. 'Go on, I'll catch you up. Pour me a cup of tea, will you?'

He heads towards the house, but as he reaches the steps, he looks back. Gwen is no longer attending to her boot laces, instead she appears to be retrieving something from under the loose brick in the gatepost.

Whatever it is, one thing is clear: she does not want anyone to see.

Jack carries out his careful study of the newspaper again that evening. There is news of the royal trip to America; of bombs exploding in post offices and pillar boxes across London, Manchester and Birmingham as the IRA terrorises the country, but there is no news from Newcastle. Once again, he shuts the paper with a sense of relief, though the twin monkeys of fear and guilt cling stubbornly to his back. As he sinks into his chair, his anxieties soothed by the gentle music emanating from the wireless, he realises his urge to run is dissipating. He steals a look at Gwen. He is safe to stay. For a little while, he cautions himself silently. Just for a little while. He cannot risk becoming complacent.

He bids the others goodnight and makes the now-familiar trek across the yard to the tack room, his way lit by a moon unfettered by clouds. When he lights the candle on the apple crate, he hears Kip whine and then a muted voice. As he goes out to investigate, Gwen appears in the stable doorway with the dog at her heels and something draped over her arm.

'I forgot these earlier,' she says. 'I just thought with the bright mornings and me padding about at all hours, you should have the option of a little privacy. They're curtains,' she explains in the face of his confusion

He expresses his gratitude. Unsure what to do, he offers to take them, but she shakes her head and brushes past him.

'I'll hang them for you.'

'Is there anything to hang them from?' he asks, rubbing the back of his neck as he follows her into the room, suddenly conscious of the unmade bed.

'There should be. The last chap had some curtains in here, but I think the moths ate them clean away.' She appears to be talking to herself as much as to him, as she peers up above the window frame. 'You see? The cord is still there. Here, take these a minute.'

She passes him the curtains and stretches up on tiptoe to reach the taut line that has been strung between two hooks. The fabric is kitten soft against his bare skin and he realises with some surprise that it is green velvet. Gwen's shirt tugs loose of her waistband. He catches a glimpse of pale skin and looks away.

'There we are, let me . . .' Taking the first panel from him she threads the cord through the open hem she has sewn at the top, then gives it to Jack to hold while she threads on the second panel, the fabric bunching as she slides it along. When she is done, they raise the laden cord between them and hook it into place. 'There.' She stands back to survey her work before pulling the material together, closing them in the room with only the candle flame offering any resistance to the darkness.

'Velvet curtains are very fancy for my humble abode,' he observes.

'It's just offcuts from a dress I'm making.'

'Must be some dress.' He notices how the material catches the candlelight and for a moment allows himself to imagine Gwen draped in that same shimmering fabric. How she would dazzle a room.

'I'm going to a ball on Saturday night . . .' Her face clouds as she drops her gaze to the floor. 'Well . . . hoping to go . . . I'd very much like to go . . .' She looks up and smiles again. 'I'm more inclined to go now, knowing you'll be here to keep Dad company. So perhaps you can see the curtains as a little thank you, from me.'

Jack doesn't understand why his presence should make all the difference, but she offers no further explanation.

'Anyway, I shouldn't delay you any longer . . . I just thought you'd like them up for tomorrow morning.'

He accompanies her to the outside door, where Kip is waiting patiently in a scoop of moonlight.

'Goodnight, Jack.'

'Goodnight, Gwen. And thank you . . . for the curtains.'

'Well, I don't want to see anything I shouldn't when I come to wake you up at the crack of dawn.'

He matches her wry grin and watches her walk away with the dog at her heels, feeling suddenly more awake than ever.

CHAPTER FIFTEEN

Jack

June 1939

The day's task is to plough up the fallow field Jack has thistled and hedged. Gwen shows him how to tack up the two Clydesdales, positioning the black leather harnesses over their broad backs before fastening buckles and girths. When the horses are bedecked and chomping the jointed metal bits lying in the hollows between their teeth, they lead them, one apiece, across the yard from the stable block to the implement shed. They hold them steady while Jim couples up the plough, attaching lengths of chain to their huge collars.

Jack expresses an interest in learning to work with the horses and Jim notes the natural affinity he shares with them. The two giants respond well to his quiet disposition, nuzzling his shoulder as he wraps an arm under their platter cheeks to whisper in their twitching ears.

'We'll soon have you working this pair,' Jim says as he gathers up the length of rein and lifts the ploughshare clear of the ground.

They walk down the lane, Jim running the plough on its

wheel while Gwen and Jack grip onto the horses' bridles. The day is overcast; the light of the watery sun is diffused by a thin film of cloud, and the damp air threatens rain.

They lead the horses through the gateway and line them up ready, leaving a margin at the edge of the field. Jim calls for Jack to join him, while Gwen remains at the horses' heads. He talks him through the handling of the reins and how to guide the plough so that its blade slices through the heavy clay, which the mouldboard behind turns over into smooth plasticine folds. He shows him how to bring the horses round at the end of the furrow and how to line them up so that the ridges form in perfect symmetry. Jack quickly appreciates there is artistry in the farmer's handling of steel and steed. Heads bowed, the horses cross the field to the rattle of chain and clink of metal as the blades catch on flints and stones. Above them, a flock of gulls whirl and cry, pitching periodically to plunder the freshly exposed earth. The threatening rain holds off.

By mid-morning, a third of the field has transformed to corrugated soil, contrasting sharply with the remaining grass. From the lane, they hear the chunter of a car engine and shortly after a figure appears in the gateway. He holds up a hand in greeting then makes his way across, waiting for them at the end of the furrow, his pocketed hands pushing back the sides of his shabby tweed jacket.

'Morning, Ted,' Gwen calls.

'Morning, Gwen. Jim.'

Jack senses the stranger's lingering scrutiny as Jim draws back on the reins, bringing the horses to a standstill.

'Ted – how are you?'

'Well, thank you. This is looking very nice.'

'Ah, it's turning well. What can we do for you?'

'I've come to ask a favour. My Judy's gone lame and I wanted to harrow the west field tomorrow. I wondered if there was any chance I might borrow one of your two?' He nods towards the horses.

'Ah, of course. I tell you what, when we've finished up here, I'll get Gwen to walk Bobby over, Brenda can get the plough home on her own. You can put him out to graze and he'll be all ready for you tomorrow then.'

'That sounds good. Thank you, Jim. I'm most grateful to you.'

'What are neighbours for, if not to help each other out? Now, I've just thought, you've not met my new labourer.' Jim leans on the plough handle. 'This here's Jack, he'll be helping me out for a few months.'

The farmer strides forward, his boots sinking into the turned earth. His paw-like hand swallows Jack's in a fearsome grip.

'Nice to meet you,' Jack says, flexing his crushed fingers by his side.

'That's not a local accent.'

'No.'

'Where are you from?'

'Sunderland,' Jack says, pleased that this time the lie falls without hesitation.

'You're a long way from home.'

He shrugs. 'I wanted to spread my wings a little, broaden my horizons.'

'You farmed before?'

'No, it's all new to me.'

'Ah, he's taking to it like a duck to water,' Jim crows from behind them, using the opportunity to fish his Woodbines from his jacket pocket. He offers the packet to his neighbour, who gladly pulls one free, but Jack, when offered, shakes his head.

'And how are you, Gwen?' Ted turns to address her, patting his pockets to elicit the tell-tale rattle of a matchbox.

'I'm well, thank you.'

'She's off to the Summer Ball at Netley Hall on Saturday,' Jim says, lighting up.

Ted locates his packet of Bryant and May, but this revelation gives him pause. 'Saturday?' He retracts his darted look from Jim and turns to Gwen. 'This Saturday?' he checks softly.

Jack notices how Gwen's smile falters. 'Jack's going to keep Dad company, aren't you, Jack?' There is a stark desperation in the look she gives him.

'Aye.' He senses a contract between them, though he is not privy to its detail. He frowns, but Gwen's apparent concern seems alleviated by their pact.

'I thought I might go down to the Hare and Hounds,' Jim pipes up. He draws deeply on his cigarette, holding onto the smoke as he removes the fag with dirt-blackened fingers. 'What do you say, Ted? Fancy joining me for a pint?'

'You said you would stay in.' There is a note of horror in Gwen's blurted interjection. 'You said you'd stay in with Jack.'

'I don't see why we should stay in when you're out having all the fun . . .'

'Dad . . .'

'Oh Gwen, can't a man go out for a jar every now and then? And if Jack wants to come, he's more than welcome. What do you say – Ted? Jack?'

For an awful moment, Gwen appears on the verge of tears,

but her features harden as she looks between the two men. Ted picks a fleck of tobacco from his bottom lip.

'Ah,' he says at last, shifting his stance. 'I don't see why not. Been a while since I was down the Hare and Hounds.'

Gwen opens her mouth to speak, then appears to rein herself in, but her tightly pressed lips still manage to convey her resentful fury.

'What about it, Jack? Will you join us old boys for a beer?'

'Not so much of the old, Jim,' Ted chuckles.

'You're a whippersnapper compared to me, it's true,' the farmer laughs, resting on the plough, smoke spiralling skyward from the cigarette caught between his fingers. 'Well, Jack?'

Jack does not want to go to the pub. He wants to stay hidden at the house, out of sight. Safe. But Gwen casts him such a look of naked appeal he knows he has no choice.

'Aye . . .' His voice catches in his throat. 'Aye, I'll join you for a pint, why not.'

Gwen attempts to conceal her trembling mouth by turning away to rub the horses' blazes. When she finally composes herself, it is Jack she seeks out.

He does not understand what he has done to earn the gratitude that warms her features.

But he knows he will do anything to keep it.

Jim attempts to goad Gwen at breakfast on Saturday morning.

'Well, I don't know, Gwen . . . I can't really let you off your chores just so you can go and get dolled up for some dance.'

'I don't mind not going, you know. If you'd rather I stay . . .'

Jack looks up from his plate. The levity that lifted Jim's words is markedly absent from Gwen's.

'Don't be daft, girl. You're going to the ball.'

'But . . .'

'No buts, you're going.' Jim waves away her doubts with his knife and fork.

Gwen does not seem relieved. Indeed, as the week has progressed Jack has noticed how quiet she has become. He has also noticed the leaden looks she exchanges with Muriel whenever Saturday is mentioned and the shallow frown that appears like fretwork on her brow.

'You do the milking this afternoon as normal, and I'll come and help Jack clean up after. How's that? Will that be time enough?'

'I'll put the copper on for you, so you can have a bath when you come in.' Muriel half-turns from the stove where she is frying off some beef for a casserole.

Gwen's expression of gratitude strikes Jack as half-hearted.

They spend the day sowing peas in the field which Jack himself harrowed the day before. He was powerless to hide his pleasure when he finished the task, with both Jim and Gwen approving his efforts.

'I'm going to have to scrub like mad to get this mud out of my nails,' Gwen says to him later, examining her grimy fingers as they go together to bring the cattle in for milking. 'Jack . . . tonight . . . could you try and make sure Dad doesn't get too carried away in the pub?'

'Is he likely to?'

She throws a glance to the horizon, sending it on its way with a slight shrug of her shoulders. 'I can trust you to look out for him, can't I?'

'He's a grown man, Gwen . . .'

'Can't I?'

'Of course.'

She tries to muster a smile, but it wilts on her lips like a parched flower.

'What exactly is it you're worried about, Gwen?'

She tips her head back. The breeze ruffles the loose strands of hair that have escaped the scarf knotted at the base of her skull.

'I'm just being foolish . . . I'm sure there's nothing to worry about,' she says at last. 'Nothing at all.'

Gwen is uncharacteristically quiet as she finishes the milking. When Jim appears to take over the cleaning up, she offers again to remain at home for the evening.

'Go away with you!' Jim protests, snatching up the broom. 'After you've spent all that time making a new dress? Gwen, there's no need to be creating all this fuss, no need at all.'

'But Dad . . .'

'Enough, Gwen,' he snaps, causing her to flinch. Jack pauses his sluicing of the floor. Jim gathers himself, his temper easing. 'Go and get ready, Gwen. I want to see you all done up.'

He leans into the broom after she has gone. 'Always fussing over me.'

Jack throws the remaining bucket of water over the stone and refrains from asking questions.

Muriel dishes up dinner, then removes her apron.

'I'm going to help Gwen get ready,' she says, folding it neatly over the chair, unable to contain her fizz of excitement. She is like the mother of the bride on a wedding day, eager for her daughter to make her entrance. 'It'll be a full house at the Hall this year, what with young Gordon being back from his travels.'

'That wastrel? I can tell you – his absence was no loss,' Jim mutters darkly over his spoonful of stew.

'Well, there's no telling all they said about him was true.' Muriel quicksteps around the table. Jim snorts and mutters again, this time about smoke and fire.

'This stew is right tasty, Muriel,' Jack says as she passes behind his chair. She lays her hand on his shoulder in appreciation of the praise, an encouraging sign of her warming regard.

A light tap on the door is followed by the click of the latch.

'Evening, all,' Ted says as he ducks under the lintel. 'Oh, I'm too early, I didn't mean to interrupt your meal.'

'Have you eaten, Ted?' Muriel calls from the step into the hall. 'There's more in the pot, help yourself.'

'If you're sure?'

'Tuck in, Ted,' Jim insists. 'Gwen's having supper at the ball, so there's plenty to go around.'

'Well, just a taste then.' Ted moves around the kitchen with marked familiarity, collecting a plate from the dresser, before lifting the ladle from the pot.

'Muriel was just saying the Allingham lad is back.'

'Gordon? He's been back a while now.' Ted sets down his plate and pulls out a chair. 'How's Gwen getting to the Hall?'

'The Hendersons are picking her up. I'll go and collect her.'

They have just finished eating when Muriel's voice carries down the stairs like a shrill bird call.

When they fail to respond, she bursts into the kitchen, bright spots of excitement blotching her drawn cheeks.

'Well? Don't you want to come and see her?'

'Ah, of course we do,' Jim says, smiling broadly as he shoves back his chair and levers himself up, the others following suit.

They traipse into the hall, Ted bringing up the rear.

Muriel arranges them by the front door with the stairs rising before them.

'They're ready for you, Gwen!'

'There's really no need for all this . . .' Gwen's floating voice contains a hint of exasperation.

She appears at the top of the stairs. There is an audible intake of breath from Ted.

'Oh now, Gwen, love . . .' Jim claps his hands together as further words fail him.

Jack cannot breathe. He stares up at her. Short cap sleeves cover her shoulders and a square-cut bodice clings to her torso, nipping in at her waist, before flowing out in an emerald skirt that skims her hips to pool at her feet, a shimmering waterfall of velvet. Her freshly washed hair is scooped back and falls around her face in gentle waves. She has kept her make-up light: a touch of powder, a discreet coat of lipstick. She is, he thinks, perfection itself.

'Will I do?' The question reveals the fragility of her confidence. It is as delicate as finely blown glass – one careless touch and it will shatter.

'Do? Will you do? By God, Gwen, you look beautiful.' Jim turns to the two men beside him. 'Doesn't she look a peach, lads?'

Ted's voice is rusty; his cheeks colour as he stumbles through his flattery. Jack remains silent. He does not trust himself to speak.

Gwen glides down the stairs, the velvet rippling with each step, clearly embarrassed by their overt admiration. Muriel drapes a fox stole around her shoulders and hands her a silver clutch.

The brass bell jangling above the front door instigates a flurry of activity. Muriel clucks over Gwen, checking she has all she needs, while Ted and Jack fall back into the shadows. Jack notices how Ted tugs at his own shirt, as if regretting his lacklustre appearance. Jim tussles with the wedged bolts on the little-used entrance until eventually they give way and, with a turn of the key, he pulls open the door to reveal a girl of Gwen's age, dressed in pink satin. A car idles in the lane.

'Hello, Lucy dear, don't you look pretty as a picture.' Jim is more jovial than Jack has ever seen him. 'I won't kiss you,' he laughs, as he hands Gwen over the threshold. 'I don't want to leave a grubby mark on your cheek. Thank your parents for me, Lucy, and Gwen, I'll pick you up at eleven.'

'Oh midnight, please, Dad.'

'*Eleven* and not a minute later!'

Though her father is ushering her out, his hand on her back, Gwen cranes around, searching for Jack. In a silent communiqué, her eyes slide towards Jim. Jack's nod banishes the anxiety that fleetingly mars her perfection and the tension in her shoulders visibly eases as she accompanies her giggling friend from the house.

Jim stands on the doorstep and waves her off until the car has pulled away. When he finally closes the door, Jack notices a wistfulness in his expression that hadn't been evident previously and his features darken as if a scudding cloud has temporarily smothered the sun. When it passes, his returning brightness seems strangely forced. 'Right then.' He rubs his hands together with the vigour of someone trying too hard. 'Let's get ourselves down to the pub.'

*

Jim has had too much to drink and Jack now appreciates the reason for Gwen's concern. He is also struggling to contain his anger at Ted, who seems not only to have condoned the farmer's inebriation, but actively encouraged it.

'Just one more?' Jim slurs, clinging to the tacky bar that seems to be sweating beer.

'Why not?' Ted's eyes shine with alcohol. He holds up his hand to catch the publican's attention.

'Don't you think he's had enough?' Jack hisses.

'What would you know about it?'

'He can barely speak.'

'He needs it,' Ted mutters. He perks up as the publican approaches, but glowers as the man looks ostentatiously at his watch.

'I rang last orders a quarter of an hour ago, Ted.'

'One more, Bill.'

Jack looks at his own watch. Beneath the cracked glass, the hands sit at 10.35 p.m. He gets off his bar stool.

'Jim, it's nearly time to get Gwen.'

'Gwen . . .' the farmer sings his daughter's name. 'My God you should have seen her tonight, Bill.' He sprawls over the bar, sopping up the spillages with his shirt. 'She looked so beautiful, the spitting image of my Vera.'

'One more for the man, for God's sake, Bill,' Ted demands, slapping the bar.

Jack catches the publican's eye. 'I think we should go.' He puts his arm around Jim's shoulders which seem somehow shrunken, weakened by the whisky he's been downing since the beer slaked his thirst. 'Let's get Gwen, Jim.'

Ted grips his arm. 'I said, let the man have one more drink.'

'He's had enough.'

The farmer tightens his hold until his fingers bite into Jack's flesh like a ferret clamping down on a rabbit's throat. 'You know nothing about this man, what he's been through. You don't even know the significance of today, do you? So don't you dare try and tell me what he does and does not need. I know him better than anybody. And I know what he needs and what he needs is one more drink.'

'Is that why Gwen asked me to watch out for her father? Because she knew you couldn't be trusted with the task?' Jack wrenches his arm free.

'Gwen asked you?'

'Perhaps I'm better equipped to know when whisky begins to drown the man and not his sorrows.' Jack cajoles Jim to his feet, but it is his firm arm that keeps the man upright. 'Now, am I dropping you home as well or are you intending to stagger back?' he asks Ted.

The three of them head out into the night, to where Jim's car is parked on the roadside. Jim is stumbling and it is all Jack can do to keep them both on their feet.

'Give me the keys, Jim,' Ted says, walking towards the driver's side with more concentration than should be necessary, banging into the front wing as he misjudges his way. 'I'll drive.'

'The hell you will,' Jack grimaces. 'You're three sheets to the wind as well.'

'I'm perfectly capable—'

'And I'm more capable.' Jack wrestles open the rear door and, with some rough guidance and a bit of shoving, he manages to fold the drunken farmer inside. Jim slumps across the back seat.

Jack curses under his breath as he slams the door and makes his way round to the driver's side. 'I'm driving.'

Ted looks set to argue. Jack draws himself up to his full height, preparing to square up to him, but at the last minute, the other man relents. Slurring some derogatory comment, Ted staggers back to the passenger side, one hand on the bonnet to steady himself. Jack gets in behind the wheel.

He grinds the gears and almost stalls the engine, out of practice and unfamiliar with the car. It's some time since he pootled around the shipyard in a borrowed truck, but before long the natural rhythm of the dance returns to him and soon his feet coordinate effortlessly with the shifting stick.

The night swallows them. The moon is waning, lying on its back as if it too has imbibed too much and toppled into slumber. Jack peers through the windscreen as he struggles to decipher the dimly lit road before him.

'She died eleven years ago today.'

Jack snatches a look at the man beside him. Ted's expression is shrouded in shadows and his voice is thick with alcohol and sorrow.

'Jim's Vera. Gwen's mother. My wife and child had died just a few months earlier. All of them TB.'

'I'm sorry.'

'So, you'll forgive us if we take a few pints this night in memory of what we've lost.' His words are edged with bitterness.

'That's why Gwen wasn't sure . . .' Jack is almost unaware he has voiced his deduction, until he senses Ted looking at him, '. . . about going out.'

'The ball was bad timing – tonight of all nights. But I say there's nothing wrong in honouring our loved ones' memories.'

Jack twists round briefly to take in the comatose figure sprawled across the back seat. He returns his focus to the road.

'He's blind drunk. He's hardly honouring any memory getting into a state like that.'

'But he doesn't drink to remember . . .' Ted's stare drills through the gloom. 'He drinks to forget. Ah, you can sit there all superior. You've no idea what grief does to a man.'

'Don't presume to know me. You don't know me at all.'

The car's wan headlights fall on the garden wall of Ted's farmhouse. Jack pulls on the handbrake, but leaves the engine ticking over.

'You should get Jim home, I'll be all right to go and fetch Gwen,' Ted tells him.

'No. You're here now and I'm nearly at the Hall. Go in and get some sleep.'

The passenger door opens. Ted hesitates.

'I would have seen him right. She could have trusted me.'

The door slams before Jack has a chance to respond. Ted's hunched figure is bathed in gold as he plunges through the car's twin beams, but he has been swallowed by darkness long before he reaches the house. On the back seat, Jim lets rip a loud snore. Jack puts the car in gear and pulls away.

It is a miracle he finds Netley Hall. He would have been hard-pressed to find it in daylight – he has only passed its pillared entrance a couple of times at best. He misses it initially and slams on the brakes with such force that Jim is almost projected into the footwells. The farmer stirs enough to right himself, mumbling incomprehensibly, before drifting back to sleep. Jack stretches his arm around the back of the passenger seat and reverses up the road. He peers up at the imposing wrought-iron gates, changes gear, and directs the car up the drive.

The house extends before him, lit up like a Christmas tree. It seems at first that every window is an open gleaming eye, but as he draws nearer he sees that some are indeed shuttered to the world. The vast gravelled forecourt is crammed with parked cars and he advances slowly until he finds a space, poking Jim's modest Morris Eight between two stately Rolls-Royces.

Turning off the engine, he sits in the darkness looking up through the small windscreen at the impressive mansion.

'Don't worry, Jim, you stay here. I'll find her,' he mutters. The sleeping farmer merely snores in response.

It is surprisingly cold and he fights the urge to flick up his collar and huddle into his cheap jacket as he might have done walking the terraced streets at home. Instead, he pushes back his shoulders and braces himself against the discomfort of the cutting chill, buttoning up his jacket so it looks of a better cut than it is. Walking with more confidence than he feels, he approaches the imposing black doors at the centre of the house.

He is embarrassed that his heart is pounding as he reaches for the brass knocker, which he brings down to echo with light apology against the glossed wood. He shifts uneasily on the limestone step, turning to look out over the expansive park, its great oaks silhouetted against a navy sky whose ghostly clouds drift lazily over the moon in a half-hearted game of hide and seek. Jack knocks again.

Music wafts on the breeze. He listens to a rakish dance of tinkling piano keys, accompanied by sliding strings and the boom of a plucked double bass. With his knocking unanswered, he allows the drifting notes to beckon him around the side of the house, where he discovers a stone terrace. Golden light floods through its row of French doors and spills onto the partygoers clustered on the lawn below. Their mingling voices are punctuated by tittering laughter and low guffaws. The men are dressed in dark dinner jackets and white bow ties and the ladies dazzle beside them in their sheaths of jewel-coloured satin. They drink from coupes of glistening champagne as if conscious this might be their last hurrah.

Jack hangs back in the shadows, acutely aware he does not belong here. He lingers by the edge of the grass looking up at the terrace where fleeting images of whirling dancers are caught behind glass. Checking his watch, he sees it is now after eleven. He wishes Gwen had been waiting for them, as she ought to have been.

Unsure what to do, he loiters, not daring to step onto the cropped grass which seems to designate some social boundary he should not cross. Instead, he keeps his feet firmly planted on the gravel, not wanting the grind of chippings to disclose his presence.

He waits with the nervous anticipation of an actor hovering in the wings, following the drama unfolding on stage, hanging on every line, awaiting his cue. And then, as if by prearranged direction, his attention is caught by a shimmer of velvet and a ripple of blonde waves. Gwen enters stage right, laughing merrily as she glides through a set of French doors that have been flung open to release the heat trapped inside. She fans her flushed cheeks with gloved fingers, her eyes alive with excitement as she half-turns to the young man who has escaped with her to the refreshing respite of the terrace.

Jack's jaw tightens. Her companion is tall and his black dinner jacket appears sculpted to his broad physique. He carries himself with the confidence of a movie star and has the looks to rival most – square chin, straight nose, strong brow, and tawny hair bearing a brilliantine glaze. Backlit by the chandeliers inside, he appears to possess a magical aura, and from the look on Gwen's face, it is clear she is entranced.

She smiles as she accepts a glass of champagne and regards him coyly over its rim as she brings it to her lips. Jack doesn't catch the young man's words, but Gwen giggles in response and lays a hand on his lapel in a display of mock chastisement. The flirtatious gesture fans the flames of Jack's irrational jealousy and before he knows it he is striding forward, his steps silent upon the lawn, until he stands below her.

'Gwen.' His voice comes softer than he intends and it fails to carry. He calls again, firmer this time, and it catches her attention. She glances about her, her nose wrinkling with confusion, convinced she has heard her name but unable to determine from where. Cursing under his breath, Jack calls again and as he does so he steps into a strip of light donated by the windows above. Gwen emits a mew of surprise and leans over the lichen-speckled balustrade.

'Goodness. Jack?'

Her voice is different, and the artificial crispness of it – the concentrated enhancement of her accent, her uncharacteristic choice of exclamation – rankles more than he can explain.

'I say, who on earth is that?' The young man's voice quivers with laughter as he joins Gwen at the balustrade, but his humour fades as he sees Jack below.

'Oh, it's all right, Gordon, it's only Jack – our farm hand.'

Her belittling remark drives a knife into Jack's chest. 'I've come to fetch you home.'

'What on earth are you doing skulking around the back? Why didn't you go to the front door?' the young man demands.

'I knocked. No one came.'

'I thought Dad was coming?'

'He's . . . feeling unwell. So, I offered to come.'

His words douse the merriment that just moments before had lit her face.

'Oh now listen, you can't leave yet.' The young man makes an ostentatious show of taking her hand. 'Stay longer, I'll drop you home.'

'No, Gordon, really. I must go.'

'Running away like Cinderella before midnight?' he teases, bringing her fingers to his lips. 'Deserting your Prince Charming?'

Gwen laughs. 'I'm sure you'll survive.'

'I might survive, but you're breaking my heart.'

To Jack his voice is like syrup – thick and rich and sickening in large doses. He steps forward.

'Gwen. We need to go.'

'Yes, yes, of course.' She retrieves her hand from Gordon's. 'I'm sorry.'

He leans close to whisper something into her ear and Jack can't help but notice the familiarity their bodies seem to share, like worn pieces of a puzzle that have been fitted together on more than one occasion.

Gwen pulls away, suppressing a smile. She gathers up her dress to safely tackle the steps from the terrace down to the lawn and when she reaches the bottom she looks back a final time at the young man she has left behind, before hurrying to join Jack. He guides her towards the gravel with a light touch to the small of her back.

'We're parked on the drive,' he says, low enough for her alone to hear.

They are lost in their own thoughts as they walk side by side towards the car. Jack cannot see Jim inside and he immediately fears the farmer has roused and taken it into his head to go wandering. He quickens his pace, leaving Gwen to trot awkwardly in her heeled shoes. He is relieved beyond measure to see the farmer's inert body curled across the back seat. When Gwen reaches the passenger side, she places her palm to the glass and peers in; her expression dissolves into one of profound sadness.

'Oh.'

Once they are inside, she swivels round to lay a fleeting hand on her father's knee, before turning back to face the front. Jack starts the engine.

'I thought perhaps . . .' She leaves the comment suspended, incomplete.

The engine whines as he reverses out from his parking spot, but it ceases to complain once back in forward gear.

'He couldn't have driven,' Jack says.

'No.' Gwen drops her gaze to her lap where her silver bag glints through the dimness. 'And Ted? He was as bad, I suppose?' Her question has a sharp edge to it.

'He didn't dissuade him, let's put it that way.'

Gwen nods and looks out of her window.

'Ted told me.' He tears his eyes away from the indistinct road before him to meet her gaze. 'He explained the significance of the day.'

She abruptly cuts off her bark of bitter laughter. 'Yes. The anniversary of my mother's death.' She glances at the back seat. Her soft sigh conveys so much unhappiness that Jack yearns to reach out and comfort her, but he thinks better of it and keeps his hands firmly on the wheel. There is something about the close confines of the darkened car that is gloriously intimate and he is more aware of her now than ever before.

'I shouldn't have gone out . . .' He strains to make out her low words. 'He used to get like this every year. Ted would take him down the pub to get his mind off it and he'd come back . . . blind drunk. Then, a couple of years ago I said, "No more." I wouldn't let him go. Instead, we sat together listening to the wireless and we talked a bit about Mum . . . that seemed like a much more fitting memorial than . . .' Jim's snore rattles behind them. Gwen bites her lip. 'I thought he'd just stay at home with you, I thought it'd be all right. I didn't expect him to go out . . . and I so wanted to come tonight. I promise you, Jack, this is out of character for him. He would never usually—'

'When grief possesses a man, he becomes capable of excesses he would never have dreamed of.' Jack knows this better than anyone. He clears his throat, embarrassed to have been so unguarded. 'It's not your fault, Gwen. I'm just sorry I couldn't stop him.'

'It was unfair of me to expect you to. When Ted and Dad set their minds to something . . . their hearts are so bruised, you see. I suppose sometimes they just need to . . . numb the pain.' She has started to shiver. She rubs her hands up and down her goosefleshed arms. 'Oh, my stole!'

Jack hits the brakes, bringing the car to a stop. The headlights catch on the open edges of the entrance gates.

'We can go back.'

'No . . . no . . . I'll collect it tomorrow. Let's just get Dad home.'

'Here . . .' Releasing the wheel, he shrugs off his jacket. 'Take this.'

'Are you sure?'

Gwen leans forward, allowing him to drape it around her shoulders. She smiles as she gathers it close.

'Thank you, Jack.'

They drive in silence the rest of the way, though Jim continues to snore on the back seat. Jack parks the car outside the farmhouse.

'You go and open up. I'll bring him in,' he says.

As Gwen delicately picks her way across the yard to the steps, he yanks open the rear door. Jim mutters in his drink-sodden sleep and offers a meek protest as Jack manoeuvres him from the car and hauls him upright. He positions Jim's arm over his shoulder and kicks the door shut before lugging him up the steps. Kip appears, tail wagging drowsily, but Jack sends him back to his bed with a gentle word.

By the time he has got Jim up the steps and along the path there is light from the kitchen window and the back door hangs open.

'Can I help?' Gwen asks, hovering on the threshold.

'No, just lead the way. I'll get him up to bed for you.'

He follows her into the darkened hall, half-walking, half-dragging the semi-conscious farmer. He jiggles him awake enough to help him manage the stairs, though Jack is forced to grab the bannister to prevent them both toppling backwards. Gwen leads him into the end bedroom, hurrying forward to pull back the bedcovers. Jim collapses onto the mattress the moment Jack releases him. He mumbles incoherently as Jack pulls off his shoes, then rolls onto his side and falls silent once more. Gwen draws the covers up.

'He can sleep like that – it won't hurt him,' she whispers, extinguishing the paraffin lamp on the bedside table.

Jack retraces his steps to the kitchen, the soft swish of Gwen's velvet dress following behind.

'Oh, you'd better take this,' she says, shucking off his jacket as they reach the back door.

'Will you be all right?' he asks, taking it from her.

'I'll be just fine. I dare say Dad will have a sore head in the morning.' She musters a smile.

'Aye, I reckon you're right about that.'

She puts her hand on the door as he slips on his coat.

'Thank you, Jack, for everything.'

'It's nee bother, lass.' He hesitates. 'Tell me, though, did you have a good time?'

'I had the most wonderful time.' The memory of the evening fans the fire in her eyes, but he suspects Gordon Allingham sparked the blaze.

He walks across the yard, tormented by the perfume lingering on his jacket. He yearns to be the man responsible for igniting such fires, but by the time he reaches the tack room he is despondent, for he knows that particular privilege will remain forever beyond his reach.

CHAPTER SIXTEEN

Jack

June 1939

Suspecting Gwen will sleep in following her eventful night, Jack rises earlier than usual – the milking will take him longer alone. As he leaves the stable block, he sees her curtains are still drawn against the breaking dawn and the farmhouse displays no tell-tale signs of life. Only Kip comes to greet him, pausing to stretch and snap off a yawn, before trotting beside him to the pasture where they find the cattle huddled at the gate.

As he drives the cows into the yard the cockerel leaps onto the fence, propelled by its batting wings. It throws back its head to wake the world, the rosy flap of skin beneath its beak rippling like a signal flag. With the morning reveille performed, it jumps down, its great pronged toes digging into the mud as it spreads its colourful wings in a vainglorious display. Jack gives it a wide berth. There is something about the cock that strikes him as arrogant and dangerous. He doesn't trust it an inch.

He has been milking for over an hour when Gwen finally dashes in, breathless and embarrassed and terribly apologetic.

She snatches up her stool and pail and hurries into the neighbouring stall where a cow waits, dragging hay from the iron basket attached to the wall. Within minutes, Jack hears the steady *whist* of milk. A short time later, she pauses on her way to the scales.

'Jack . . .'

He stops and swivels on the stool to better face her.

'Aye, lass?'

'I'd be grateful if you didn't say anything, to Dad . . . about how you found me last night, about me being with someone.' Her lashes lower. 'He's just a bit . . . funny . . . you know, about things like that. Overly protective. I'd just rather we kept it between ourselves.'

'Your business is your business, Gwen. I'll not say anything.'

She smiles and says no more.

They are arranging the churns on the milk stand in the lane when Jim finally appears, walking carefully, pulling deeply on the stub of a Woodbine. He coughs, looks sheepish, and never quite manages to hold Jack's eye as he enquires about the morning's yield. He nods when Gwen gives him the figures, flicking his cigarette into the long grass of the verge.

'That's good.'

Gwen folds her arms. 'And how are you feeling this morning?'

'Ah, Gwen . . .' The farmer's weather-beaten cheeks grow ruddy as he has the decency to look abashed. 'I'm sorry about last night. Jack, lad . . .'

'Say no more, Jim,' Jack says, lifting the final churn onto the platform.

Ringing hooves cut their conversation short. Jack looks up, squinting against the low morning sun which silhouettes the approaching horse and rider. Jim regiments his posture, his brow knitting as Gwen gasps and sweeps off her headscarf, shoving it into her pocket. Jack's stomach drops as the horse, a sleek hunter with a twitching cropped tail, draws close enough for him to identify its rider.

'Good morning!'

Gordon Allingham doffs his bowler hat. Gwen's face breaks into a smile as she pushes past her father, self-consciously brushing at her buff trousers.

'Good morning.'

'I came to return this – I believe it's yours.' Gwen's fox stole is draped across his thighs; he lifts it up, displaying it like a trophy from a victorious hunt. 'Mother was most perturbed when she found it abandoned in the cloakroom this morning, but I noticed your name tag on it.'

'Oh yes, thank you!' Pinpricks of pink delicately colour Gwen's cheeks. She starts forward, but as she reaches the hunter Gordon jumps down from the saddle, landing surefooted before her. He hands her the stole; she clutches it to her chest.

'I was also going to see if you were free to ride out with me?' The invitation is delivered in a low voice, but not low enough to escape Jim's sharp hearing.

'I'm afraid she can't, we've sheep to dip this morning and Gwen's help is needed.'

'Oh, Dad . . .' She whirls round to him. Jack is unable to tell whether her face is flushed from disappointment or embarrassment. Jim remains defiant.

'I'm afraid that's how it is with us working folk, Mr Allingham. No time for idle pleasures.'

Gwen glares at her father. Even Jack is discomfited by the

farmer's pointed remark, but the young man appears unmoved either way, though his manner is more reserved as he expresses his understanding.

'Perhaps another time?' His charming demeanour returns as he smiles down upon Gwen. Jack thinks he whispers something to her, but if he does, it is drowned out by the raucous crowing of the cockerel in the yard behind them. Yet as Gwen steps back to give Gordon room to remount, he notices a fresh glow about her. Allingham gathers up his reins before tipping the brim of his hat.

'Good day to you.'

He brings his heels sharply back into the hunter's flanks and the horse flicks up its head before walking on. Gwen waits until he is out of hearing before rounding on her father.

'How could you be so rude?'

'I thought I'd made myself perfectly clear the last time he came sniffing. I'll not have you running around the countryside with the likes of him.'

'Dad!'

'He's one hell of a reputation, Gwen. I'll not have him sully yours, even by association.'

'Village rumour and tittle-tattle.'

'Where there's smoke there's fire.'

'You don't know him.'

'And I don't want to! I know quite enough about him already.'

Gwen grits her teeth, her breathing fast and furious. When she speaks again, her voice is cold and determined. 'Well, you can't stop me. I shall see him if I wish. And if he asks me out riding again, I will go.'

Jim takes a threatening step forward; there is a blatant

warning in the subtle tilt of his chin. 'You will not, young lady. I will not be swayed on this, Gwen. Now you will mind your manners and you will do as I say.' His voice rises in the face of her contempt. 'I will not have you associating with that young man, do you understand me? I absolutely forbid it.'

Jack stares at the ground, his fists balled in his pockets. He risks a look at Gwen and sees she is keeping her emotions in check through sheer force of will.

'Perfectly,' she replies.

Her begrudging acquiescence defuses Jim's ire. His shoulders relax, he draws in his chin and grunts with satisfaction. 'Now hurry up and take that bloody thing up into the house. Those sheep aren't going to dip themselves.'

Her lips part, but she seems to think better of whatever she is going to say and instead they wither into bitter twists as she hurries past him, breaking into a sprint that Jack suspects is spurred by anger or tears – or both. He turns to watch her go. Jim delves into his pocket for his Woodbines and taps one free.

'That lad keeps trying it on, Jack, but I won't have it, I tell you. Nothing good would come of it, I know that damn well. Only heartbreak lies that way for my Gwen.' He rests his cigarette between his lips and talks around it. 'I'm looking out for her, that's all. Protecting her from the truth.'

But Jack is beginning to suspect Gwen is taking the same course of action with her father.

'She'd never be good enough for the likes of him,' Jim mutters.

Returning the packet to his pocket, he leaves the cigarette unlit as he walks back up the yard. Jack gives him a head start. Jim, he thinks, has it all wrong. There is no doubt that Gwen is good enough for Gordon Allingham. The doubt in Jack's mind is whether Gordon Allingham is good enough for Gwen.

It is left to Jack and Gwen to prepare for the dipping. Jim, mindful of Gwen's tight mouth and red-ringed eyes, absents himself to bring in the sheep.

Gwen is sullen as they fill the concrete tub in the back field with water and, when the task is complete, she strides off towards the barn without a word, leaving Jack to hurry after her. Tucked in a murky corner, amongst hessian sacks of seed and feed, is a bag of powder detergent. They both reach for it at the same time.

'I can manage.'

'I don't doubt it.'

Recognising her fight is with her father alone, Gwen relents with a peevish sigh and steps away. Jack grips the top corners of the sack but makes no move to lift it.

'You're already seeing him, aren't you? That lad.'

'It's hardly any of your business.'

'No, lass, it certainly isn't,' he admits quietly. Still he does not lift the sack.

'You won't say anything, will you? To Dad, I mean?' she says at last.

His breath escapes through his teeth. 'Like I say, lass, it isn't my business to get involved.'

'He's done nothing wrong, Jack – nothing to earn Dad's contempt.'

'Jim's just trying to protect you.'

'From what? Life?' Her hands lift in frustration. 'I'm old enough to make my own decisions and, if necessary, my own mistakes. But it's not a mistake. Dad can't believe that someone like Gordon could ever truly want someone like me. But he does. It's not Gordon who cares about the differences between us – it's my own father. That's the irony. He should be happy for me.'

'So instead you're running around behind his back? Hiding notes for each other, is that it?'

'You did see me then.'

'At the gate? I did.'

'Well, how else are we supposed to communicate when Dad refuses to let him anywhere near the place?'

He does not want to know about her affair, and yet now the secret is shared between them, he is greedy for more information, even though each morsel sticks in his throat and once swallowed rests like lead in his stomach.

'So, if you don't mind me asking, how long has this been going on?'

'A couple of months.' Her voice warms with the reminiscence. 'Long enough for us to know how we feel about each other. We met at the Hunt Ball. He came up to the house a couple of days later to ask me out, but Dad sent him packing. We found a way, though, to see each other.'

'And has he tried talking with your dad since then?'

'Gordon? Why would he want to? You've seen for yourself how Dad is with him.'

'Has he tried though? Walked up to the door and asked to speak to him, man to man?'

'Well . . . no . . . because we both know what sort of reception he'll get.'

Jack rests his weight on the sack, the hessian crushed in his tightening fists. 'But he's going to have to sometime, surely?'

'In time, I suppose.' The petulance of her one-shouldered shrug irritates him.

'No time like the present, lass. If he means well, let him come.'

'You make it sound so easy.'

'Perhaps it's easier than you think.'

She says nothing, allowing herself to be distracted by the flapping of a pigeon that has become trapped inside the barn. It flutters about the rafters until, exhausted by panic, it perches on a beam to take stock of its predicament. Gwen gestures towards the sack. She is sullen again, and for a moment Jack fears he has crossed a line and claimed a familiarity he has no right to, but he cannot square the young man's behaviour with his own sense of what is right. Nor can his envy see past Gordon's indifference.

He heaves the sack onto his shoulder with a sigh. He does not want to afford Allingham room between them and so seeks to change the subject in the hope of winning back her easy companionship.

'Why do you dip them, the sheep?' he asks as they slice through shafts of sunlight on their way to the open doors.

'To protect against scab.'

He meets her terse explanation with a bewildered smile and watches her petulance fight her instinct to return the gesture. He is relieved when it loses the battle. 'It's a disease. There's a mite that lives in the skin and lays eggs. It causes irritation, makes the sheep itch, so they rub themselves against anything they can. Eventually, they rub away their coats, create sores, and the skin scabs up. It's horrible – they spread it to one another, it can devastate a flock. So, we try and make sure that they're not harbouring any insects before the autumn – the mites tend to lay eggs when the sheep are in their full fleeces.'

Back at the tub, Gwen measures out the disinfectant. She leaves Jack to swirl it through the water, while she checks the gated run that connects the holding pen to the dipping tub and then the field beyond. It is not long before they hear the sheep bleating in the distance and Kip's excited barks. They stand by, their overalls tied tight with string around their waists, their sleeves rolled above their elbows.

'Here they come.'

Jim drives the sheep up the yard. Kip skirts behind those lagging at the back, sweeping left to right, rounding them together, funnelling them between the barn and the stable block and into the pen in the field beyond. Jim swings the gate shut as the last ewe pushes into the huddled flock.

'Ready?' he calls.

Gwen gestures for Jack to stand beside her at the tub. 'Push them right under, any way you can. You must douse them fully. Just do as I do,' she instructs as Jim begins to open the gates, urging the first sheep through, the next one following, until they are trotting down the narrow run in single file, bottlenecking at the final gate, just above the dipping tub.

'A firm hand is what's required, Jack,' Jim shouts, as he climbs up onto the bottom rail of the run to release the last gate.

The first sheep barrels towards Gwen. She grabs two fistfuls of fleece and unceremoniously pitches it into the water, pushing it down until it is completely submerged before hauling it up to the surface again, water sloshing against the sides of the tub, splashing her overall and even her cheeks. She thrusts the animal towards Jack.

'Dunk it again,' she orders as she reaches for the next one, leaving Jack to grope inexpertly for the animal that is battling through the water to reach the far edge of the tub, freedom in its sights. He buries his fingers into its dense wool and, feeling the sheer strength of it as it struggles against him, he tightens his hold and attempts to force it under. He has just managed to submerge it when it strikes free of his grip and scrambles away from him. He gasps at the shock of cold water on his sun-warmed skin. The next animal is already paddling past him.

'Grab it, quick,' Gwen shouts, amusement playing in her voice.

Cursing, Jack grabs the rear of the escaping sheep, dragging it back as its front legs find purchase on the edge of the trough.

'You make it look so bloody easy!'

Gwen and Jim laugh.

'You need to be quicker, lad,' Jim tells him, knocking the next sheep through.

It takes concentration for Jack to establish a rhythm. His shoulder knocks Gwen's as their hands feed over each other passing the sheep between them, pushing and pulling, dunking and hauling, the air filling with the trepidatious bleats of the flock pressed together in the holding pen. Jack begins to relax into the motion, his spirits lifting at the sight of the released sheep shaking themselves like wet dogs as they scrabble free of the tub before trotting out into the daisy-speckled field behind.

The ring of a bicycle bell catches Jack's attention. He is laughing at something Gwen has said when the shrill sound draws his eye to the side of the building. He fights to maintain a semblance of a smile as he sees a tall figure in a blue uniform wheeling the bike over the worn track towards them.

The vein in Jack's neck begins to pulse as his breaths shorten and his chest becomes strangely tight. He feels the bob of his Adam's apple.

'Jack, focus!' Gwen chides as he is splashed by a careering sheep. He rips his eyes away from the approaching policeman and drags the errant creature back, plunging it into the trough. But he cannot focus. His mind is as numb as his water-frozen hands.

'You started without me, Jim,' the policeman calls, resting his bike on the back wall of the stable block.

'Well, I haven't got all day to wait for you, Vic.'

The policeman appears unruffled by the criticism scantily clad in jest. He calls out a greeting to Gwen who responds as she pauses to wipe water from her face with the back of her hand. Jack can feel the policeman's eyes upon him. Sweat beads his forehead, but he tells himself it will be put down to exertion and nothing else. It is, after all, hard labour, dipping sheep. Hard labour. Better than what awaits him. He keeps his head down. He refuses to be drawn by the constable's stare.

'I heard you'd acquired some help.'

The words are conveyed over the cacophony of thrashing water, terrified sheep, and Kip's incessant yapping. There is a lump in Jack's gullet, a blockage. Gwen's hands graze his in the unthinking exchange of an animal. Not here, he thinks, not like this. He calculates the route over the field to the lane and wonders if he – the younger man – can beat the policeman to it.

'Ah, this is Jack.'

'Hello there, Jack.'

Jack cannot find a voice to return the greeting. Gwen appears amused by his gaucheness, but then her expression changes and her brow furrows. He clears his throat and finally manages a response.

'Ah, a northern lad, with an accent like that,' the policeman says, pleased with his powers of deduction. He unbuttons the top pocket of his uniform jacket and takes out a black notebook. 'So, where do you hail from?' he asks, producing a pencil stub. He flips back the pages of his pad and begins to write. He pauses, his eyes narrowing. He is waiting, Jack realises. He is waiting for Jack to speak.

He tries to concentrate on the sheep, the wash of water over his arms, the strain in his muscles as he holds them down. He tries to remain calm. 'Sunderland.' The lie falls with the easy slip of chiffon and Jack experiences a frisson of satisfaction that he has kept to his story. He has not faltered under pressure.

'Sunderland? Well, you are a long way from home. My wife is from Durham, so I know just how far you've come. She insists on us making the journey up to see her family on a fairly regular basis and it's a bloody long way, I can tell you.'

Jack schools his composure in the light of this revelation. 'Aye, that it is,' he says, wrestling with a frantic sheep.

'A fairly regular basis? Bah, Vic, you can't tell me you go more than once a year,' Jim shouts across.

'Once a year is regular, thank you very much. She's a big family and makes us do the rounds – a whole week gone visiting one relative after the next. I don't mind seeing my brother-in-law, though, at least we get to talk shop.'

'Talk shop?' Gwen asks.

'He's a policeman up there. So, what takes you so far from home, Jack?'

Jack's blood roars in his ears. 'Work,' he manages.

'We're making a farmer of him,' Jim laughs.

'So, I see.' The policeman's smile fails to reach his eyes. 'How many you done?' He advances but refrains from getting too close – he does not want his uniform splashed with filthy water. He stretches his neck to look in the field beyond, carrying out a rough head count of the soaked sheep, wet and pathetic in the brightening sun as they crop the grass, sodden tails flicking.

'Twenty-five I reckon, another forty to go. Muriel's inside, she'll make you a cup of tea if you ask,' Jim calls.

'I have my duty to fulfil here, Jim. I need to keep my eye on you.'

'Don't you trust me?'

'I don't trust anyone, Jim.'

Jack's skin prickles as if the mites have abandoned the man-handled sheep and are crawling up his bare arms, worming into his flesh to twitch and feast and irritate.

'In this job, you learn that pretty damn quick. Always keep an eye out. You never know what – or who – is going to turn up unexpectedly.'

'You're shaking,' Gwen murmurs as she passes him the next ewe.

Jack looks down at his hands with an air of bewildered detachment. They are indeed trembling, like the legs of a new-born lamb. He buries his fingers into the sheep's water-matted coat. 'The water's freezing.' Seeing her suspicion, he looks away.

The policeman makes no attempt to conceal the yawn that prises open his mouth. He ambles over to one of the fence posts supporting the corrugated iron sheets walling the run and rests against it. He fishes out a packet of cigarettes.

'Smoke?' He offers the box to Jack then grins. His front teeth overlap. 'You've got your hands full, I suppose.' He laughs at his own joke, a throaty cackle that seems strangely feminine. Jack swallows his contempt.

'Aye, something like that.'

'Well, my Iris will be delighted to hear there's a fellow northerner around. I'll have to get the two of you introduced.' He grins again at Jack, though with his uneven, tobacco-stained teeth, it seems more like a leer. 'She'd love to have a natter with someone from home.'

Jack does not respond, he merely pushes the next sheep below the churning water, wishing the policeman would go. He has no desire to meet his wife. He wants nothing to do with home.

Gwen is tacking up Arthur when Jack returns to the yard that evening, having safely restored the milking herd to pasture.

'Riding out?' he says as she throws the saddle over the stallion's back.

'Yes.' She strains to fix the girth. 'Stop breathing out, you bugger,' she mutters, squeezing the buckle prongs into the correct holes. Jack strokes the horse's blaze. Its ears twist as Gwen joins him. 'I'm . . .' she starts, but then busies herself checking the fastenings on the bridle.

'You're what?'

She shakes her head. 'Nothing.' She collects her riding crop from the window ledge. 'You seemed surprised, earlier. To see Vic – Constable Jennings – at the dipping.'

Jack continues to stroke the horse's nose. 'Did I? Well, I suppose I was.'

'He has to come, to check we're doing it. There's all sorts of paperwork we have to fill in. It's a legal requirement, having Vic supervise.'

Jack nods. He does not trust himself to say anything, so instead he takes hold of the bridle, keeping Arthur steady as Gwen fits her boot into the stirrup. With two bounces, she swings herself up into the saddle. The leather creaks beneath her as she gathers up the reins and finds her other stirrup.

'You looked as white as a sheet when you saw him,' she says. Jack releases the horse and steps back, unable to meet her eye. With a click of her tongue and a dig of her heels she pulls Arthur round. 'It's funny,' she shifts in her saddle to look back at him, 'it was almost as if you thought he'd come looking for you.'

And without waiting for his reply, she urges the horse to walk on.

CHAPTER SEVENTEEN

Jack

June 1939

Jack is leaning against the back wall of the farmhouse eating a handful of raspberries while he waits for Gwen. He is captivated by a small bird that scurries up and down the trunk of the silver birch.

From the corner of his eye, he clocks Gwen emerging from the privy. She stops to rinse her hands under the outdoor tap, then walks over to him, wiping her palms on the thighs of her trousers. Squinting against the sunshine, she follows his rooted gaze.

'What are you looking at?'

'That bird.' He nods towards the silver birch. 'What bird is that? I swear I've never seen anything like it.'

'It's a nuthatch.' She nudges his arm with her elbow. 'City boy,' she teases.

'It's beautiful. The colours on it.'

'I'll let you into a secret – it's my favourite garden bird.'

'No?'

'It is. I'm not just saying that, it really is.' She helps herself to a proffered raspberry. 'Pretty, isn't it?'

'Aye, it is that.'

'When I was little, I was given a bird-spotting book by my great aunt one Christmas. Each page was dedicated to an individual bird – you know the sort of thing, a little bit about its habits and where it could be found, what it ate and so on – and each had a watercolour illustration. I spent hours going through that book, but out of all the birds it was the nuthatch that caught my eye.'

She leans against the wall beside him, her shoulders curving against the render. 'I said to Dad, "I'd love to see a nuthatch" and he just laughed and said, "Spend some time in the garden with your eyes open and you'll see your nuthatch." I didn't believe him – I wouldn't accept that I could have missed something so beautiful. How could that bird be found in our very own garden and me not notice it? But I did as he said, and sure enough a couple of days later I saw one skittering over the bark of the apple tree, and it was even more beautiful in the flesh than it was in the book.' She shades her eyes with her flattened hand. 'Isn't it funny how sometimes the very thing we long for can be right in front of us and we just never see it?'

Jack says nothing. He keeps a steady watch on the grey-blue bird hugging the rippled bark, his heart too full to muster a response. In a rapid flutter of wings the bird is gone and the moment is lost. Gwen pushes herself from the wall.

'Come on, work to do.'

They have been set the task of weeding the sugar beet. They work a few rows apart, their hoes scraping against the flints in the soil as they prise out the charlock and the groundsel, the chickweed and the shepherd's purse. They bend and pull, and shake the earth loose from the roots, before tossing the vanquished growth into a pile to be burnt later. They are easy with each other and the silence between them is comfortable. A buzzard glides above them, its plaintive mew drawing their attention. They watch it land on a fractured branch of the dead elm that stands in the corner of the field and Gwen tells him how the tree, now the colour of weathered bone, was struck by lightning when she was a little girl. She wipes the sweat from her forehead with the heel of her hand, leaving a streak of dirt. It is all Jack can do to stop himself reaching over to brush it away.

They work on. Every so often Gwen straightens up, poised to speak, but then appears to change her mind and, blushing furiously, returns to her task with renewed vigour. Her behaviour strikes Jack as curious. She reminds him of the nuthatch – striking, but nervous.

'Jack . . .' she starts at last, resting on her hoe.

'Let's have it.' He smiles. 'You've been trying to say something since we got here.'

She laughs lightly. 'Yes, yes I suppose I have. I was just wondering . . . there's a dance on next Saturday. Would you want to go?'

'A dance? Are you asking me to a dance?' he blurts out, unable to contain his surprise.

'I'm just asking if you'd like to go.'

'Aye,' he says quickly. His smile is broad. He feels strangely lightheaded. 'Aye, I'd like that. Very much.'

'Good!' She twists the hoe in the soil. 'Perfect,' she says, more to herself than to him.

There is a bounce in Jack's step as they return to the farm for lunch. At the table, Gwen raises the subject of the dance with her father.

'The one at Hawbury village hall? You can go, the two of you, I don't see why not.'

Gwen springs up to press a kiss on her father's cheek. Jack is pleased to see her so happy, but his pleasure is overshadowed by a sudden recollection of Jenny dancing into the parlour one evening, her spirits high, her colour up, as she twirled away from his curious enquiries as to where she had been.

When Gwen leaves to use the privy, he leans over the table and speaks to Jim. His voice is shy and halting as he confesses he has nothing suitable to wear for a night out. He asks for an advance on his wages.

'Ah, lad, don't waste your money on clothes you'll hardly wear,' the farmer scoffs. He calls for Muriel. She has been grading eggs in the larder and emerges with an egg tray in her hands and a quizzical look on her face. 'My old suits, Muriel,' the farmer says. 'Can you look one out for the lad? A shirt and tie too?'

'I should think so. There's some in mothballs in the spare room wardrobe that I'm guessing you've not had on your back for years.' She peruses Jack, her eyes narrowing as she sizes him up. 'They should fit.'

When she returns to the larder, Jack thanks the farmer.

'There's one other favour I have to ask,' he says as he rises from the table. 'I see there's some pine logs in the back of the barn. Would you mind if I took one, just a small one, like?'

'Lad, help yourself. There's plenty of beech in the store. They're better for the stove.'

'I don't want it for burning,' Jack says, but he offers the farmer no further explanation as he bids him farewell and returns to his chores.

*

It is the morning of the dance and Gwen asks Muriel for help washing her hair. Jim is talking to Jack about seed drills and ratios, but Jack is struggling to focus. His eyes stray to the sink where Gwen and Muriel are whispering between themselves so as not to disturb them. Muriel part-fills a white enamel jug with water from the kettle, while Gwen undoes the top buttons on her shirt and wriggles the loosened fabric down around her shoulders, exposing the greying straps of her brassiere. She holds the scrubby towel that Muriel drapes around her neck in place, then hangs her head over the Belfast sink, her golden curls tumbling forward. Jack forces himself to look away.

He tries to tune into Jim's droning monologue, but the sound of flowing water steals his attention and his eyes slide to the sink once more. Water cascades from the jug's broad spout, catching the light from the window as it streams over Gwen's head. Setting the jug down, Muriel lathers up some soap and attacks the saturated hair. Gwen is tugged and turned by her vigorous ministrations.

'So, I think it should be all right, you see,' Jim concludes, getting to his feet. 'But we'll make a start and see how we get on.'

'Yes,' Jack stutters. He has failed to absorb anything the farmer has said, but he covers his distraction by following his lead and rising from the table.

'Gwen, will you be along?'

'Yes, Dad.' Gwen's response is drowned by pouring water. Soap suds slip down the length of her slick hair. 'I'll be as quick as I can.'

'No rush,' Jim says as he makes his way outside. He lights a cigarette while Jack balances against the doorjamb to shove on his gumboots. 'She'll be as pretty as a picture tonight.' Jim winks. 'You'll be proud to have her on your arm.' He calls to the waiting dog and sets off towards the yard.

Jack follows on, painfully aware his rising anticipation is nothing short of foolish.

Later, in the tack room, he dresses with care. Muriel has indeed found a suit and has made it fit, lengthening the leg by taking down the hem; the faded line in the material that betrays the alteration can barely be seen. Dressed only in his trousers and vest, his braces hanging by his sides, he lathers up his face and bends to the mirror as he drags the razor over his stubble. When its head blossoms with foam he rinses it in the small bowl before him, swirling it until the water laps it clean. Angling his jaw to the glass, he draws the blade down again.

When he is done, he dabs his face dry with the towel draped over his shoulder and pulls on his shirt. Muriel has done her best to air it, but it still bears a faint trace of mothballs. He hopes Gwen will not notice. The buttons are fiddly; he refuses to put his fumbling down to nerves. He pushes the tails under his waistband and pulls up his braces. Turning up his collar he threads the borrowed tie around his neck and effects the neatest knot he can.

He shrugs on the suit jacket, leaving it loose, but on catching a glimpse of himself in the small mirror he thinks better of his decision and buttons it up. He dips his toothcomb into the ewer water and rakes it through his short-cropped hair. He wishes he had a drop of cologne.

Retrieving his wallet from the windowsill he thumbs through the notes tucked inside. Satisfied he has enough, he slips it into his inside pocket. His hand hovers over a small object sitting on the apple crate. He vacillates over whether to take it or not, but in the end his fingers close over the sculpted wood and his heart dares to lift. He drops it into his side pocket, strangely fortified by its featherlight presence. He pushes back his shirt cuff to check his watch, and realises it is time to go.

The back door is whipped open before he reaches it. Gwen stands framed in the open doorway, and for a moment he feels his balance waver. She wears a white full-skirted dress covered in the palest of pink roses. Her hair, washed that morning, has been wound around thick rollers all day, protected by a head-scarf. Now, released and pinned, it falls in luxuriant rolls around her lightly rouged cheeks. Her broad smile wears a shimmer of lipstick. She dangles the car's ignition key from satin-gloved fingers, while her other hand keeps the cardigan draped around her shoulders from slipping free.

'Do you want to drive or shall I?'

Jack takes the key with a slow smile just as Jim appears behind her.

'You scrub up well, Jack – that suit fits you right tidy.'

Jack tugs self-consciously at the jacket. 'It does, thank you.' But having seen Gwen, he wishes he was not wearing her father's cast-offs, but a suit cut to fit him alone.

'Be back by eleven, you've both got work tomorrow.'

'Oh, Dad!' Gwen spins around to her father, the petticoats beneath her skirt whispering their dismay. 'The dance finishes at midnight. Just for once, can't I stay to the end?'

'Gwen, you know fair well that this house is locked up when I go to bed at ten thirty. I'm giving you leeway tonight as it is.'

'I have the spare house key. There's no need for you to wait up and watch me in.' She snatches a glance at Jack. 'You trust Jack to see me home, don't you?'

'Of course I do, but . . .'

'Then midnight, just for once, shouldn't be an issue, Dad. I'm not keeping you up. Jack will see me in, won't you, Jack? And I promise I'll be up for milking.'

Jack is unable to resist the pleading look she throws him. 'She's right, Jim. She'll be quite safe with me. I won't let anything happen to her – you have my word on that. And I'll be up in the morning – you have my word on that too.'

'Well . . .' The farmer's protests falter in the face of their joint appeal. 'All right then,' he concedes with a huff. 'But make sure you leave at midnight sharp – not sometime after. And I'd better see you both bright and early in the morning.'

'You will!' Gwen kisses his cheek.

Jack follows her down the path to the car. She is clearly excited and Jack dares to wonder whether he plays a part in that, but he quickly stamps down on the foolish fantasy. It matters little. His time here is limited, his presence is temporary.

He pushes the sour thought from his mind. He will make the most of what time he has. He opens the passenger door for her and she gently mocks his chivalry as she drops into her seat.

They barely exchange a word as he drives to the next village. The summer evening is bright. Gwen cracks the car window and the warm air that rushes in carries with it the sweet scent of freshly cut grass. She tucks buffeted strands of hair behind her ears. Jack's eyes slide surreptitiously towards her. He has never seen her look so beautiful.

The village hall car park is already packed with vehicles

by the time they arrive and bicycles stand propped against its boundary fence. The large windows glow with yellow light and, as Jack parks up, music flows through the hall's open doors. Gwen's eyes burn bright.

He gets out first intending to open her car door, but Gwen is clearly impatient and eager and unable to wait and throws her door wide while he is still feet away, bringing him to a halt. He is burdened by a profound disappointment, as if she has stolen an opportunity from him, robbed him of a moment of intimacy. Oblivious, she beams as she smooths down her skirt and any disappointment he has melts away – the simple reward of being in her company is enough. He closes the door as she steps away from the car.

'Oh, I'm so looking forward to this!' she declares, and to his surprise she slips her arm through his, pressing against him, and his heart sings in response. He knows he must tamp down the glowing embers within him that threaten to burst alight. He cannot stay; there is no future for him here. And yet, those embers refuse to die. In a show of weakness, he permits them to flare. Just for tonight, he tells himself.

The village hall is a throng of bodies. An unsavoury fusion of perfume, sweat and beer hangs in the thick air trapped beneath the pitched roof with its darkly stained joists. The whole room reverberates with tunes belted out by the band – a loose, dinner-jacketed ensemble brought in for the evening, not quite the right side of professional. Their music is fast and loud and intoxicating, and Jack sees its giddying influence on Gwen immediately. There is a bounce to her step that proclaims her a slave to its rhythm.

Jack follows as she winds her way amongst the flush-faced

revellers downing pints of ale and glasses of gin and orange, their spirits high. She presses forwards, towards the dancefloor that lies in the shadow of the stage at the far end of the hall. Periodically she stops, grabbing his arm to steady herself as she rises on tiptoes to survey the crowd like a watchful rabbit at twilight, and it crosses his mind that she is searching for someone. But then she drops down again and her smile is so carefree he convinces himself he is wrong.

They find themselves at the edge of the dancefloor. Exuberant couples whirl and pitch as they sweep across the parquet to the roaring music.

'Will you dance with me?' Jack asks.

Her lifting smile is his answer. He brings her round to face him, his hand resting lightly on her waist. He takes a deep breath to steady himself.

The bombastic beat ends abruptly. Applause ripples around the hall, accompanied by a few whoops and cheers from the out-of-breath dancers. Almost without pause, whispering brushes on the snare drum set a slumbering pulse and a solitary clarinet rises from the ashes of the previous trumpeted chorus to sing a melancholy tune, with muffled trombones humming melodiously behind.

Jack hesitates, unsure Gwen will welcome the intimacy afforded by the sensuous music, but to his delight she makes no attempt to pull away. The air around them seems to contract as if the room itself is holding its breath in anticipation and, as their bodies draw together without discussion, their feet begin to move with slow purpose. They circle in unconscious movement, relinquishing themselves to the music, allowing it to carry them on its gentle swell. As they skirt the edges of the dancefloor,

Gwen's warm breath skates across Jack's skin and he realises *this* is happiness.

'I say, mind if I cut in?'

The voice interjects like a stick thrust between the spinning spokes of a wheel. Jack's steps falter. He catches the edge of Gwen's shoe, feels the give of its soft leather and gasps an apology as they stumble to a stop.

Gordon Allingham stands in a sharp suit, his hair slickly parted and gleaming under the hall's bright lights. He proffers his hand and Gwen springs from Jack's grasp with such unbridled joy that he realises at once he is a dupe. He steels himself against the icy shaft thrust between his ribs as she withdraws the last vestiges of her warm touch and slips seamlessly, without apology, into Gordon's waiting arms. Before Jack even has a chance to draw breath, she is whirling away, as elusive as a dandelion clock borne on the wind. He thinks she looks back at him, just once, before she disappears behind scudding couples, but when she finally emerges, skimming the far side of the floor, she is gazing so intently at Gordon he knows he was mistaken.

He is sitting on the outside steps when Gwen comes to find him, smoking a cigarette that he has cadged from the girl serving behind the bar, though he failed to return her flirtation and had declined her offer to meet later, delivered as a hot whisper into his ear. The cigarette was the only thing he wanted, something to blur the edges of his regret and dull his sense of disappointment. The barmaid had eventually surrendered it with an arched brow, her puckered lips transforming into a hard line of displeasure as she moved away. Jack made no apology; he had merely picked up his pint and the cigarette and headed for the door.

'There you are! I thought perhaps you'd already gone,' Gwen says, descending a step so she can sit beside him, her shoes clacking on the wood. 'Gosh, it's boiling in there!'

He glances across at her and notices the sparkle of sweat on her forehead. It reminds him of a rose garnished with morning dew. He turns his eyes out front.

'I won't go until you're ready,' he tells her, grinding the cigarette under his shoe.

'The thing is . . . Gordon's offered to take me home . . .'

'Your dad . . .'

'Doesn't need to know.' She looks at him beseechingly, but she cannot face him for long. Her gaze drops to her satin-encased fingers, as they fiddle nervously with the clasp on her clutch. 'Please, Jack.'

'You could have told me, Gwen,' he says at last. 'You could have told me this was all a ruse.' She has the decency to appear embarrassed, and he is struck by how young she looks – how young she is. It is so easy to forget her youth when she is labouring beside him, as sturdy and competent as any man. But all dressed up, her hair prettily curled, her cheeks flushed, she looks little more than a girl, a girl who hasn't yet experienced enough of life for it to curb her optimism or tarnish her innocence. For a second, Jenny flashes before him and he is forced to look away, the pain in his chest so sudden and so penetrating that it takes his breath away. 'I promised your father I'd bring you home.'

'Oh, please, Jack!' She swivels to face him, her knees catching his leg. 'Gordon will take me straight home, I promise. And Dad need never know. He'll be fast asleep snoring his head off by now . . .'

'I gave him my word, Gwen.'

'And I'm asking you to help me . . . please, Jack, help me.' Her hand rests lightly on his arm. 'Just this once? I should have told you, you're right, and I'm sorry I didn't, that wasn't fair, but I was so worried Dad would find out and stop me from coming. I promise, no harm will come of it. And we're friends, aren't we, Jack? Don't friends help each other out?'

They are forced to shuffle aside as a drunken couple stagger out through the open doorway. The girl is giggling, collapsed against her partner whose arm is wrapped around her narrow waist. He casts Jack a knowing look as they stumble down the steps and onto the gravel. He leads her towards one of the parked cars and she slumps against the side as he opens the passenger door. Their murmurous interchange as he helps her in is too low to decipher. The door slams and he is whistling as he scoots around the back of the car, his hand skimming the boot, before he climbs into the front and starts the engine. As the car passes them, the woman slides across the front seat and nestles into his shoulder.

Jack looks up at the dark sky pinpricked with light. He believes he has seen more stars in the last few weeks than he has seen in his entire life, for here their beauty is unobscured by murky Tyneside smog. The whine of the car's engine fades into the night.

'Jack?'

'All right then.' He stands. Offering her his hand, he pulls her up. He tilts his watch towards the light slanting through the hall doors. It is half past eleven. Half an hour, he thinks, what harm is there in that? He wonders if he should ask to speak to Gordon, man to man, to look him in the eye and check for himself that his intentions are honourable, but even as the thought crosses his mind, he realises it is ridiculous. 'You must leave at midnight though, Gwen, and come straight home. That was the agreement you made with your dad.'

'Oh, Jack! I will, I promise. Thank you.' She lurches forward and plants her lips on his cheek. It is so fleeting he wonders if he imagined it, but his skin is seared by her touch and its burn confirms he did not. 'You're a brick, Jack.' She rewards him with a beautiful smile and he knows he is lost, adrift in an ocean he has no chance of navigating, on a journey he is not even sure he can survive.

She spins away, her full skirt lapping against his leg before receding like sea surf.

'Gwen.'

She turns back.

'Here.' He delves into his pocket, then holds out his hand. She cocks her head, an uncertain smile on her lips as she offers him her open palm.

'Oh!' She looks down at the little wooden bird he has placed into her care. It is accurately sized and carved with unsuspected skill. She lifts it up to examine, her expression wondrous, as if she were holding not a wooden creation but the real thing, for it is flawless and so realistic that for a moment she might believe he has by some magic delivered a live bird into her hand. 'It's a nuthatch.' Their eyes meet over its exquisitely painted body, the blue-grey back the colour of a stormy sky, while its underside is reminiscent of a setting sun and the black-banded eyes a streak of night. She touches the sharp tip of its pointed bill. 'Jack! It's perfect. You never made this?'

He pushes his hands into his trouser pockets. The shrug he offers is bashful and modest.

'You said they were your favourite . . .' he says at last. 'I was just whittling some wood to pass the time.'

He does not reveal how closely he has watched the little bird over the past number of days, committing its form to memory. Or the careful hours he has spent sat on the edge of his camp bed in the lamplight, carving a piece of pine log into shape before sanding it with glass paper, following the grain with patience and care until the wood became so warm in his hands it was as if he had given life to his creation. Nor does he reveal his special trip into the village to order paints from the store, returning to collect them a couple of days later, or how he has painstakingly experimented with colour, blending globules of pigment on a broken saucer he found discarded behind the shed until he had perfected the shades required.

And never will he reveal that the fashioning of the nuthatch was not simply a way of passing the time, but an expression of the love he has come to feel for the farmer's daughter. He knows it is pointless to lose his heart to her, but it is too late. She has elicited his love as unwittingly as she has received the nuthatch. He has begun to dread the day that he knows must come, the day he must leave her, for he cannot stay – for his own preservation, *he cannot stay*, and yet his own preservation seems so inconsequential now. Indeed, the delight in her face seems to confirm this conviction, for surely nothing that might await him, should he survive, could surpass the joy of witnessing her present pleasure and knowing he is responsible for it. But he is aware his feelings are unreciprocated, though he can't help but wonder . . . if he *was* able to stay, if a future with possibilities – a future unblemished by his past – now stretched before him, might he be able to win her heart? It grieves him that he will never be free to try.

'You're very clever.' She gifts him a smile so generous his chest must expand to take it. 'Thank you.'

'I say, Gwen! You're taking an age, come back inside.' Gordon emerges from the doorway. He glances between them, his eyes narrowing a fraction as he places his arm around Gwen's back. 'Is it all arranged? I'll bring Gwen home, there's no need for you to trouble yourself.'

'It was never any trouble,' Jack says quietly.

'Look what Jack made!' Gwen holds up the nuthatch for Gordon's inspection.

'Oh, how quaint. Can we go and dance now?'

'Yes, yes, of course.' For a moment, Jack thinks she means to say something to him, but she appears to change her mind and instead releases the clasp of her clutch. She drops the little bird inside; it clatters against her compact. She snaps the bag shut. 'Actually, I just need to pop to the powder room – shall I meet you by the bar?'

'Yes, all right, but do be quick.'

'Goodnight Jack, I'll see you in the morning.' She smiles with gratitude, then returns to the bright light and the noise. Jack expects Gordon to follow, but he pauses while he extracts a gold cigarette case from his pocket.

'You should speak to her father, you know.'

Gordon flicks the case shut and looks at Jack in surprise. 'I beg your pardon?'

'You should come to the house; tell her father you're courting her.'

Gordon snorts. 'Well, thank you for that advice.'

'You shouldn't have Gwen sneaking around behind her father's back. It isn't right. It isn't decent.'

'I hardly think it's any of your business.' He puts the cigarette between his lips and slips the case into his inside jacket pocket before taking out a lighter.

'Her dad has a right to know what your intentions are.'

'My intentions? What? If they're honourable or not?' Gordon sniggers as he drags his thumb against the lighter's wheel. Its flame burnishes his curved palm as he brings it to his cigarette. As the tip burns, he pushes back the flap of his side pocket and drops the lighter inside. He takes the cigarette from his mouth. 'And what are you going to do if they're not?' he asks, his eyes narrowing at his smoke-laced words. 'Challenge me to a duel for the lady's honour? Pistols at dawn?'

'I'm more of a fists man myself.'

For a moment Gordon has the good grace to look startled. Then he laughs, but his humour is short-lived. He takes a deliberate step in Jack's direction. 'Why don't you mind your own bloody business?'

'Speak to her father.'

'I'm seeing Gwen, not her father,' Gordon hisses. He turns on his heel and stalks back into the hall. He does not acknowledge Jack's parting words.

'A gentleman with good intentions does both.'

CHAPTER EIGHTEEN

Gwen

May 1945

It takes all day for Gwen and Nora to sow Top Field. They complete the task just as the herd's impatient bellows begin to drift across the valley. By the time they have finished milking, rolled the churns down to the stand and sluiced the parlour, Gwen is exhausted. She is relieved when Nora offers to take the cows back to the field.

She uses the lip of the back step to prise off her boots, knocking them against the outside wall to dislodge the worst of the muck, contemplating as she does so the work that needs to be done the following day.

As she pushes open the kitchen door, a flash of blue-grey catches her eye and she pauses to watch a nuthatch fly from the apple tree to the silver birch. Suddenly she finds herself thinking of the wooden bird, so carefully carved and painstakingly painted, that sits upon the mantelpiece in her room. It has become lost amongst the detritus that has gathered on the shelf over the years and reminded of it now she resolves to tidy away the items that detract from its beauty. It is a gift she has overlooked for too long.

She calls a greeting to Muriel, who is standing at the table mashing potatoes. Hearing her voice, Tom charges in from the sitting room and barrels into her legs, flinging his arms around them, pressing his cheek against her thigh. She laughs, rubbing his back. She has made him stay in with Muriel today, but in truth she has missed his company.

She is washing her hands at the sink when Nora comes in, Ted following behind. He sweeps off his flat cap and makes his greetings. Gwen feels his eyes settle upon her a little longer than the rest, but for some reason she is reluctant to meet them so she busies herself lathering her hands. With all the day's labours, her impromptu invitation of the night before had completely slipped her mind, and now, as she rinses the suds from her fingers, she experiences a niggling regret that it was made at all.

She has never felt Ted's presence in her house before. He has been such a constant over the years that her father used to joke he was part of the furniture. He required no special treatment, no acknowledgement, he was just there – in the same way that Muriel was. But something has changed, Gwen realises, a seismic shift she can't quite fathom and suddenly she is conscious of Ted's every move, his every word. She can feel the intensity of his focus and her skin begins to crawl with it, as if some part of her has tuned in to him as one might tune a wireless to obtain a clearer signal. But Gwen does not feel comfortable with Ted's broadcast – its underlying static conceals hints of a message she does not want to receive.

She is grateful for the distraction of Tom's constant gabbling as they take their places around the hastily cleared table. Muriel ladles out the rabbit stew that has been incubating in the hay box all day rather than simmering away on the range using up precious fuel, and Gwen distributes the plates accordingly. Ted laughs at something the boy says and Tom grins with pleasure, but soon the laughing has turned to a coughing fit. The farmer pitches to the side to retrieve a grubby handkerchief from his trouser pocket. He uses it to smother the noise. Gwen sets a glass of water before him.

'You've had that cough since winter.'

'Oh, it's nothing to worry about.' He wipes his mouth and balls his handkerchief back into his pocket.

She lightly rests her hand on his shoulder as she stretches to put his plate before him. 'You should go and see Dr Penny.'

Ted's hand traps hers in place. 'Are you concerned about me?'

He delivers the words with conspicuous levity, but it fails to conceal the gravity that lurks beneath. An awkward stillness embraces them. Muriel is chatting to Tom, oblivious to the interchange at the head of the table. Gwen slips her hand free, her skin scorched by his touch.

'You need to look after yourself is all I'm saying,' she says quietly, taking her seat. She is aware of Ted's lingering gaze, but she avoids it by pouring herself a glass of water from the jug on the table. He picks up his cutlery. Recognising the moment has passed, Gwen gathers up her own and forks in a mouthful of stew, suddenly eager for the meal to be over.

'There's talk in the village of having a party,' Muriel pipes up, 'to celebrate the end of the war.'

'But it's not over yet, is it? There's still Japan to contend with,' Gwen points out.

'Well, that's the thing, what with the Johnson boys both out in the Far East and Mrs Moncton's husband and Geoff Browne too. Some are arguing we should wait until all our village lads are safe before having some shindig. I mean, the Japs can't hold out for much longer, surely? Now Germany is out of the picture us and the Yanks can turn all our might on them, we'll soon bring them to heel.'

'Determined buggers, the Japanese. They might prove difficult to defeat,' Ted warns.

'Victory in Europe gives us something to celebrate, at least. No more air raids, no more blackouts, hopefully no more rationing. Things might start getting back to normal,' Muriel says.

'I reckon we'll have rationing for a while yet.' Ted chews his meat thoughtfully. 'This rabbit tastes lovely, Muriel.'

'Yes, it does – well done me for snaring them,' Nora chips in. 'And as far as I'm concerned, the more parties the better. I'm happy to celebrate until the cows come home.' She grins, flaring her eyebrows.

But Tom is the only one who laughs.

Muriel doesn't stay long after dinner, instead she cycles home as soon as the clearing up is done. Ted shows no signs of following suit so Gwen has little choice but to invite him through to the sitting room. She turns on the wireless ready for the evening news while Ted goes down on one knee to feed another log into the fire. Nora persuades her to break out the sherry and she pours them each a small glass. When she finally sits down, Tom crawls onto her lap and rests his head against her chest. She can see him fighting the urge to suck his thumb, but he eventually succumbs.

Nora jiggles her knee restlessly as she gulps down her drink. Gwen can see she is distracted, impatient . . . bored . . . and so is not surprised when the Land Girl leaps to her feet.

'Do you know what, I might pop down to the Hare and Hounds, see who's about. Anyone fancy joining me?'

'You're not going out this time of night, surely?' Ted says, throwing a glance at Gwen but she fails to acknowledge it. She has long been used to Nora's impetuous ways. She stopped trying to rein the girl in years ago – let her reap what she sows, she thinks. Instead she gently eases Tom to his feet.

'Come on, Tom. Time for bed, I think.'

'Right, well I'll just get ready then,' Nora declares. They listen to her bound up the stairs. Her bedroom door creaks and slams.

'Say goodnight, Tom,' Gwen prompts as the tired boy drags his feet towards the door.

He murmurs sleepily over his shoulder. Gwen ushers him into the hall. She hesitates, expecting Ted to take the opportunity to excuse himself for the evening, but instead he reaches over to pick up the newspaper from the floor besides Nora's vacated chair. He shakes it open and begins to read. Uncertain what to say, Gwen follows her son.

She takes her time putting Tom to bed. She lifts into place the blackout blind which – though no longer needed – effectively blocks the invasive light of the lengthening evenings, helping Tom to sleep. She does not chivvy him while he changes into his pyjamas. She neatly folds each piece of discarded clothing and puts it away. She reads him a story, and when he asks she reads him another, though on other nights she would adopt a strict tone and say 'No more, sleep now' before turning down the dial on his paraffin lamp. She hears the clack of Nora's door latch and her unguarded steps on the landing just before she peers into Tom's room to mouth goodnight, fresh lipstick gleaming on her lips.

She pauses in her reading, listening to Nora's heels clump on the stair runner and her muted call of 'Goodnight' to Ted. His low response rumbles up through the floorboards. He is still here. She picks up the thread of the story and continues reading long after Tom's silken lashes have dropped and his breathing has become soft and peaceful. She falls silent. Her pulse beats a little faster.

She closes the book and sets it down on the bedside table. She stands for a minute in the same pool of light that gilds her son's slumbering features, then she turns down the lamp to a firefly's glow, before plunging them into darkness. Still she makes no move to leave. She is aware of her shallow breathing, of her nervousness, but she gives herself a shake and scolds her foolishness. He is an old friend, she reminds herself, a neighbour . . . a stalwart in time of need. He regards her fondly and nothing more. She has wilfully misinterpreted his demeanour of late and by doing so she is putting their easy familiarity at risk. If she is not careful, she warns herself, her fearful notions will ruin their friendship beyond repair.

She leaves Tom's door ajar and makes her way downstairs. She is reluctant to enter the sitting room, but she gives herself another no-nonsense talking-to and finally walks in as if nothing is wrong. Ted looks up over the top of the paper and smiles, and she knows at once – from the light in his eyes, the lift of his expression – that she has not been foolish in her suspicions after all, and her chest tightens with panic. The smile she summons feels more like a grimace, but she covers it by contriving a yawn which thankfully morphs into a natural one, rendering her less guilty as she hides it behind her hand.

'Goodness, I must be more done in than I thought,' she says, her voice artificially bright.

Ted averts his gaze to the fire – she suspects to cover the disappointment that troubles his features. Recovering himself, he closes the paper and neatly folds it in half, before setting it down upon the settee beside him. He pushes himself up.

'I'd best leave you to it. I've probably overstayed my welcome as it is.'

'Oh no, I didn't mean . . .' Gwen feels wretched. More wretched because he is exactly right.

'No, no . . . it's getting late . . . and you'll be up early with the milking.'

'Yes.' She offers him a grateful smile.

'Right, so I'll be off.'

He leads the way, as comfortable in her home as he is in his own, perhaps more so, she thinks suddenly. The kitchen's darkness is alleviated only by the light that spills in from the hall, but it is enough for Ted to make out his jacket, hanging on the hooks by the back door. He shrugs it on. Gwen crosses her arms, shielding herself as she wills him to be gone.

He bids her goodnight but makes no attempt to leave and for an awful moment she thinks he is going to kiss her, but instead he reaches past her to collect his tweed cap from the sideboard.

'Gwen . . . I just wanted to say . . .' But his words seem to elude him like leaves snatched up by the wind. He scrabbles to collect them and she can barely breathe, trapped as she is, unable to escape. 'I know you haven't heard from Jack for some time . . . you must be wondering about him, now it's all over . . .' He looks down at the cap he is running through his hands. 'I meant what I said the other night. I've been glad to help you out, you and little Tom, I've enjoyed doing so . . .' He lifts his eyes to hers and she wants to weep at the intensity of feeling they contain. 'You need never be alone, Gwen. Whatever happens. I just wanted you to know that . . . and if, for whatever reason, Jack doesn't come home . . . I will always be here for you, Gwen, for you and Tom. Always.'

He does not wait for her reply and for that she is pathetically grateful. He turns away, pulling his cap low over his brow before tackling the door. She thinks he mutters a final farewell as he steps out into the gloaming but she is unsure – he may have just issued a weary sigh. The dog is lying on the path and lifts its head the moment the door opens but, as if attuned to the unusual tension, it makes no attempt to rise and fuss as it usually would. Instead it hunkers back down, its dark eyes regarding them with uncertainty.

Gwen drifts to the doorway, the blood sluggish in her veins. She watches him descend the steps to the yard and hears him stifle a cough.

He does not once look back.

CHAPTER NINETEEN

Jack

June 1939

He wakes with a shout and is out of his bed before he is fully conscious. He stands in the pitch-black, his chest heaving, his heart beating so violently it pains him. He gropes his way to the makeshift washstand he has fashioned out of an old tea chest and splashes his face with water from the ewer. His rapid breaths cut the still air. The image of Jenny, blood-soaked and lifeless, burns in his brain. He slams his palm against his forehead to dislodge it, but his efforts are in vain. Another bloody image slips into his mind with the sharp sting of a thorn and though he tries to claw it out it works its way in to fester. He will not think on it. He cannot. His anger frightens him.

As his heart steadies, he sits on the edge of the bed, the wooden frame cutting into the back of his thighs. He feels for his wristwatch and sees it is gone half two. He sinks his head into his hands and tries to purge his thoughts, wondering whether he will ever be free of the images that terrorise his sleep and shadow his waking moments – though it crosses his mind he does not deserve such release.

From outside he hears a muted clatter, loud enough to cause the horses to shift in their stalls. He hears it again and it brings him to his feet. He edges aside the velvet curtain but can see nothing but night through the grimy panes. He suspects a fox might be prowling around the poultry again. One had dug its way under the chicken wire the night before and killed three hens. Jack had found two headless corpses in the paddock and a pile of bloodied feathers near the edge of the copse. Fearing it has returned, he quickly pulls on his trousers and jams his bare feet into his boots.

The evening's rainstorm has left the yard peppered with dark puddles. The night sky is smothered in a layer of smoky cloud and Jack struggles to decipher the darkness. He starts down the side of the stables, heading for the chicken coop, but as the noise comes again he realises it does not originate from the paddock but from the implement shed. His steps quicken as he strides diagonally across the yard, puzzled by Kip's failure to raise the alarm. As he approaches he catches the flash of the dog's white ruff, luminescent against the night. He can just make out a figure struggling behind the plough.

'Gwen?'

She gasps and almost drops the ladder she is attempting to retrieve from the back of the shed.

'My God, Jack! You scared me half to death.'

'What on earth are you doing?'

She sighs and lowers the ladder to rest on its side. 'I'm locked out.'

'What?' His mind is still fuddled by nightmares; he cannot fathom why the farmer's daughter is in a shed in the early hours of the morning, wearing a pretty frock and a cardigan and a pair of her best shoes. 'It's two in the morning, Gwen, where on earth have you been? What's going on?'

'I'm locked out, that's what's going on, and I'm trying to get back in.' There is clear irritation in her carefully formed words. 'I forgot to pick up the spare key and Dad's locked up. I can hardly hammer on the door this time of night, can I? So I'm just going to climb in through my bedroom window, I've done it before.' She lifts the ladder. Its ends tip up and down like uneven scales as she tries to pass it over the plough. It crashes against the metal frame and the stillness of the night amplifies the din. Jack winces.

'You're going to wake the dead, lass,' he hisses, darting a glance at the blinkered farmhouse, relieved when no light appears. He rubs his hand over his face then winds his way between the plough and the seed drill to take the ladder from her before she creates any more of a disturbance. Up close, he smells the sickly taint of whisky clinging to her skin. Her sideways glance skates off him.

'Your dad has no idea you've snuck out, does he? What have you been up to, Gwen?'

And then, as Kip idly scratches behind his ear and a tawny owl's hoot echoes from the woods, he takes in the puzzle pieces set out before him – the misbuttoned cardigan, the Dutch courage, the luminous glaze to Gwen's eyes and the secretive curve of her lips – and with lightning speed he slots them together: *Gordon*.

He doesn't know whether he has said the name aloud or simply screamed it in his head, but it makes no difference. Gwen perceives his deduction.

'Dad's got him all wrong, Jack. He loves me, he's serious about us.'

'Then let him come here and make that clear to your dad.'

'Oh Jack, you've seen how Dad is. He wouldn't give him the time of day.' Slick with drink, her words slip into each other, though he can see the effort she is making to form each one, like wary footsteps on ice.

'You can't sneak around like this, Gwen. Your dad is going to find out.'

'Then let him. And when he sees the lengths we're prepared to go to in order to see each other, perhaps he'll realise he can't keep us apart – not when we so want to be together. And we do, we want to be together.'

'And when does Gordon plan on letting your father know his good intentions? Are you really telling me it's fear of your old man that's keeping him away? For God's sake, lass . . . can't you see there's nothing really stopping him from being open and honest about all this?'

'Dad . . .'

'Your dad would be more likely to believe him if he did the right thing and came here to explain himself, rather than encouraging you to be slipping out of doors and climbing in through windows like a thief in the bloody night! I bet Gordon's not scaling a damn ladder to get into his home right now, is he? Did he not even wait to see you safely in?'

'He dropped me at the end of the drive, we didn't want to risk waking Dad . . .'

Jack curses under his breath and shakes his head. 'And what do his parents think about all this running around?'

'Well . . . I . . . I don't know. That is, we haven't told them yet, either.' In the face of Jack's scepticism, she quickly adds, 'We can hardly tell them and keep my own father in the dark, can we?'

'Is that what's happening, Gwen? Gordon won't admit it to anyone?'

'I'm admitting it to you, aren't I?'

'Only because I've caught you out. Gwen, if he really cares about you the way he says he does then there's no reason for the two of you to be creeping around behind everyone's backs like this.'

'You don't understand . . .'

'Oh, I do understand, all too well.'

'Oh, you're just like the rest of them!' She tries to wrestle the ladder from him, but Jack doggedly maintains his hold, to her growing vexation. 'You don't understand . . . you don't understand anything at all . . .'

'No, you're right, I don't understand, because if I was lucky enough to be in his position I'd be so damned proud I'd want everyone to know.'

They fall still, eyes locked over the ladder that hangs between them. Jack takes its full weight as Gwen abruptly relinquishes her hold. She steps back but does not speak. She drops her gaze, self-consciously brushing her hand over her dress. She will not look at him.

'We'd better get you inside,' he mutters, lifting the ladder clear of the implements. Unsettled by the change in atmosphere, Kip slinks off to the straw bed in the corner. He circles three times and lies down.

They do not speak as they cross the yard. Jack leads the way with Gwen trailing behind as he moves quietly up the steps to the back of the farmhouse. He hoists the ladder and carefully props it against the render beside Gwen's casement window which rests ajar.

'I can manage now,' she says, but aware of the drink coursing through her veins and her heightened emotion, Jack shakes his head.

'I'll go up first and open the window wide for you.'

'There's no need.'

'That may be so.' He already has his boot on the second rung.

The ladder dips and wobbles under his weight. Once alongside the window he reaches across and knocks up the stay, then draws the casement wide. Conscious of the drop, he wonders how safe it is for Gwen to try and clamber in but, short of waking her father, he sees no other way.

'Are you sure?' he asks as he reaches the bottom. His unguarded admission appears to have sobered her.

'I've done it before.' She pushes past him and begins to climb. He holds the ladder steady, weighting the bottom rung with his booted foot, careful not to look up until she has reached the window. He watches with naked concern as she stretches across, one hand on the window frame, one hand on the ladder. His breath catches as she pitches herself through the gap, her feet scrabbling against the render as she slithers inside head first. She manages the perilous manoeuvre with such aplomb he wonders how many times she has executed it – how often has he slept through her comings and goings? How many more secret rendezvous with Gordon Allingham has she had?

He continues to watch the window. When she finally appears she does not call down her thanks or acknowledge him in any way. She merely reaches for the stay and pulls the casement to, then draws the curtains, signalling the end of the evening's performance.

Kip does not stir when Jack returns the ladder to the shed.

As he makes his way back across the yard to the stable block, he looks up at Gwen's window for a final time, his heart heavy with knowledge it would rather not hold.

CHAPTER TWENTY

Jack

July 1939

Gwen is standing by the range reading an oat-coloured pamphlet when Jack and Jim come in for lunch. The paper quivers in her hand.

'You should probably read that,' she says to her father, placing it on the kitchen table before him. Jack notices how pale she has gone.

Jim reaches for the pamphlet. '*Some things you should know if war should come*,' he quotes in a monotone. '*Public information leaflet number one*.' He shakes his head with slow resignation. 'Number one of how many, I wonder.'

Gwen carries the kettle from the range to the sink, but she seems to forget her purpose and stands staring out of the window, the kettle in her hand. Jack moves forward to take it from her, startling her from her reverie. She looks at him blankly, then retreats from the drainer.

'They're on about the light restrictions again,' Jim says, looking up from the pamphlet. 'You'd best get the blackout screens up from the cellar, Gwen. I thought we'd seen the last of those after all that Munich nonsense. It's a good thing we didn't chuck 'em out after all.' His tone is sombre. 'Jack, will you help her?'

'Aye, no bother.'

She leads him into the hall and opens the cellar door, pausing to light the paraffin lamp that hangs from a protruding nail just inside. Gwen goes first, holding the lamp aloft so that its light trickles over the descending steps, while Jack follows behind, instinctively hanging his head under the low ceiling. The cellar is cool and dark and filled with an assortment of wooden crates, cardboard boxes, and bits of discarded furniture.

Gwen takes him further in, past a pair of dining chairs with broken rush seats, to where a set of simple wooden frames rest against the wall. Black fabric has been stretched across them and tacked into place. Gwen pulls the first one free.

'I had hoped we wouldn't be needing these.'

Jack steps forward and relieves her of the frame that has D/R, FRONT chalked on its side. Gwen brushes against his shoulder as she brings the lamp closer.

'*Dining room, front window,*' she interprets. 'There's a system, you see.'

He nods. 'Is there one for every window?'

'Almost. I think the crisis was averted before we got them all done. Looks like we'll have to finish the job now.'

'Aye, it does.'

'Do you think that, Jack? That war is inevitable?'

He is reluctant to be the harbinger of doom, but there is no avoiding it. He nods.

She places the lamp down on a stacked tea chest. 'What will happen, do you think? Will it be like last time? Conscription?'

'I would imagine so. I suspect . . .' he sighs. 'Men didn't know last time what it was going to be like – they expected an adventure and were keen to volunteer for that. But we know better now and I can't see it happening this time. I think men will have to be compelled to do their bit. They'll do it, like – when asked – but I think they're going to have to be made to go.'

'And what of you, Jack? You said you'd sign up.'

'And I will.'

'When?'

'Eager to get rid of me?'

'No!' She offers him an apologetic smile, then asks softly, 'Do you think they'll wait? Wait until war is declared before starting conscription?'

'Well, they've started the process already, remember, with the young lads doing military training . . . but full conscription? Aye, I reckon when war is announced, then we'll hear.'

'Gordon will have to go.'

'Yes, more than likely he will.'

She nods. 'He's ready. We've talked about it, but it just never seemed real. Then that bloody leaflet came through today and . . .' She covers her mouth with her flattened hand and turns away.

'Ah now, lass.'

She shakes her head and lowers her hand, her eyes glistening. 'We're getting married, Jack.'

Like a boxer on the ropes, he steadies himself, struggling to conceal the effect of the unexpected uppercut.

'Married.' His voice is hollow.

'Gordon knew war was coming. He says it's been inevitable since the Germans invaded Czechoslovakia. He . . . he said . . .

we don't know what time we have left together. He doesn't want to waste a minute of it.'

He nods, his grip tightening on the wood. 'So now you'll tell your dad?'

She avoids his question by levering another frame from the stack. She makes a show of looking for the chalk mark identifying its destination. 'This one is for the other dining-room window. At least all that work wasn't in vain, though I can't help wishing it was.'

'He *is* going to come and speak to your dad, Gwen?'

'Of course.' A nervous laugh escapes her. 'Can you imagine his face when Gordon turns up asking for my hand? After all he's said, after all his doubts. I've proven him wrong, Jack! He should have had more faith in me. I knew from the start that Gordon and I would go the distance. Sometimes, you just do, don't you? The first time I met him, it was like fireworks between us. I'd never felt anything like it . . . and it was the same for him. I knew then we were meant to be together. And I know we've been skulking around behind Dad's back, but really, Jack, we've had no choice and, at the end of the day, we've made such an effort to carry on seeing each other, it just proves it, doesn't it? That it's the real thing. It's true love.'

Jack forces a smile. Fireworks, he thinks, are funny things. They erupt with such drama – deafening explosions resulting in a kaleidoscope of colour – and yet, moments later, when their ghostly trails have faded from the night sky and their resonance has been lost to the breeze, there is nothing to see, nothing to hear, just the whisper of the air and the pitch of the night sky. Their impact is so transient it is as if they had never been there at all.

They carry the frames from the cellar one by one, depositing them in the rooms they were made for. When they are done, Gwen asks Jack to help her measure the windows yet to be addressed and she leads him upstairs.

He demurs in the doorway when she enters her own room, but she beckons him in. He unfolds his wooden rule and holds it against the window's width. Gwen's pencil scratches across her notepad as he reads out the numbers etched in black.

'I'll have to go into the village tomorrow to buy some more blackout fabric,' she says, as he changes the angle of the ruler to measure the window's height. 'I do hope they haven't sold out.' She jots down the measurements he gives her. 'Perhaps I'll cause a scandal and purchase my wedding lace too,' she whispers, an impish grin dimpling her cheek.

'Have you and Gordon a date in mind?'

'No . . . not yet, but . . .' She tucks her hair behind her ear. Jack is struck by her sudden nervousness. 'It's the summer fete in a couple of weeks. It's held up at the Hall, and . . . Gordon wants to wait until then. I think perhaps that's when he's planning to introduce me to his parents.'

'But your father, Gwen, he can't find out then. You must have plans to tell him before that?'

'Yes . . . yes, of course.'

'Or are you thinking of coming home tomorrow with an armful of lace, hoping he'll draw his own conclusions?'

The teasing note in his voice elicits a smile. 'No . . .' she laughs.

'But you're clearly hoping to start your wedding dress?'

'I won't be making my wedding dress. I'm going to wear my mother's. It's wrapped in tissue paper in a box in the attic as perfect as the day she wore it. I take it out, every now and then, just to have a look. It will be my way of having her at the wedding, wearing her dress. She was so happy with Dad . . . perhaps it will bring me the same good fortune.'

'Do you think you need a good luck charm to find happiness with Gordon?'

'Of course not!' She pulls an indignant face. 'Gordon and I are very happy together. Dad will come to see that – hopefully sooner rather than later. He'll come to realise Gordon's intentions were always honourable.'

'And you'll get to wear your mother's dress.'

'Carrying a bouquet of white roses and trailing ivy, symbolising friendship, fidelity and love – all things I want my marriage to have.' She smiles. 'That's what I've always dreamt of, and that's all that I want for my wedding day – my mother's dress and that bouquet.'

'Then I hope your dreams come true.' He clears the gruffness from his voice and takes a new tack. 'It might be best to try out these blackout frames. We'll get them in place later and I'll take a walk around tonight to check they're doing their job.'

'Are you questioning my abilities?' She laughs.

But it wasn't her abilities he was questioning. Just her judgement.

CHAPTER TWENTY-ONE

Jack

July 1939

They wake to rain on the morning of the fete. Gwen pulls back the curtains in the kitchen and lets out a cry of dismay. Jim is on his knees, lighting the range. He sits back on his heels, unperturbed by the haze beyond the speckled panes.

'Oh, don't you worry, girl, it's nothing more than a scud. It'll turn out nice by this afternoon, you mark my words.'

'I hope so. I have my dress and shoes all chosen and rain won't do with my outfit.'

'You're going to a lot of trouble this year,' Jim observes, clanking the range door shut as flames lick the wood. He reaches for the rail and hauls himself up.

Jack is at the dresser collecting mugs for the tea. He catches the furtive look that flickers across Gwen's face, but it is gone before her father draws himself up to full height.

'Oh, you know how I enjoy the fete,' she says brightly, 'and there's nothing wrong with making a bit of an effort once in a while.'

'No, nothing wrong in that at all,' Jim agrees, pulling out a chair.

Muriel arrives, huffing and puffing about the shower, her raincoat glistening.

'I hope it clears up or this afternoon will be a washout,' she declares, tying up her apron.

'You girls . . . it's a shower, nothing more,' Jim grumbles.

Gwen cries off her chores that morning in order to help Muriel bake for the cake stall. Jim chunters under his breath as he strikes a match to light his Woodbine and rolls his eyes at Jack as the women flour the scrubbed tabletop, ready for patting out scone mix, the fluted cutters already retrieved from the pantry shelf.

The two men spend the morning snagging hedges. The blades of their billhooks flash in the sunlight that breaks through the lingering cloud, and by the time the foot of the hedgerow is trimmed with unruly ribbons of cut shoots and hacked brambles, the clouds have been banished to distant lands. The cobalt sky above them soon plays host to little more than wisps of white, and the rising heat has their shirts soaked with sweat.

They break off at midday. With the fete due to start at two, they need to eat and make ready in good time, bearing in mind Gwen has to arrive early to help set up. They will burn the rubbish the following day, Jim announces as they walk back to the farmhouse, the wooden handles of their blades clamped in their damp palms.

They find the kitchen crammed with the fruits of the women's labours. Jars of jewel-coloured jam lie nestled in straw-bedded crates. Wooden trays – so many Jim wonders aloud where they have come from – cover the table, each bearing plates of sugar-dusted buns, fruit tarts and sponge cakes filled with buttercream.

They resist the precious culinary offerings and instead carve themselves hunks of bread which they slather in butter that is overly soft and top with cheese that has begun to sweat in the heat. They eat standing, one leaning against the dresser, the other against the draining board, crumbs dropping to the floor, too afraid to sit at the table lest they disturb something and incur the women's wrath.

'You've been busy,' Jim says when Gwen finally appears in the doorway.

Jack swallows his last mouthful of food and draws himself up. She is wearing a dress he hasn't seen before, a pretty tea dress that suits her well. She sets a broad-brimmed straw hat and a pair of lace gloves upon the dresser top and smiles.

'Not bad, eh?'

'You've gone to town,' Jim says, studying her, and for a moment it seems Gwen is unsure whether her father is referring to the baking or to her appearance. An attractive blush spreads across her cheeks.

'Oh well . . .' she shrugs lightly, then instructs them to hurry up and get ready.

'Don't fret, it shan't take Jack and I long to titivate ourselves.' Jim winks at Jack as he dabs the crumbs from his mouth.

'Perhaps not, but it will take a good while to get this lot in the car,' Gwen says, brooking no nonsense as she ushers them both from the kitchen.

At a little before half past one, the men – washed and spruced – help Gwen ferry the cakes and jam into the car, until the vehicle is so tightly packed they barely have room for themselves. Gwen squeezes into the back, shuffling forward on the bench seat to smooth down Jim's hair which is sticking up at the back, making him look in her estimation 'like a country bumpkin'. Jack stares through the windscreen, sour with disapproval. He knows all too well the real reason for Gwen's extra efforts and her concern over her father's appearance. Jim swats away her hand, cursing her fussing as he starts the engine. They turn into the lane and head in the direction of the Hall.

On arrival they see the huge marquees that have been erected on the front lawns. Groundsmen in ill-fitting black suits and bowler hats direct them through an open gate onto the meadow, where a handful of cars have been parked in a neat row and a few motorcycles loll on their stands.

Jim parks up and Jack gets out to open Gwen's door. She looks nauseous, but soon rallies as Jim, ill-at-ease in these surroundings, barks at her to hurry.

Between them, they load up with crates and trays. Gwen picks her way across the sun-bleached hassocks in her high-heeled shoes and the men follow. They pass through a narrow iron gate onto the velvet lawns. She pauses to survey the scene before her, then dispatches her father with his tray of cakes to a tent shaded by a cedar tree, while she and Jack take their crates of jam to the large marquee in front of the house.

Gwen, Jack realises immediately, is in a heightened state of alertness. She appears to be on constant lookout, though she attempts to mask her sweeping study of the fete. They are greeted by people Jack doesn't know, mostly ladies wearing pearls, neat hats, white gloves and smart dresses that fall well below the knee. When he asks, Gwen whispers they are members of the church committee which organises the event each year. But he knows her interest does not lie with such pillars of the community.

'Looking for Gordon?'

'He's here somewhere, I know.'

'I'm sure he'll be looking out for you.' The reassurance feels hollow, even to him. Some instinct, deep in his gut, belies the words.

'Yes . . . yes, he will,' she says, improving her grip on her crate.

They enter the marquee, the close-cropped grass a plush carpet beneath their feet. Trestles have been set up end-to-end to run its length. The first table is arranged with plates stacked with pies of all sizes – pork pies, picnic pies, meat pies – their contents hidden beneath thick layers of grease-sheened pastry with pinched rims, all jealously guarded by a plump middle-aged woman with tightly curled hair. Beads of perspiration cling to her furred upper lip as she battles off a persistent bluebottle. The warm air trapped inside the canvas is as thick as treacle.

'Jams, preserves and pickles – far table,' she snaps, as Gwen shyly proffers her wares.

Jack follows Gwen along, observing her as she receives nods and greetings from the other ladies setting up their stalls. The far table is unmanned and unadorned, so they set down their crates and while Jack unloads the jars Gwen starts to arrange them into colourful pyramids.

He is just stacking the empty boxes when he detects a frisson of excitement pass through the marquee as an older woman with regal deportment dips with practised elegance under the tent flap. Her dress is simple and unfussy, yet its discerning cut reveals it has been made for her and her alone. Strings of pearls cover her chest in ever-decreasing loops, and her narrow-brimmed hat bears a pretty arrangement of flowers at its front which sets off her outfit to perfection. The smile that graces her features is practised and cold.

'Good afternoon, ladies.'

Her greeting is met by a jumble of gauche responses. Patches of pink have appeared on Gwen's cheeks and at once Jack realises that this woman – this grand dame of local society who now glides from table to table exchanging a few polite words with the tongue-tied women standing to attention behind – can be none other than Gordon Allingham's mother. Lady Allingham. The woman Gwen soon hopes to call 'Mother'. As she draws ever nearer, he is aware of Gwen's breath catching.

'Don't they look pretty arranged like that . . . all those lovely colours? So eye-catching.'

And then she is gone, leaving behind a subtle hint of lily of the valley.

'Did you see?' Gwen's face is alight with excitement, as she leans towards him in confidence. 'Did you see how she singled me out?' Jack can almost hear her heart thudding against her ribcage. 'I'm sure she did it on purpose. He's spoken to her, he must have. The way she smiled at me!' Her joy is tangible. 'Don't you see, Jack? She knows. She knows who I am and, more importantly, she knows exactly who I am to Gordon!'

CHAPTER TWENTY-TWO

Gwen

15th August 1945

Iris Jennings, the constable's wife, bundles into the kitchen without invitation as they are eating their dinner to share her elation that Japan has surrendered and the country is finally at peace. There has not been the spontaneous celebration that followed the announcement of VE Day. The village has, for some time, been planning for a more organised event to celebrate the end of the war and has been patiently waiting for the day those plans could be set in motion. That day has at last arrived.

'We now have a military-style operation of our own to launch, ladies,' Iris declares pulling back a chair and settling herself down. She rests her arms on the table. 'There's not much time, so it's going to be all hands to the deck. It's lucky we have the plans already prepared.'

The victory celebration is to be held on John Powell's meadow next to the church, right in the heart of the village. Had Lord Allingham been in better health it would, no doubt, have been hosted at the Hall, but the present arrangement pleases Gwen.

'Now,' Iris continues, 'I've got the marquees going up this evening – Gwen, you said you had some bunting we could use?'

'Yes, that's right. Dad got some in for the coronation. It's in a box in the cellar somewhere.'

'Well, I'd be most grateful if we could borrow it. We want the whole area decked out the best we can. I won't disturb your dinner for it now, but is there any chance you could drop it down to the church later?'

'Yes, yes, of course. I'll dig it out and bring it over.'

'Perfect! Now, Muriel, you know what you're doing – cakes and sandwiches?'

'Yes, I've had a look through the recipes the Ministry of Food sent through,' she shakes her head in despair, 'I'll rustle up what I can.'

'Marvellous, ladies. And Nora, have we discussed your contribution yet?'

'Not formally.' Having already finished her dinner, Nora is smoking a cigarette. She taps its flaking tip onto the ashtray beside her. 'But I know what I'll be doing.'

'And what's that?' Iris asks suspiciously.

Nora hitches an eyebrow and holds her cigarette aloft. 'Looking lovely and showering kisses on our returned heroes, of course.' She blinks with feigned innocence.

'Oh you,' Iris huffs with little humour, pushing back her chair in disgust. 'Gwen, I'll see you later. Muriel, Tom . . .' She glares at Nora as she draws the door to behind her.

Catching Tom's eye, Nora sits back in her chair and laughs.

Gwen goes alone to the church. She leaves Tom with Nora and Muriel, who stays later at the house during the summer, while the nights are drawn out. Gwen suspects the widowed housekeeper finds her own cottage lonely these days.

The church is alive with people when she arrives, though the pews themselves are filled with produce and props rather than worshippers. Villagers have gathered in clusters in the side aisles and nave to discuss the setting up of stalls and the practicalities of entertainments. Iris flits between them, loud and energetic, her voice ringing out as she directs operations. It is clear she is in her element.

Gwen stands with her dusty box, trying to determine where best to leave it. She approaches the nearest group, but a rather harassed young woman with blemished cheeks abruptly explains they are only responsible for children's events, before returning to her group's animated discussion.

Gwen moves up the nave but finds everyone too involved with their own preparations to assist her. Finally, Iris spots her hovering and from her position in the transept she raises her arm and waves her forward.

As Gwen approaches, she sees the policeman's wife is not alone – she is in conversation with a stooped man Gwen does not recognise and a well-dressed older lady who stands with her back to the church.

'Gwen, my dear! Come, come.' Iris beckons her closer as if she were child shy of taking centre stage.

'I've bought the bunting.' Gwen gestures with the box and, as she does so, the older woman turns. Gwen's heart seizes as the woman offers her a practised smile.

'Oh, that's perfect!' Lady Allingham dips her gloved hand into the bunting and lifts some clear of the box. 'And in such better condition than what we have brought. Mrs Jennings, I do fear ours is going to look a little shabby, but it has done us good service – why, my father-in-law purchased it for Queen Victoria's diamond jubilee! I'm concerned it may fall apart as soon as you start to unravel it.'

'Mummy!'

Gwen spins round at the echo of the familiar voice. Tom is racing up the nave and her first words are to chastise him for running in church. Only after he sheepishly apologises, pressing against her leg, suddenly shy before strangers, does she question his presence, but then she sees Nora sauntering up the aisle with another box of offerings.

'Muriel dug out some more things for you, Iris.'

The Land Girl smiles as she sets the box down on an empty pew, but it fades to a look of bemusement as she catches sight of Gwen's alarm.

'What?'

Gwen's arm snakes around Tom's shoulder, fixing him against her. She is unable to give voice to her concern.

'Tom wanted to come,' Nora says, her manner defensive.

'Mummy,' Tom wraps his arm around her thighs, tipping his head back to look at her, 'will you give me a piggyback home? My legs are very tired! Nora walks so fast I had to run to keep up.'

Lady Allingham laughs, charmed by the boy. Tom coyly basks in the warmth of her attention and, as he does so, Gwen notices something play across the older woman's features, as if her son has stirred a deep-seated memory, and now, put to mind of it, she desires to remember it anew. But it remains tantalisingly beyond Lady Allingham's grasp and she soon abandons her efforts and loses interest in the boy.

'Now, Mrs Jennings, I'm afraid we must be off. Gordon has made a number of cine films during his time abroad and Lord Allingham and I have committed to watching them this evening. I left him setting up a large screen. I fear it will be a long and sobering show.'

Iris thanks her for her donation. Gwen steps back, pulling Tom with her. Lady Allingham casts them a bland smile as she pulls her mink stole further around her shoulders. The clip of her shoes on the stone flags echoes as she walks away. The stooped man, who Gwen now suspects to be her chauffeur, hurries behind.

Gwen does not watch her leave. Instead she tightens her grip on Tom's shoulders and persuades herself that Lady Allingham has no idea who she is. She has no idea at all.

She sends up a silent prayer that it will stay that way.

CHAPTER TWENTY-THREE

Jack

July 1939

Jack is not enjoying the fete. Gwen has committed to the opening stint on the jam stall and at first he thinks he will stay with her, but as the marquee becomes packed with plump farmers' wives and young children overflowing with reckless energy, he makes his excuses and ducks out. The grounds are filling up now. The domed roofs of cars cobble the front meadow and abandoned push bikes decorate the iron railings, while the Hall looms in the background, disapproving of the hoi polloi now milling over its manicured lawns.

It is unbearably hot. He pulls his handkerchief from his pocket and dabs at his forehead. He yearns to strip off his jacket and roll up his sleeves, but he notices a decorous standard is being maintained amongst the crowd, with everyone suffering the heat in their hats and suits, and he has no intention of letting the side down. So, his jacket remains on, though his body leaks through his shirt into its seams.

He passes the coconut shy where a group of giggling girls are trying their luck with little success, and then an apple-bobbing barrel with a line of boys egging each other on to get wet, much to the consternation of the stallholder. The enticing scent of honey and hops emanates from the open-fronted beer tent, but though sorely tempted, Jack decides against joining the old men and lithe lads lingering around its guy ropes supping their nectar-filled glasses. He walks on.

An eight-piece ensemble is playing on a raised dais erected in the middle of the lawn, and as the violins' soft strains float through the air Jack is struck by how unimaginable he would have found his present situation a few weeks ago. He thinks back to that night in June, huddled against the shuddering boards of the coal wagon, with his throbbing knuckles and smarting eyes, and he remembers the plan he managed to extricate from his racing thoughts. He marvels how that very plan – formed from a desire to redeem himself – has so unexpectedly brought him here to this new life – a life that he now longs to pursue.

But he knows it is an impossible dream. He must fulfil his original intentions. He has no choice in the matter – he must escape to the war that draws ever closer. It remains the only way he can atone for what he has done – and perhaps secure a future. War will be his trial and fate his hanging judge. If he is to sacrifice his life for his crimes at least it will be on his own terms, and that way he can accept its loss – for its loss, he suspects, is inevitable. The black-bordered photographs on his mantel at home reveal how battlefield odds play out for men like him.

The insistent call of his name startles him from his reverie. Jim is standing a short distance away before a red-striped tent in the company of Ted and another couple. He arcs his arm to catch Jack's attention and, raising his own hand in acknowledgement, Jack starts towards him. His steps slacken as the couple turn to greet him. It takes him a minute to place the man – he looks different out of uniform – but by the time he realises it is Constable Jennings, and the woman beside him presumably his Durham-born wife, it is too late to walk away.

'And here he is.' Vic Jennings holds out his arm to gather Jack in. 'Come on, lad, I want you to meet someone. I know you'll make her day.'

There is not a cloud in the sky and yet a cold chill insinuates itself up Jack's back and his sweat-dampened skin turns to ice. He musters a smile which even to him feels thin and insubstantial and certainly no match for the broad beam that brightens Mrs Jennings' eager features. She is shorter than the constable, and large. She playfully swats her husband's chest and the fatty flesh sagging from under the short sleeves of her cotton dress quivers.

'Oh, Vic, you are a daft bugger.'

The accent of home jars for Jack. Its cadence is out of place here and brings him no comfort. It reminds him of things he'd sooner forget.

'No, come on now, Iris,' her husband chides, 'how many times have you said to me you get sick of hearing our bland southern voices and yearn for a good old northern accent?'

'Well, yes, I do love to hear the northern intonation every now and then, that's true.' She smiles at Jack. The warmth of her attention is almost unbearable. 'So, tell me – Jack, is it? – whereabouts are you from? I've family all over the north-east so I'm bound to know it!'

'Sunderland.' This time he stumbles over the lie. It rises unexpectedly to trip him. Her presence has rendered the landscape uneven and the level path he has been confidently treading is suddenly fractured and dangerous.

'Sunderland? I have family there! Whereabouts in Sunderland?'

'By the infirmary.'

Every large town has an infirmary, he thinks. He hopes it will be the end of the matter, but her eyes widen with interest.

'Oh really – which area? Tunstall, Hendon?'

He schools his features. He does not know if there are two infirmaries, or whether one infirmary sits in the middle of the two areas she has mentioned. *Tunstall or Hendon.* He fights the urge to lick his lips.

'Tunstall.' He sees at once from her flash of surprise that he has guessed incorrectly.

'Tunstall?' The hitch in her voice speaks volumes. His ignorance has led him into a mistake. 'Goodness. That's a nice area,' she says a little too brightly, while wearing the perplexed look of a shopkeeper who has discovered a discrepancy in the day's takings. 'You must miss it.'

'He doesn't miss it, do you, Jack?' Jim's robust voice echoes in his head. 'He prefers farming to the shipyards, I'm sure.'

'You were employed in the yards, were you? What did you do?'

Her ongoing confusion is now ill-disguised and Jack can see she is intent on prising apart his story. She does not approve of its construction; there are elements which, to her eyes – with her knowledge – are misaligned. By breaking them apart, perhaps she hopes to reconstruct them in a manner that will make more sense to her. But Jack is aware her well-meant enquiries are in danger of stripping away his cover – his ability to hide is in jeopardy. Desperate, he gropes for a suitable role, a role a man from Tunstall might conceivably have at the yards, but he cannot think of one. He suddenly feels weary.

'Riveter.'

He sees at once his honest answer has reinforced her doubts. She seems almost embarrassed by it, as if it is an unwelcome gift. She blusters a moment, deciding what to do with it, before kindly saying – 'That's tough work, isn't it? I've family who are shipbuilders, hard men all of them.'

'Aye, it is.'

'I don't know much about the Sunderland yards, mind, but my uncle was an overseer at Swan Hunters. That's how it is up there, isn't it? Coal or shipping. My dad went down the mines. Mind you, I think he was more than relieved when my brother Bob decided to join the police rather than follow in his footsteps.'

'I didn't know you had a brother in the force, Iris,' Ted pipes up.

'Yes, indeed. Well, it was him who introduced me to Vic. Vic was in the military police, weren't you Vic, and Bob was his sergeant.'

'Never.'

'That's right. He's done well for himself, our Bob. He left the army after the war and joined the civilian force and he's a detective now,' she turns back to Jack, 'up in Newcastle.'

'Is that right?' Jack resists the temptation to tug at his collar. It feels tighter than when he left the house. He puts it down to the heat.

'He picks up a lot of work around the shipyards, he says. There's some rough streets down by the river . . . some of the things he's seen,' she makes a soft tutting noise as she shakes her head, 'terrible. He always tells Vic he doesn't know how lucky he is, having a quiet country patch like this.'

'Supervising sheep dipping is probably a little different to dealing with murders and such, I'm sure,' Ted observes dryly.

Vic's hitherto broad smile compresses to a thin line.

'I keep my wits about me, Ted, don't you worry. I'm more than man enough for any task that might come my way.'

'And what are your plans, Jack?' Iris breaks in, keen to avert a confrontation. 'Are you down here to stay now or do you see yourself going back?'

'I won't be going back.' He hopes it is enough, but there is a look of expectation on her face. She waits for him to continue. 'I'll stay and help Jim for the rest of the summer . . .'

'But then you're moving on,' Ted qualifies.

Jack studies the farmer next to him. He could not have been more pointed if he had tried. 'Aye, then I'll be moving on.'

'To do what?' Iris asks.

'I expect I'll be joining the army if things don't settle down in Europe.'

'You'll wait for conscription, surely?'

'I intend to volunteer.'

Her head tips to the side as she adopts a baffled expression. 'You know, listening to your accent I'd swear you were from Newcastle not Sunderland. Are you sure you're not from the other side of the Tyne, because I'd honestly say—'

'For God's sake, Iris, do you really think the lad doesn't know where he's from?' Vic protests. Jack's limbs suddenly feel loose and bloodless.

'All I'm saying is I can usually tell Geordie from Mackem and I swear, Jack, you sound like a Newcastle lad. I can hear it clear as day!'

'I have family . . . over Newcastle way . . .' Betrayed by the flex of his vocal folds and the intimate touch of tongue to palate, Jack gropes for a feasible explanation, aware that even Ted is now paying keen attention. 'My mam . . . she was from Newcastle . . . I probably picked up my accent from her.'

'Sunderland born and bred you said . . .' Ted mutters darkly.

'My dad, his family are all Mackems, though . . .'

He never anticipated an encounter with someone from home, and now Iris's sharp ear has detected the loose thread of his story and, with her persistent tugging, his lies are unravelling, as one stitch of fabrication gives way to the next.

A bell clangs across the garden and Jack spins around, blessing its interruption.

'That'll be the speeches . . . we'd best go and listen,' Jim says, shepherding them towards the dais.

Jack picks up his pace, eager to escape their company, and soon the space he has created between himself and the others fills with the gathering crowd. He spies Gwen, standing by herself at the far side of the platform, and makes his way to her.

'There you are.' Her smile is remedial. His racing pulse abates as his rising panic recedes like a withdrawing tide. Alone in her company he is at last able to breathe.

'I was with your father.'

'Oh, yes, I see him over there.' She peers into the crowd, tracking her father as he finds a place towards the back. 'He's with Ted, I see. And is that Vic Jennings and his wife?'

'Iris, yes.' But Jack doesn't look round. He has no desire to draw their attention. Not when he feels safe at last.

Gwen nods absently as she continues to look around her, constantly searching.

'Have you seen Gordon?' Jack asks quietly.

'No, have you?' The words fly from her, urgent and hopeful. When he shakes his head her eyes dull with disappointment. 'I don't know where he can be. I've been looking for him all afternoon.'

The crowd falls silent as the front doors of the Hall are thrown open and an older, upright gentleman Jack takes to be Lord Allingham, dapper in a dogtooth suit, strides out with the vicar. The woman who Gwen has already identified as his wife follows with another lady who, from her general demeanour, Jack deduces to be the vicar's wife. He hears a sharp intake of breath from Gwen as Gordon Allingham and a young woman Jack presumes to be his sister bring up the rear.

Someone at the back of the crowd begins to clap, opening a smattering of applause that is uncomfortably insipid. Lord Allingham mounts the steps onto the dais, holding up his hand in grateful acknowledgement, before taking a spot front and centre. With his hands clasped behind him, he rocks on his well-polished heels while the rest of the group form a neat row behind. When there is satisfactory quiet, disturbed only by the cooing of a pigeon, he begins.

'My dear friends, neighbours and fellow parishioners, welcome to Netley Hall. I am delighted to see so many of you here today in support of St Peter's Fete. Reverend Hardman . . .' he twists to acknowledge the gracious man of God behind him, 'and I are eternally grateful for your generosity, especially those of you who have donated time, energy and endeavour to make the fete the success it always is.' He pauses, his smile fading to genial regret. 'I am glad the rain that threatened our festivities today moved off in good time to see us blessed with this wonderful sunshine and warmth. I can only hope that the storm clouds that have been blighting our far horizons in recent days will similarly disperse, and I pray we find ourselves blessed by clear skies there also, in the not too distant future. We must keep faith with our politicians during these difficult times and trust them to steer us safely through this crisis. We must not give up hope. We must also remember that however dark the days may seem there is always joy to be found, and I am delighted to take this opportunity to share some good news with you now. I cannot think of a more appropriate setting to make such an announcement than this.'

As he pauses, a crow heckles from the branches of the cedar.

'My son, Gordon, this morning asked Lady Helen Ashworth to be his wife, and to all our great delight . . . she said yes.'

CHAPTER TWENTY-FOUR

Jack

July 1939

Jack is acutely aware of Gwen's calcifying figure. She stares at the dais, her eyes glazed. It is as if Lord Allingham's announcement has drained her soul and now only a lifeless shell remains.

A murmur whips around the crowd like a crisp leaf carried on a gust, rising and falling. Lord Allingham beckons his son forward and Gordon brings with him the young woman he had escorted from the Hall. Jack had benignly identified her then as a sister, but now she takes on a more sinister role. She is a blight on Gwen's blooming heart, a canker set to devour her hopes and dreams.

Lady Helen is certainly a beautiful girl – it would be pointless to deny it. Fine-featured with high cheekbones and a long nose sculpted to perfection, her bud-like mouth creases with suppressed pleasure. She is all honey and roses and perfect for the summer afternoon setting, which seems to further enhance her natural charms. Gordon grips her hand. They bask in the light applause and calls of '*Congratulations!*' that ring out from the crowd, beholding each other with ill-masked satisfaction that seems to say, *This is it, we are born for this*. In this moment they are adored. The announcement of their union has brought happiness to those they do not even know. It is a gift they bestow with benevolence.

Gwen's breaths are ragged. The colour recedes from her cheeks and her eyelids flutter as her lips fall apart. Jack darts his arm around her waist as she begins to sway.

'Stand tall, lass,' he whispers, his lips so close to her ear strands of hair catch upon them. 'Don't become the object of idle gossip.' His muscles strain against her weight as his fingers bite into the soft dip of her waist. His body becomes her scaffold.

From the dais, Gordon begins to speak, thanking those gathered for their good wishes.

Gwen turns to Jack with blind eyes. Her confusion is palpable. Her knees buckle again, and he grits his teeth as he struggles to keep her on her feet.

'Walk with me.' He speaks softly, trying to penetrate her blank gaze. Her lips move, but no sound comes out. Tears begin to swell at the corner of her eyes. As the rapt crowd listens to Gordon's silken speech, Jack draws Gwen away, keen their departure should attract as little attention as possible. As they fall back through the rows, his grip slips from her waist to her stone-cold hand. Once free of the gathering, he tugs her behind a marquee.

Now hidden from view, she snatches herself free of him and stumbles forward. She clamps her hand over her mouth to gag her mournful cries. Her whole body begins to tremble, and Jack finds her sudden fragility unbearable. This is not the Gwen he knows. This is not the sturdy girl who labours beside him with robust energy and a speedy smile. Her treacherous lover has stripped the strength from her bones and left her brittle. She is breaking before his very eyes and he cannot stand it.

'It's a mistake . . .' He catches the words amongst her faint mutterings as she begins to pace, her aimless steps driven by confusion and disbelief. 'His parents . . . corralled him . . . they don't know . . . he hasn't been able to say . . . When they know . . .'

She brings to Jack's mind the woman who lived three doors down from them in Newcastle. She would walk the cobbled pathway behind the houses unkempt – her hair matted, her face smudged, a holed cardigan over a nightdress drab with wear – muttering to herself, fingernails bitten to the quick bunched at her cracked lips, her downcast eyes raking left to right as she searched for something that could never be found. The young children were all afraid of her, for she would reach for them adoringly, then cry with pain as they shied away, while the older ones mocked her for her madness. And she was mad, Jack's mother said, driven mad by the death of her only bairn. Her child's sudden passing had been incomprehensible, and unable to fathom her loss, her sanity fractured. Her husband had abandoned her and she was left alone, her mind rotting, just as their narrow terrace, neglected, began to rot around her. That Gwen's behaviour should now cause him to recall that grieving woman frightens Jack. He takes a step towards her.

'Gwen—'

'I have to see him.'

She lifts her head. Her eyes shimmer with fervour. 'I need to see Gordon . . . now . . . I need to speak to him, to . . . don't you see? He hasn't told his parents about us, so they've arranged this marriage without his consent. I must go to him now, so we can tell them together . . .'

He blocks her attempt to pass, grabbing hold of her arms as she struggles to push him aside.

'Let me go!'

'You can't speak to him, Gwen. Not here, not now, not like this.'

'I can . . . I must . . .' She claws at his chest. 'Blast it, Jack, let me go!'

But he clenches his jaw and bears the violence of her frantic struggle, a struggle fuelled by panic and rage and grief in equal measure. He murmurs her name softly, begging her to stop and think. He will not let her subject herself to the raw humiliation such a confrontation is sure to bring. Gradually, the fight ebbs from her as the reality of her situation dawns. She emits a low moan as her knees give way; he pulls her to him. Enclosed in his embrace, she sobs against his chest. Jack rests his chin on her bowed head, her tears dampening his skin. By some form of osmosis, he absorbs her grief, her disappointment, until soon his own heart is breaking.

'Let's get you home,' he says, hoarse with emotion.

The crowd beyond the marquee are clapping again. Winners are being announced and prizes bestowed.

'Dad will wonder where I am . . .'

Gwen decides she will make her own way home. She knows the paths between the Hall and the farm like the back of her hand. Jack does not ask her how – he does not want to think why. She asks him to reassure her father with tales of a headache and the intolerable heat, but Jack will not let her go alone, not when her tears are only temporarily dammed and her suffering is still so raw. He begs her to wait for him, and though he can see she yearns to be gone, in the end, she relents.

He hurries to the place he last saw Jim, his harried breaths drowned out by hearty applause, but the farmer has gone. He spots Ted, though, clapping mechanically, clearly bored of the prize-giving, and decides to entrust him with Gwen's message. Ted listens to Jack's stumbling explanation with increasing concern.

'Well, I'll take her home if you can't find Jim. I've got my car. I'll drive her now . . .'

'No, no need.' Jack holds up his hands to stop him. 'I'll see her back safe.'

'She shouldn't be walking in this heat if she's unwell. *I'll* take her.'

'No.'

And before Ted can protest further, he turns away. 'Tell Jim,' he calls over his shoulder, grateful for the dispersing crowd that traps the farmer behind him.

They walk back in silence down an old drovers' path overhung with bushy elder and banked with blackthorn. The verges are thick with nettles and wild garlic and clumps of honesty, its green coins yet to silver into mock riches. The air is thick with heat and cloying scent and swarming midges, but Jack is too preoccupied with Gwen to notice.

They soon reach the stile leading onto the lane. She grabs the post, but she does not plant her foot on the raised plank before her, instead she remains frozen in place, lost in thought.

'There will be a reasonable explanation,' she says at last, 'and I'm sure it will all be sorted out. I just need to speak to

Gordon . . . but you're right, Jack, I shouldn't have tried to speak to him at the fete. There were too many people . . . it needs to be just us . . .'

'Gwen—'

'I'll go back later . . .'

'Gwen, lass—'

'No, no – I'll go to the kiosk in the village and telephone him from there first.' She breaks into a smile and the optimism behind it steals Jack's breath. 'You see, Jack . . . there are things you don't know,' she says quietly. 'And I know those things will change everything.'

True to her word, Gwen dashes down to the village on their return, though she is back by the time Jack brings in the herd. The milking is long completed by the time Jim finally appears, the thread veins in his cheeks rosy from a bevvy or two.

'I told you, didn't I?' he crows, drawing out a chair from the kitchen table. He sits down to undo the laces of his best shoes. 'He's a chancer, that lad. He would have broken your heart, Gwen – there would have been no future in it. He's a bloody cad. To think he was here not that long ago asking you out riding, when he must have already been seeing that girl. You can't tell me that's the behaviour of a gentleman.' Laces loose, he sits back in his chair. 'Well, I tell you now, I pity that poor girl. She's welcome to him – she'll find out soon enough what a bounder he is.'

Gwen is at the sink washing up the crockery that has been left to languish on the drainer. Her father's words break the rhythm of her movements, the dish mop momentarily idle in her hand. Gathering herself, she rinses off the final plate and picks up the tea towel. She dries it briskly, before slotting it into the dresser.

'I'd better go and collect the eggs,' she says. The door latch clatters and she is gone.

Jim glances across at Jack and shakes his head as he prises off his shoes. 'I suppose she's still carrying a torch for him, but in time she'll come to realise the lucky escape she's had.'

But Jack wonders if she will.

Later that evening, as the sinking sun stains the horizon gold, Gwen tacks up Arthur outside the stable block. Jim watches her tighten the horse's girth as he assists Jack in the making of a new gate for Top Field. Jack is also alert to her presence, but he keeps his focus on the saw biting through the wooden bar braced before him. A muscle in his jaw flexes as Gwen rides from the yard.

When she fails to return by twilight, Jim becomes anxious. They had, as usual, retreated to the sitting room at the end of the day's labours and for a while Jim was distracted by the newspaper, but now he rises from his chair and crosses to the window, where the curtains are yet to be drawn against the failing light. The clock strikes nine.

'Where the hell is she?' he mutters.

Jack has also been monitoring the passing time with growing concern. He suspects Gwen's absence is the consequence of her earlier telephone call to Gordon, but he knows he cannot use this information to allay the farmer's fears.

'Perhaps she's had a fall,' Jim says, turning away from the window.

'It's been a lovely evening, perhaps she just went further than usual.'

'No, she never stays out this late. What time did she set off? She could be halfway to Helvedon and back by now. No, no . . . something's happened, I'm sure of it. That bloody horse, I should have sent it to the knacker's yard long before now . . .' Jim heads for the door. 'I'm going looking for her – I'll take the car, drive around.'

'She could be anywhere, Jim,' Jack reasons, fearing what Jim might stumble on if Gwen is indeed with Gordon. 'I'll come too. I'll take the push bike and head up the track, see if I can spot her up there.'

But as they are bundling into their jackets, they hear the snort of a horse, and the slow clop of hooves. Jim's relief is evident as he yanks open the back door in time to catch sight of Gwen riding up the yard. It is her slumped shoulders that Jack notices first and, edging past Jim, he says he will help her untack.

He hurries to the stable block, half-walking, half-jogging. Gwen swings down from the saddle just as Jack arrives.

Her red-mottled face tells him everything he needs to know. 'Oh, lass . . .'

She merely shakes her head in response and leads the horse through the open door into its waiting loosebox. Jack follows her in, closing the gate behind him. He does not attempt to question her, instead his fingers work the buckle on the horse's chinstrap as she runs up the stirrups. Jack gathers up the reins and relieves Arthur of his bridle, as Gwen slides the saddle from his back. The horse moves forward to snatch hay from the iron basket on the wall, its grinding teeth the only sound that disturbs the silence. For a moment, Jack and Gwen look at each other across the horse's curved rump, their hands full of leather. Gwen lowers her gaze first and pushes open the gate with her hip. She rests the saddle on the wooden divide of the next loosebox, while Jack hangs the bridle on the nail jutting from its post.

'Your dad was getting worried. You were gone a long time.'

Her head drops. She nods and looks away. 'Yes.'

'Did you speak to him?' Jack asks, his voice gentle.

'It seems . . . I've been a fool.' She raises her face to him just as a tear trickles down the length of her cheek. She strikes it away with a determined swipe of her hand. Her lips form a mournful twist. 'Dad was right all along. I could never be . . . *a serious contender*, as Gordon put it.'

Jack swears under his breath.

'He thought I knew it was just a bit of fun. Except, of course, it wasn't . . . not for me at least.'

A breath shudders from her, but no more tears. She has exhausted her supply it seems.

'Gwen, I . . .'

'There's nothing more to be said.' She covers her face with her hands, but after a sharp intake of breath she lowers them again. 'I should have known better. I've learnt a hard lesson. A very hard lesson indeed.'

She swallows. He can see her struggling to maintain her dignity, struggling to keep her emotion in check. 'Anyway, what's done is done. No point crying about it. Everyone suffers a broken heart sometime, I suppose.'

The smile she conjures is a brave one and though precariously thin it does its job and papers over the cracks. She makes to leave, but then hesitates a moment before turning back.

'Thank you, Jack.'

'For what?'

'For listening. For keeping my secrets. For helping me when I asked you to. For letting me talk. If I'd had to keep all this to myself, I think I'd have gone mad.'

And before he has a chance to respond, she presses her lips to his cheek, and hurries out into the night.

CHAPTER TWENTY-FIVE

Jack

August 1939

July slips into August with days of smothering heat broken by thunderstorms that rumble up the valley, their progress accompanied by sheet lightning as dazzling as a photographer's flash.

Jim walks the bristling fields of corn every day, running his hand over the bowed heads that slowly turn the colour of sun-scorched sand. He pauses periodically to break off the tip of a head, rubbing it between his palms before gently blowing across the fragments to separate the wheat from the chaff. He takes a teardrop nugget between his teeth and bites down, his eyes closed in concentration as he assesses the ripeness of the grain.

For days, he brushes his hands free of the discarded corn and mutters under his breath while studying the sky above. Then one morning, as the blossoming sun begins to test its building strength on the back of his neck, he takes a golden grain between his teeth, and a slow smile spreads across his burnished cheeks. As a flock of skylarks dance through the blue expanse above him, he rubs his hand across his unshaven chin and nods. It is ready.

Harvest comes as a welcome distraction. Gwen has done her best to suppress signs of her heartbreak, but Jack sees through her façade. Her broad smiles vanish as soon as she looks away and her hacks on Arthur now bite deep into dusk and see her return with bloodshot eyes.

Whilst her father seems oblivious to her silent suffering, Jack suspects Muriel has detected something is amiss, but Gwen rebuffs the housekeeper's kind enquiries with irritable comments and snapped denials. To Jack, Gwen confides nothing more, but when her father walks up the yard with a spring in his step and announces they will begin harvesting that day, she whispers, 'Now we'll be busy – we won't have the energy to think of anything else,' and her relief is tangible.

They waste no time tacking up the Clydesdales and leading them to the implement shed, where Jim is sharpening a scythe with a whetstone, the edge of the brown blade turning silver with every singing swipe. Hearing the jangle of the horses' bits, he looks up, eager and joyful, for the forthcoming task is the symbolic culmination of the year's labours and the ultimate example of the earth's alchemy. Propping the long wooden snath of the scythe against the wall, he introduces Jack to the reaper-binder, a peculiar-looking piece of machinery that will be critical to the day's endeavours.

He leads Jack down the length of the broad canvas conveyor belt, which runs just above the ground to the left of the raised driver's seat. He points out the iron teeth lining its front edge which will shunt back and forth, cutting the corn's stalks, and describes how the broad batons that rise before it will sail round, knocking the cut corn onto the canvas belt, which will then elevate it past the driver's seat and over to the right-hand side of the machine. There the stalks will be bundled into sheaves mechanically secured with string before tumbling to the ground. It will be Jack and Gwen's responsibility to gather those sheaves and place them in stooks around the field, so the warm air can circulate amongst them, drying the corn.

Jack listens intently, asks intelligent questions and, from the corner of his eye, watches Gwen as she attaches chains between the implement and the horses' harness. When she is done, Jim passes Jack the scythe he has just sharpened, then lifts down another one from the wall behind him. Bobby whickers as Gwen slaps the reins against the horses' broad rumps and issues them with the instruction to walk on.

The two men reach the cornfield in advance of Gwen. Before the binder can be put to work, they will need to scythe through the scutch grass and scarlet poppies, the oxeye daisies and blue cornflowers that spill from the margins into the crop. Jack is surprised by the weight of the scythe and pays close attention as Jim shows him how to roll his body with the snath, sweeping the curved blade as he goes. Soon, with some sadness, he has cut a swathe through the pretty borders and, rather than bobbing in the breeze, the colourful flowers now dapple the ground.

The sun climbs in the azure sky. Jack's shirt becomes tacky and sweat stings his eyes. Around him, grasshoppers sing with the discordance of an orchestra tuning up in the pit. Before long, the *clip-clop* of horses' shoes rings out on the lane alerting them to Gwen's arrival. Clambering down from the binder's raised seat, she readies the machine for her father, replacing the large carriage wheels with the smaller field ones, before winding down the main wheel to its correct working height.

It is not long before the men have finished cropping the margins. Jim climbs up into the binder's seat and plants his boots on the metal footrests stretched before him. He urges the horses on and, with their heads hung low, they draw the machine forward, setting the toothed blade shuddering left to right as the sails begin to turn, reminding Jack of a paddle steamer he had once seen upon the Tyne. Jack and Gwen fall in step behind, deafened by its cacophony, and as the sheaves fall they stand them in stooks of six, clumped across the field.

Ted joins them just before lunch, a .22 rifle slung over his shoulder. Jim halts the horses and leans down from his seat to talk to him.

'What's with the gun?' Jack asks Gwen, as he props a sheaf on their half-formed stook.

She adjusts its position, so the grain-swollen heads catch the breeze.

'Rabbits. They hide in the crop and as the binder goes through the field, they dart out into the hedgerows for cover. Ted'll shoot them and give them to Muriel to make a stew, most likely. He'll help us make stooks now he's here too and we'll return the favour when he harvests.'

Jim slaps the reins and the horses traipse forward, shaking their heads against circling flies as the noisy machine clatters back to life. Gwen and Jack finish their stook, then fall in with Ted behind the binder to continue gathering the falling sheaves.

At lunch time, Muriel arrives with a picnic of pies fresh from the oven. They sit beneath an old oak tree, relishing the shade it affords them as they rest against its wrinkled trunk. Gwen pours cold black tea from a flask and when the pies have been polished off, they peel the shells from boiled eggs and sink their teeth into the jellied whites.

Gwen rises, brushing flecks of pastry from her trousers before accompanying her father to fetch water for the horses, now tugging leaves from the hedge. Jack offers to help, but Jim waves him back down, and so he watches father and daughter walk away across the stubble.

Ted swats at the midges flitting around him and suppresses a belch before draining his tea. Jack can feel the burn of his scrutiny, but he ignores him, giving his attention instead to Kip who failed to return to the farm with Muriel. The poor dog is suffering in the heat and pants heavily, even though it is cooler in the shade of the oak. Jack strokes his head.

'I saw Vic Jennings this morning.'

Ted's announcement is abrupt, bursting into the awkward silence that has existed since Gwen and Jim's departure.

'Is that so?'

'I bumped into him and his wife coming out of the grocer's first thing. You remember his wife?'

'Aye.'

'They were stocking up, it seems.'

Jack says nothing.

'All excited she was, Iris. Her brother is coming down to stay.' Blood roars through Jack's ears, distorting Kip's panting, and muffling Ted's words. 'He's the one from Newcastle, the detective . . .'

'I remember,' he snaps.

Jack burrows his fingers deeper into Kip's fur until they are trembling against the creature's skull. The dog ceases to pant. Its dark eyes lift to Jack. He pulls back his hand.

'You know . . .' Ted starts, a hint of cunning in his voice, 'I can't get over how certain she was that you were from Newcastle and not Sunderland.'

'It was a mistake, that's all.'

'Funny how locals can pick up on variations in accents like that.'

The weight of Ted's gaze is unbearable. Jack scrambles up, his heart hammering. Kip rises, ears pricked, alert.

'Jim and Gwen are back.' Relief floods over him as they appear in the gateway, water slopping over the tops of their pails. 'I'll go and help them.'

'He's coming for work,' Ted calls after him. Jack stops. He does not turn around, though he is aware of the farmer getting to his feet. 'Iris's brother. I thought he was coming down for a holiday, but no . . . it seems something more serious is bringing him this way.'

With the horses watered, they start work again, moving through the crop until the field is dotted with clumped stooks and there is only one corner left to harvest. Ted retrieves his rifle and wraps the shoulder strap around his wrist, stalking forward as Jim turns the horses into the final quadrant of the field. He brings the stock to his shoulder and sights his aim.

There is a flash of grey from the stand of corn, closely followed by another leaping dart, and behind that a dashing white scut. The rifle cracks. Ted rattles the bolt and swiftly lifts the gun again; it bucks into his shoulder, another shot splitting the air. He breaks it open, fumbling in his trouser pocket for more cartridges, slotting them down the barrel, before snapping the gun shut. The action is swift and practised and Jack starts as the gun blasts again and again.

Eventually Ted walks back to them, the rifle broken over the crook of his arm, holding six limp rabbits by their back feet. Blood drips upon the golden stubble.

'It's instinct, you see,' Ted says, holding the dead animals aloft, a curious glint in his eye that renders Jack ill-at-ease. 'When there's nowhere left to hide there's only one thing you can do – take your chances and run for your life.'

CHAPTER TWENTY-SIX

Gwen

August 1945

Gwen and Nora are weeding the swedes in Ten Acre. A fine rain has been plaguing them since mid-morning, just enough to soak the ground and make the task muddy and unpleasant. Tom has remained at home with Muriel, and seeing the dark clouds building on the horizon, Gwen is pleased he has.

She pauses to stretch out her bent spine and roll relief into her knotted shoulders. Her fingers are black with dirt and her nails lined with grime. She wipes the sleeve of her coat across her face. The rain might be fine but given long enough they will be soaked through. She looks again at the sky. The draining light and building wind suggest there is a downpour on the way. She grips the long handle of her hoe and digs under a thick mat of chickweed, ignoring the sting of a burst blister at the base of her right thumb.

'Did I ever tell you how much I hate weeding?' Nora calls out, her hands pressed into the small of her back. Strands of dark hair have sprung free from her headscarf and now stick to her forehead like kiss curls.

'On many occasions.'

'Just checking. It's even worse doing it in the rain in case you were wondering.'

Gwen snorts and wields her hoe once again, its metal head chinking against the bone-coloured fragments of flint embedded in the soil. She is pleased to see the swedes' broad leaves so thick and healthy. The summer has not baked them, and whilst the rain is unpleasant to work in, it's much needed.

The wind whips up. The trees in the hedge line creak and groan as it bullishly makes its way through their laden branches. Nora yelps as she is forced to slap a hand onto her scarf to prevent it lifting away. Gwen looks across the furrow and laughs. The gusting wind sends needles of rain into her face. She bows away from it.

As quickly as the wind blows up, so it dies, leaving heavy rain in its wake. Gwen can feel it trickling under the collar of her shirt and the earth slickens beneath her feet. The softened soil releases the weeds with good grace, but even though it is mild the wet chills her and her fingers are soon numb. She glances at her watch, wiping droplets from the glass so she can see the face clearly. In the distance, there is a rumble of thunder.

'Oh, for goodness' sake, this is miserable,' she cries to Nora. 'Let's break early for lunch, see if we can't give it time to clear.'

There is another grumble from further down the valley, where inky clouds are cloaking the sky. Nora throws down her hoe.

'I'm not going to argue – and I don't fancy being turned into a lightning conductor either.'

'Nor me.'

Abandoning their tools, they squelch their way down the

muddy furrow, their boots slipping and sliding beneath them until they reach the grass margin. In the lane, they hunch against the inclement weather, chilled to their cores and longing for the warmth of indoors.

They pay little heed to the roar of the motorbike in the distance. As it careers around the approaching corner they edge to the side of the road, but the bike drops down a gear and soon slows to a stop, waiting for them.

'Not the best weather to labour in, ladies.'

The rider's head is protected by a leather aviator's cap, its flaps hanging loose over his ears, while his face is obscured by a pair of goggles which he now pushes back onto his forehead.

'You can say that again.' Nora's smile is more dazzling for the sheen of damp it defies. 'A hot cup of tea is all I want right now . . . well, that and to get out of these wet clothes . . .' She allows her gaze to linger. The rider chuckles, studying her afresh. She boldly meets his curiosity.

'Now that sounds like an eminently sensible plan.'

'That's a rather fancy bike you're riding.'

'It's a new acquisition. You like bikes?'

'I'm rather partial. It's a Vincent Comet, isn't it?'

'I'm impressed.'

'She's a beauty,' Nora says, an impudent smile gracing her lips.

'Yes, she is.' His words seem to convey double meaning. 'We'll have to see about taking you for a spin, since you like bikes so much.' He throws her a lopsided grin as he lowers his goggles. The engine roars as he twists the throttle.

'Ladies . . . till we meet again.' With a mock salute and a devil-ish grin, he is gone. Nora lets out a low whistle.

'Blimey, who was that?'

Gwen shakes her head, professing ignorance with a twitch of her shoulders. The rain's cadence is drowned out by the thud of her heart.

They run the last couple of hundred yards, as the heavens sicken of the rain and seek to unload the clouds in a thunderous deluge. They burst in through the back door, Nora squealing as she shakes herself off like a dog. Muriel puts on the kettle.

Gwen yearns to be alone. Her thoughts are a churning torrent that she cannot fight free of. She is about to slip away to her bedroom when Muriel calls for her to rid herself of her coat, and she stops, confused, until she sees rain dripping from her mackintosh, staining the flags. Her numb fingers fumble with its fastenings. She passes it into Nora's waiting hand and steps up into the hall.

Tom runs in from the sitting room, holding out a picture for her approval. She casts an absent appraisal over it and delivers empty words of praise.

'You didn't even look at it properly,' he pouts.

'I'm wet through, Tom, let me change,' she says, stepping past him. She takes hold of the newel post. 'As soon as I'm in my dry clothes, I'll take a good look, I promise.'

He watches her go, brimming with disappointment.

In her room, her fingers shake as she struggles to relieve the sodden knot of her headscarf. She finally works it loose and the drenched material slaps onto the floorboards. Her knees give way and she collapses onto the stool before her dressing table. She studies her reflection, dwelling on the dark crescents below her eyes and her sunken cheeks, stripped of their youthful plumpness and leathered from the summer sun. She lifts her finger to the fine strands of grey that now blight her temples though she is barely old enough to warrant them, even if life has, over the past six years, been hard enough to earn them. She splays her hands. They were never soft, dainty things, but now they seem bloated by work, calloused and tough, her nails bitten and broken. She does not notice the thin band of gold.

She buries her face in her palms, struggling to breathe. He had not known her. He had not shown even a flicker of recognition. Nora had distracted him with her brazen smile and the sultry suggestion in her voice. And Gwen is glad – relieved, even. She had avoided all tell of him for years, apart from the odd bit of gossip muttered over shop counters in the village – Lord Allingham ailing, but clinging on to see his son and heir safely home. He must be a happy man.

She has never given much thought to Gordon's return. Even when in church Lady Allingham had spoken of him being back, he seemed too far removed to be real. The concept of his near presence was intangible. Seeing him in the road has left her stunned, shocked, and empty inside – whatever feelings she had once nurtured for him died long ago. And since then, she has been too preoccupied with keeping the farm going – meeting her quotas, surviving the war – to contemplate what would happen when the men came back.

But the men are coming back.

Gordon Allingham is back.

She meets her own gaze in the mirror and studies herself anew. Has she really changed so much as to be unrecognisable?

Tom's voice drifts up the stairs, an impatient whine, demanding of her attention.

Her breath catches.

Gordon Allingham might not have recognised her . . . but would he recognise his own son?

CHAPTER TWENTY-SEVEN

Jack

August 1939

Jack loiters in the yard, waiting for Gwen as dawn paints the sky pink. Her bedroom curtains remain drawn. He checks his wristwatch. The herd's impatient bellows are just discernible in the distance. He can wait no longer.

She is at the back door pushing on her gumboots when he returns, the cattle ambling before him, snorting and shitting as they plod towards the pen by the milking parlour. She hurries down the steps to join him, absentmindedly ruffling Kip's fur as he trots across to greet her. Jack is immediately struck by her pastiness. She catches him up as he closes the five-bar gate on the pen.

'I'm sorry, Jack.'

'You look awful.'

She makes no attempt to contradict him, she merely responds with a rueful smile, before heading into the adjacent building. He follows her under the low lintel. She moves slowly, mechanically, collecting her stool and pail, chewing her blanched lips as she buttons up her milking coat.

'Gwen, if you're unwell I can manage . . .'

'I'm fine. I just . . . overslept, that's all.'

'You look done in.'

'I'm fine,' she reiterates, brushing past him to fetch in the first of the herd.

They work in a silence that is broken only by sawing milk, the stomp of an impatient hoof, and the occasional bovine snort.

Jack finishes draining the engorged udder of a cow called Bess. He stands up and slips the halter from her neck, slapping her rump to drive her from the shed. Hooking the pail on the hanging scales, he squints at the flickering needle before recording the figure in the milk ledger. He upends the pail into the cooler, pleased that her yield has increased on the previous day's. As he sets off down the aisle to bring in the next cow, he passes the stall where Gwen is working. He notices that she is gulping for air.

'Gwen?'

She leaps to her feet and dashes through the door into the brightening morning. Seconds later, he hears her retching.

He finds her with one hand braced against the wall, while the other rests on her hip as she heaves again. Little more than liquid splatters the bottom bricks.

'Jesus, Gwen, you should have stayed in bed if you're sick.' He places a hand on her back, but she shakes him off.

'That fish Muriel served last night, I said it smelt funny.'

'It tasted all right.'

'It was on the turn. I told her.'

She keeps her face angled away as she wipes her mouth with the back of her hand.

'Let me get you some water.'

'No. I'm fine.'

But the words have only just left her when she whirls back to the wall and spews again.

'You're not fine, lass. Go on, get yourself inside, I'll finish up.'

'It'll take you ages.'

'I'll manage. Get away with you now.'

She considers protesting, but seeing reason, she nods. 'I'll just clear this up.'

'I'll do it,' he says gently. 'Go on now. Get some rest.'

Biting her lip, she takes a few steps towards the house, then stops.

'Thank you, Jack.'

He watches her go, then fills a bucket from the pump and sluices down the wall, before returning to the milking parlour to do the work of two.

She has surfaced again by the time he goes in late for breakfast. Jim is already seated at the table, an empty plate smeared with egg yolk before him, a half-drunk mug of tea at his elbow.

'Finished at last, eh?'

'Aye.'

'Sit down, I've got your breakfast here.' Muriel sets a laden plate in his place as he takes off his boots. His eyes stray to Gwen as she pours his tea.

'Sorry to dump you in it.' Her voice is soft as she sets the mug down beside him.

'It's nee bother.' He is unsure whether he should enquire about her health in front of the others.

'Clean overslept!' she says brightly, as if reading his mind. She holds his gaze for a moment before turning away. 'Haven't done that in a while.'

'You should have knocked on the door, lad, rather than plough on single-handed,' Jim says.

'Oh, it was no bother. I got into my rhythm and time flew by.' He takes a sip of tea.

'I think I'll go back to setting my alarm clock.' Gwen smiles brightly. 'It won't happen again.'

But the following morning, it does.

She makes it to the privy. Jack follows her out, leaving the cows restless in their stalls. He waits a discreet distance away. When she finally emerges she looks drained, but there is something else festering beneath the surface. He sees it immediately, though she stalks past without acknowledging him. She makes her way to the pump in the yard and cranks the handle with angry vigour, scooping the water with her free hand, splashing it into her face. She dries her dripping cheeks on her sleeve.

'We should get back to milking,' she says.

'How far gone are you, Gwen?'

The flare of her eyes betrays her, though she blusters with indignant denials.

'Don't take me for a fool, lass. Green-gilled every morning? What else do you think it is?'

'An upset tummy, nothing more.'

'Aye, you keep telling yourself that.'

'How dare you.'

She walks away from him, but he catches her easily and, though she protests with the vehement outrage of a manhandled suffragette, he marches her through the open mouth of the barn.

'You said there were things I didn't know . . .' he fights to keep his voice even, '. . . when Gordon announced his engagement – things that you said would change everything. You thought the fact you were carrying his child would bring him round, didn't you?'

She is breathing hard. Her limbs quiver.

'Does he know?' Jack demands, standing before her, hands on his hips. 'Allingham? Did you tell him?'

'Yes, he knows!'

He absorbs the blow of her anger. 'And what did he say?'

'To get rid of it.' She spits the words out. 'Even told me where to go. Some woman in Helvedon who's helped him out before apparently.' She cannot hide her rancour.

'A backstreet abortion? That's what he's told you to do?'

'What other choice is there? I can hardly have it, can I? I can hardly have a baby.'

She reaches out to steady herself on the wagon, resting her forehead against its painted wooden side.

'What am I going to do?'

'I'll tell you what you're not going to do.' Jack moves towards her but holds himself back. 'You're not going to some backstreet abortionist to have some old biddy stick you with a bloody knitting needle and leave you hoping for the best.'

The brutality of his words brings Gwen round. His passion lays him bare and he finds he cannot stand her scrutiny. He stifles a guttural curse and works out his agitation by pacing away from her, shuddering breaths wracking his frame.

'Do you want to get rid of it? The bairn. Is that what you want?'

'I don't know.'

'You could have the bairn and give it up.'

She ejects a bitter laugh. 'Even if I wanted to, how can I do that? You know how word gets about here. Everyone would know . . .'

'You could go away to have it.'

'What? Say I've gone to stay with some maiden aunt in the next county and then come back a discreet time later? Do you not think everyone will guess? There is no such thing as idle gossip around here, Jack, just avid speculation and a love of scandal. I couldn't possibly subject Dad to that, the shame would kill him! Without Gordon's ring on my finger I have no choice but to get rid of it.'

'No, Gwen, I can't let you do that.'

'Jack, it is nothing to do with you—'

'I can't lose you the way I lost Jenny!'

He does not mean to shout. The silence that follows is deafening.

'Jenny?' Gwen drills him with the piercing look of a prosecutor interrogating a witness. 'Who's Jenny?'

'My sister.' He drags his hand across his face. 'Jenny was my sister.' He tries to shut out the images that flash in his mind's eye. His stomach grips at the rusty scent of blood, even though he knows it is only his cruel imagination at play. He finds himself compelled to cross to the barn's open doors, to fill his lungs with fresh air.

'Jack . . .'

'She got into trouble. Fell victim to some silver-tongued charmer who promised her the world and instead left her in a world of trouble. If she had just come to me . . . but she panicked, I suppose. She never said anything.' He rubs the back of his neck. 'I came home from work one evening and found her soaked in her own blood. She had tried to get rid of it, found a woman who said she could help. Oh, she'd done away with the bairn all right, her with her knitting needle, and in doing so she had turned our Jenny's insides into a pin cushion. There was no saving her. She was seventeen. Barely more than a bairn herself.'

'Jack . . . I'm so sorry . . .'

He spins around. Backlit by the sun, his expression is concealed in shadow. 'So, when I say you can't go to some backstreet abortionist, I mean it, lass. I'll not let you go.'

'But, Jack, there's no other way.'

'Aye, lass, there is. There is another way.' He catches his breath. 'You could marry me.'

The shock of his proposal is a physical blow that sends her staggering back.

He draws away from the door into the shade of the barn and in the even light his features are once again discernible and reveal the earnestness of his offer. 'Now this might sound mad, like, but hear me out, that's all I ask.'

'Jack, I like you, I really do . . .' he cannot tell whether Gwen is fighting tears or laughter, 'but marriage would be for the rest of our lives . . . Marriage is forever, Jack.'

'Nee, lass. Not necessarily. I've good reason to suspect this marriage wouldn't be forever.' He can see now that he has frightened her. Her eyes dart past him; she is like a trapped deer looking for escape. He curses himself for his impetuosity. He gathers his arguments and allows his passions to drain away. When he starts again, his voice is soft, his manner calm. He has one chance, he realises, one chance to avert a looming tragedy.

'There's a war coming, Gwen, sure as houses, and me? Well, I intend to go and do my bit as I always have done, just like the men in my family did in the last one.' Weariness suddenly overwhelms him, and he is troubled by an unexpected ache in his chest. 'And if the last one's anything to go by, the chances of a bloke like me coming home are pretty slim . . .' She starts to protest but he raises his hand to stop her. 'And I'm all right with that. I'm not asking you to marry me, Gwen, because I want anything from you . . . I don't expect anything. But I could give your bairn my name. No one needs to know it's not mine, not unless you choose to tell them, because I'll never give the game away. Some might gossip it must have been conceived out of wedlock, if they trouble themselves to do the maths, but we wouldn't be the first couple who shut the door after the horse has bolted, so to speak. And I reckon no one will care – they'll see we've done the right thing.'

'Jack, this is . . . this is very kind of you, but . . . even if there is a war, even if you do go to fight . . . you're making huge assumptions. You might survive. And then what, Jack? What happens if you do come back?'

'I can't come back, Gwen.'

'You say that now, but you might . . . and . . .'

'I can't come back, Gwen, because I can't be here. I shouldn't even be here now. I've stayed too long as it is.'

'What do you mean?'

'I didn't come down this way for a change of work, Gwen. I was running. I should still be running.'

'Running from what, Jack? Jack?' Her tone hardens as he fails to meet her eyes. In a moment of prescience, it hits her. Her voice fades to a whisper. 'Oh God, Jack . . . what have you done?'

CHAPTER TWENTY-EIGHT

Jack

Newcastle upon Tyne, June 1939

Years of exposure had rendered him deaf to the clanks and groans of machinery, the harassed shouts of men, the hollow clanging of hammers on steel and the whine of slow-moving derricks.

Inured to their distractions, Jack focused on his own task. He braced the rivet gun against his hip as his holder-upper inserted a furnace-fresh rivet through the punched plate before him. His frame shuddered as the pneumatic hammer pummelled the white-hot tail with the thundering sound of a titan rolling its tongue. When the rivet was flattened and firm he stepped back and wiped the sweat from his forehead, a fleeting pause before the next molten tip was presented and vibrations wracked his body once again.

The end of shift whistle shrieked as he secured the last rivet in place. He stripped off his gauntlets and ignoring the ache in his muscles made his way from the ship's vast belly. His hobnail boots echoed off the wooden gangplank as he passed through the forest of slender boles scaffolding the ship's growing hull onto the yard below.

He paid no attention to the crane booms swinging above him, or to the men traversing elevated girders like tightrope walkers working without a net. He merely joined the army of shipbuilders in their uniform of rolled sleeves, waistcoats and flat caps as they flooded out through the yard's yawning gates to the screams of circling gulls, all eager to escape the taint of diesel and smoke and the sour miasma that characterised the dockside.

He was invited to the pub on the corner for a swift half, but he was in a strange mood and had no desire for company or drink. His hunger was starting to gnaw and he wanted to get back, so he made his excuses. Tipping his cap in farewell, he thrust his hands into his trouser pockets and set out across the cobbles for home.

His street was quiet when he finally turned into it. Mrs Higgins from number thirty-three was on her knees in her housecoat scrubbing her front doorstep, the bristles of her brush rasping against the stone. She looked up to him in greeting, her expression devoid of any warmth, but Jack knew that was just her way and took no offence; he merely nodded and offered her a curt 'Evening' back.

Further on, a group of boys were kicking a ball across the street, their boots thudding against the stitched leather. A miss kick sent it skittering Jack's way and on another occasion he would have knocked it back, but today – though they waited expectantly, bracing themselves for its return – he just glowered and stepped past it. Their mocking taunts rang in his ears as the smallest lad trotted forward to retrieve it.

He glanced back at them as he mounted the step to his front door, but they had lost all interest in him and had returned to passing the ball with whooping jests and jeers. He pushed the door open and stepped inside.

He knew at once something was wrong. When he had left for work before seven, Jenny had been preparing the washing, while their mother sat at the table, smoking her first fag of the day. And yet, as he walked through the front room, there was no sweet smell of soap suds freshening the air and no damp clothes drying on wooden airers before the fire. He set down his knapsack. The house was quiet. The wall clock ticked through the silence, but beneath its soothing rhythm was a peculiar frisson. He became aware of his own breathing. He stood, listening, the hairs on the back of his neck rising.

'Jenny?'

His call was tentative. He walked through to the back room, passing the steep staircase that divided the house. The steel wash tub stood under the window that overlooked the back yard. The door of the understairs cupboard listed open and he could see the scrubbing board still hanging from its peg. In the galley kitchen, the sink was full of the morning's dishes, and the saucepan used to cook his porridge remained on the drainer, a thick milky mucus clinging to its sides. The bluebottle preening on its handle took flight, buzzing as it knocked against the window. Its escape thwarted, it landed on the side, restoring the room to its eerie silence.

'Mam?'

Jack's heart began to beat faster as he climbed the narrow staircase. It rose steeply, the wallpaper on each side grimed from years of steadying hands.

He stepped onto the landing that was not a landing at all, just a three-foot-square platform large enough to take a man.

His mother's bedroom door to his left was open. The curtains were drawn back and the evening sun was slanting across floorboards strewn with her cast-off clothes. To his right, the door to his own room – which led in turn to Jenny's – stood half-open. He placed his hand against the wood and pushed. The hinges creaked as it swung wide.

His room was just as he had left it. The sash window before him was still open a crack and the permitted breeze lifted the flimsy curtains. His bed was roughly made and his pyjama bottoms draped over the rush-seated chair in the corner. The other furniture in the room – the small wardrobe and dilapidated tall boy – was shared, through necessity, with Jenny. Her little box room, accessed through the door tucked away in the corner of his, was barely big enough to take her slender bed. He saw that door was ajar.

He trod lightly as he crossed the room, his fingers catching the finials of his metal bedstead. His heart hammered against his chest as he raised his hand to the door.

'Jen?' he called softly.

It was the smell that hit him first. The harsh metallic taint of a butcher's shop. As the door inched open, it exposed the bottom of Jenny's bed and the sheet folded back over her upright feet.

'Jenny?' He pushed the door wide.

She was lying on her bed, face up, her beautiful blonde curls spread across the pillowcase, her sightless eyes staring at the mould-speckled ceiling. Her blanched skin was as white as the nightdress that covered her. But Jack did not register any of this. It was the scarlet pool that soaked the garment below her hips that trapped his gaze, a bloody flood that oozed from her to cover the bedsheet beneath and smear the exposed skin of her calves.

He stumbled down the steps beyond the door, a cry of disbelief crawling out from the depths of his body. He whispered her name, his eyes wildly roaming as he tried to comprehend the horror before him. The bedsheet she lay upon was bunched in her clawed fingers.

'Jesus, Jenny!'

He reached to touch her cheek, but instantly recoiled, burnt by the iciness of her skin. A keening cry escaped him as he took in the waxy sheen of her face, the blue lips, the vacant stare. He did not need a physician to tell him she was dead.

It was then he saw his mother, cowering in the corner of the room, her eyes wide – whether with shock or fear, he couldn't tell. She was clutching a towel that might once have been a faded blue, but was now crimson. From its bottom edge, blood dripped to stain the worn slippers on her feet.

'Mam . . .' Jack gasped. His jaw moved impotently as he tried to raise his questions, but there were so many crowded in his mind, churning chaotically amongst the confusion and despair that he was unable to voice them. Darkness edged his vision. He feared his chest would burst with pain. He forced himself to breathe.

'Mam . . . what . . . what . . .'

His mother's fingers tightened on the blood-sodden towel.

'Our Jenny . . .'

'Mam, for God's sake – tell us what happened?'

Her lips quivered. She retreated further into the corner, until her shoulders were hunched against its edges.

'I couldn't stop it . . . I couldn't stop the bleeding.'

'But why was she bleeding? Mam, the blood! What the hell happened?'

'She said there'd be a bit of bleeding as it came away, like, but it just flowed from her, flowed and flowed, it wouldn't stop, it ne'er stopped, and our Jenny was moaning in agony and I couldn't do a thing . . .'

'Who said there'd be bleeding?' It only took one stride for Jack to reach her. He grabbed the tops of her arms, his fingers biting cruelly into their loose flesh as he bored into his mother's empty expression. 'Mam, tell us . . . tell us now,' he shouted, shaking her once, twice, until her head tipped back and forth.

'Oh, damnit it all, Jack, she had gotten herself into trouble,' his mother cried out. 'She got herself knocked up and the dad didn't want to know so I told her she'd have to get rid of it. I got a woman in to sort her out.'

'Jesus, Mam, what have you done?' His fingers flared open as he staggered back. He clutched his head as he caught sight of his sister's ruined body, lifeless on the bed. 'What have you done?' he echoed.

'She used a knitting needle . . .' his mother gasped. 'And every time she pushed it up, Jenny screamed out, but I thought . . . you know, it was just the way of these things. And she kept sticking her and sticking her, saying she had to make sure.'

'Jesus Christ.'

'I sent her packing after that. A week of Jenny's wages she cost me! But Jenny, she just kept crying and moaning, and dear God, the blood!'

'Did you not get the doctor to her?'

'I couldn't have called a doctor, Jack – are you mad? He'd

have known straight away what's what and got the police, and then where would we have all been, eh?'

'Jenny's dead, Mam!' Jack's voice cut through the room. His chest heaved as he stared at his mother, struggling to conceive how she could have seen her own daughter dying before her and not lifted a finger to help. 'Jesus Christ, did you not think to get her help? Did you just stand there and watch her die! Look what you've done!'

The silence that followed was ghastly. His mother's shoulders sagged, yet her eyes did not stray towards the bed. It was a wonder to Jack that in such a small room she managed to avoid it. Her lips pinched together.

'I couldn't do nothing,' she said at last, her voice quiet.

'Who did this to her?'

His mother shrugged. The action, he realised, was not callous, but resigned. 'Just some backstreet biddy I was put in the way of. It makes no difference.'

'And who knocked her up? Eh? You tell me that.' His voice rose as he warmed to the subject. 'What bastard had his way and then left her to pick up the pieces?'

'You don't know?' His mother's mouth had a cruel twist to it. 'You're telling me you don't know who she was stepping out with?'

'I didn't even know she was stepping out!'

She snorted, but the dark amusement that momentarily lifted her features departed as she caught sight of the bloody towel in her hands. Her breath shuddered. A tear ran down her cheek.

'Your pal Mickey Jones.' She skewered Jack with her loathing. 'He wouldn't leave her alone. Round here all the time, he was, while you were at work. Always cosying up to her, giving her gifts, whispering sweet nothings in her ear until her head was turned.'

'Mickey? No.'

'Aye. You brought him here. You introduced them.' Her voice hardened to flint. With a sharp cry, she threw the towel to the floor. She drew forward, her eyes fiery now, shock giving way to furious grief. She thrust a finger in the direction of the bed as she stood toe to toe with her son, her chin thrust up. 'Look what you've done, Jack Ellison.'

She held herself together for a few seconds more then, like a blasted chimney stack, her knees buckled and she crumpled in a vertical descent, and before Jack could catch her she was spread across the floorboards, lamenting her loss.

'Mam . . .' Her name escaped him as a broken whisper. He reached for her, but she blindly slapped him away, sobbing her daughter's name. Jack relished the sting on his flesh. He backed towards the doorway, tripping up the steps to his own room. A gauze of tears obscured his vision as he made his way to the stairs. He descended with reckless speed, his heel slipping off the edge of a tread so that he bumped to the bottom on his rear, but he cared not for the sharp pain in his back. He hauled himself up and, battling emotion, groped his way to the front door.

The boys in the street gave him a wide berth, instinctively detecting from his harried movements and stricken features that now was not the time to provoke him. When he reached the main road, he dodged around pedestrians and crossed recklessly before a delivery van, earning a blast of its horn, but he didn't care. He only wanted one thing – to get to the Queen Victoria before it was too late. He ran down side alleys and back lanes, using every shortcut he knew, until he arrived, breathless, before the pub's etched windows. He paused only to catch his breath, before shoving the door open and stepping inside.

It was full, as he had expected. Men clustered around squat tables, all pointed knees and sharp elbows as they leant forward in conversation. Barks of laughter carried above the deep hum of voices. Tobacco smoke filled the air and men lined the length of the bar. A few drinkers hailed Jack as he paused inside the door. The Queen Victoria was a regular haunt for shipyard workers and the establishment gratefully accepted a goodly portion of their weekly wages. But Jack failed to acknowledge any of the faces he knew. He wiped his mouth with the back of his hand as his breathing steadied, then began to shoulder his way through the throng, constantly searching for the one man he had come to find.

'Alreet, Jack? Let me stand you a pint.' Jack's arm was grabbed from the right. He whirled around, his left fist already clenched, but he checked himself as Ben's beaming face came into view, though the man's broad smile quickly faded. 'You all right, man?'

He shook his friend's hand from his arm. 'No. No I'm not.' He moved off, pressing into the wall of backs before him, but Ben tugged him again. He came in close, his voice low.

'Jesus, man, what's wrong?'

Jack didn't trust himself to speak. He caught the edge of his lip between his teeth and squeezed back his threatening tears. 'Have you seen Mickey Jones here?'

'Mickey? Aye, he's down the end of the bar.'

Jack nodded and, leaving his bewildered friend behind, he fought his way through the crowd. He was beginning to think that Ben was mistaken when finally he saw him – sitting on the last stool, talking to a couple of lads Jack recognised from work. He felt a fury rise within him, a black rage that was hot and demanding. He wet his lips, his fists closing at his side.

'Mickey. Mickey Jones.'

Distracted from his conversation, Mickey swivelled round on his bar stool. He had wide features blighted by a boxer's nose, its broken bridge leaving his face looking creased. He brightened on seeing Jack.

'Ye alreet, Jack?'

'You'd better stand up, man.'

He let out a shout of laughter. 'And why's that?'

'You've been messing with our Jenny.'

He chuckled, raising his hands in appeasement. 'Well, a pretty lass like your Jenny is hard to resist, like.'

'She's dead, man.'

Mickey's features flickered. 'Dead?'

Jack took a step closer. He leant down until he was close enough to hiss in the man's ear. 'Aye, dead. Dead trying to get rid of the bairn you put inside her, you dirty bastard.' He stood back. 'Now stand up.'

But Jack didn't wait for him to rise. Seeing guilt inhabit the man's features, he darted forward and grabbing his waistcoat, dragged him from the stool. It tumbled to the floor with a tell-tale crash that instantly drew the attention of those around them, but Jack's only hesitation was the time it took to draw back his fist before letting it fly. Mickey Jones's head snapped back. He staggered, swiping drunkenly, but he was no match for the fury that fuelled Jack's knuckles. Another blow to the jaw sent him reeling and it was only the steadying hands of the crowd around him that kept him on his feet. There was a sense of dark excitement in the hushed air, a bloodthirsty anticipation. Mickey dabbed at his mouth and stared at the blood that glistened on his fingertips.

'Come on then,' Jack goaded. 'Let's have you.' And when the man failed to advance, he let out a holler and charged forward with such ferocity that the crowd about them fell back. Exposed, Mickey took the full force of Jack's tackle; the two men sprawled onto the floor.

'That's enough!' the publican cried out, jangling the bell behind the bar like a referee calling time. 'That's enough or I'm calling the coppers!'

The threat fell on deaf ears. The men grappled wildly until strong arms banded Jack's chest and hauled him backwards. His feet scrabbled against the bar's scuffed floorboards.

'Jesus, Jack, get a hold of yourself, man,' Ben hissed, holding him firm. 'They've called the police, get the hell out of here while you can.' Ben half-dragged, half-carried him up the length of the bar, stunned drinkers parting like the Red Sea before Moses. Mickey Jones grabbed onto a table and dragged himself to his knees, his wheezing voice raised in insults as he explored his damaged face with bloodied fingers.

Ben didn't release Jack until the pub door had swung shut behind them. As soon as the warm smog hit him, Jack wrestled himself free and stumbled sideways, reaching out to steady himself on the outside wall. Ben stood behind him, his expression grim.

'What the hell, Jack! I reckon you would have killed him.'

'I wish I had,' Jack hissed, flexing his raw knuckles. Tears pricked his eyes. 'He killed our Jenny.'

'What are you talking about? Jack, for God's sake – what's happened?'

Jack shook his head, his throat constricted against a surge of emotion that threatened to overwhelm him. 'Some backstreet abortionist did a hatchet job on her. She's dead, man.'

'Jesus . . . I'm so sorry.' Ben groped for understanding. 'But Mickey?'

'Knocked her up and wouldn't stand by her. Her blood is on his hands.'

'Christ, Jack.' Ben rested a cautious hand on his friend's shoulder. 'I don't know what to say, I can't believe it. I'm sorry about your Jenny, she was a fine pleasant girl. You've given Mickey Jones what he had coming to him . . . But it's time to go home now, Jack. Go back to your mam . . . sort things out for Jenny. There's no more you can do here.' Jack wiped the back of his hand across his eyes. 'Look, I'm off on the trains tonight, but I'll be back tomorrow. I'll come over, we'll down a pint or two.'

'Aye, you're a good pal, Ben,' Jack muttered at last. A drinker left the pub. Noise spilt out into the street as the door opened and was cut off as it closed. Jack rubbed his chin. 'You're working tonight then?'

'Aye. Heading south from the depot on a midnight wagon run.' Ben glanced at his watch. 'Listen, man, I've got to get on. Will you be all right now?'

'Aye . . . reckon I will. Thank you, Ben.'

Ben clapped him on the shoulder. 'Get back to your mam, Jack,' he called as he headed down the street.

'Aye,' Jack murmured.

But he didn't go home.

He had to wait for hours, but it didn't bother him. Jack Ellison had long been a patient man. When Ben left him, he set off at a quick pace to the terraced street where Mickey Jones rented a room in his aunt's house. He waited on the corner, sinking back into the shadows, leaning against the brick wall where the street curved into the alley that ran behind the terraced yards. There were no streetlamps, and as the hours ticked by the dying light took on a sickly yellow hue before fading to grey and gradually lapsing into the silvered ink of night. The shadows embraced him and claimed him as their own. And still he waited.

His heart throbbed faster when he finally heard Mickey's voice in the distance, but his stomach knotted as it became apparent he was not alone. All his careful planning, his patience, hung on a thread as he peered down the dark street. Frustration balled inside him.

But then, just as he could have wept for the injustice of it all, Mickey's companion dropped away, his departing words growing fainter, lost to the neighbouring street. Mickey called out a farewell. Then he walked on alone.

Jack's heart was beating at such a rate he was almost heady on the blood pulsating through his veins. His breaths shortened. He could practically smell Mickey Jones he was so close. He risked a glance up the street. There was no one around and curtains were drawn at the overlooking windows. A scrawny cat slunk across the alley and then it too was gone. Only he and the unsuspecting Mickey remained.

Jack stepped from the shadows into his path. The other man was startled; bleary eyes squinted against the gloom. Jack caught a waft of rancid breath and his insides heaved.

'For fuck's sake . . .' Mickey muttered, but his words died as his sight sharpened. 'Ah, now listen, Jack . . .'

But the incident in the pub had forewarned him and the

words were simply a ruse for his rapid jab into Jack's stomach. Jack buckled, the wind knocked out of him, and before he could recover, Mickey's meaty knuckles slammed upwards through his chin. He reeled back, his head exploding in pain as he lost his balance and fell.

'Go fuck yourself,' Mickey hissed. He hawked noisily before spitting on Jack's sprawled body. Hitching up his trousers, he stepped around him.

But Jack was quicker. Grabbing the man's ankle, he wrenched as hard as he could. Mickey thundered to the ground and before he could right himself, Jack was upon him, straddling his chest, pinning him down. His fists rained onto Mickey's face, strike after strike. He felt the man's cheekbone give way, he heard his nose crack, and when he pulled back his hand a string of blood and mucus came with it. Tears streaked his own cheeks and sobs burst from his chest as he thought of Jenny's lifeless body at home. Gripping Mickey's battered head, now crudely painted with bruising and blood, he raised it from the ground and with a heart-broken cry slammed it down onto the pavement. He doubled over, sobbing, his gore-covered fingers hiding his face. When his tears finally subsided, he dared to lower his hands. Mickey Jones lay motionless beneath him, his head lolled to the side.

Jack could barely breathe as he scrabbled from the man's prostrate body. He whispered Mickey's name. Receiving no reply, he rose unsteadily, stealing fretful glances at the dormant windows and the empty street. His stomach contracted. He staggered back, appalled by what he had done.

And then, unable to think of anything else, he ran.

CHAPTER TWENTY-NINE

Gwen

August 1945

Gwen decides to start the milking early on the afternoon of the VJ celebration. Tom is giddy with excitement, talking nonstop about the promised firework display, due to culminate in a moving elephant that must be seen to be believed. He is quite beside himself at the prospect – the thought of delaying their arrival is too much to bear.

Nora also welcomes her decision. She wants time to get dolled up and Gwen agrees to return the cows to the pasture so she can have first dibs on the hot water in the copper. Once washed, they don flimsy summer dresses, cardigans draped upon their shoulders for later. Gwen dips a pencil into the gravy browning to draw a line up the back of Nora's slender legs. With her summer bronzing, it lends itself well to the illusion of seamed stockings.

They walk to the village swinging Tom between them. He squeals with delight, tucking up his knees with each forward sweep, before landing on both feet and begging for more. Gwen tries to smile at his ebullience, but she is struggling to allay her fears. There is safety in numbers, she reasons. Lost amongst the crowds, there will be little chance of the Allinghams crossing their path. And yet her rationale fails to alleviate the increasing weight of her anxiety. When they reach the brow of the hill, they see the marquees in the meadow beside the church, the fete laid out in miniature before them. As Tom lets out a holler of wonder, Gwen's insides contract.

It seems the whole village has turned out. Union Jack bunting flutters above them as the crowd mingles happily, with neighbours sharing news of boys coming home. There are relieved smiles all round. Gwen thinks back to the last fete she attended. Her hand strays to Tom's shoulder as she pushes the memory away.

Nora soon peels off, skipping over to a bunch of lads milling before the beer tent. Tom is hungry and mithering for food, so Gwen allows him to lead her to the trestle tables within the main marquee, laid out with plates of sandwiches and cake, the array impressive given rationing restraints.

'Just don't ask what's in them,' Muriel says sourly, manning the tables.

'It's lovely to see so many people turn out,' Gwen says, gently chastising Tom for overloading his plate.

'All and sundry are here, it seems. There's a party from the Hall. They must feel inconvenienced having to drive down here rather than have people flood to them to pay homage.'

Gwen is a taken aback by Muriel's caustic comment. She had no idea the woman's antipathy towards the family ran so deep. She wonders whether her housekeeper's feelings are motivated by loyalty and, suspecting they are, she can't help but feel grateful.

*

The party runs on into the night. Gwen is tired, exhausted by the vigilance that has her looking over shoulders, craning to spot those she wishes to avoid. She has taken little pleasure from the celebration and would have left hours ago, but Tom is determined to see the much-lauded firework elephant and she cannot deny him that pleasure.

Storm lanterns have been hung from the tent poles and candles in jam jars set upon the ground. A big bonfire has been lit, and it roars and crackles, hungry flames licking into the night sky, devouring the blackout at last.

She sips the cup of warm wine someone has pressed upon her, while Tom – defiantly wakeful – sucks on a barley sugar and clings to her hand. She has not seen Nora for an hour or more. A new band has taken to the stage at the top end of the meadow and the sedate music playing earlier has been replaced by raucous jazz. The trumpet player, a middle-aged man Gwen does not recognise, is thrilling the crowd with his skill. People are dancing and amongst them Gwen finally spots Nora, flying from the hold of some young chap like a spinning top, her skirt whirling high, her head thrown back, a joyous laugh ripping from her throat, as her feet twist and jab with such speed they blur before Gwen's eyes.

'Can I tempt you?'

Gwen starts as Ted appears beside her. Having not seen him all evening she had presumed he had decided not to come and, to her shame, she had been relieved. He has dressed up for the occasion, though she sees the collar of his shirt is a little frayed. Detecting an uncharacteristic hint of cologne, she quickly turns her attention back to the dancers, drawing Tom closer to her side.

'Oh no, my feet are killing me as it is.'

'Do you want to find somewhere to sit down?'

He turns, searching the darkness, but what chairs have been brought out from the marquees are occupied.

'No . . . no, honestly, it's fine,' Gwen assures him. Tom is resting heavily against her leg. 'I hope they're going to light the fireworks soon – this one can hardly keep his eyes open.' She scoops Tom up, placing him on her hip. He offers Ted a sleepy grin.

'Waiting to see the elephant, Tom?' Ted smiles as the little boy nods before resting his forehead on Gwen's cheek.

They stand in silence, watching the dancers twirl before them, tapping their feet to the irresistible rhythm of the band. There is a smattering of applause as the song draws to end. The trumpet player lowers his instrument.

'Right, folks,' he shouts, 'I've just been told it's time for the fireworks.'

There are cheers of excitement. The dancers drift away from the clearing before the stage, as a crowd gathers in the direction of the bonfire. A few men run behind the blaze, racing between objects on the ground, almost lost to the encroaching darkness. Gwen jiggles Tom on her hip until he rests more comfortably and has a good view. Ted stands beside her, patting his pockets for his cigarettes.

The first firework screams skywards. It explodes against the pitch-black, showering red sparks that fall and fade. It is closely followed by two more, whooshing and cracking, spurting colour across the sky, accompanied by an appreciative chorus of *oohs* and *aahs*. Tom bounces excitedly on Gwen's hip and his exuberance delights her. On two posts planted either side of the bonfire, Catherine wheels whiz round firing a cascade of light as they go. Tom points in delight, imploring Gwen to watch. Ted chuckles beside her. Tom's enthusiasm is contagious.

More rockets shoot into the night sky. The pricking stars pale in comparison to the triumphant display. Tom's upturned face is illuminated in colour.

And then finally, the pièce de résistance. The crowd falls silent with anticipation. The large board looks innocuous. Gwen can just make out the vague outline of an elephant. There is a collected intake of breath, as a shadowed figure squats at the far side and strikes a match. Something fizzes as he hastily retreats. Tom is deathly still, spellbound in her arms.

A run of sparks races around the outline, magically transforming into a shimmering elephant. When it reaches the head a sparkling trunk lifts into the night sky, creating a breathtaking moment of awestruck delight. The crowd erupts into cheers. Tom bounces with sheer ecstasy in Gwen's arms, gabbling wildly as he recounts the wonder just witnessed in case she had blinked and missed it.

People start to drift away once the elephant has faded. Gwen's arms ache from holding Tom up. He is fully awake now, fired with enthusiasm and gusting along on a second wind. She is keen to walk him home while she can make the most of this renewed vitality – she doesn't fancy carrying him all the way. She tells Ted that she needs to find Nora and fearing he will suggest escorting her, she walks away before he has a chance to process her words. She feels guilty and relieved in equal measure when he remains where he is, abandoned.

The band are reassembling on the stage and the dancers are

waiting impatiently for the music to begin. Nora is amongst them, with a different partner this time, Gwen notes.

'We're going back,' she calls out when Nora glances her way, but the Land Girl merely wiggles her fingers in farewell.

Tom yanks on her arm as he hops and skips, still full of the firework display. She sees Muriel clearing up in one of the marquees and feels guilty for not stopping to help, but then, she reasons, she has Tom. She must get him home. A few people call 'Goodnight' as she makes her way over the grass, her shoes tipping on the tussocks. The gate hangs open before them. The balloons attached to it have shrunk to woeful crinkled sacs that hang limply against the wooden bars.

Distracted by Tom and his endless monologue on the elephant, she does not notice the parked car alongside the church until they are almost upon it. A stooped chauffeur holds open the rear door for the two ladies – one young, one old – while two men stand by, discussing the Hall in cut-glass accents as they wait for the women to settle.

The Hall.

Blood hums in Gwen's ears as her steps falter. The old man ducks inside the car and as he does so the younger one looks round, attracted by the sound of Tom's high-pitched excitement.

Their eyes lock.

Gwen suddenly feels faint. Her grip on Tom's hand becomes so fierce he calls out in complaint. She cannot breathe.

'Do hurry up and get in, Gordon,' the older man's upper-class drawl drifts from the car, rallying his transfixed son.

'Yes, of course,' Gordon says at last, though he remains distracted. He slides into the car and even after the chauffeur has clicked the door shut behind him, he continues to watch her through the window.

And then, what Gwen has been fearing comes to pass. His gaze drops to the boy clutched to her side and even as the car eases away, there it stubbornly remains.

CHAPTER THIRTY

Jack

August 1939

'I didn't mean to kill him. Or maybe I did. I don't know.' Jack lets out a ragged sigh. He dares to lift his eyes to Gwen; the new wariness in her expression breaks his heart. 'I didn't think I was a violent man, Gwen, but maybe it's there in all of us. I had a rage on me like never before, and I hadn't got the self-control to stop it.' He shakes his thoughts loose. 'I just couldn't stop myself.' He pauses for a deep breath. 'But anyway, the point is this: I've killed a man, and I reckon the coppers must have a pretty good idea it was me that did it. I had enough witnesses when I had a go at him in the pub. I've tried to cover my tracks, but I've not done a decent job. Did you know Iris Jennings' brother is a detective – in Newcastle? Apparently, he's coming here. I can't help but think he's coming for me.'

'You don't know that.'

'Iris told Ted he was coming down for work.'

'If he was coming for you, he'd be here by now, wouldn't he? He'd have got Vic to arrest you. Your own sense of guilt is making you leap to conclusions,' Gwen adds quietly.

'Maybe. Oh, Gwen, I don't know. All I know is . . . I can't stay here. This damn war can't come soon enough. I reckon no one's going to ask too many questions about a man willing to give up his life for his country, not when his country needs every willing man she can muster. And I reckon I should let fate decide what happens to me next . . . perhaps I will survive. Perhaps fighting this war will be my redemption. But even if I do live, I can't see how I can come back here, to England. I'd spend my life looking over my shoulder, waiting for my past to catch up with me. I can't live my life in the shadow of the hangman's noose, Gwen.'

'But what will you do?'

'If I survive the war, I reckon I'll hop on a ship somewhere, start afresh. America maybe. Or maybe I'll stay in Europe and just not come home – there are many ways a man can disappear and start again. But if you let me do this for you, Gwen – marry you, I mean – you'll be able to keep your bairn, without disgrace, without fear. Your dad'll look after you. And if I don't survive, you'll at least have a widow's pension, and that'll help down the line.'

'I couldn't take your money.'

'If you're getting my war pension, lass, I'm in a place where I won't be needing it.'

'But your own family . . .'

'I have no family. Jenny was my only family.'

'Your mother . . .'

'She was never much of a mother to me, Gwen. She's only herself to take care of these days and she's more than capable of doing that. I would rather you had the benefit of the money.' He hesitates. 'You've come to mean more to me than my own flesh and blood, Gwen. I'd want you to have it.'

'To even talk about this is madness. I'll not talk about it anymore.' She tries to walk past him, but he catches hold of her arm. Gently, he brings her round to face him.

'Gwen . . . do you want this bairn?'

She bites her lip and looks away. Slowly she nods.

'Because it's his?' he asks, for no other reason than to torture himself.

'Because it's mine!' She faces him, radiating defiance.

'Then let me help you. Let me do that? One last act of friendship before I go.'

'I can't marry you, Jack. I don't love you.'

Her honesty shouldn't hurt him but it does, though he knows he has no right to her affections. It was foolish to expect them, ridiculous to hope. 'I promise you, Gwen . . . I won't come back. Whatever happens, I won't come back. I can't, don't you see? And if Jerry doesn't get me first, in seven years you can have me declared dead. You can get on with your life while you're waiting for the legalities to pass. You and your bairn.' He takes her hands. 'Don't run the risk of getting rid of it, lass, especially if that's not what your heart wants anyhow.'

'I need to think.'

'Aye, I understand. Think on it, think on all I've said.'

He releases her, but she remains enveloped in his heart, whether she is aware of it or not.

It seems to Jack that Gwen drives herself harder that day than on any other. She hoists two sheaves at a time onto her shoulders, so bent beneath their weight she can barely lug them across the stubbled field to where the horses stand, shackled to the haycart with its growing load. She grunts with effort as she flings them up one at a time, before clambering aboard to haul them to the far end to make space for more. It is not long before her hair clings to her forehead and her shirt is dark with sweat.

'Working like a Trojan, Gwen!' Jim calls, his voice ringing with admiration.

Gwen does not acknowledge her father's compliment. She jumps down from the back of the cart and strides off to dismantle another stook. Jack cannot help but wonder whether she is trying to dislodge the tiny creature embedded in her womb, so that she might be absolved from making the difficult decision before her. He reflects that perhaps they are both more comfortable with their courses being decided by fate.

They ride the wagon back to the farm, strands of straw shedding onto the warm evening breeze to land like flotsam in their wake. When they pull into the yard, Gwen jumps down and runs in to see if Muriel has the copper on.

Once in the rickyard, she stands tall on the back of the wagon and pitches sheaves over the side for the men to stack into a towering rick, storing the crop until threshing time.

They break briefly for tea, a simple meal of bacon rashers and broad beans sprinkled with mint from the garden, and new potatoes glistening from a liberal dressing of the meat's hot fat. They eat hungrily. Gwen complains her portion is not enough and she takes her empty plate to the range where she raids the saucepans for more. Jack notices how Muriel's eyes follow her.

They finish building the rick as the light begins to fade and when they are done they head back inside, hot and sticky and weary. Jim breaks open a flagon of beer and offers Jack a glass to slake his thirst. Gwen takes the tin bath down from its hook in the pantry and sets about filling it with water from the copper, while Muriel fetches clean towels from the press. She sets them on the pantry shelf while Gwen retrieves the cracked soap from the dish by the kitchen sink. As Muriel turns to leave she dips her hand in the water and lets out a cry.

'Good God, Gwen, you'll boil alive in there. Put some cold water in before you scald yourself.'

But Gwen steps into the pantry and edges the door to, securing her privacy, all the while claiming she doesn't find it too hot . . . to her, it is not hot at all. As the door shuts, Muriel's lips purse and her brow knits. She gathers up her things preparing for home, distractedly offering her farewells. Only Jack notices how she dithers on the threshold, half-turning towards the barred pantry, as she contemplates the swish of water coming from within.

That night, Jack awakes with a start. In the looseboxes beyond the tack room door the horses sidle, their hooves catching on the cobbles beneath the straw. He swings his legs over the side of the bed. Sitting on its edge, he cocks his ear to the darkness and concentrates. His senses tingle with alertness. Getting to his feet, he steps into his trousers and pushes on his boots. He is careful as he lifts the latch on the door to make as little noise as possible.

Through the threads of moonlight he sees Gwen, sitting on an upturned bucket in front of Arthur's stall. The horse's head hangs over the wooden gate; he snorts softly, nudging her shoulder with his velvet muzzle.

Gwen twists round to face Jack. She is nursing a bottle of whisky and he sees at once she has been crying. The streaks on her cheeks glisten in the darkness.

'I thought about what you said,' she says at last, 'about letting fate decide. I thought I'd let my body decide whether it kept this baby or not. So, I worked hard today. I worked until I thought I would drop, until every inch of me was screaming with pain. Then I had that bath – I could hardly stand it, it was so hot, I thought I'd be blistered all over when I got out. And then finally I took this from the bottom drawer of Dad's desk. He doesn't realise that I know it's there. I just . . .' Her chest heaves and falls on a sob. 'And then I started thinking – what if what I'm doing doesn't cause me to lose the baby, but just damage it in some way? What mother does that? What sort of mother harms the innocent life inside her?' Her gaze drills into him. 'You asked me if I wanted this baby . . . if I wanted to keep it. And the thing is, Jack, I do.'

She whispers her confession, then abruptly thrusts the bottle aside and stands up, walking over to the gaping doorway. She tips her face towards the full moon, the goddess of fertility shining in the night sky like an omen. 'This is my baby as much as his. It has as much of me in it as it does of him. He can reject it . . . but I won't. It is growing within me, becoming more a part of me every day. It is *my* baby.'

There are no tears on her face as she turns to address him, though there is profound sorrow, perhaps regret. He stands rigid, aware of the distant bark of a fox and the soughing of the wind in the trees. But all he wants to hear are her words.

'I won't abandon my baby, Jack, and I don't want to hurt it. If it stubbornly wants to stay and live, I must respect it for wanting to be. The fault is mine, not my baby's, so I'm not going to try and get rid of it anymore.' She walks towards him until there is barely a breath between them. She lifts her chin, but he immediately sees the confidence is feigned and when she speaks there is a tremor in her voice. 'Make your offer again, Jack.'

He does not hesitate. He has no need to. He knows the words she wants to hear and, though he will never confess as much to her, he longs to say them.

'Marry me, Gwen.'

'Yes.'

Her voice is dull. There is no yearned-for sparkle in her eyes, just resigned defeat.

Without waiting for his response, she turns away and walks out into the night.

CHAPTER THIRTY-ONE

Jack

August 1939

'No.'

The force of Jim's refusal causes Jack to step back, panic rising. This was not part of the plan.

'Jim . . .' He grapples for words, words that will convince the dour farmer to give him permission to marry his daughter.

'No, Jack, I can't give my blessing. I'm . . . well, to be honest, I'm totally taken aback. You and Gwen? Lad, you hardly know each other.'

'We know what we want.'

'I didn't even realise the two of you were . . . well, are you? Courting? You've been to a dance, I'll give you that, but you've not exactly stepped out – gone to the pictures or . . .'

'We've worked beside each other day in, day out for nigh on three months now, Jim. I reckon that's a better way of getting to know someone than taking them to the pictures a couple of times a week, don't you?'

'But you've given no indication . . .'

Jack rubs his forehead, his mind racing. They are in the

orchard behind the house, picking apples. It is not an ideal time, but Jack has been struggling to find a suitable moment since Gwen finally accepted his offer. They had agreed he would ask to speak to Jim that first evening, but Ted had turned up unexpectedly and they had ended up drinking beer and discussing the deteriorating situation in Europe, speculating on the possible implications of Britain's pact with Poland.

'When are you going to say something?' Gwen had demanded after.

So, he promised her it would be today, and here in the orchard with the birds warbling and the air sweet with the scent of sun-warmed apples, the time seemed ripe. He waited until the wooden crates at their feet were full and, against a hovering wasp's ominous drone, he pitched his request. But he was careful not to convey the full truth in his heart – it rendered him too vulnerable. But now, in the face of the farmer's refusal, he realises a full confession is his only hope.

'I love her, Jim.' Gwen's father mutters in disbelief, but Jack continues undaunted. 'From that first day, I knew. I knew how I felt and, in truth, that's what's kept me here. It wasn't the offer of work or the money. There was something . . . something about her . . . something which struck me that day – I don't know what you'd call it, a sixth sense maybe – and I knew I couldn't leave, I couldn't walk away from her. My feelings haven't altered since that day, Jim . . . they've only grown.'

'Well, that's as may be, but it's all too sudden for my liking. It's not you, lad, I like you, don't get me wrong, and I'd be more than happy to welcome you into the family, I really would. But all I'm asking is that you wait a bit longer, until you're sure . . .'

'I am sure, Jim. I've never been so sure of anything in my whole life and neither has Gwen. Ask her, she'll tell you herself.'

'If you feel that strongly about each other I don't see what the rush is. A few more months, is all I'm asking – let all the giddiness of young love settle down a bit before you make such a commitment.'

'There's going to be a war, Jim. It's inevitable, I think we all know that, and I'll have to go and do my bit. If we get married now, well, if anything happens to me Gwen will be looked after.'

'No.' Jim holds up his hand. 'No . . . this war is more reason to wait, not less. I'll not have my Gwen made a widow before she's twenty. I'll not have her go through that. You go and you do your bit for King and Country, lad, I wish you all the best with it, and I hope to God you do survive whatever's coming. And if, when it's all done, the two of you still feel the same way, well, I will happily give you my blessing. But I won't have my Gwen rushing up the aisle like this, I just won't . . .'

'Jim, please.'

'No!' There is anger edging his voice now. 'I don't want to talk about this any further, Jack. I will not give you my blessing.' He pauses, relenting. 'I'm just asking you to wait. I'm not saying never – you're a solid chap, Jack, she could do a lot worse than you. *Wait*, that's all I'm asking. Now take these crates inside to the girls, will you?' He starts to climb the short ladder resting against the tree behind him. 'We'd best get on, get these apples in before the wasps get them.'

Jack searches for words of persuasion, but he cannot find them. He has laid his heart bare and revealed more than he has ever dared reveal to Gwen, and yet he has been thwarted. He tries to stifle his anxiety as he thinks of the secret hidden deep inside her – a secret that cannot be concealed for much longer. His failure pains him.

The stacked crates are heavy as he lugs them through the back door. Gwen is standing at the kitchen table wrapping apples in newspaper, ready for storage in the cellar. She looks up and sees at once the apology on his face. The colour drains from her cheeks.

'He said no.' It is barely more than a whisper; Jack could weep for letting her down.

'Who said no – to what?'

Muriel stands in the hall doorway newly returned from the cellar, an empty crate hanging from a hand smudged with newsprint. Her beady eyes dart between them. She tilts up her chin, her nose twitching to detect the stink of collusion, hidden beneath the sweet mustiness of apple.

'Come on, let's have it.' Her manner is as sharp as a paring knife. She means to cut out their secrets.

'Jack and I . . . we . . .'

Jack moves to Gwen's side. 'I asked Jim for Gwen's hand and he said no. That is, he said we have to wait . . . until after the war.'

'He said no, did he?' Muriel's mouth pinches with displeasure. She thrusts the empty crate into the vacant space on the table. 'Stupid bugger. You leave this to me – I'll sort it out.'

'What are you going to do?' Gwen follows her to the door.

Muriel glowers at her. 'I'm going to tell him exactly why you cannot wait.'

'What's that supposed to mean?'

'Did you honestly think that I – having looked after you most of your life – wouldn't notice? Thickening waist, growing bust, green in the morning. Oh, he's tried to cover for you, I know,' her spindly finger flies out in Jack's direction, 'and your dad's been too daft to question any of it, but I wasn't born yesterday, missy. So now, if you don't mind, I'll go and have a word with your father and make it plain why he will *not* make you wait. When I've done with him, he'll make sure you're up that aisle the minute the banns have been read.'

Gwen tries to stop her, her pleas breaking like smashed china, but Muriel throws her off and storms through the door. With a cry, she dashes to the window to observe the scene unfolding beyond the glass. Jack lays a tentative hand on her back, but she tenses at his touch and so it drops to his side once more.

Muriel strides up the path with purpose, knocking Kip out of her way as the dog prances about her feet. Jim is up the ladder, picking apples into the canvas bag slung around his neck. Alert to Muriel's approach, he slowly descends until they are standing toe to toe in the shade of the tree. Muriel bats away a wasp, but it is clear it does not distract her from her purpose.

In the kitchen, Gwen and Jack are unable to hear what is said, but they see Jim's chin drop and his shoulders slump. His slackening stance conveys far more than mere words. Unable to bear the sight of his broken heart, Gwen turns away. Brushing past Jack, she stands by the range, absorbed in thought. Jack pushes his hands into his pockets and stares at the runnels in the wooden drainer.

Muriel returns alone. Jack looks through the window, but there is no sign of Jim: he is no longer humming a melody while picking apples in the afternoon sun.

'It's done.' The housekeeper dusts off her hands, as if glad to be rid of the tawdry business. 'Your father is going to go and see the vicar this evening. He'll get the first reading of the banns this Sunday.' She glares at Jack. 'I know you're not one for church, but you'll be there, do you understand me?'

He mumbles his assent. Gwen runs from the room. They hear the rapid thud of her feet on the stair treads and the slam of her door. The fight leaves Muriel. Her gnarled fingers grip the dresser edge.

'It's not yours, is it?' She looks directly at him. Jack holds her gaze and says nothing. 'Oh, I'm no fool, Jack, she doesn't see you that way, even though I think you wish she did. Your eyes linger on her long enough, but hers skid off you like skates on ice.' He tries not to flinch; her blunt words wound deep. 'I found a note, doing the washing. She must have forgotten to empty her pockets. Full of daft lines it was, silly frivolous things, things that would soon turn a foolish girl's head. I always warned Jim he was sheltering her too much. Signed with a G, it was. I wonder who that could be?' But her tone tells him she already knows. 'So, you see, I know it's not yours.'

'It's my bairn now and that's all that matters.'

Tears fill her eyes like a flash flood, but she rapidly blinks them away. 'I hope you know what you're doing. Now you'd best get back out to those apples, they're not going to pick themselves.' She pushes herself away from the dresser and crosses to the table. Snatching up a sheet of newspaper, she whips it around a piece of fruit, the paper crackling with every fold.

Jack glances up at the silent floorboards above them, then lifts the latch of the door and is gone.

CHAPTER THIRTY-TWO

Gwen

August 1945

Gwen rises the next morning with the feeling of dread weighing heavily in the pit of her stomach. As she splashes her face with water, she tries to console herself that Gordon is now merely aware she has a child. He has no reason to think Tom is the same child she warned him she was carrying – the child he instructed her to get rid of.

And yet . . .

She forces her fears from her mind. She hears Nora moving about in the room next door, yawning loudly, cussing when she bangs into something as she leaves to bring in the cattle. There is milking to be done. Gwen chides herself for her distraction. She is worrying about nothing. The façade she has crafted all these years with the help of Jack's selfless gift is faultless. Let Gordon have his suspicions, there is enough evidence on show to create reasonable doubt. Even so, as she lifts the latch on her door, she cannot help wondering what Gordon looked like as child and whether there are photographs of him at Tom's age, displayed in silver frames around the Hall. She wonders what similarities there might be.

She cannot resist the temptation to look in on Tom. He sleeps peacefully, his thumb fallen free of his mouth, his cheeks flushed with the cosy warmth of his bed. She has never seen him look sweeter; she has never been so aware of his vulnerability. She wishes a German bullet had served to protect her son and is immediately ashamed of her callousness.

Muriel cycles into the yard just as the first of the cattle appear in the lane. She enters the house full of gossip from the night before, but Gwen cuts her off mid-sentence.

'Do you think Tom looks like me?'

'What do you mean?'

'Does Tom look like I did, at his age . . . as a child?'

'Well, I . . . well, of course there's bound to be a look of you about him . . .'

'But I mean more than that.'

'I . . . I don't know, I never thought about it . . . he has your eyes. I've always said that.'

'But he isn't the spit of me.'

Muriel blusters. 'Well, no, not exactly.'

'Do you . . . do you think . . .' But Gwen cannot bring herself to finish her question. She is too afraid to hear the answer.

'Gwen, love, what on earth is it?'

'Gordon Allingham . . .'

'Oh yes. He's back, of course.'

'He saw us . . . last night, leaving the victory party . . . the two of us. He saw Tom.'

'Oh.' Muriel sits heavily on the chair beside her. 'Oh, I see. And did he . . . did he say anything?'

Gwen shakes her head. 'But he saw us.'

'Look, Gwen . . . I can see why you're worried, but . . . it's been nearly six years.'

'Does Tom look like him?'

'No!'

'What if he looked like Tom as a child . . . what if . . .'

'Don't waste your time on what ifs.' Muriel leaps up, leaning into hands firmly planted on the table. Conscious of her raised voice she glances up at the ceiling to where the very boy sleeps above them. 'You're a married woman,' she continues quietly. 'You were married before that boy was born and you knew your husband in time for him to be the father. That's all that matters. No one has ever questioned that boy's parentage, not for one minute. You stick to your story and there'll be no need to worry about Gordon Allingham. Do you hear me? Don't you start to wobble, because folk will sniff you out and there's many around here with nothing better to do than put two and two together and gossip about the five they make.'

Gwen hugs herself, gooseflesh running across her back. 'I never thought it all through, you know. None of it. I didn't think about what would happen when the war ended. Jack made me a promise and that was good enough for me. I didn't stop to think about Gordon, about what would happen if *he* survived . . . if *he* came home. I think as the war went on and so many people lost their loved ones, I just presumed – hoped even – that he wouldn't make it. But he has. He has made it. He has come home.'

'Pull yourself together.' Muriel draws herself up to her full height. 'There's no use sniffling now, what's done is done. You stick to your guns. There's no need for Gordon Allingham to get suspicious.' Her severity relents on a sigh. Softer she says, 'He'll want to get on with his life, now the war is over. He's got his wife – she's been waiting for him all this time. They'll be wanting a family of their own, no doubt. Even if he does have suspicions about the boy, he's hardly going to show interest in his . . .' she stops herself then she spits out the word with an air of defiance, '. . . *bastard*, is he? There'd be shame for him as well as for you – ramifications I'm sure he'd want to avoid.'

'Yes . . . yes . . . his wife, of course . . . I'm sure you're right.' Gwen forces a smile and tries hard to take comfort from Muriel's sensible reassurance, but somehow it proves elusive. She cannot quite find the sure footing the words appear to offer; every step seems to land on quicksand that sucks her further into despair. She hears the cows calling outside and forces herself to rally. 'I must go and help Nora,' she mutters, passing behind Muriel to retrieve her boots from the doorstep. As she readies to leave, Muriel calls out to her.

'Don't think on it, Gwen, do you hear me? Don't waste your time worrying about things that will never come to pass.'

But the anxious expression on Muriel's face belies the confidence of her words.

CHAPTER THIRTY-THREE

Jack

3rd September 1939

'What a day for the banns to be read,' Gwen mutters to Jack as they wait for Jim to join them for the walk to church.

Hitler has been given until eleven o'clock to withdraw his troops from Poland. Gwen has already declared herself fearful for what the day might bring, but Jack suspects it is the prospect of their public marriage announcement that has put her on edge, rather than the nation's perilous position. The thought that their forthcoming nuptials are weighing so heavily on her mind saddens him.

Jim is grim-faced and silent when he finally appears. He has barely spoken to either of them since the fateful day in the orchard when secrets dropped like windfall. That night, Gwen had gone straight to her room after dinner. Jack had intuitively known he would not be welcome in the sitting room, so instead, he had busied himself with chores – shutting in the chickens, feeding Kip, refilling the horses' water troughs. When he was done, he returned to the stables, intending to take to his bed in the tack room. He had been surprised to find Jim waiting for him, nursing a tin mug that Jack knew immediately did not contain tea – the smell of whisky was too strong.

'Muriel's told me everything. I thought you should know that. So there's no need for any pretence between us.' His breath was ripe with tobacco and spirits.

Jack had shifted uneasily. 'It makes no difference to me – I want you to know that. I've taken responsibility for the child and I won't shirk it.'

Jim had merely huffed and nodded, clutching the chipped tin mug to his chest as he hovered in the doorway. 'Looks like you've come to my girl's rescue twice, lad.'

'And I'll happily keep coming,' Jack replied softly, 'for as long as she needs me. I promise you, Jim, anything I do will be done in Gwen's best interests.'

In that moment, he had considered sharing with the farmer his plan and his promise not to come home, that Gwen would – when she chose – be free to love another, someone lucky enough to capture her heart. But Jim had stalked out on unsteady legs before he had a chance to explain his intent: to join the army and fight – not for his country per se, not even for his life, but for bettering her future. He would fight recklessly and without fear, knowing if he fell, she would benefit.

After what he had done, the life he had taken, it seemed a suitable penance.

Muriel is already waiting for them outside the church. They take their places in a row halfway down the aisle. Jim exchanges greetings with a few neighbours as they slip into their pews, but for the most part he keeps his eyes front and centre and his mouth grimly set.

Gwen unhooks her hassock and drops to her knees to offer a brief prayer. Jack remains seated beside her, though he bows his head to stare at his knotted fingers resting in his lap. The church is filling up. The places of worship he knew in Newcastle were vast affairs which afforded a degree of anonymity, but in this quaint village church, with its modest number of pews and narrow aisles, there is nowhere to hide.

Hushed activity at the church door incites the organist to break into a flourishing voluntary. Jack peers around as Gwen retakes her seat and hangs up her hassock. He catches his breath.

The last of the congregation has arrived. The Allinghams have appeared in full force – the parents, the son, the pretty fiancée. Jack watches Gordon shake hands with the vicar but returns his eyes to the front as the family begin to glide up the aisle with an inherent air of privilege, bestowing a gracious nod here and a beatific smile there.

But there is no such offering for Gwen or her father. They walk straight past, the click of their heels just discernible beneath the sound of the organ as it builds to a wheezing crescendo in perfect time for them to take their seats. Jack notices how attentive Gordon is to his fiancée, placing his hand on the small of her back as he guides her into the family's boxed pew. He is struck by the adoration in her eyes as she darts him a grateful look, her pink-painted lips twitching. Gordon pinches up his trousers and sits down beside her. He does not once look at Gwen, and her head remains bowed.

There is a flow to the service that Jack, to his surprise, finds calming – stand, sit down, stand and sing, sit down. The vicar's words wash over him and for a while, he almost forgets why he is there – until his name is read aloud for all to hear. He looks up, blinking, confused as it resonates into Gwen's. She stiffens beside him. Whispers circle the congregation.

For a fleeting moment, Gordon Allingham unwittingly betrays some emotion that Jack can't quite construe, before his mask of idle disinterest returns. As the vicar concludes, Gordon's gaze sidles across the pews until it settles on Gwen. And then his eyes snag on Jack's. They stare at each other down the length of the nave. The muscle in Jack's jaw twitches.

He takes some satisfaction from the fact that it is the other man who looks away first.

Nobody lingers in the graveyard after the service, which has served as little more than a prelude to the day's main event. All feel an irrepressible need to return to their wireless sets and tune in for the latest developments. There is a sombre air of expectation.

They walk quickly back through the village. Muriel invites them into her little cottage, but hearing the banns read has left Jim agitated and he wants to get home. He carries on walking, leaving Gwen to mutter their apologies.

Jim strides through the kitchen straight to the sitting room. He flicks on the wireless and throws himself into his chair, his elbows resting on the arms, his fingers steepled before him, while Gwen comes to a standstill before the set. Jack follows cautiously behind and, receiving no objection, draws beside her. The minutes tick by on the mantel clock. The eleven o'clock deadline comes and goes. Gwen presses her fingers to her lips. Through the background hiss it starts:

'*This is London. You will now hear a statement by the Prime Minister . . .*'

Chamberlain's clipped voice begins from the hollow confines of the war rooms. He speaks slowly, pausing between clauses, and then his strict tone relents to one of sadness as he confirms the nation's fears:

'*Consequently, this country is at war with Germany.*'

Bells peal across the radio waves following the conclusion of his statement, filling the deathly hush as they await the public information announcements they have been warned will follow.

'Well, that's that, then,' Jim says, his manner subdued.

They listen closely as information is relayed on the immediate closure of theatres and cinemas, '*If they were hit by a bomb, large numbers would be killed or injured*', and description is given to the different methods of alarm – the sirens, hooters and whistles that will signal an impending air raid, and hand rattles for gas. They listen to information on school closures and the call for empty streets; they absorb instructions for carrying identification and how luggage labels bearing names and addresses should be sewn into children's clothes. It is impossible not to be affected by the unspoken reasoning behind these rules.

The details begin to wash over them as the information ceases to be directly relevant – the prohibition of Underground stations as air-raid shelters and the practicalities of benefits collection will not affect them. By the time the sobering relay has concluded, they are numb. There is a hiss-filled pause and then the national anthem strikes up loud and clear.

Jim pushes himself up from his seat. They stand listening to the stirring notes passionately played by the brass band and just as the final chord is struck, Jack feels Gwen's fingers slip into his.

CHAPTER THIRTY-FOUR

Gwen

August 1945

Tom is up by the time they finish milking. He runs down to the gate as they are placing the last of the churns on the milk stand, collapsing to his knees to fuss over Kip, who placidly submits to his suffocating embrace.

Nora is to return the cows to the field. Tom leaps up begging to go with her and when the Land Girl offers no objection, Gwen agrees. She watches him skip after the departing herd, before returning to clean out the milking parlour.

She feels a tug of concern when they fail to return by the time she has completed her task. The enticing smell of frying bacon is wafting through the open kitchen window – a decided benefit of partaking in the pig club – but rather than go in to see Muriel, Gwen wanders down to the gate. She looks up the empty lane, wondering where they might be. She is about to turn back when something catches her eye. Her stomach lurches, and for a moment she is catapulted back in time. A brick juts out from the gatepost.

At first, she persuades herself it is nothing – that it is the angle she is standing at which makes the brick appear proud. She alters her position; the brick signals to her still.

She decides it must be Tom's doing – he has noticed it is loose and fiddled with it out of curiosity. She will not touch it. But she knows, deep inside, it is not Tom's handiwork. Her body begins to shake, as if she has heard the wail of an air-raid siren. The signal before her denotes just as much peril.

Her fingers tremble as they close over the coarse brick. It scrapes her skin as she wriggles it loose and, just as she feared, she sees a fold of paper skulking behind it. Though she knows no good can come of her actions, she feels compelled to retrieve it.

The paper is crisp and thick – good quality – folded in half and then folded again. She looks up and down the lane to ensure no one is coming, for she has no desire to be caught with this missive. Her concern for Tom and Nora is temporarily forgotten.

She stifles a moan as she summons the courage to open it. There was a time when she would have eagerly ripped such a note apart, desperate to devour the words it contained, but now she feels only terror. Biting her lip so sharply she tastes blood, she unfolds the paper.

We need to talk.
Usual place, 8 p.m.
About the boy.

Her stomach spasms and bile scorches the back of her throat. She grips the top of the gatepost, heaving, though nothing comes out. Her panic refuses to be purged.

About the boy.

'Mummy! Mummy!'

She spins around at the sound of Tom's voice and her heart fills with love at the sight of him. Tears spring to her eyes as, fighting back a sob, she drops to a crouch and welcomes him into her embrace, crushing him against her until he wriggles to get free.

'You took your time! What kept you?' she says, relief giving way to annoyance as Nora comes sauntering up behind.

'Mummy, I sat on a motorbike!'

'What?'

'It was really fun, and the man said I should learn to ride a bicycle so that I can have a motorbike one day. Can I have a bicycle, Mummy?'

'What man?' Gwen asks sharply, but something has caught Tom's eye in the verge and he drifts away to investigate. Squatting down, he starts poking the long grass with a stick. Gwen looks at Nora. 'What man?'

'That rather dishy chap we saw the other day.' Nora grins. 'You never told me he was the local gentry. Unfortunately, it appears he's married . . . not that that necessarily matters.'

'What were you doing talking to him?'

'He just happened along as we were putting the cows back. We got chatting, that's all.'

'About what? What did he want?'

'Nothing, he was just being friendly, charming . . .'

'He asked me what my name was and then he managed to guess how old I am,' Tom chirps up.

'Yes, he took quite a shine to young Tom here, didn't he, Tom?' Nora grins.

'He was really nice. Look, Mummy, a toad!'

'Leave it alone, Tom,' Gwen snaps, and when he fails to comply she grabs his arm and hauls him to his feet. 'I said to leave it alone! Now go on inside and get your breakfast.'

'I've had my breakfast.'

'Go inside to Muriel, Tom.'

He pouts but wisely decides not to press his luck and kicking up every stone he can find, he wanders up the yard. Gwen rounds on Nora.

'I don't want you encouraging Tom to speak to strangers.'

'I was hardly encouraging him, and Gordon's a neighbour, not a stranger.'

Gwen is shocked by how casually Nora dispenses his name.

'I don't want my son anywhere near that man. Do I make myself clear?'

'Why on earth not?'

'I'm your employer, Nora. I pay your wages, I put a roof over your head and food on your plate. I don't answer to you.'

Nora expels an exasperated breath. She shakes her head, her features pinched with contempt. 'Fine. Whatever you say, Gwen.' She stalks through the gateway, turning back to offer a mocking tug of her forelock. 'Ma'am.'

Gwen tips back her head and blinks to keep her tears at bay as the note bites into her balled palm. She forces herself to look at it one last time then, gritting her teeth, she reduces it to paper petals that flutter down to speckle the verge.

CHAPTER THIRTY-FIVE

Jack

September 1939

The country might be at war but there is no discernible difference to their daily lives. Jack takes the bus to Helvedon to register with the local authorities. He takes his place in a queue of men largely silent, though a few brazen lads mouth off, eager to get stuck in. The fear lurking behind their bravado is painful to see.

He is nervous when his turn comes. Asked for his name, he hesitates, earning himself a look from the clerk. He contemplates giving a false one, but in the end he gives an honest account of himself. He has seen nothing in the papers for nearly three months and Iris Jennings' brother has not come to visit after all. He reasons he is here to register for active service – why hang him when he is willing to die fighting? The clerk inscribes his name in the ledger in cramped black ink.

He knows he will not be called up straight away. He is beyond the first age bracket – the youngsters have been chosen to lead the charge – and then there is his occupation:

farm labourer. The clerk pulls a face, and Jack can't be sure that it isn't disappointment.

The banns are read again the following week. This time Gordon is absent – he has already departed for officer training. Jack is standing beside Gwen when they overhear Lord Allingham informing the vicar. Colour flees her cheeks as she looks away.

At home, on the farm, the atmosphere has become charged. Jim is withdrawn and sullen. The cheeriness that characterised him has vanished. He barely speaks, except to bark orders – even Gwen suffers his silence. They labour side by side, only speaking when the task necessitates – *bring the horse round, loosen that chain, spread the seed thinner.* Jack is no longer invited into the sitting room each night. Instead he retreats to the tack room, sometimes with Kip for company. He misses the comfort, the enveloping warmth, of family life but he has found a task to occupy him.

He has made some space beyond his bed and fashioned himself a workbench from bits and bobs gleaned from the sheds. He unravels his leather roll of tools and sets to work on wood pilfered from the store, sawing and planing, carving and nailing. Every so often he will stretch out the muscles bunched in his back, stroke the dog's head and step out into the yard to take in the evening air. The nights are drawing in and temperatures have dropped. He looks up at Gwen's blacked-out window and yearns for her company.

Conscious his time with her is ebbing away, he gladly steps in when Jim leaves her with the evening chores. He downs tools on seeing her pass by his window and joins her to shoo the hens into their coop.

'Have you noticed? He can't even look at me anymore,' Gwen says, as Jack carries the last bantam inside. 'My own father. He hates me.'

He shuts the door and lifts the bar into place. 'Ah lass, he doesn't hate you.'

'He's disappointed in me. I've disappointed him.' She crosses her arms against a stiffening wind. 'He took great satisfaction in reminding me earlier that he had warned me to stay away from Gordon. If I had just done as he said . . .'

'No use crying over spilt milk. What's done is done.'

'And now you're paying the price. I'm ruining your life.'

'Gwen.' He lays his hand on her arm. 'You could never ruin my life.'

'I don't understand why you're helping me at all. What do you stand to gain?'

His hand drops. He longs for the courage to speak the truth, but he knows his confession would be pointless and futile. So instead he summons a half-truth. 'Maybe it's just my way of making amends for Jenny. I couldn't help her, but I can help you.'

'This war . . .' she shakes her head, 'it doesn't even feel like we are at war.'

'Aye, it's strange, isn't it? Nothing's changed. No bombers over the south coast . . . no invasion ships.'

'What if it stays like this? What if they sort things out and there isn't an actual conflict? What if it's all resolved through diplomacy? If that happens, Jack, we'll be married in the eyes of the law and you won't need to enlist . . .'

'You're worried you'll be stuck with me. God forbid . . .'

'I didn't mean it like that . . .'

'Aye you did, lass.' He does his best to conjure a smile. 'And you've every right to think that. For what it's worth, I think Hitler is just biding his time. He'll have us in his sights in due course. I will be off to fight, lass. Look, I know you're worried, but I meant what I said – I have no hold on you, that's not why I'm doing this. I just want to help. Once I leave here – and I will leave, war or no war – I'll not come back.'

'I feel so awful for—'

'Not wanting me?'

'You're so very nice.'

'Aye, but that's not enough, is it? Despite all he's done, your heart belongs to another.'

'But it's not as if you love me.'

'Would it make any difference to you if I did?'

He holds his breath, waiting for her reply. Seeing her flicker of surprise morph into wariness, he regrets voicing his question. There is nothing to be gained from examining their feelings, or from exposing the open wound of his love.

'I'd best get back inside,' she says at last. From the gloom beyond the chicken coop, one of the Clydesdales whickers.

'Aye, it's getting late.'

She pauses at the paddock gate as if intending to say something more, but in the end she simply says, 'Goodnight, Jack' and returning the farewell he watches her go, taking his heart with her.

In the middle of the month, Jim caves to pressure from the WarAg and decides to sell his sheep. On the morning of the Helvedon livestock market, they corral the flock in the yard. The animals anxiously bunch together, their plaintive bleats deafening. Gwen has suffered another bout of morning sickness and Jim has told her in no uncertain terms to remain behind. She stands on the top step overlooking the fretful creatures, her arms wrapped around her.

Ted arrives to help and Jim, crook in hand, works his way through the shuffling mass to greet him. Jack takes the opportunity to edge his way to Gwen.

'There's always been sheep on this farm,' she says as he reaches her. 'I remember my mum having the cade lambs by the range in the kitchen. I used to help feed them as soon as I was able to hold a bottle.' She shakes her head. 'This doesn't seem right.'

'You can raise sheep on hill farms that are no good for crops, but this land can be cultivated,' Jack says, leaning on the crook he has been given as he recalls Jim's last meeting with the WarAg rep.

'And they'll take the farm if Dad refuses. So, I suppose this is the lesser of two evils.'

'How are you feeling, now? Are you well enough to come with us?' He does not relish the idea of being alone with Jim and Ted all day. The latter has been distinctly cold with Jack ever since he learnt of their engagement. Jim had promised Gwen he would not tell anyone the true circumstances of their hasty betrothal, but Jack wonders whether he has confided in his friend and neighbour after all.

'You heard Dad. I'm staying here. Anyway, Muriel needs a hand grading the eggs.'

He nods, hoping his disappointment doesn't show. Jim raises his crook to catch Jack's attention.

'We're off,' he shouts.

Jack straightens up, lifting his own crook in acknowledgement.

Ted swings open the gate and with a whistle from Jim, Kip, head low, pressures the sheep from the yard.

The flock trot gamely down the narrow lane, filling its breadth. Jim works his way to the front, while Ted falls in with Jack at the back.

The pace is slow, but the lane is thankfully quiet. A couple on bicycles pull into a gateway and call out 'Good morning!', laughing as they wait for the sheep to pass, before remounting and pedalling on. A car coming up behind them is less patient. The driver revs his engine and, when they show no sign of facilitating his passage, he blares his horn.

Ted glares at him and with an ill-tempered gesture indicates there is nowhere for them to move the sheep aside.

The driver leans out through his rolled-down window. 'Can't you hurry the buggers up?'

'Bloody idiot,' Ted mutters under his breath.

When they reach a spot where the road widens, they spread the flock thinly along its edge, working Kip to keep the sheep tight to the verge, leaving just enough space for the car to squeeze past. Fumes billow from its exhaust as it speeds away.

They release the sheep back across the road and Ted and Jack fall in step once again.

'I never offered you my congratulations.' The farmer's belated good wishes appear begrudgingly bestowed. Unsure how to respond, Jack avoids commenting at all by catching the rump of a straying sheep with the tip of his crook and chivvying it on. 'You're a lucky man, Gwen's a peach.'

'Yes, she is. Yes, I am.'

'You must have set your sights on her from the minute you arrived.' Jack regards him sharply. There is bitterness in Ted's voice, and regret. 'Well, you'd better be good to her, because if you're not . . .'

'What?'

Ted stops him with a hand on his arm. He steps in close. 'Just know this: if you ever hurt her, so help me God, I'll kill you.'

They catch the bus home in order to be back in time for milking. They look odd, the three of them, armed with crooks, folded into bus seats. Jim argued with the driver to get Kip on board. The dog lies on the vibrating floor by Jack's feet. Some wit calls out from the front of the bus, asking if Little Bo Peep has lost her sheep.

Ted gets off first. He says goodbye to Jim but only nods at Jack. He starts to make his way down the length of the bus, swaying as it jounces over potholes, holding onto the backs of seats to steady himself. The doors crank open and he climbs down at the crossroads leading to his farm. He holds a hand up to Jim as the bus pulls away.

The driver lets them off just outside their gate, at Jim's request. Kip races into the yard.

'Come in for a cuppa and then we'll go for the cattle,' Jim says, his manner still brusque.

They find the kitchen deserted. Jim calls out. A faint response is heard from the front of the house.

Muttering, Jim heads into the hall and Jack follows. The dining-room door at the far side of the stairs is open. Muriel is talking to Gwen – *'Turn my way, stand still a minute, all right, now turn that way . . .'*

Jim stops dead in the doorway. The Singer sewing machine

is set up on the dining table. Gwen is standing on the footstool Muriel uses to reach the top shelves in the pantry.

She is wearing a wedding dress.

She gasps when her father appears, then pulls herself taller, pushing back her shoulders. Her hopeful expression breaks Jack's heart. She looks beautiful.

'What are you doing?'

Jim's whisper of words is a warning. Gwen stutters, but Muriel gathers herself quickly.

'The wedding is only a week away. I need to do the alterations.'

'You'll not touch that dress.'

'But, Jim, the waist needs to come out a bit and I need to take a good inch off the hem or she'll be tripping up the aisle . . .'

'You'll not touch that dress – do you hear me!' They jerk at the ferocity of his roar. Muriel blanches. 'You get that dress off, right now. You've no right, no right at all to wear it!'

'But this is Mum's dress. She would have wanted me to wear it to my own wedding, Dad. I want to wear it – I want to have her there . . .'

'I said, get that dress off!' For a big man, Jim moves quickly. Darting forward he grabs Gwen's arm and yanks her down from the stool. She cries out in shock. 'It's an insult to see you in that dress, do you hear me? Your mother wore white that day for a reason! I'll not have you make a mockery of all it means – of all we had. I'll not let you sully your mother's memory with your whoring.'

'For God's sake, Jim!' Muriel cries.

Gwen struggles against her father's iron grip, sobbing as the words he hurls at her land like blows – *whore, slut, tart.*

'Jesus, Jim, stop!' Jack pulls him round by the shoulder and places himself between Gwen and her father. He grasps the man's wrist in a tight manacle and prises his fingers from Gwen's arm, left red and raw from his unrelenting grip. Released, Gwen falls back.

'Don't you interfere, this has nothing to do with you, lad!' Jim shouts, spittle flying from purple lips that look fit to burst.

'It has everything to do with me.'

'I don't understand you. Why are you even helping her? Are you one of those nancy boy types? Is this just a way to hide your own perversions, taking on my tart of a daughter and her bastard child?'

'Don't you speak about her like that.'

'She's my daughter and I'll speak about her any way I bloody well please and not you nor anyone else will stop me! Get out of that bloody dress, you whore!' he bellows like a wounded bull. 'Get out of it now or so help me God I'll rip it from your body!'

He throws himself forward, his hand raised above his shoulder. Gwen screams and cowers into Muriel's arms, as the housekeeper prepares to shield her – with her own body if needs be. But Jack is already there. He grabs Jim's raised arm. The farmer is strong and sturdy, but Jack is tall and tough and more than his match.

'Jesus, Jim, get a hold of yourself, man, before you do something you'll regret. And believe me, regret it you will, for the rest of your life, because neither of you will ever forget, or ever move past it.' The farmer continues to struggle. 'I'll not let you lay a finger on her, Jim.'

With a broken cry, Jim stumbles back, snatching himself from Jack's grasp. He lands heavily against the drinks table tucked into the corner. One of the glasses set out upon the silver tray topples and falls. The fine crystal explodes as it hits the floorboards. Splinters of glass skitter across the polished wood.

Jim's anger broils and yet his face crumples as he sees Gwen sobbing in her mother's wedding dress. Fighting his conflicting emotions, he draws himself up.

'You'll not wear that dress, Gwen, not over my dead body. Ours was an honest love, a true marriage of hearts – I will not have you desecrate that with this charade the two of you have concocted.' He swings back as he reaches the door. 'I'll not have you make a show of yourself. This,' he waves vaguely between her and Jack, 'it's all face-saving nonsense.'

He rubs his hand across his mouth as he tries to regain control of his temper, but his anger continues to resonate in his voice. 'Now I'm not saying I'm not grateful to you, Jack, but I do wonder what your motivations really are. And Gwen, there are dresses already in your wardrobe, girl, that'll have to do and flowers to be had in the garden. That might make you look a second-rate bride, but in my eyes, in God's eyes, and in your mother's eyes, a second-rate bride is all you are, and all you have the right to be. Now there's a herd to milk. You get out of that dress and you come and do your bit. You need to give me a reason why I'm still letting you sleep under my roof. You'll earn your way – do you hear me?'

He leaves in a maelstrom. Gwen buckles to the floor, inconsolable, and all Jack can do is watch, his heart breaking, helpless to offer solace.

CHAPTER THIRTY-SIX

Gwen

August 1945

Ignoring his protests, Gwen insists Tom stays in with Muriel all day. She can barely bring herself to speak to Nora, she is so angry. Having picked up on the resentment crackling between the two girls, Muriel corners her after breakfast and demands an explanation. She listens stony-faced as Gwen tells her of Nora's crime, and of the message behind the brick. Though she passes no comment, her knuckles blanch around the tea towel screwed in her hands, and when she returns her attentions to Tom, her voice is artificially bright. Gwen leaves to carry out the day's labours, knowing her son is safe from all harm.

There is little conversation to be had during the evening meal. The silence is punctured by cutlery scraping on the stoneware plates. Gwen picks listlessly at her food. Nora is still smarting from her earlier reprimand and Tom is tetchy from having been cooped up all day.

'Let's go to the pictures,' she says suddenly. 'Tom? What do you say? A special treat. Nora, wouldn't you like to come? Muriel, you'll join us, won't you?' And in a fit of spontaneity, she abandons her meal and hurries to retrieve the evening paper from the letterbox. She leafs through its pages as she walks back from the hall, eager now to be away for the evening, to not be sitting in the house, watching the hands of the clock move ever closer to an appointment she has no intention of keeping.

She spreads the paper on the table and runs her finger down the local listings.

'Here we are, a Charles Hawtrey comedy – wouldn't that be fun, Tom? We can catch the bus into town and back. What do you say, shall we go?' Even to her ears, she sounds desperate.

'Yes, yes, all right, a trip to the pictures would be very nice,' Muriel admits.

'Nora?' She does not particularly want the girl's company, but she is afraid that if she fails to turn up to Allingham's rendezvous he might come to the house and she does not want anyone to be in if he does.

Nora purses her lips and for a horrible moment Gwen fears she is going to decline the invitation, but the Land Girl has never been one to sulk, and to Gwen's relief she now shrugs her shoulders with a wry smile. 'Go on then, why not?'

Reassured that Gordon Allingham will now be thwarted should he come to call, Gwen sinks back into her chair and picks up her cutlery. She finds her appetite fully restored.

It is almost dark when they return. They catch the last bus home and climb down when it stops in the village. They walk through the deserted streets together, Tom riding on Gwen's back. They pause at Muriel's picket gate and watch her safely into her cottage before carrying on their way. They talk of the film and the joyous return of streetlights and gaiety, and they talk of the work that must be done in the morning. But there is no mention of the charming man on the motorbike.

Gwen puts Tom to bed as Nora boils milk for cocoa and then, without bothering to change, assumes the task of shutting up the farm for the night.

The tang of ammonia hits the back of her throat as soon as she opens the coop door. She delivers the hens to the straw-strewn shelves and soon they are chirruping with contentment as their thin eyelids beginning to droop. She fills their hoppers with grain and water, then draws the door shut behind her. A vixen screams from the copse behind the farm as she lifts the bar into place.

The night is still as she walks from the paddock, the leftover grain shushing over the bottom of her pail. She closes the gate and crosses the rough ground behind the buildings, before plunging into the shadowed passage between the stable block and the milking parlour.

'You missed our meeting.'

She lets out a throttled cry as Gordon Allingham emerges from the darkness. He draws towards her, moonlight throwing his face into relief, revealing features that once quickened her heart with joy, but which now instil sheer terror. Her fingers tighten around the pail's wooden handle.

'What do you want?'

'I want to talk to you. About Tom.'

Bile rises from her gullet as his voice caresses the name of her son.

'There's nothing to talk about.' She attempts to pass him, but he sidesteps to block her.

'We both know that's not true.'

'I know no such thing. You're not welcome here, Gordon.'

'Well, I've no intention of leaving. Not until I've said what I've come to say.'

'And what's that?' Gwen's temper bites. 'What could you possibly have to say to me after all these years?'

'I want my son.'

She thrusts out her chin, her heart hammering against her chest. 'I can't help you there.' Her bravado is like gossamer. 'I don't know what delusion you're labouring under, but if you think Tom is your son you are wrong.'

'You can tell yourself that as much as you like, but we both know it's not true.' He moves closer. 'Tom *is* my son. You seem to forget you told me you were carrying my child . . . and I have your letters to prove it.'

Gwen's blood runs cold. *Christ, the letters!*

'They prove nothing,' she says, buying for time.

'Really?' He chuckles; the sound is chilling. 'So, who are you claiming Tom's father to be?'

'My husband is Tom's father.'

'Is that so? That's not what you wrote.'

Gwen had almost forgotten about the existence of her desperate missives, posted in passion. It had never crossed her mind that Gordon might have kept them, but if he has, they now put Tom in more danger than she could ever have imagined. She needs to mitigate their significance – by any means.

'The letters?' Her laugh is hollow. 'You didn't believe them, did you? Oh dear, it was rather conniving of me but . . .' She rejoices as his arrogant certainty gives way to ill-concealed confusion. She has wrong-footed him. She presses her advantage, no longer caring what he or anyone else thinks of her. She cares only for her son. 'You see, Gordon, I was in a bit of a predicament. I had been . . . how do I put it . . . playing the field. You were the first to capture my heart but Jack Ellison . . . well, he proved persistent. He was so flattering and attentive and we were thrown together hour after hour, day after day and I found myself unable to resist . . . and unable to choose between you. And then I realised, perhaps I didn't have to.'

'You're lying.'

'I'm rather ashamed to say it, but I'm not. I suppose all the attention quite turned my head. But then I realised I was pregnant, and I knew from the timings . . . well, let's just say I knew it couldn't be yours. But I liked you Gordon and, even more, I liked the life you could give me. But then of course you announced your engagement and I realised just as I had been having my fun with you, so you had been having your fun with me. But I didn't want to abandon the game straight away – I thought I'd try one last throw of the dice. So, I wrote those letters, to see if I could trick you into marrying me after all. But when it became clear you had no intention of standing by me or the child I was trying to palm off as yours, I had no choice but to ask Jack to do the right thing.'

'Do you honestly expect me to believe that cock-and-bull story?'

'It's the truth. I'm not proud of what I did, what I've done, but it's the truth. Jack Ellison is Tom's father, not you, and those letters are just a pack of lies.'

'I don't believe you.'

'Why? Because you can't believe that I slept with another man while I was sleeping with you? What's good for the goose is good for the gander, isn't that what they say? Weren't you making love to your fiancée at the same time you were making love to me? Two can play at that game, Gordon, and I certainly did. So, rest assured, Tom is nothing to do with you and never was. Now get the hell off my farm. You have no right to be here.'

She shoulders past him, forcing herself to take confident strides, willing her legs to hold though she is as unsteady as a newborn foal. She gets as far as the corner of the stable block before Gordon yanks her round.

'You're lying!' His spittle lands on the soft skin beneath her eye. 'That boy is mine – good God, he's the spitting image of me at his age – you can't tell me that's a coincidence. I will have him. He is my son, my heir, and I won't let you take him from me.'

'He's mine.'

'He's mine.' He snaps her arm down. She clenches her teeth to staunch a cry of pain. 'Now, we can sort this out between ourselves like two civilised people and do what's best for Tom, or I warn you now, I will take legal action to secure his custody.'

'You can't do that.'

'Oh yes, I can. And who do you think is going to win?' He relinquishes his hold. 'I've had an interesting little chat with your Land Girl. This husband of yours . . . it seems very strange that he never writes; that he shows no sign of coming home, and yet there's no sign of him being dead either. An arrangement that seems to suit you very well. She told me in all the time she's been here she's only seen you write or receive a handful of letters from him. That all seems very peculiar to me. The letters from my wife were like a lifeline when I was serving and I know she lived to hear from me.'

'Jack's never been one for writing . . .'

'No leave, no letters – one begins to wonder whether he was

ever really a husband at all. He certainly wasn't a father. It makes me think the whole marriage might be nothing more than a façade of respectability. Is that what it was, Gwen? It's all very convenient, isn't it? You get married, he disappears off to war and Tom is born not quite the right side of the blanket. How much did your father pay him?'

'Nothing. He paid him nothing! How dare you stand there and speak to me like this? Jack cared for me . . . and he was decent enough to do the right thing, even though he knew I could never love him the way he loved me!' As the words fall unconsciously from her lips, she realises their veracity. Their inherent truth renders her defiant. 'Whether you like it or not, Tom is Jack's son, not yours. You have no right to him, no right at all. Do you understand me? Now get off my farm and don't you ever come anywhere near me or my child again, because if you do . . . I will not be held responsible for my actions.'

'This isn't over, Gwen. I warn you now, I know you're lying. I know that boy is mine, and I will go to the highest court in the land if I need to.'

'Just you try,' she calls back over her shoulder. 'Just you bloody try!'

CHAPTER THIRTY-SEVEN

Jack

September 1939

Jack rises early on the morning of the wedding. The rippled clouds have been stained red by the river of molten lava flowing across the horizon, and the old adage of shepherds and their skies springs unwelcome to his mind. He hopes the scarlet-streaked heavens are not an augur for all that is to come.

The milking must go ahead as usual, but the rest of the day's labours are to be set aside. The wedding will not be a grand affair. Gwen wrote out invitations in her best hand, sending them only to a few of her closest family friends. She is not having a bridesmaid, nor a maid of honour, though Jim has, for the sake of appearances, agreed to give her away. There was a moment, just after she had garnered the courage to ask him, her voice small and pleading, when it seemed he might refuse. Muriel had taken him into the kitchen and shut the door, leaving Gwen and Jack in the sitting room, Gwen gnawing on her fingernails as they watched the minute hand on the mantel clock move slowly round. When Jim returned, he had reluctantly agreed to walk her up the aisle. He grunted and rustled open his paper when she thanked him.

Jim is already waiting when Jack emerges from the stable block.

'She's not coming.'

The gruff announcement knocks Jack for six. Thoughts racing, he stares at the ground to hide his dismay that Gwen has reneged on their arrangement.

'It's just us milking, Gwen needs to get ready,' Jim calls back over his shoulder as he strides towards the gate.

'Right.' Jack's relief is profound. Feeling the blood return to his cheeks, he clears his throat and follows on.

Later, when they are milking, he stops by the stall where Jim is working.

'What is it?' the farmer asks without looking up, his hands unfaltering in their task.

'I need to pick something up in Helvedon this morning, before . . .' He is too shy to say the word. 'I was wondering whether you might lend me the car?'

The farmer sits back and looks directly at him. 'You're not doing a runner?'

'No, no,' Jack is quick to reassure him. 'Just need to pick something up, like. I'll be back in good time, if you don't mind me heading out when we're done here.'

The farmer releases a burdened sigh. 'If you must. This day is wasted already. You swear you're coming back?'

'I'll be back,' Jack promises. This time.

His errand has taken too long. There was a broken-down wagon on the outskirts of Helvedon, and he wasn't familiar enough with the back lanes to find an alternative route. It ended up with him snatching the toolbox from the car boot and fixing the broken wheel shaft himself. By the time the horse dragged the cart clear of the lane, he knew time was against him – but he couldn't turn back. He raced through the town's streets, earning more than a few curses, but he managed to do what he needed. He had sped all the way home.

He parks the car in the yard without care and throws open the door, hurrying around the warm bonnet to the passenger's side. With great care he lifts the box from the front seat.

He bounds up the steps to the kitchen door and reaches for the handle but stops himself. He can't simply walk in, not this morning of all mornings. So, he raps his knuckles against the wood and waits, attempting to steady his frantic breathing. When his knock goes unanswered he peers through the kitchen window, but the room is deserted and dressed in gloom. He looks at his watch then hurries through the garden, reasoning that if they are upstairs getting ready, he has more chance of being heard at the front door. He is conscious of precious minutes ticking by. Balancing the box on his upturned arm, he lifts the brass knocker and brings it soundly to bear.

He waits. Sweat clings to his temples. He has yet to change – he is still dressed in his work shirt and rough trousers. He needs a shave.

Bolts grate behind the door.

'Jack, what the devil?' Jim looks uncomfortable in his best suit, the jacket a tad too tight on the shoulders.

'I just . . .'

'You're not even dressed. Good God, you have, haven't you? You've changed your mind.'

'No!' Jack pushes the box into his hands.

Jim frowns. 'What's this?'

'For Gwen.'

'Who is it, Dad?' Gwen's voice drifts down from the landing. Jim half-turns and Jack looks up. She is standing at the top of the stairs dressed in a blue suit he hasn't seen before, presumably one that has been languishing in her wardrobe. Her hair has been rolled and the sides clipped back from her face. He catches his breath, and though he knows he should avert his eyes, he is unable to do so. Seeing him, she looks fearful. 'What's going on?'

'Get away, Gwen, a bride shouldn't be seen before . . .' Jim starts, but Gwen ignores him and pads down the stairs, her stockinged feet whispering with the carpet. 'It's bad luck . . .' Jim protests feebly, as she elbows him aside.

'It's a bit late for that.' She looks at Jack, then her attention moves to the shallow box her father is holding.

She pushes the lid back on its cardboard hinge. She gasps.

Nestled on the bed of tissue paper is a bridal bouquet.

White roses. Threaded with trailing ivy.

Friendship, fidelity and love.

There are few people in the church. Muriel is already seated in the front pew and nods at Jack with something akin to gratitude as he walks up, his steps echoing on the worn stone flags. He clasps his hands before him, his heart pounding. He has no best man. The ring, unboxed, weighs heavy in his jacket pocket. He slips his hand inside to reassure himself, careful to leave it pushed into the corner fold. He clasps his hands before him once again.

The silence is stifling. They have only paid for the organist to play the wedding march, but perhaps out of sympathy – or plain discomfort – the organ wheezes into life and an intricate weave of notes fills the awkward emptiness. Jack glances behind him as footsteps announce the arrival of more guests. Gwen's best friend Lucy slides into the pew behind Muriel accompanied, Jack presumes, by her parents. She looks at him with blatant curiosity and he wonders if Gwen has confided in her. A vague smile passes across her face as she looks away. Jack is painfully aware there is no one to fill the rows behind him.

Muriel swivels in her seat, then levers herself up and sidesteps from the pew. The click of her heels bounces off the arched ceiling above them and Jack cannot resist his curiosity to see what she is up to. Ted has slipped into the back row. Muriel grips the polished pew in front of him as she leans down to speak, and though Jack cannot hear what she is saying, it is clear Ted is being chastised. He rises and demurely follows her forward, running the rim of his trilby through his fingers. Muriel edges her way back into the front pew and Ted sits down beside her. He does not once look at Jack.

The organist comes to an abrupt halt. A side door bangs and the vicar glides across the tiles of the transept, his gowns rustling faintly as he takes his position before Jack. He smiles as he opens the bible in his hands. The organist hammers out the opening chords of Mendelssohn's wedding march and on cue those seated stand. Jack's heart begins to beat faster; his palms are clammy. Unsure whether to look round, he instead focuses on the majestic stained-glass window towering before him.

Jim walks his daughter up the aisle with more speed than is perhaps customary, as if eager to get her off his hands. He reaches the front too soon and is forced to wait while the organist catches up. Jack is alert to Gwen's presence. His whole body seems to tingle and finally he permits his eyes to skim across his bride's face. Sensing his scrutiny, she meets his gaze. Her nervous smile fails to brighten her features.

The organist concludes with a triumphant chord and the vicar begins to speak.

Jack takes a deep breath and prepares to play his part.

Muriel has laid on a simple buffet of sandwiches and cake at the farm, for the vicar and the handful of guests. The atmosphere is strained, the celebration muted. Perhaps there is an underlying suspicion the wedding is a sham, or perhaps it is the talk of war, discussed discreetly in corners by those not wishing to bring doom and gloom to a supposedly happy day.

Jack catches Gwen's eye across the room and offers her a smile. He is bolstered by her response: the shy lowering of her eyes, the hint of colour in her cheeks before her gaze lifts to his once more.

When the first of the guests leave, Jim takes him aside for a quiet word. 'I've booked you a room at a hotel in Helvedon. People would have talked otherwise. I don't know how you'll manage it.' He is unable to hide his embarrassment.

'We'll manage,' Jack says. He catches sight of Gwen in the far corner talking to her friend, Lucy. She still carries her bouquet and, as Lucy appears to comment, she lifts it to savour its scent. Jack fights to maintain his impassive expression.

Later, when all of the guests have finally departed, they travel by bus to Helvedon, their things packed into the small suitcase at Jack's feet. It had felt peculiar, to place his clothes upon Gwen's – strangely intimate.

The hotel is a red brick establishment in the centre of the high street, an old coaching inn, Jack guesses. The names Mr and Mrs Ellison lodge in his throat as he stands at the reception desk, and the woman behind it regards them suspiciously until Gwen pipes up that they are newlyweds and flashes her thin gold band. The woman's manner brightens at once. She laughs about a day of change and regales them with stories of her own wedding day thirty years previously, as she leads them up the rickety staircase to their room, reflecting on how quickly the time has passed.

She unlocks their door and walks in, checking the top of the dressing table for dust as she reels off the arrangements for dinner and breakfast. She reminds them to ensure the curtains are drawn in good time for the blackout and warns them each room will be checked before sunset. She leaves them be with an indiscreet wink.

Jack sets down the case. Gwen drifts towards the window, pushing aside the sheer curtain to look out onto the pretty high street of black-and-white Tudor buildings crammed amongst Georgian brick and Victorian render.

Jack clears his throat. 'Shall we go for a walk by the river?'

Gwen spins around. 'Yes, please.' Her gratitude is tangible.

They walk down shop-lined streets, then wind their way through the town until they reach the river, the evening sunlight spangling its surface. They amble beside it, past the locks and into the meadows, watching swimming coots leave sparkling chevrons in their wake. They turn back as the draining light swathes the landscape in drab grey. By the time they reach the town, the blackout is in force. The trees stand inky black against the sky and the river is reduced to a lead ribbon. Streetlights stand idle, and the few cars that rumble down the narrow streets have shades fitted to their headlamps. Jack catches Gwen's arm as she trips on the edge of the pavement. They take a wrong turn and end up down a side street of timbered properties, the white plaster glowing in the dim light.

'This way,' Jack says at last, recognising a shop front, and instinctively he reaches for Gwen's hand. She makes no attempt to resist.

They eventually find their way back to the hotel, laughing with relief that their little adventure is over. The landlady apologises that the kitchen has closed. She offers to make sandwiches, but neither of them has any appetite and so they politely decline.

'Well, I'll leave you to head for bed then,' she says, vanishing out the back, having unknowingly whipped the wind from their sails.

They climb the stairs side by side. They hesitate at the top, both struggling to remember the way back to their room through the jumble of crooked corridors, laughing as they each suggest opposite directions. The moment of levity is welcome relief to the building tension that neither wishes to acknowledge.

At last, they find their door. Jack is clumsy fitting the key into the lock. The blackout curtains have been drawn on their behalf and the features of the unfamiliar room are barely discernible. All levity is lost.

He leaves the door open allowing the dull glow from the landing light to guide Gwen safely to the bedside lamp. When she shunts the bayonet across, Jack closes the door.

'I'll take the floor.'

'Are you sure?'

'Yes. I'll go for a walk, let you get sorted, like. Fifteen minutes?'

'Ten is plenty.'

He heads back along the landing. Unsure where to go, he sits down on the top step of the stairs and waits.

The landlady appears at the bottom. She huffs for breath as she hauls her great weight upwards, a sympathetic smile plumping her cheeks.

'Everything all right, dear?'

'Yes, she's just . . .' But words fail him.

'Don't you worry about a thing, dear,' she says, patting him on the shoulder as she passes. 'It's a wonderful thing. A wonderful thing.'

He gives Gwen fifteen minutes, just to be sure. He knocks lightly and hears her hushed call.

The lamp glows. She is tucked in bed, the coverlet hiked high to her chin, the empty space beside her a chasm that he cannot cross, though in his dreams he does. A pillow and two folded blankets lie on the floor on top of the eiderdown.

'I'll turn out the light, so you can . . .' She plunges them into darkness. The blackout curtains prevent even a trim of moonlight. He quickly undresses down to his underwear, then unfolds the bedding by touch alone. He lies upon on the eiderdown. Pulling the blankets over him he tries to get comfortable, but they ruck up each time he moves, exposing his toes to the chilly air. Giving up, he rests his head on the pillow and exhales.

He closes his eyes. He listens to the glug of water in the pipes beneath him; to the gentle patter of rain as it starts to fall against the windowpanes; to Gwen's steady breaths. In. Out.

From the bed, a rustle of movement.

'Are you terribly uncomfortable?'

'It's not so bad – and I'll have to get used to worse. This'll seem like luxury where I'm going.'

The bedstead creaks as she lies back. 'When will you join up?'

'As soon as we're back.'

'Tomorrow?'

'The day after maybe.'

They absorb the silence.

'What do you want from me, Jack?'

He stares at the darkness pooling above him.

'Nothing, Gwen.'

'Then why are you doing all this for me?'

'A letter maybe,' he says, avoiding her question. 'And a picture of you and the bairn when it's born.' He stops to consider his words. 'I have no one, Gwen. A letter from a friend now and then would be a welcome relief from what is to come – if you could bear to write to me, that is.' He holds his breath, awaiting her response.

'I can bear that, Jack.'

He stares into the dark haze, then closes his eyes. And sleeps.

CHAPTER THIRTY-EIGHT

Gwen

September 1945

Her encounter with Gordon leaves Gwen unnerved and his threats frighten her. She is painfully aware that the law has a tendency to favour men – especially those with wealth and social standing. She curses herself for her stupidity, for ever having set her cap at Gordon Allingham, for thinking her father was wrong, when – in truth – her father had never been wrong about anything in his life – a realisation she has come to far too late.

She longs to lock Tom away in the house. She will do anything to keep him safe. She is terrified of what measures Gordon might take, what extremes he might be capable of to achieve his ends. It is all she can do to stop herself from packing a case of their things and fleeing.

Fractured sleep leaves her sombre and quiet, though she dismisses Muriel's concern and Nora's genial enquiries. Tom begs to come with them to the fields, and she is about to dismiss his request when she pauses, contemplating that it might be better if he is with her, if only for her own peace of mind. So, to Muriel's surprise, she agrees, scooping the boy up, hugging him close, smothering his neck with kisses until he is squirming in her arms, giggling, demanding to be put down.

They are going muck-spreading. Tom comes with her to bring Bobby in from the paddock, running unevenly over the tussocks, whooping with excitement as he goes. Ted has borrowed the tractor to plough his thirty-acre field, but Gwen is glad of the opportunity to put her remaining Clydesdale to work. She knows, with great sadness, that these heavy horses will soon be a thing of the past. She intends to make the most of him while she still can.

Tom helps brush the dried mud from Bobby's bay coat, standing on an upturned bucket so he can reach the withers. He talks incessantly, barely pausing for breath, rolling comments directed to his mother into those meant for the horse.

Once Bobby stands between the shafts of the manure-laden cart, they are ready to go. Gwen climbs onto the bench seat at the front of the wagon and picks up the flat leather reins. Nora grabs Tom and pretends to throw him into the back with the stinking pile of muck, and he screams in mock terror. He scrambles to Gwen for protection and she relishes the warm press of him. They jerk forward as Bobby takes off, plodding from the yard, Kip trotting alongside.

Nora jumps down to open the field gate. There is a harsh wind, a reminder that September is well under way. It brings the first of the copper beech leaves from the branches; they drift lazily to pepper the ground. Gwen slaps the reins and drives Bobby through the gate to the top of the field. She jumps onto the rain-softened soil and then reaches up for Tom. Before she can say a word, he is off running, calling for Kip. She watches him go, absently freeing a strand of hair from her lip, her chest aching with love for the blond-haired boy that is hers and hers alone. She is still savouring the sight of him as Nora hands her a fork from the back of the wagon.

'Everything all right, Gwen?'

Gwen finally looks away. 'Yes.'

She thrusts the fork's broad prongs into the straw-laced muck piled above her, then steps back to shake its load loose over the furrows at her feet.

By mid-morning, they have covered half the field and the air is pungent. Tom entertains himself by collecting blackberries from the hedgerow. Periodically, he runs back to Gwen to reveal his stained tongue, his chin dribbling with juice. When he tires of blackberries, he moves onto the hazelnut bush growing halfway down the back hedge. He stuffs his pockets with the husk-wrapped shells missed by the squirrels, though Gwen warns him they are unlikely to ripen.

'Hello, hello, who's this?' Nora wipes her nose with the back of her hand. The prongs of her fork sink into the ground as she leans her weight upon it, her attention taken by something at the bottom gate.

'What?' Gwen scatters her forkful of manure, breaking up the clods of muck with a bash of its prongs. Squinting, she follows Nora's gaze. A maroon-coloured car has pulled up in the gateway. The driver's door opens and a woman stands out. She turns to regard the field over the roof, shielding her eyes with the flat of her hand, though the sun is far from dazzling. She pushes the door to and picks a delicate path around the front of the vehicle until she is standing in the open gateway. She holds up a gloved hand.

'I don't know who she is but she's going to regret it if she tries to walk up here in those shoes,' Nora mutters, wrenching her fork free.

The woman is waving now, eager to draw their attention, impatient for them to come. It seems she has no intention of tackling the muck-coated field.

'Shall I go?' Nora asks, when Gwen makes no attempt to respond.

'No . . . no, stay here.' Gwen's mouth is suddenly dry. 'Keep Tom with you, will you? I don't want him getting in the way.' She rests her fork against the side of the wagon as her eyes rake the hedgerow, searching for her son. She finds him balanced in the lower branches of the hazelnut bush, only a matter of feet off the ground. Deducing he is perfectly safe, she wipes her damp palms on her trousers and sets off down the field, her arms swinging purposefully by her sides. By the time she reaches the woman, she is breathing hard, but it is not exertion that has shortened her breath. It is fear.

'Hello, Mrs Ellison.'

Gwen is irked by her visitor's advantage. She is unsure how to address the beautifully presented woman before her – she is not versed in titles and decorum – but then she remembers how Gordon Allingham's wife is referred to in the village and she finally finds her voice.

'Lady Helen.'

The responding smile suggests her greeting is satisfactory.

'I thought I should come and see you. I know you had an encounter with my husband last night and I wanted to . . . apologise . . . He had no right to ambush you like that. Gordon is like a child sometimes. His petulance can make him a little bombastic.'

Gwen tries to hide her surprise, but her raised eyebrows give her away. 'Your apology is accepted. Now if you don't mind, I have work to do and, as far as I'm concerned, there is nothing further to say on the matter.'

'I would appreciate the opportunity to talk with you, Mrs Ellison.' Lady Helen's step forward is accompanied by a fleeting glance at her shoe, wary of what she might be tramping in, but she swiftly meets Gwen's eye again. She produces a detached smile. 'I believe a heart-to-heart between us would be far more conducive than Gordon's hot-headed threats.'

Gwen is stunned. She stares at the woman before her. 'Forgive me . . .' she stutters at last, '. . . you know? You know what he came to discuss with me?'

'Yes, yes, I know all about it.' She looks past Gwen. Shielding her eyes again, she allows her gaze to linger on Tom. He is dangling now from a branch of the hazelnut, shouting to Nora, but the distance and the building breeze prevents them from deciphering his words. 'Tom. He came to speak to you about his son.'

'Tom is not Gordon's son.' Gwen is relieved by the steel in her voice. 'How many times do I have to say it? He is *not* Gordon's son.'

Lady Helen blinks slowly. 'But your letters . . .'

'Look, I'm not proud of what I did. I wrote those letters hoping to trick him into marrying me.'

'Yes . . . he told me last night that was your story.'

'It's not a story, it's the truth. Now look here, there really is nothing left to be said. I'm sorry I misled him all those years ago – it was a shoddy thing to do, I admit, and I'm not proud of my behaviour that summer, but I was young and stupid . . .

ignorant . . .' She brushes her hair back from her face and catches a waft of manure. She realises she must stink. 'Anyway, he quite rightly ignored my letters then and he should ignore them now. I don't know why he should suddenly care—'

'Because he can't have any more children.'

Lady Helen observes Gwen's shock, her own dull eyes betraying her suppressed emotion. 'He didn't tell you that, did he? He sustained an injury while fighting in North Africa. No other lasting physical effects . . . just that one. So, you see, Tom takes on a new significance. He is the only natural son and heir that Gordon will ever be able to have.'

'He is not Gordon's son. He's my husband's.'

'Ah, yes . . . your husband. He was your father's farm labourer, wasn't he? You see, Mrs Ellison, I've read your letters – so powerful, so desperate . . . pitiful even. I don't believe you could have fabricated that passion . . . and I don't believe you could have whored yourself about when you had that depth of feeling for Gordon. This tall tale of stringing both him and your husband along at the same time . . . I don't buy it, Mrs Ellison, and neither does Gordon.' She sighs as if Gwen is some troublesome conundrum. She cocks her head to one side and pulls a sympathetic moue. 'What a predicament you found yourself in; how impossible everything must have seemed.' Her focus trails over Gwen's shoulder to Tom. 'Gordon is of the opinion that this "husband" was a convenience, paid for by your father.'

'That's not true.'

'Isn't it?' Her voice peaks with disbelief as she studies Gwen, the ghost of a smile on her lips. 'Then why hasn't he come home? We've made some enquiries, you see. Between us, Gordon and I have some useful family connections. Your husband, Mrs Ellison, isn't dead . . . he's not listed as missing, he is not a POW – in fact, your husband was demobbed several weeks ago, which begs the question – where has he got to? What husband . . . what father . . . doesn't leave the army and rush home to his family?' She tips her head to one side. 'Perhaps one who never really had a family in the first place.'

Her smile is chilling. Gwen turns towards the field struggling to absorb the information, unsure how to react to the news that Jack is not dead and that he is thankfully keeping his promise.

'So you see, Mrs Ellison . . . *Gwen* . . . why Gordon and I should have our suspicions . . . and why this news should convince us all the more about the veracity of those letters. I'm not here to defend Gordon's behaviour – then or last night. He treated you a little shabbily, shall we say – I fear he took advantage of your naïvety, as so many men do with young girls.' Lady Helen shrugs lightly. 'They are simply men, after all.' She sighs and contrives a look of apology. 'But I digress. Mrs Ellison, I have come to speak to you woman to woman. I think I understand you in a way Gordon never will and so I have come up with a proposition for you, one which I hope will prove . . . well, beneficial to us both.' She folds her gloved hands together and Gwen catches a drift of her fragrance, an artifice of floral scents too exotic for this land. 'I think we all know the truth of Tom's paternity, let us not pretend otherwise now.'

She draws closer to the hedge. Gwen studies the fine line of her jaw, the perfect cut of her clothes, her neat chignon, jealously aware of how shabby she must look in comparison, in her shit-stained trousers and mud-covered boots with their broken laces. She longs to tear Helen Allingham's eyes out so she can no longer watch Tom as he races happily across the field, Kip yapping at his side.

'I always think back on those Jewish women in Germany,' Lady Helen begins softly, 'the ones who put their children on ships and sent them over here before the war. The Kindertransport – I think that's what they called it. You know, I'm struck by what courage, what *love* . . . what selfless devotion . . . that took. Of course, at the time some thought they were being rather heartless and reckless, but now we realise how sensible they were to see which way the wind was blowing. Their selfless sacrifice saved their children's lives, provided them with a future that they would otherwise have been denied. I suppose one might also think of those mothers here who had their children evacuated from the cities. What greater demonstration of love is there, than what a mother is prepared to do in the best interests of her child?' She holds Gwen's gaze.

'Mrs Ellison, I am here today to appeal to you to do the same for your child. I am asking you to put his life and happiness – his future – before your own. I am asking you to give Tom up, to give him to Gordon and myself.'

'That's madness!' Fear flares Gwen's temper. 'How dare you? How dare you come here and say these things to me? He is my son – I carried him for nine months, I gave birth to him, I have cared for him single-handedly all these years. I love him more than life itself. I will never give up my child, never!'

'Mrs Ellison, put your emotion aside for a moment and think of your son – think of Tom and Tom's best interests. Look at what you can offer him, compared to the life we can give him. He will have the best education money can buy: Eton, Cambridge. He will be the friend of aristocrats and men of power. He will be heir to a mansion and five thousand acres in Northumberland, as well as other properties around the country, a townhouse in London . . . He will never want for anything. He will be a beloved son and a cherished heir. His future will be glorious.

'He won't be spreading manure across some muddy field in Berkshire. He won't spend his life getting up at the crack of dawn to milk cows and muck out stables. He will travel, he will see the world, his life will be rich with experiences and opportunities, the like of which you can't even begin to imagine. Would you really deny your son all of that? Is that what a loving mother would do? Wouldn't she sacrifice herself, to give the son she loves all of those things?'

Gwen is too stunned to respond. She stares at the woman before her. When it does come, her voice is faint with disbelief. 'How can you even expect me to give up my boy?'

Lady Helen draws closer in confidence. 'I understand it might prove difficult to explain away this turn of events to friends and neighbours and so on, but I have thought on that and I have a proposal that would, I think, work for everyone. Gordon's father is dying. He has mere weeks to live according to his doctors. When he is gone, Gordon will inherit the estate. He will sell up and we will move to my family's estate in Northumberland – the five thousand acres I mentioned – which I will inherit on my father's death and which ultimately Tom will inherit from me.

'I would suggest that we purchase your farm the moment Gordon's father passes. It can then be absorbed into the estate prior to any sale. With that money, you would be free to leave here and start a new life either somewhere else in the country, somewhere where no one knows you – knows of your past, or your son – or you might wish for a greater adventure, and start afresh in . . . America, perhaps. So many opportunities over there for someone with a little money and ambition. We would take Tom north and he would start his new life with us. So you see, no one around here need ever know about our arrangement.' She pauses, trying to decipher Gwen's expression.

'The fact is this, Mrs Ellison, you are still a young woman. You have your life ahead of you. This marriage of convenience I suspect you have arranged can no doubt be dissolved, one way or another – perhaps that was part of the plan all along? With what I have suggested, you would be a woman of independent means, able to marry for love this time and start a new family of your own. You are, in some ways, more at liberty than I am. You have the potential of bearing more children. I know now that I shall never have a child of my own. I know we could adopt, but one never really knows what one is getting . . . whereas with Tom, I do at least know that he is partly my husband. I know therefore that I could love Tom, love him as if he were my own. And at the end of the day, he *is* my husband's son, his rightful heir.'

'He is not your husband's son . . .'

'Oh, come now, Mrs Ellison, we both know that is not true, however many times you say it.'

'It is true.' Gwen fights to keep her voice even. 'He has no claim on him.'

'Mrs Ellison.' Lady Helen's mask of amiability is starting to slip. Gwen senses her patience is wearing thin. 'If you insist on playing this game, I must warn that you my husband is prepared to go to great legal lengths to secure custody of the boy. I can hardly think *that* will be an enjoyable experience for any of us.'

'He is not his son. Those letters prove nothing.'

'Perhaps, perhaps not. But there are other means of proof available to us.'

Gwen's blood runs cold. 'What means?'

A sly smile plays across Lady Helen's perfect features. 'As I say, Gordon is prepared to go to any length to get his son. You are a single mother . . .' she waves her hand over the field, 'working every hour God sends, no doubt. How much attention can you really spare a young boy? So, I ask you this, Mrs Ellison – as a mother, wouldn't you rather do what is best for Tom, rather than what is best for you? What if those German Jews had held onto their children, rather than sending them abroad, where would they be now? Dead in those awful camps, no doubt. But instead, those children, the children of those brave mothers, have life and a future, and opportunity to make something of themselves. Wouldn't you want Tom to have the best in life?'

She makes her way back to the car and opens the driver's door. Gwen bites her lip, refusing to watch.

'Give him up, Mrs Ellison. I assure you he will be treasured, and we will go to every length to ensure that the situation is managed in such a way that no one need ever know the truth. You have my word on that. You will be free to start a new life, financially secure. And it can be a happy one if you choose to make it so.' She rests her arm on the top of the doorframe to make her final appeal, her voice softening with persuasion. 'Give your son the chance of a wonderful life – a life without financial concern and blessed with possibilities. It is the life every good parent *dreams* of for their child, and so few have the resources to make it happen . . . but we do, Gordon and I. Do what is best for your son, Gwen.'

Scooping her skirt under her, she drops into the leather driving seat and pulls the door to. Gwen shudders as the engine starts. She looks away as the car pulls out into the lane.

From up the field, Tom's joyous whoops carry like bird calls on the wind, accompanied by Kip's frantic barking as the two of them chase across the furrows. Gwen's eyes fill with tears.

She will not let him go. The life he has with her is good enough. She refuses to entertain Helen Allingham's arguments. She will not succumb to her manipulation. No matter what type of mother it might make her, she will fight for her son.

CHAPTER THIRTY-NINE

Jack

September 1939

Jack is overwhelmed: they have all come to see him off. His orders to report for duty came through with lightning speed and now he stands on the platform of the village station, his knapsack slung over one shoulder. It is the same one he arrived with, but it is heavier now and, though he cannot think what items he has added to it, he is acutely aware he is leaving with much more than he brought.

Jim is coughing into his fist. The weather has turned in the last week. It is damp and colder now. Jack worries for Gwen, but she gently rebuffs him when he expresses concern about her waiting on the chilly platform.

Muriel has insisted on joining them. She gives him a string bag containing two jars of her homemade strawberry jam which she knows to be his favourite. She ignores his protests and pushes the bag into his hand, shushing him when he tries to object. Accepting defeat, he kisses her cheek. She bats him away, coyly delighted by his affection.

A whistle screams. The approaching train clatters towards them. Jack clears his throat to cover his sudden nervousness.

They step back from the platform edge as the leviathan slides alongside, belching great clouds of steam. Doors clang. Jack is one of only a few passengers waiting and he knows he will have to be quick. The train will not suffer tardy goodbyes.

He shakes Jim's hand, thanking him sincerely for all he has taught him. He has, in a few short months, thrown off his mantle of city dweller and donned a farmer's garb and it suits him well. He has been transformed in a way he would never have thought possible. His smog-filled lungs have been cleansed; the love of countryside floods his veins and he feels a better man for it. Only it has come too late.

The guard looks up the length of the train. He glares at them, his whistle ready.

Gwen steps forward. Things have been strange between them since the wedding.

'Take care of yourself now, lass.'

It is all he can do to get the words out. He drinks her in, memorising her face.

Her hands alight on his shoulders and his arm instinctively slips around her waist as she rises on her tiptoes, but he does not pull her to him – he merely holds her, as innocently as one might hold a maiden aunt in a waltz. Her lips graze his cheek.

'Goodbye, Jack,' she whispers.

She drops down, but before his arm falls away, he murmurs for her alone to hear.

'I've left something for you. In the tack room, under the blanket.'

The guard's shrill whistle splits the air. There is no time

to explain. Jack climbs up into the carriage and slams the door behind him. There is not even time to lower the window before the train jerks away. He presses his palm against the glass, watching the three of them grow smaller and smaller, knowing that for him there can be no return; that he will never see Gwen again.

CHAPTER FORTY

Gwen

September 1945

Gwen throws herself into work after Lady Helen's unwelcome visit. She labours from dawn until dusk and then beyond. She does not want idle time on her hands, she does not want to give her thoughts time or space to roam. She is afraid of where they will go.

She confides only to Muriel the contents of that fateful conversation. They sit at the kitchen table in the gloaming, both too preoccupied to muster themselves to light the paraffin lamp before them. Instead, they leave their faces to fall into shadow, grateful that the failing light masks the extent of their concern. Neither are willing to tempt fate by lending voice to their fears.

Nora laughs when she finds them. She strikes a match and the paraffin lamp flares into life. They contrive their self-deprecatory smiles and exclaim how quickly the night has come on, but as soon as the Land Girl has left them, their expressions grow grave once again.

Muriel pats Gwen's hand as she leaves. 'They don't have a leg to stand on,' she says, but they both suspect that isn't true.

Gwen had returned to the field that day promising Tom a bicycle. He listened in wide-eyed wonder as she boldly made her guilt-fuelled pledge, triggered by Helen Allingham's words. She was determined her boy would have all the gifts she could give him.

So, as Tom sleeps above her and while Nora hums along to the wireless in the front room, she descends to the cellar searching for treasure to sell. She opens boxes of bits collected over the years, but with a sinking heart realises there is little of value, little that will raise the sum she needs.

Even so, she sweeps the cobwebs from Tom's highchair and lugs it up the narrow steps, planting it in the kitchen, before descending again. She remembers his pram in the barn, splattered with bird droppings and crusted with dust, but nothing a good scrub couldn't fix.

In a damp cardboard box nibbled by mice, she finds an old china tea service wrapped in yellowed newspaper and thinks it might fetch a bob or two, and then – to her surprise – a copper tea urn, a little battered perhaps, but with a spot of Brasso and a bit of elbow grease it would gleam.

As she delves deeper, she comes across a large blanket-wrapped bundle and a memory tugs. She brings the paraffin lamp closer and, setting it down, crouches in its puddle of gold. As the blanket falls away, the light catches on a beautifully crafted cradle in darkly polished oak and her heart forgets to beat.

Her fingers trail over the scrolls and flowers and the carved lamb gambolling on its side. She sits heavily on the brick floor, unable to breathe, as she recalls finding this very cradle all those years ago, wrapped in the same blanket, on the camp bed in the tack room – the parting gift of a husband she could not bring herself to love.

To everyone's delight the weather has turned fair. There is talk of an Indian summer, with cloudless blue skies and unseasonable heat. It is perfect weather to bring in the farm's final hay crop, a late mowing of rye grass and red clover, rich feed for the cattle over winter.

Gwen and Nora are in Worm Meadow. It is only five acres, steeply banked and of awkward shape, so they have decided to cut it by hand. The warm air vibrates with a blackbird's mellow trill, and the repetitive chorus of a song thrush is interspersed with the *pip pip pip* of a redwing newly arrived for the winter. Their scythes, whispering through the dry grass and clover, add to the symphony with a rhythmic *shush shush shush*.

Tom charges down the field margins, squatting periodically to cup butterflies in his hot hands – admirals and peacocks and cabbage whites – but with little success. He accepts his failures with good grace and rises to chase them instead, but soon he catches sight of the swallows slicing through the air like Spitfires as they depart for foreign shores, and he spreads his arms to join them.

Gwen pauses to wipe the sweat from her forehead and peel her shirt from her back, where it sticks to her skin like gummed paper. The drab canopies of the spinney behind her lift and fall, sighing with placid satisfaction at the soothing ministrations of the much-needed breeze. A fleeting movement catches Gwen's eye and she twists to follow it. From the shadow of the wood, a cock pheasant shouts his throaty alarm. For some reason she tenses, troubled by a strange sense of foreboding though she cannot think why. It turns out to be little more than a darting squirrel; she feels a profound sense of relief as it scampers up the tree to its drey, the messy ball of twigs and moss just visible through the thinning leaves.

They work on, progressing up the banked field until they are nearly at its top. The breeze drops away and the sun beats down unchallenged, fierce and punishing. The final wisp of cloud drifts from the sky and all that is left is blue. Tom, puce-faced, his hair plastered to his forehead, complains he is too hot, and Gwen sends him to sit still in the shade of an old oak, where he gleans fallen acorns from amongst the gnarled roots, favouring those still sitting in their hatched cups.

'Hello . . . we have a visitor.' Nora leans on her scythe, tipping her head towards the gate far below them.

Gwen finishes the sweep of her blade, then turns to follow the Land Girl's gaze. The sky shimmers with heat and she is forced to squint against the sun. There is indeed a figure at the gate.

'Must be Ted,' Nora says and turns away in disinterest.

But there is something about the visitor's manner as he opens the gate that seizes Gwen's attention. As he begins to approach through the haze, light catches on brass set against khaki and she is powerless to look away.

It is not Ted.

Her scythe thuds to the ground.

She is vaguely aware of Nora calling her name as she drifts forward, her eyes pinching. Tom comes up behind her – she cannot see him, but she knows he is there. They are one, the two of them; they share an inseparable bond.

Her mouth is so dry she struggles to swallow.

The visitor comes to a stop before her. His kitbag lands

heavily beside him. For a moment they stare at each other, as if trying to determine whether the moment is real or merely some mirage resulting from the heat. Gwen fears she has somehow conjured him and, if she has, what the consequences will be.

'Hello, Gwen.'

Her husband has returned.

PART TWO

Sicily, 1943

Jack found a quiet spot by a tumbled section of wall, a little removed from the rest of the lads who had sat in sociable groups to share a few smokes and tuck into their rations. He swept away the worst of the rubble with the side of his boot, then eased himself down, resting his back against the bullet-bitten stonework. Tipping back his head, he closed his eyes and wondered, once again, why he was still alive.

He rubbed his dusty face with a hand rusted with blood and, when he was done, his fingers strayed to the breast pocket of his uniform. Working free its brass button, he took out the small black-and-white photograph of Gwen tucked inside. She was crouched down, smiling, her arm around the little boy in shorts coyly looking up at the camera as he leant against her. He smoothed his thumb over the image, a wistful expression occupying his face as he studied every line and shadow of their features.

'I have no idea why you take the bloody foolhardy risks you do, sergeant.' His lieutenant squatted beside him, an unlit cigarette propped between his lips. He searched his pockets for his lighter. 'How you pulled off that stunt today I've no idea.

You're like a cat with nine bloody lives, but you'll come a crop-per one of these days if you don't learn to pull your neck in.'

Jack said nothing but thought, That's rather the point, sir.

The officer lit his cigarette and screwed up his eyes as he inhaled. Smoke escaped between his teeth as he moved to get a better look at the photograph in Jack's hand.

'All I know is if I had a beauty like that waiting for me, I'd be doing my utmost to stay alive, not trying to get myself killed.' He bounced up to standing. Jack did not respond to the man's continued scrutiny – he had no desire to break off his study of Gwen's face to meet it. The officer sighed.

'You're a brave soldier, Jack, no one could say otherwise. But death is stalking all of us, you've no need to court it. Just . . . take it easy, stop being so reckless . . . and then maybe we can do our best to make sure you get back to them. To that family of yours. That's all I want to say.'

Jack did not look up to see the melancholy smile the officer presented, nor did he see the baffled shake of his head. He was grateful when the man finally moved away, his boots crunching on debris as he crossed to join the men feasting on the contents of their billy cans.

Jack caressed Gwen's face with the side of his thumb once more, then secured the photograph inside his breast pocket. He rested his head back on the wall and closed his eyes.

He wondered what his lieutenant would think if he knew the truth: that they were not his family; that he could never go home; and that his getting killed would be the best outcome for them all.

CHAPTER FORTY-ONE

September 1945

Jack's heart is pounding like a jackhammer.

He feels suddenly lightheaded, perhaps due to the heat of the day, or lack of sleep, or his empty belly – or maybe because he is here at last. And so is she.

He has done his best not to imagine this moment – though on occasion he has succumbed to the sweet torture of this particular fantasy. But standing here now, seeing the blatant shock on Gwen's face, he becomes painfully aware of the promise he made – the promise he is now breaking.

'Jack.' She croaks his name, then wipes a bead of sweat from the corner of her eye with the tip of her finger. 'Jack,' she says again, her tone disappointingly leaden. His shy smile falters.

He is aware then of the boy. He has crept forward, stealthy and unsure, like a curious kit exploring beyond the safety of the burrow. He peers out from behind his mother's legs, his expression wary. Jack meets his solemn eyes and is overcome by the realisation that *this* is the child, the child it was all for – the façade of their marriage, the promise made and now broken. *This* child drew them together and forced them apart. And yet he has an overwhelming sense of this being *his* child, and suddenly a sob chokes him. He covers it with a cough and hopes that Gwen remains oblivious to the rush of love that has caught him unawares. Of all things, it is his reaction to the boy that is the most unanticipated.

He crouches down, fearful his knees might give way, for he is trembling as if possessed by a fever. He looks at the boy with wonder, studying his every feature – the curve of his brow, the sweep of his mouth, the line of his button nose. He has been absorbing the same features in miniature every night for the past five years, tracing their black-and-white outlines. And now he sees them in the flesh: the boy a little bigger, the features more defined.

'And you must be Tom.'

His voice gives way on the boy's name. He tries to smile, but the swell of his emotion is so great it fails to become the bold expression he intended – though it is charged with joy all the same. The boy nods, before ducking behind his mother's legs. Jack thinks his heart might burst.

'Don't be shy, Tom, say hello to your daddy! He's back at last – back from the war. What a lucky boy you are to have your daddy home.'

It is the Land Girl who speaks. Previously, she has been little more than a sketch in Gwen's occasional letters, but now she sidles forward in full embodiment, a scythe in her hand, her face alive with devilment.

'I think you've stunned them both into silence,' she laughs. Gwen shoots her an annoyed look, but the girl is unrepentant; she merely leans on her scythe and settles in to enjoy the show.

Jack pushes himself up to standing. He had not factored in the presence of a stranger. There is a confidence to the Land Girl that unnerves him and he wishes she was not there. He had never wanted his first meeting with Gwen to be a spectacle, but she is turning it into one and he resents her for it. The words he has practised are lost in the stage fright of an actor facing an audience for the first time.

'This is Nora . . . my Land Girl,' Gwen says, as if sensing – and perhaps sharing – his disquiet.

'So I gathered,' he says, before mumbling a greeting.

'I'm glad to meet you,' Nora replies, putting the emphasis in all the wrong places.

'I wasn't expecting you. You should have warned me.' The note of accusation in Gwen's voice stings.

'I'm sorry.'

'Oh, Gwen!' Nora laughs. 'Where's your sense of romance? I'm sure Jack wanted to surprise you – and what a surprise it is! You must be delighted.' She grins, apparently relishing the fact that Gwen is clearly not.

Gwen touches the belt of Tom's arms around her legs. 'Well, let's get this finished up and we'll go and get a cup of tea.' She retrieves her fallen scythe. 'You can go on up to the house and wait if you like,' she says to Jack.

He watches Tom as he scurries back to the shade of the oak tree. 'No . . .' he says quietly. 'I think I'll stay here until you're done. If you have no objections?' he adds, taking a careful step forwards, conscious Nora has finally returned her attention to her labours.

'I don't mind,' Gwen says at last.

But it looks for all the world as if she does.

Gwen cuts the remaining hay with a vigour fuelled by terror and suspicion. She cannot fathom the reason for Jack's return, but she fears he intends to extract some recompense for the service he has rendered.

They walk back to the house as soon as the hay is done. Jack offers to carry Gwen's scythe, but she shakes her head, then calls Tom to come. He scampers to her side, clawing for her hand, even though he can see her hands are full. It is all she can do not to snap at him, hot and irritated as she is. And anxious. Above all, she is anxious, but then, she realises, so is he. The man before him has never been more than a monochrome image but now he has materialised in living, breathing Technicolor – it is understandable that Tom should be perturbed. How can she possibly expect him to adapt to Jack's arrival without fear or question? God knows, she has questions enough of her own. And she is afraid.

Tom drops back to the safety of Nora's side. The Land Girl's curiosity is so blatant it is almost obscene, and Gwen wishes she hadn't witnessed Jack's return. It will make his imminent departure all the more difficult to explain, but explain it she will, for the one certainty she has been clinging to since seeing him walk up the field is that he cannot stay. She will not allow it. There is no place for Jack in their lives. He made her a promise, a promise he has reneged on, and now she is terrified to discover the reason why.

She sneaks a glance at him as he walks beside her taking in the landscape, a hint of a smile on his face and a softness to his expression that reminds her, disturbingly, of bliss. He tips his head back to watch the buzzard lazing in slow circles above them, and then cranes his neck to look over the hedgerow into the field beyond.

'More grazing gone,' he comments.

'We ended up ploughing under most of the pasture. The WarAg demanded it. The herd has had to survive on the bare minimum to make way for more crops,' Gwen explains. It is safer to talk of the farm than of anything else, especially with Nora earwigging behind.

'It must have been hard. All that change.'

'Yes, well . . . there have been a lot of changes around here. We've just had to get used to them.'

'I was so sorry to hear about your dad.'

To her surprise, Gwen's throat clogs at his quietly conveyed sympathy. She is grateful that they have reached the farm gate, for she finds she is unable to respond.

They have barely crossed into the yard when Kip comes haring towards them, barking wildly, his tail oscillating through the air at a rate of knots. Jack's face explodes with joy. He drops to his knees as the ecstatic creature bowls into him, licking and climbing and nuzzling and whimpering with unadulterated affection. Jack laughs with delight, mussing the animal's thick fur, pulling a face as it slathers him with its tongue. Even Gwen finds a smile tugging at the corners of her mouth.

'At least someone's pleased to see you,' Nora laughs, pointedly catching Gwen's eye above the ecstatic reunion.

'All right, lad, all right,' Jack chuckles. He gently pushes the cavorting dog away and gets to his feet. He gazes up at the house.

Gwen observes his rapt expression and thinks of his covetous inspection of the land and suddenly it hits her: he has returned to lay claim to the farm – her farm – just as Gordon has returned to lay claim to her son. She is under attack on all sides and though once she might have considered Jack an ally, he is clearly an ally no more. The realisation knocks the breath from her body and she no longer cares about Nora's suspicions, because Nora's suspicions are right.

She is not pleased to see him. She is not pleased to see him at all.

CHAPTER FORTY-TWO

They go in via the back door. There is a muted hubbub as Gwen and Nora rid themselves of their boots and Tom chucks off his wellies before running to hide in the front room. Jack sets his kitbag down in the corner and unties his laces, as Gwen snatches up the kettle from the range. She fills it at the sink, then plants it on the hotplate before lighting the paraffin. Another change, Jack notes without comment – the coal-burning range replaced in the name of economy.

Nora brings a cut fruit cake and a jug of the morning's milk out of the larder and sets them upon the table, while Jack hangs back, absorbing every aspect of the familiar interior. He is overcome by a joyful sense of belonging he knows he has no right to feel. Gwen's frostiness reminds him that even though he might long to consider it as such, this is not his home; he has no claim upon it. He does not even have the right to be here and yet he could not have stayed away. He watches Gwen as she takes the whistling kettle from the flame. For so many reasons, he could not have stayed away.

'Take a seat, Jack, you must be exhausted.' Nora draws

out a chair and gestures him into it. He glances at Gwen and when she shows no objection – indeed, she does not look at him at all – he settles himself down. 'I thought all you demobbed boys were supposed to get a suit?' Nora continues. He cannot tell whether she is unaware of the simmering tension in the room or simply entertained by it. She slides him the mug that Gwen has poured.

'Aye well, let's just say the old demob suit wasn't up to much, so me and some of the lads decided we'd rather keep with the uniform.' He takes the proffered milk jug. 'I've kind of got used to it, I suppose,' he adds softly. 'It's done me proud.'

They drink their tea and pick at slender slices of cake in awkward silence. Gwen's relief is evident as she looks at the clock.

'Time for milking.'

Nora stands up and begins to gather up the mugs. Jack pushes back his chair.

'I can help—'

'No need,' Gwen cuts him off. She already has the back door open, waiting for Nora, who glances between them, eyebrows hiked.

'Mummy! I want to come!' Tom races through from the hall and it crosses Jack's mind that he has been listening, out of sight, the whole time. He darts Jack a guarded look as he snatches up his wellies from the floor, putting them on in record time to join Nora outside. Gwen draws the door to behind her.

Jack sits in the silent kitchen, his heart breaking. His return has not been well received, that much is painfully clear, but even so, he does not regret it. He always knew his chances of being welcomed back with open arms were slim, but he could not let the poor odds deter him. He had to come back. He had to try.

The door opens behind him. He twists round and seeing Gwen, he gets to his feet. She takes a deep breath and steps inside, resting her weight against the door as she pushes it shut.

'What are you doing here, Jack?'

He has pictured this moment so many times: telling her everything. But now he is here, alone with her at last, he struggles to find the words, unsure where to begin.

'I went home to Newcastle . . . The town was badly damaged, like. The shipyards took a battering . . . the city around . . . my street was gone.'

She appears taken aback. 'Your mum . . .'

'I heard the drink got her before all that.'

'I'm sorry.'

He shrugs awkwardly, wondering how he came to be talking about his mother. 'There was nothing for me there.'

'But there's nothing for you here either, Jack.'

Her voice is firm, her manner cold.

She stands her ground and suddenly he realises she too has changed since he left – matured, strengthened – perhaps even hardened. And yet, he instinctively knows her essence is unaltered, that her sweet heart remains. She is still the same Gwen he laboured beside, stood beside . . . *loved* . . . all those years ago. He has seen it in the unguarded comments and subtle observations contained in her occasional letters. And though he cannot explain it, he feels it keenly now.

'Tom . . . he's a fine boy.'

'He is.' Her chin juts up. He sees the wariness in her eyes

and wonders where it comes from. 'And whilst I'll always be grateful to you, Jack, we're doing just fine the way we are.'

'I just . . .'

'He's mine, Jack.'

'I know . . .'

'You have no claim on him.'

'I know that, Gwen . . .'

'Just like you have no claim on this farm.'

'Of course I don't. Gwen, this is your farm, your land . . .' He cannot hide his confusion. He does not understand what he has said – what he might have unknowingly implied – to make her so defensive.

'Jack, I agreed to do what I did because you made me a promise: no ties; no comeback. Now don't get me wrong, I'm glad you're alive . . . I'm pleased you survived the war . . . but I don't want you here. There is no place for you in my life or in Tom's life, and your coming here will only confuse and complicate things. So, you need to go. You cannot stay here. Do you understand? You cannot stay.'

'Gwen, I need to . . .'

She holds up her hand to stop him. 'I don't want to hear it, Jack. Now so far, only Nora and Tom know you're here. I can explain away your departure to them both, but you need to leave at once.'

They hear the faint lowing of the cows being driven into the yard. Gwen bites her lip, her hand on the latch.

'I'm going to help Nora do the milking. I want you gone by the time we're finished.' She pulls open the door. 'I'm sorry, Jack,' she says gently. 'I really do wish you all the best.'

And before he can answer, the door closes against him.

He slumps, defeated. He feels like a potter who has patiently crafted a delicate vase from the shapeless lump of clay spinning on his wheel. But in a moment of clumsiness his touch becomes too firm, his pressure on the pedal too great and, before he can prevent it, his object of beauty topples into a useless fold of clay, spinning beyond his control.

Sinking his head into his hands, he wonders how his return could have so quickly gone wrong. He has squandered his one chance to secure the future he has longed for, shattering the dreams that have sustained him for the past year.

His head jerks up as the kitchen door is flung open. Muriel stands in the open doorway, breathless and pale. He instantly pushes back his chair and gets to his feet, a tentative smile lifting the corners of his mouth. She lets out a mew of relief and dashes forward, cupping his face with her hands in an extraordinary display of affection.

'Heaven be blessed,' she exclaims, drinking him in; she is sensitive enough not to mention his hollowed cheeks or the weariness in his eyes. 'Mrs Hamer said she was sure she'd seen you at the train station, then Bob Collins said he'd seen you walking past the pub and I hardly dared to believe it!' Tears glint as she releases him. 'I knew you'd be back,' she whispers.

'But not for long, it seems.'

He meets her puzzlement with a sad smile. 'I made a promise and I broke it, without any right to do so. Gwen's asked me to go, and that's fair enough.'

'Go?'

'Aye.'

'When?'

'Now. She's doing the milking. I have to be on my way before she's done.'

Her mouth tightens as her eyes harden to flint. 'Is that right?' She spits out a noise of disgust and grabs the door handle. 'Just you leave this to me.' She points a finger at his chest. 'Sit back down, my boy. You're not going anywhere.'

CHAPTER FORTY-THREE

Gwen is trembling when she enters the milking parlour. Nora is at work in the second stall. Tom squats by the side of her milking stool, the soles of his wellies flat on the ground, the backs of his thighs plastered to his calves, his arms wrapped around his knees as he watches the jets of warm milk squirt into the pail. They both look around as Gwen comes in. She pauses while her eyes adjust to the dim light after the glare of the sun. Amusement plays across Nora's pretty features and Gwen has to bite her tongue to stop herself from lashing out at the girl, for mocking what she doesn't have the wherewithal to understand.

Tom scampers over to her as she buttons up her dairy coat. He shyly whispers for her attention.

'Not now, Tom.' She cannot bring herself to look at him, so profound is her sense of guilt. She has betrayed him his entire life, boldly feeding him lies, confident that she would never be caught out. All that mattered was that Tom should feel loved and cherished – by her and by his 'father'.

Over the years she has constructed a castle for him built from untruths and mortared with falsities, never once considering how one crumbling block might bring the whole edifice tumbling down, never once considering that the king might one day return to reclaim his citadel and the little prince trapped inside.

And now Tom is looking at her with a blend of excitement, confusion and fear and she cannot bear it – she cannot bear the damage she has done.

'Later,' she says at last, cupping his chin in her hand and smoothing his cheek with her thumb. 'Let Mummy get on with the milking for now. Why don't you run and have a look in the pen and decide who I should bring in first? I think maybe Petal.'

He pulls a face. She knows Petal is his least favourite cow. 'Tulip,' he decides.

Gwen frowns playfully. 'Are you sure? Mabel maybe? Go and have a look and I promise I'll bring in the one you say.'

Placated, he races down the length of the building and out through the door to the pen. Gwen's smile fades. She collects a pail from the stack by the doorway and nearly collides with Nora as she turns back. The Land Girl's grin seems almost malicious.

'You're a sly one,' Nora says, lifting her pail onto the hanging scales. 'You never said your fella was such a looker.' Noting the result, she lifts the pail clear and faces Gwen. 'That photograph on your mantelpiece doesn't do him justice.'

Gwen is unable to summon a reply. For some inexplicable reason, her cheeks grow hot. She is infuriated by Nora's impish glee.

'Hurry up, Nora, we're running late as it is.'

'Yes, I'm sure you're eager to get back to him – I know I would be.' Nora saunters to the cooler and sloshes in the milk.

'Although I have to say, it wasn't the fond reunion I'd been expecting.'

'Well, I'm sorry to disappoint you.' The girl has stretched Gwen's patience like a rubber band and now it breaks. The words snap from her, sharp and stinging, leaving Nora looking so startled that Gwen is on the brink of apologising when the light from the doorway disappears.

'A word. Now.' Muriel glowers at Gwen.

'How did you find out?' Gwen asks as soon as they have left the building and retreated a safe distance from the Land Girl.

'It's all over the village,' Muriel hisses, grabbing her arm. She marches her across the yard and pushes her into the barn. For the first time in her life, Gwen feels lost in the cavernous space. 'You little fool.'

'I've told him he can't stay.' Gwen spits like one of the feral cats that slink around the buildings. 'How was I supposed to know he'd come back? He promised me, promised me faithfully that I would never see him again!'

'I have never encountered a girl as soft-headed as you.' Muriel folds her arms across her chest, fury etched upon her narrow features.

'I don't care what you say to me, Muriel. I did what I had to do to protect my child – I wasn't about to have him labelled a *bastard* if he didn't need to be – and I will do whatever is necessary to carry on protecting him now.'

'Then why the devil are you trying to send Jack away?' Muriel's voice erupts, echoing through the barn. She glances nervously behind her, checking Nora is still safely ensconced in the milking parlour and that Tom hasn't come to eavesdrop. She drives Gwen further into the pooling shadows, scattering a clutch of sparrows feeding on spilt grain in the corner. They flit across the rafters, objecting noisily.

'He can't stay, Muriel! For God's sake . . . it's not as if we were ever really married.'

'But in the eyes of the law you are and that's all that matters right now. Gordon Allingham is threatening to assert his rights as Tom's father and, like manna from heaven, the one man who can stop him returns to you in the nick of time, and what do you want to do? You want to turf him out on his ear.'

'What?'

'For God's sake, think about it, Gwen! Gordon is claiming paternity of Tom. If you send away now the man everyone in this village thinks is your husband, the man who in the eyes of the law is Tom's father, you'll be handing *on a plate* all the evidence Gordon needs to make the world suspect he might be telling the truth, and that your marriage was nothing more than a sham to cover up your pregnancy with *his* illegitimate child. But if Jack stays and the two of you play doting parents to that little boy, Gordon'll find his pleas falling on deaf ears. No one will believe him. No one will *want* to believe him. There'll be no question of who Tom's father is if Jack stays to play his part. Your boy will be *safe*.'

'Oh, God.'

'So you get back into that house and you get down on your knees if you have to, but don't you let Jack walk away today, because if he does . . . you'll have lost your best weapon against Allingham and you'll end up fighting alone for Tom – and Gwen . . . I don't know if you'll win.'

Gwen covers her mouth against a wave of nausea, as the full effect of Muriel's words comes to bear.

'I can't be his wife . . .'

'Oh, Gwen. Jack will do whatever is necessary to protect you and Tom . . . and he won't ask for anything in return.'

'How do you know? How can you possibly know that?'

Gwen is unable to interpret the strange look on Muriel's face. 'Because I do. The thing I find most incredible is that you don't. But then . . . we only see what we want to see, I suppose. Now, get on up to the house and tell Jack what's been going on and ask him to stay. And if you can't swallow your pride and put your own foolish fears aside to do that, you'd best start imagining life without your boy because that's the future you'll be looking at. Right now, Jack Ellison staying is the only way to safeguard your son.'

When Gwen bursts into the kitchen a few minutes later it is empty. Muriel's warning ricochets inside her head as she runs through to the sitting room, thinking perhaps he has made himself comfortable for a little while, but the room stands stagnant and undisturbed. She hovers in the hallway wondering if he might be somewhere else, but in her heart she knows the house is empty – she can sense its vacancy, its air unmoved by another's presence. The silence cuts her to the bone. She is too late.

Perhaps she can catch him. The thought flashes through her mind, reinvigorating her static body. Racing to the back door, she shoves on her gumboots and sprints along the path, leaping the steps. She lands with a jarring thud and runs on down the yard to the lane. She stops, breathless, just beyond the gate, spinning left to right. There is no sign of Jack. She has no idea which way he might have gone – she had shown no interest in his plans, she had thrown him out without so much as a good-bye. After what he has done for her, she cannot help but feel she has been handed her just desserts. It is all she can do to contain the scream of despair building inside her.

Defeated, she remains in the lane until her breathing has become sluggish and her heart as heavy as lead. She turns back to the yard, barely able to put one foot in front of the other, cursing her stupidity, wishing she had done so many things differently in her life. She wonders what she will say to Muriel.

The cows bellow in the holding pen, disgruntled with the slow progress of the milking. She needs to return to her duties; she needs to fabricate some story about Jack's departure for Nora. Her insides clench as she wonders how to explain to Tom that his newly returned father has left already.

She spots Kip waiting expectantly outside the stable block door and her steps stutter as hope dares to flare in her chest. The dog's head whips towards her. He emits a short whine then looks back towards the gaping door.

'Jack . . .'

She hurries past and on to the straw-scattered cobbles inside. The air remains redolent with the musty scent of horses though the stalls all stand empty, with Bobby grazing in the paddock. The tack room door hangs ajar. Timidly, she pushes it wide.

Jack responds to the tell-tale creak of hinges, a leather roll of some kind caught in his hands. His kitbag is on the floor by the camp bed.

'I left my tools behind last time I—'

'I need you to stay.'

Her blurted confession takes him by surprise.

'Please, Jack.'

Gwen moves to the window to gather her thoughts and form her appeal. Cobwebs matt the glass and in the corners hapless flies dangle in gossamer shrouds. The velvet curtains she made all those years ago hang limply from the sagging wire above, moth-eaten and damp, speckled with mildew and mould. She doesn't dare to touch them – she fears they will crumble if she does.

'Gordon Allingham came home,' she says quietly. Jack does not utter a word and yet the air is alive with his presence. 'He was injured, apparently . . . North Africa somewhere . . . he can't have any more children.' Steeling herself she turns to face him. 'So, he wants Tom.'

She watches Jack absorb her bombshell. A muscle ticks in his jaw. 'He can't have him.'

'He's threatened to get lawyers involved, if I won't surrender him.'

'But he has no firm evidence that Tom is his son.'

'He has letters.' Gwen's voice fades to an ashamed whisper. She cannot look at him as she makes her confession. 'I wrote to him . . . begging him . . . before . . .'

'Oh, Gwen.'

'I just thought if he understood all I felt he might . . . I never expected him to keep them all this time, not after . . .' Her tears well. 'Anyway . . . I told him that the letters are full of lies, that I'd been . . . seeing . . . the two of you at the same time and that I knew Tom was yours.' She finally braves a look at Jack, but he gives nothing away. 'He doesn't believe me. He says there are means available to prove he's the father.'

'What means?'

'He didn't say.'

'Have you seen a lawyer yourself?'

She shakes her head. 'Not yet. He said a woman like me, on my own . . . against him . . . that I wouldn't stand a chance.'

'But I'm here now.'

'I need you to be my boy's father, Jack. I need you to stay . . . at least for a while . . . so there's no room for doubt or suspicion . . . or gossip. I can't lose my boy, Jack.'

Tears slide down her cheeks. She gasps for air, her chest cracked open, her heart exposed. Jack comes to her without hesitation. He gently guides her into his embrace and she surrenders willingly, surprising them both. It is what she needs in this moment. She is too tired to fight; she is too exhausted to be strong.

'I can't lose Tom,' she sobs into his shoulder.

'You won't, lass,' he promises her softly. 'While there's breath in my body, you won't.'

CHAPTER FORTY-FOUR

Jack is aware of the boy staring at him as they eat the meal Muriel has set before them, but every time he attempts to make eye contact, Tom buries his face into Gwen's arm, earning himself a gentle reprimand, so in the end Jack ceases to try. He does not want to get the boy into trouble.

He finds it strange how things have changed. He misses Jim's cap and coat, absent from the hooks by the back door. He misses the smell of coal smoke from the range and even the distinctive tang of Woodbine stubs in the ashtray. He finds Nora's bold presence disconcerting. The kitchen strains under the pressure of her energy, her buoyant personality, as if struggling to contain her. He is glad for Muriel's extended company, though, for since Jim's death he learns she now stays for dinner and often lingers after. He finds her maternal disposition comforting. She, at least, is free with a ready smile. Gwen keeps her head down and her gaze averted, with whatever closeness they momentarily experienced in the tack room long forgotten – and he fears regretted.

They stop in the kitchen talking until Muriel takes her leave at half six. Jack joins Gwen, Nora and Tom in the sitting room. Gwen takes her father's chair and turns on the wireless. Jack is left with the settee when Nora lays claim to Gwen's old seat.

Tom scurries into the corner behind Gwen where he clearly considers himself safe from Jack. He lies on his tummy, opening a sketch pad. The scratch of his coloured pencils on the paper is interrupted by the occasional sigh and wriggle of limbs.

Gwen takes out mending from the knitting bag beside her chair and proceeds to push a darning egg into the heel of a sock. She licks the end of her thread into a sharp point, then feeds it through the eye of her needle, cutting off the excess with her teeth. Nora meanwhile is engrossed in a lengthy letter received that morning. She nibbles a broken nail as she reads, giggling as she turns the sheet over to follow the scrunched writing along.

Jack picks up the evening paper but though he unfolds the pages he has no interest in the stories it contains, and instead he uses it to conceal his observations – of Tom's raised heels as they absently kick the air and of Gwen, her top teeth tugging at her bottom lip as she guides her needle through the sock. He has imagined such simple domestic scenes as these over the years and now he intends to enjoy them while he can, for he suspects his reprieve will be short-lived. But he will savour them gladly for now.

When the mantel clock chimes seven, Gwen puts away her darning and rises from her chair, calling Tom to bed.

'Goodnight, Tommy boy,' Nora says, looking up from her letter as Tom dashes to join Gwen at the door.

Jack closes the paper. He smiles at the boy. 'Goodnight, Tom.'

But the boy merely buries his face into Gwen. She casts Jack an apologetic look, then ushers him from the room. Jack listens to the boy's rapid ascent of the stairs.

'Poor Tom, I think he's finding your sudden return a bit overwhelming,' Nora says, folding her letter.

'Aye . . . I can understand that.'

'He'll get used to you, I'm sure.'

Laying down the newspaper, Jack gets up to attend the fire which is burning low. He pushes another log into the flames and takes the poker from the companion set to nudge it into place.

'You must be so pleased to be back.'

'Aye.'

Nora is suddenly beside him. She takes down the framed wedding photo from the mantelpiece. He replaces the poker and rises from his crouch, careful to keep a safe distance between them.

'What an attractive couple you make.' She beams, but there is a brashness to her that he does not trust. 'All those years away . . .' She puts the picture back. 'I thought everyone got a bit of home leave.'

'I never quite managed it, what with one thing and another.'

'I'm sure you and Gwen are looking forward to getting reacquainted after such a long time.'

He does not appreciate the mischief dancing in her eyes. He retreats to the settee as flames take hold on the new log.

Gwen appears in the doorway. She looks between them. Nora grins, then performs an exaggerated stretch like a poor actress.

'Tom down, is he? Well, I'm clean tuckered out and I'm sure you two have a lot to catch up on, so why don't I go and shut the chickens in and then make myself scarce? I wouldn't mind an early night.'

She brushes past Gwen in the doorway, pausing to say '*Be*

good' in a stage whisper punctuated by a crass flare of her eyebrows. Gwen's features harden with contempt as she watches her disappear into the kitchen. Once she has heard the back door bang, she addresses Jack.

'We'll have to think about where you're going to sleep.' She perches on the edge of her chair and stares into the licking flames. From her evident disquiet, Jack deduces she has been thinking of little else since she took Tom to bed. 'Nora loves to gossip. She'll talk, you see . . . if she suspects . . .'

'I see.'

'She's in the spare room.'

'I presumed as much.'

'We will have to be careful . . . pretend you're in with me, I suppose . . .'

'I can take the tack room again.'

A guilty look of relief flashes across Gwen's face. 'Are you sure?'

'Aye . . . and if Nora says anything you can tell her that I get nightmares . . . and that I was worried about frightening Tom.'

She nods, then after a while she asks quietly, 'Do you?' Seeing his blank expression, she adds, 'Get nightmares?'

It is now his turn to look at the dancing flames. 'Sometimes.'

She says nothing. Eventually, she rises from her chair. 'I should get the mattress and bedding now, before Nora comes back in.'

'I'll give you a hand.'

The stairs creak as they walk up, one behind the other. Gwen opens the door of the linen press and Jack experiences a curious sense of déjà vu, but he knows it is only his memory playing tricks on him, sending him back in time to when he stood on this very landing with Muriel, feeling just as unwelcome as he sadly feels now. Tom's door is ajar, and he fights the temptation to sneak a look at the slumbering child. Gwen hands him the mattress roll – cinched once again with belts – and a feather pillow whose cotton cover sports pale yellow stains, while she takes an armful of pressed sheets and a thick woollen blanket.

They hurry downstairs to secrete the stash in the sitting room, hiding it behind the settee as they hear Nora enter the kitchen, whistling, her outside chores complete. They wait in silence, listening to her retreating footsteps and the clack of her bedroom door, and when all is quiet, they retrieve the bedding and creep out to the stables.

Jack pauses at what was once Arthur's loosebox, noting the absence of bedding and the lack of hay in the wall basket.

'Where's Arthur?' he asks, dreading the answer.

'Sold, years back.' She looks down, but not before he sees the flash of pain in her eyes. She shakes her head, as if to dispel the unpleasant memories he fears his question has evoked. 'It quickly became apparent I wouldn't be able to look after him. Dad made it clear that if I couldn't exercise him myself then the kindest thing to do was to let him go.'

'I'm sorry, lass. I know what he meant to you.'

She accepts his sympathies with a curt nod, then briskly leads him into the tack room, setting down the paraffin lamp she has been using to light their way. Jack looks around him and considers how, compared to everything else, the tack room at least has remained unchanged.

He drops the rolled mattress onto the wooden slats of the camp bed, then takes the bedding from Gwen's arms.

'I'll make it up for you . . .' she offers, but he shakes his head.

'I can manage. You'd best get in.'

She drifts to the door. 'She said it would be selfish of me to try and keep Tom.'

'Who?'

'Gordon's wife. She tried to persuade me that if I really loved Tom, I'd give him up . . . so he could have a chance at a better life. A better life than the one I can give him, anyway. Am I being selfish, Jack?' Moonlight falls upon her through the window. 'Am I putting myself before my son? Am I denying him a life of riches and opportunity, just to safeguard my own happiness?'

'Gwen . . . you know that's not right.'

'Do I? She made a convincing argument.'

'Life's real riches can't be bought, Gwen. Life's real treasures are not gilded mansions and fine possessions. Happiness, love, *knowing* you are loved . . . those are the things that truly matter.'

Seeing his words fall on fallow ground, Jack advances towards her. 'Listen to me: what Tom needs is his mother's love, his mother's presence. What message would you be sending if you gave him away now? What damage would be done to that little lad? He won't understand the supposed sacrifice you're making. All he'll understand is that his mother didn't want him, that his mother gave him up, when there was no real reason for her to do so. The life you can give him is as good as most of us get, better even. And all right, maybe with all their money and their fancy friends they can give him things you can't, but I don't think those benefits would serve to heal the injury of your abandonment. He would suffer that hurt forever, and the damage of that . . . it would never mend, Gwen. And money makes a paltry plaster over a wound that size. Your love, your support, those are the greatest assets Tom can ever receive and they will stand him in better stead for the rest of his life than anything Gordon Allingham can buy. What you can give Tom is priceless and everlasting and its effects have greater significance than you will ever know.'

A moonlit tear trickles down Gwen's cheek like a droplet of liquid mercury. He traces its descent, watches it cling to the precipice of her jaw and, as she nods, whispering her gratitude for his reassurance, it vanishes from sight.

'It's the truth, Gwen. Don't let them turn your head . . . or your heart.'

She wipes her hand across her cheek. 'You were always too good to me. I don't deserve your kindness – I'm not sure I ever did. But I want you to know I'm grateful to you. I didn't exactly go out of my way to welcome you back, today . . . and I'm very aware you didn't have to stay when I asked. So . . . thank you, Jack.'

He speaks only when she has her hand on the door, preparing to leave.

'You had every right to send me away. I made you a promise and I broke it coming back here. But I also promised your father that you would have my help whenever you needed it. So, you don't need to thank me for staying, because that's one promise I will always keep; that I choose to keep . . . for as long as you will let me.'

Gwen rises earlier than usual and dresses swiftly, eager to wake Jack before Nora gets up in case she stumbles upon their arrangement. Though his nightmare excuse is plausible, she would rather not use it – she would rather Nora believe he is sleeping under her roof.

When she opens the back door, she is startled to see Jack waiting in the grey light, dressed in his uniform, crouched down stroking Kip. The dog whines with disappointment as he stops his fussing and rises to his feet.

'I wasn't sure if you still milked at five thirty. I thought I might as well help out while I'm here.'

'Oh.'

'That is . . . if you don't mind.'

'No . . . you remember what to do?'

'I figured it would be like riding a bike – it'll all come back to me once I start.'

'Well . . . we'll have to test that theory, won't we?'

They walk down the lane together, Kip gambolling ahead. Blue tits and blackbirds, concealed by turning leaves, warble and peep. A robin, its red breast puffed, flies across the lane before them to land on a briar protruding from the hawthorn. Jack pinches himself that he is alive to revel in nature's glories.

The cows welcome them with throaty bellows. Gwen grabs the gate and they lumber out, shuffling past each other to fill the lane.

'Do you think they remember me?' Jack calls across the array of broad bodies plodding between them, as a freckled cow he recalls as 'Glenda' butts him with her wet nose before walking on.

'Perhaps.'

'I remember them.'

They fall in step behind. It is as if no time has passed, and yet, Jack thinks, so much has changed. The drifting clouds marring the sky are like smudges of smoke from the bonfire of his dreams.

'We were friends, Gwen,' he says at last, unsure at first that the words have escaped his thoughts. 'Is there any chance we can at least be friends again?'

When she fails to respond, he summons the courage to look her way.

Finally, she tilts her face towards him. And smiles.

CHAPTER FORTY-FIVE

Nora is leaning against the back wall of the house, a mug of tea nestled against her chest, a cigarette smouldering between her fingers. She takes a deep drag as the cattle trudge up the yard, then angles her head back to blow out a stream of smoke, before tossing the dregs of her tea into the garden and grinding the cigarette under her boot.

'Are you planning on making me redundant?' she calls out as Jack and Gwen amble past.

'I thought you might have appreciated the lie-in.' Gwen leaves Jack to drive the cows on, while she waits for the Land Girl as she clumps down the steps.

'I might have done if anybody had thought to tell me,' Nora grumbles, pulling a headscarf from her trouser pocket. She knots it over her hair. 'I would have thought you and the returning hero would have been the ones in need of a lie-in this morning.' She pushes past Gwen and jogs towards the milking parlour, slowing to shout back, 'Tom was asking for you, he's inside with Muriel.'

*

Jack smoothly settles back into the milking. He derives such pleasure from the simple task that the events of the past six years fall away and he is almost lulled into believing they are little more than troubling figments of his imagination. In the cool gloom of the parlour, with the sharp tang of cow dung, the slosh of milk and the steady chomp of hay, the war becomes nothing more than a faded nightmare, its residual fear dwindling as each waking moment strengthens the reassuring reality of the here and now.

'All coming back to you, is it?'

He is startled from his reverie by Nora. She props herself against the wooden side of the stall, an emptied pail in her hand. The cow he is milking sidles, her hooves catching against the stone.

'It is. Like I've never been away.'

He lowers his head, his hands moving steadily. She remains, watching him. He is relieved when Gwen arrives and Nora pushes herself up and finally moves away.

He offers to drive the herd back to the field and savours the peace of his solitary return. He relishes the beauty of the countryside around him – the wood's verdant robes turned to glowing hues of yellow, bronze and red; the shadows of clouds scudding across the harrowed fields; the harmonious bird song that sends his spirits soaring. He has traipsed across Italy, France, Belgium, into Germany even, and seen these changes in foreign climes over the years, but nowhere has the changing season been as beautiful as it is here. His cautious heart lifts with the joy of being home.

There is a figure loitering just shy of the farm gate as he approaches. He takes a fortifying breath and subconsciously straightens his spine when he realises Ted has seen him. The farmer takes a final drag on the stub of cigarette caught between his yellowed fingers, before tossing it into the nettles and long grass of the verge.

'So, it is true then,' he says by way of greeting as Jack draws up short. 'I heard you were back.'

'Aye.'

'Didn't think you would be, what with one thing and another.'

Jack's brow flickers. He is unsure whether there is hidden meaning in the farmer's words. 'Got lucky, I guess.'

The wind whistles between them. Ted takes a step closer. He lowers his voice.

'I know.' When Jack maintains his bland expression, Ted snorts and looks away, muttering something that Jack fails to catch. 'Jim told me everything, just before he died. So, like I say, we weren't expecting you back.'

'Well, I'm sorry to disappoint you.'

'What are you doing here?'

Jack watches as cloud shadows the hills shouldering the horizon, rendering the wood's jewelled canopy drab.

'I just came back, Ted,' he says at last.

'She doesn't need you here.'

'Gwen seems to think differently.'

'She's asked you to stay?' Ted's surprise is stark. Jack sees his confidence falter. 'Why?'

'Right now, I'm needed here and while Gwen needs me, I'll stay. Now, I've got to get on.'

Ted catches his arm. 'Something's happened. Tell me – what's going on?'

'Ask Gwen.'

'I'm asking you.' Concern replaces Ted's animosity and faced with Jack's stubborn silence, he resorts to appeal. 'For God's sake, Jack, what is it?' Jack can almost see the rapid deductions spinning through the farmer's mind. His fingers slacken their grip. 'It's something to do with Allingham, isn't it?'

Jack shakes him loose. 'It's not my place . . .'

'Jesus, lad.' Ted's hand stays him again. 'You know what they mean to me. If he's said something to her . . .'

'He wants his son.'

Ted releases him abruptly. 'What?'

Jack knows he has crossed a line, but it is too late to go back. 'He suspects Tom is his and he intends to try for custody . . . by whatever means.'

Ted utters a profanity and turns away as he tries to absorb the news. 'He hasn't got a chance, surely?'

'As long as I'm here . . . I hope not. I'm not going anywhere, not until this is resolved, until Tom is safe . . . until Gwen feels safe.'

'I can keep Gwen safe . . .'

'But for all intents and purposes, I'm the boy's father. I'm the one who needs to be seen making a stand.'

'And is that what you're going to do? Make a stand?'

'I'm prepared to fight for that boy as if he were my own flesh and blood.'

Ted prepares a retort but at the last minute thinks better of it. Instead, he sweeps off his cap and rakes his fingers through his hair. By the time he sets his cap back, his flare of temper has been suppressed, but he remains grim-faced.

'Did she write to you about Gordon?' he asks at last, a quiver in his voice. 'Did she ask you to come back?'

'No.' Jack shuffles his boot in the dirt. 'No, she didn't. I only just found out.'

'Then I can understand why you're staying.' Ted levels his gaze. 'What I don't understand is why you came back in the first place?'

Jack does not answer him. He looks up at the house and sees Gwen appear on the top step, her arms crossing her front. She raises a hand in greeting and begins her descent.

'I'd better get in.' Jack starts towards her, but Ted calls after him.

'If I'd have known what was going on back then, I'd have happily stepped in.' Jack turns back, but Ted won't look at him. 'But I didn't know,' he admits. 'I just wish . . .' He starts to cough. He pulls a handkerchief from his pocket and wipes his mouth as the fit subsides. 'I just wish I had,' he concludes quietly.

Unable to find words of solace for the farmer, Jack continues up the yard. Gwen comes to meet him.

'He knows . . . *everything*,' he says as he passes her.

Gwen watches him stride on towards the house, her jaw slack. Thoughts racing, she forces herself to join Ted hovering awkwardly at the gate. He starts coughing again, but this time he resorts to another cigarette to stifle the attack.

'Have you seen anyone about that yet?' she asks.

He continues to cough as he lights up. He waits, letting the smoke settle in his lungs before he responds. 'Dr Penny's arranged for me to see someone at the hospital next week, but he's not too concerned.'

She nods. She feels a spit of rain on the wind. 'So, Jack told you, did he?'

'Not Jack, Gwen. Your dad. He told me all of it a few days before . . .'

'Oh.' She studies the horizon, then looks away. 'You never said anything,' she says, her voice little more than a whisper.

'I was waiting. I think . . . I was hoping that you might confide in me.'

They stand, abashed in each other's company. It is Ted who speaks first.

'If you need anything—'

'I know.'

'I meant what I said before, Gwen. I'll always be here for you, for you and Tom.'

'I know.' She takes a deep breath. 'But right now, I need Jack. I need everyone to see Jack here, taking care of us.'

He averts his face so she cannot read his expression. 'I understand,' he says gruffly. 'But he won't stay forever, will he?'

Remembering Jack's crimes, Gwen shakes her head. 'No, he won't. He can't.' But she offers no further explanation. Jack's secret is his own and she suddenly realises the risk he is taking now, staying on at her request, and she wonders anew why he has chanced a return in the first place. Still, she has no intention of betraying him to Ted.

Satisfied with her answer, the farmer nods.

'Well . . . when he's gone, I'll still be here. For you. Always.'

He does not stay to hear her response.

CHAPTER FORTY-SIX

Gwen finds them all in the kitchen finishing off breakfast when she finally returns inside. Nora has a half-empty mug of tea before her, and a half-smoked cigarette clamped between her fingers, its end bearing a ring of lipstick. Gwen passes no comment on the girl's enhanced appearance.

'It's blowing cold now,' she says, although she is unsure whether it is the weather or Ted's words which have chilled her the most. 'The weather's definitely on the turn.'

'It'll be Christmas before you know it,' Nora says, drawing on her cigarette.

'Will it really? Will it be Christmas very soon?' Tom bounces in his chair.

'It will, Tom.' Nora leans forward. 'And what do you want Father Christmas to bring you?'

Gwen wishes Nora would not stir the boy up, though she is relieved that he appears to have forgotten her rash promise about the bicycle. Her pathetic haul of things to sell would not raise anywhere near the funds needed. She watches his eyes widen as he imagines what gifts will await him on Christmas morning and feels horribly inadequate. Helen Allingham's words ring in her ears.

'A train set!' He has clearly given it much consideration and Gwen's heart breaks that she will be unable to fulfil his wish. For the last few Christmases she has been able to use the war to explain why there is so little in his stocking, so little under the tree. With factories commandeered for the war effort, there was never much to be had in the way of toys and trinkets, and what there was had been prohibitively expensive – but what will her excuse be this Christmas? Factories will be returning to normal. Families will be celebrating in style, reunited in peace after years of conflict and separation. She has no doubt there will be plentiful riches beneath the Allinghams' tree. There would be treasures in abundance for Tom there. She cannot bear to think of it. Instead, she gently sweeps his blond hair into a parting.

'That's a very big gift, Tom. Probably best to set your sights on something a little smaller.'

When she lifts her head, she finds Jack watching her. He looks away.

'Right, we'd best get on,' Nora says, shunting back her chair and stubbing out her cigarette in the ashtray. 'Still planning to sow Mere Field today?'

'Yes, yes that's right. Beans.'

'Can I come, Mummy?'

'Perhaps not today, Tom. Stay with Muriel.'

'But I don't want to, I want to come.'

'Tom, we're in Mere Field and I can't keep a close enough eye on you if I'm working.'

'I promise I'll stay away from the water.'

'You promised that last time, remember?'

'What happened last time?'

Jack's enquiry is unexpected. 'He got too near the edge and fell into the mere. I don't like him being in the field now unless I can give him my full attention.'

'I don't want to stay with Muriel,' Tom whines, earning himself a sharp reprimand from the housekeeper.

'What if I come? Keep an eye on him?' Jack waits for Gwen's answer as Tom darts her an apprehensive look.

'Yes, why not?' Nora chips in. 'That seems like a good compromise to me.'

Gwen realises she has been boxed in. Tom is notably quiet. The tension emanating from his little body is palpable, but before she can provide him with an honourable withdrawal, Nora tugs his chair from the table. 'Come on, young man, let's get you kitted up and out. You can help me get the seed sacks. We'll be like Jack and the Beanstalk today.'

Cornered, Tom scrambles off his chair and allows Nora to lead him to the door. Gwen helps him on with his coat and boots and without further discussion he heads outside with the Land Girl.

'I hope you don't mind,' Jack says when they are gone.

'It'll do Tom good,' Muriel pipes up, clearing away the breakfast things. She meets Jack's eye. 'It'll do him good to spend some time with you.' She shoots Gwen a pointed look.

Gwen chooses to ignore her and takes her jacket down from the peg and pulls on her boots. The door shudders to behind her.

'They need time, Jack,' Muriel says, her hands in the sink. She looks at him over her shoulder. 'They both need time.'

*

Gwen and Nora are attaching the seed drill to the Fordson when he joins them. Tom is sitting in the tractor seat, his hands on the steering wheel pretending to drive. He falls silent as Jack approaches and casts a nervous look towards his mother.

Nora's broad grin is more welcoming. 'I don't suppose you fancy giving me a hand with the bean seed?'

Gwen glances up, but quickly looks away. With no reason to refuse, Jack accompanies the Land Girl across the yard to the barn.

'It's over here,' she says, her voice echoing under the pitched rafters. She leads him into the far corner, where hessian sacks are stacked against each other. She searches through until she finds the bean seed. 'Here we are. Can you take one and I'll grab the other?'

'Aye, no bother.' Jack heaves the sack onto his shoulder. Nora grins. Her fingers casually touch his upper arm.

'Nice to have an extra set of muscles about the place.'

'It seems you've been managing right tidy as you are.'

She pulls a face and hefts the other sack into her arms. 'All the same, it's nice to share the load.' She sidles up to him. 'Nice to have a big strong man to help out.'

She is so close their arms brush. He is relieved that the sack is too heavy for her to tarry for long, but it is long enough for her to convey all she wants. Her eyes trail over him as she moves away, leaving a hint of musky scent suspended in her wake.

Jack stands on the field margin watching Gwen bring the tractor round, the seed drill jouncing behind her with Nora positioned on its running board. Tom waits beside him, taut with discomfort, his screwed-up features betraying bemusement at Jack's admiration. Jack grins.

'I've never seen your mam drive a tractor before.'

'She drives it every day.'

'Not when I was here. It was Bobby and Brenda.'

'Who's Brenda?'

Jack looks at him, startled. 'You don't have Brenda the horse now either?'

The little boy offers him a cautious smile. 'No.'

'Aye, a lot's changed since I was here last,' Jack muses. The boy fidgets beside him, disinterested in his observations and resentful of being forced into his company. 'Are you bored, Tom?' He knows the question is unfair. The boy's expression is so solemn the corner of Jack's lip creeps into his cheek.

Squatting down, he works to hide his disappointment as the boy steps back. He remembers Muriel's words – *They need time.* 'What do you say we go into the copse and make a shelter? Much more fun than standing here watching your mam – as impressive as her tractor skills are, like.' He looks over his shoulder towards the fume-belching Fordson then bounces back up to standing and holds out his hand. 'Come on, let's go and have an adventure.'

The boy doesn't move but continues to study him steadily, cautiously, and Jack's heart grows heavy as the seconds tick by. He is expecting too much, pushing too hard, he thinks, and he is about to allow the suggestion to fall when tentative fingers slip into his. His smile erupts. He holds the boy's wary gaze, then tips his head towards the trees.

*

Gwen eases her foot down on the Fordson's throttle, her brow furrowed with concentration as she makes minute changes to the steering to keep her straight line. Movement plays in the corner of her eye. Jack is lifting Tom over the tangle of briars and bracken that separate the top margin from the beech copse beyond. The boy grins broadly as Jack flies him through the air. From the shake of his shoulders, she can tell he is laughing.

'Gwen!' Nora's hail over the throb of the engine jerks her back and she eases off the accelerator as she realises how close she has come to the edge of the field. She brings the steering wheel round, focused again on the task in hand, but once the tractor has turned, dragging the seed drill with it, she sneaks another glance at the treeline above her, where man and child walk, hand in hand, into the sun-dappled depths.

Jack helps Tom select a tree first. He warns him that the trunk will be the backbone of their shelter, so they must choose wisely. He guides the boy's attention to the tree's setting – its position within the wood, the nature of the ground – and at last they find one set a good distance from those around it, with a sturdy trunk and bare earth at its base, free of ground elder and dog's mercury and away from spurting holly bushes. Tom puffs out his chest and solemnly agrees.

They gather fallen branches, the boy dragging ones as long as he is tall from the undergrowth. Jack is careful to employ Tom in every aspect of the shelter's construction. He helps him lift the branches upright rather than take on the task himself, though he could do it in a fraction of the time. When the boy struggles, huffing and puffing, weak but showing effort, he grins at him and ruffles his hair and says, 'Hard work, isn't it?' and

'You're doing a canny job, there lad' and then finds himself having to explain the northern meaning of 'canny'.

'You talk funny,' Tom says boldly.

Jack roars with laughter. 'I'll have you know that's a fine Geordie accent I have there. Don't worry, lad, we'll have you speaking proper in no time.'

When the tree is thickly ringed with bent props, the boy scampers off to gather bracken with which to carpet the shelter's floor. When he is done, Jack stands back, arms crossed, as the boy, red-cheeked, his hair damply tacked to his forehead, looks eagerly for his approval. He nods his satisfaction.

'Can I go inside now?'

'Aye, I reckon you can.'

The boy dashes forward, collapsing to his knees. He crawls into the tepee-like structure, wriggling himself around until he is sitting with his back to the smooth bark of the beech tree, his knees tucked against his chest.

'There's room for you too.'

Jack's heart swells and for a moment he cannot speak. He squats down and peers in through the triangular doorway. The boy draws in his feet and pats the ground beside him.

'Come on!'

Jack laughs, then carefully, on his hands and knees, he crawls inside and sits, hunched over, too tall for the cramped space.

'Did you sleep in shelters like this when you were in the army?'

'No . . . we didn't really have time to build things like this.'

'Where did you sleep then?'

'Sometimes we slept in buildings or barns, but most of the time we were just out in woods and fields in shell scrapes or trenches, or just lying on the ground.'

'Under the stars?'

'Aye lad, under the stars.'

'I want to sleep outside one night, but Mummy says I'm too little.'

Jack wisely remains neutral on the subject. 'Well, you listen to your mam for now. She probably knows best.'

The boy nods. 'Is that the same uniform you wore when you were fighting?'

Jack laughs. 'Aye, it is.' He lifts his arm and sniffs the coarse khaki fabric. 'Does it honk a bit?'

Tom giggles and shakes his head. Silence descends again like a stage curtain.

'Were you scared?' the boy asks at last.

'Aye . . . sometimes.'

Tom rests his forehead on his bony knees. They listen to the crackle of a squirrel racing up a tree and the resonant hammer of a woodpecker in the distance. Beyond the shelter, bronzed leaves drift lazily to the ground, tipping and falling on the breeze ruffling the canopy.

Tom raises his head. 'When you were away . . .' His voice is little more than a shy whisper, but it catches Jack's attention immediately. The bravery behind it is tangible. '. . . Did you think of me and Mummy?'

Jack finds he is unable to answer. His throat is too tight. He swallows down emotion he did not think himself capable of until, finally, he trusts himself to speak.

'Aye, lad. All the time . . . all the time.'

Gwen notices the sea change straight away. On their return to the farmhouse Tom chatters away nineteen to the dozen, firing questions at Jack and making demands on his attention without stopping for breath. They are carried into the kitchen on the incessant tide of his voice. Jack gamely tries to find pause to answer the boy as best he can, before being cut off by the next enquiry that springs from his inquisitive mind. Gwen does not know how to react to the delighted amusement playing in Muriel's eyes, while Nora just laughs as she ducks outside to make use of the privy. At last, Gwen takes pity on Jack.

'That's enough, Tom, give your father a rest.'

And suddenly the kitchen falls still; only Tom carries on, oblivious to his mother's choice of words. Jack lifts his gaze to Gwen and in the ensuing moment they flounder in things left unsaid. She is relieved when Tom asks Jack a question, forcing him to break away.

Now he has discovered his father, Tom is reluctant to let him go. He trails after him, faithful and reverent. Gwen is astonished by Jack's endless patience, but the growing attachment renders her uneasy: she knows it cannot last and she fears the damage that will be wrought when it ends.

That night, when the time comes, Tom asks Jack to put him to bed. Jack mirrors Gwen's surprise. He looks to her for permission.

'Why don't we both take you up, Tom?' she says, finding her voice.

Nora waits on the landing for the three of them to ascend. She is going out, her face made up, a cloud of perfume enveloping her. She calls 'Goodnight' as she thunders downwards. From upstairs they hear the back door slam.

Gwen readies Tom for bed, while Jack hovers near the door. The little boy is unabashed by the novel arrangement and pulls away from Gwen to show Jack a painting he has done, a blue eggshell he found under the apple tree, his collection of acorns. He races around his room, thrusting things into Jack's hands, seeking his approval, his admiration, before Gwen catches him and drags him back to unbutton his shirt or tie his pyjama bottoms. But the moment her hands leave him he dashes away again to collect some other treasure from the windowsill or the mantelpiece, or he is scrabbling under his bed for the old shoe box that contains his prized collection of feathers.

Finally, adopting a stern tone, Gwen ushers him under the covers and picks up his book from the bedside table. Tom springs back up and begs Jack to read to him. She can feel the warmth emanating from Jack's body as he takes the book from her hand. She steps away as he sinks down onto the edge of Tom's bed. The boy lies back, his head nestled into his pillow, his little fingers gripping the coverlet resting on his chest.

Jack begins to read, hesitantly at first, as if embarrassed to have an audience, but as Gwen falls back to the door, he appears to grow in confidence, slipping into different voices for the characters. She finds herself smiling as he reveals a talent she had not anticipated. The boy giggles. When the story is finished and Jack has delivered the final line with suitable aplomb, Tom squirms onto his side and pleads for one more. Jack turns to look at Gwen. She concedes with a smile.

She withdraws onto the landing and stands in the faint glow that slants across the runner from Tom's open doorway. She continues to listen for a moment before padding softly into her own room.

Once inside, she carries the stool from her dressing table to the wardrobe and climbs up, stretching to reach down a battered suitcase from its top. Though not heavy it is cumbersome and she grunts as she struggles with it, wobbling precariously before stepping down onto the floorboards. Heaving the suitcase onto the end of her bed, she flicks open the fastenings and lifts back the lid. Her fingers skim the men's clothing neatly folded inside – shirts, trousers, jumpers – and she experiences a pang of melancholy, but she has become hard and practical over the years and refuses to be maudlin. She begins to unpack.

Soon she hears Jack bring the bedtime reading to an end. She smiles as he sidesteps the boy's drowsy request for '*just one more*' and when the floorboards creak, giving away his departure, she gathers up the pile of clothing and heads to her open door.

He turns towards her. The landing is gloomy, grey with the sinking light that strains through the window at its end. She holds out the bundle in her arms.

'Some of Dad's things. I thought you might fancy a change from your uniform.'

She is careful not to meet his eyes as he relieves her of them. 'Are you sure?'

There is a tenderness in his voice that takes her by surprise. 'He doesn't need them anymore. There's no point them going to waste, is there?' She tries to keep her manner light, but seeing her father's things after all this time has unsettled her. She appreciates his sensitivity.

'Thank you, lass. As Nora's out for the evening, I'll take them to the tack room now . . . and I'll leave you in peace.'

He does not wait for her to reply. Keeping his tread soft as he passes the boy's door, he crosses the landing and quietly descends the stairs.

'Jack!' Gwen catches him as he reaches the kitchen. 'I didn't mean to turf you out.'

He smiles. 'Don't fret, lass. It's probably easier to be gone before Nora gets back . . . and I have something to be getting on with.'

Wishing her goodnight he lets himself out, leaving Gwen feeling strangely bereft once the door has closed behind him.

CHAPTER FORTY-SEVEN

'Someone was burning the midnight oil last night.'

Nora pulls out a chair to take her place at the breakfast table. It crosses Gwen's mind that she has deliberately taken the seat opposite Jack, as she folds herself over the scrubbed pine, smiling at him. 'What were you up to so late at night in the tack room?'

Jack slices into his fried egg with care. 'Was it late?'

Nora sits back. 'Well, I came back after eleven and I saw light in the window.'

'I didn't realise it was that late,' Jack says easily, loading his fork. 'I must have lost track of time.' He looks directly at Gwen, standing rigid by the range. 'I hope I didn't wake you when I came in, pet.'

She shakes her head, forcing a smile, her heart beating a little faster as she waits to see whether Nora has swallowed the bluff.

'What on earth were you doing out there?' Nora persists.

'I'm working on something. A surprise, like. I'd rather not say.' He holds her inquisitive gaze, then takes his last forkful of breakfast.

'I'm intrigued now. Aren't you going to give me a clue?'

'Afraid not.'

'What a spoilsport.'

'What will we be doing today?' he asks Gwen, keen to change the subject.

'Potato picking.'

'You'll need Bobby hitched up to the spinner?'

Gwen suppresses a smile. 'Not Bobby, Jack . . . the Fordson.'

He chuckles at his foolish mistake. 'Aye, the tractor, I meant. I'm still getting used to the changes around here.' He gets up. 'I can go and get the spinner ready.'

'I'll come and show you how to link it to the tractor,' Nora offers, springing to her feet.

She detects his reticence and grins, clearly relishing the fact her presence unsettles him. He stands to the side allowing her through the door first. She angles her body towards him as she slips past. The subtle flirtation is not missed by Muriel, who shakes her head when they have gone, scowling.

'I'll be glad to see the back of that girl.'

'She's harmless enough,' Gwen says, though she is beginning to wonder.

'I'm going to do the washing today. It's dry and there's a good wind, it should do well on the line. Oh,' Muriel slaps her hand against the edge of the sink, 'I should have asked Jack if he has any dirty clothes he'd like me to do.'

'His uniform needs doing – if you can manage it.'

'Well, of course I can.'

'I'll go and get him to bring it in.'

Gwen expects Jack and Nora to be at the implement shed but when she fails to find them there she deduces they must be in the barn, where the tractor is stored. As she approaches, she hears Nora's throaty laugh and wonders what Jack has done to evoke it. She comes to a standstill just beyond the door. She tells herself she is being foolish but, as Nora begins to speak, she finds herself listening in.

'Ughh, I hate potato picking. It always means sore shoulders and an aching back.'

'It has to be done.'

'I know. I wouldn't mind so much if there was someone on hand to give me a back rub at the end of the day . . .'

Gwen does not wait to hear Jack's response. She strides out across the yard, putting as much distance as she can between herself and the barn and whatever is going on inside. She does not want to know. She wants no part of it. She is breathing rapidly by the time she reaches the stable block. She plunges into the dreary interior, fusty with the smell of horse muck and hay, and pushes open the tack room door.

The camp bed is neatly made, its corners tucked in with military precision, while the makeshift workbench has been covered with a horse blanket. Jack's kitbag is on the floor and his khaki uniform is draped across the arched back of the chair. She lets out a sigh and picks up the jacket but feels at once the bulk of its pockets. It seems intrusive to empty them but it has to be done. She removes a few coins and a box of matches, a penknife and a small tin of mints. She thinks she has finished, but as she gathers it to her something crinkles in the breast pocket. Laying it flat on the bed, she undoes its brass button and pushes back the flap.

She withdraws a photograph, a monochrome image trimmed in white, crumpled and creased, and catches her breath as she sees her own smiling face in pale shades of grey. She is crouched down with Tom clutched to her side, his head tilted so that it rests against hers as he squints up at the camera. She remembers the photograph being taken, by Nora, in the summer of '43, and how she included it with a single-page letter when she could think of nothing else to write. She had, after all, made a promise years before that a letter now and then, and a picture of the growing child, was not too much to do for the man who had saved her from social disgrace. It had never crossed her mind, not even for a second, that the photograph might be carried in a breast pocket, or that it might one day show such signs of cherishment.

There is a rusty smudge on one corner, the fine lines of a fingerprint caught in its midst, and suspecting it to be blood, she gasps. The photograph flutters from her fingers to land askew upon the jacket. The kitbag in the corner beckons her.

She advances on it slowly, drawn in by something beyond simple curiosity. She checks behind her, conscious suddenly that her actions are invasive, but she cannot rein herself in, she is unable to stop herself. Loosening the cord threaded through the eyelets at the top of the bag she sees clothing. She pushes aside the spare shirt, the rolled socks and braces, and underneath she comes across envelopes – letters – tied together with string.

She recognises her own handwriting immediately. The flimsy paper package crackles as she takes it from the bag and she feels intense shame that after six years there are so few – a mere token gesture, the half-hearted fulfilment of a pledge. Self-loathing rises from the pit of her stomach. She is about to replace them when she notices another bundle and tucked beneath that yet another string-tied stack, both significantly bigger than the humble collection in her hand. Her brows knit. The top envelopes are addressed to her.

'Were you looking for something?'

She drops the letters and whirls around, her cheeks flaring. Jack stands in the doorway.

'Muriel's doing a wash,' she blurts out. 'I came to get your uniform. I . . . I didn't know whether there was anything else you needed doing.'

'Everything in that bag is clean.' She shrinks from his steady scrutiny. 'Thank you,' he adds.

'Right.'

Desperate to escape, she bustles over to the bed to gather up the abandoned khaki clothing. She stiffens as he joins her. The photograph still lies upon the jacket. When she makes no attempt to pick it up, he reaches past her and wordlessly removes it. She does not dare to look at him. She simply gathers up the uniform, clutching it against her.

'I'm sorry,' she whispers, and before he can ask her to explain, she rushes from the room.

Nora has taken to going out most nights since Jack's return, but Gwen does not miss her company. As soon as she leaves, with Tom safely tucked in bed, Jack excuses himself and retreats to the tack room. It is only then that, to her surprise, Gwen feels the loneliness of her home.

With too much time to think and too little interruption, she sits before the smouldering fire and traverses the corridors of her past, hovering beside doors she wishes she had opened, curious now as to what they might have revealed. The clock on the mantel ticks her solitary evenings away and she is always grateful when it reaches the hour for her to shut up the farm.

She checks on Tom, sleeping peacefully in the darkness, before softly descending the stairs. She pulls on her worsted jacket, for the nights are cold now with October baying at September's door. She is just pushing on her boots when Nora lets herself in and they both exclaim in surprise, coming so suddenly face to face.

'You're earlier than I expected,' Gwen says.

'Oh, the pub was dead – except for Ted, he was there, drinking by himself. He offered to walk me home and since no one else was around to entertain me, I didn't see the point of stopping. Are you shutting up? Want a hand?'

'Yes, don't worry, though, I'll do it.'

'Where's your chap? Isn't he going to help you close up?'

'He's still working,' Gwen says quickly, 'in the tack room.'

'What on earth is he doing out there?'

'You heard him, it's a surprise.'

'I have to say, you two are rather odd,' Nora says, resting against the table.

'What do you mean?'

'After all those years apart, I would have thought you'd be keen to spend every second together, but instead you seem determined to avoid each other's company.'

Gwen forces a smile. 'Well . . . it's strange, isn't it? Having someone back after all that time. Takes a little getting used to.'

'Seems to me you're not making a huge effort, though . . . and I have to say, he is rather easy on the eye – I think I'd be more inclined to have him stay in with me rather than disappear off to his tack room project every night. I just hope you're not feeling shy because I'm here. I wouldn't want you to be holding back because of little old me. If you like . . . you could go to him now. The stables afford you a bit of privacy.' Her eyebrow lifts suggestively. 'I can keep an ear out for Tom.'

'That won't be necessary.'

Nora's chuckle has a condescending bite to it. 'Gwen . . . let yourself go. You've been so tightly wound for all these years, it's about time you showed a bit of passion.'

'I don't need your advice, Nora, on how to conduct myself.'

'*Conduct yourself*? Good God, Gwen, he's your husband. You don't want to risk losing him, do you?' She folds her arms, her chin lifting. 'Or perhaps you do? Perhaps you rather liked not having him around. I can't help but notice Ted's a little put out now he's back.'

'Oh, for God's sake, Nora, just go to bed, will you – and keep your nose out of other people's business,' Gwen pushes past her to get to the door. 'And if I want your advice, I'll ask for it. In the meantime, don't try and interfere with things you know nothing about and couldn't possibly understand.'

Outside, the night sky is thick with cloud. Moonlight is a fleeting gift and she relies on the luminescence of Kip's white patches of fur to guide her down the yard. She unhooks the farm gate and begins to walk it shut. As the moon breaks free its silver light spills across a car parked a little way up the lane. Her strides shorten. She cannot tell whether there is anyone inside, but then she sees the ephemeral glow of a cigarette tip behind the windscreen and she realises there is. Someone is watching her.

She picks up her pace. The car door clicks and slams. A tall figure starts towards her.

'Hello, Gwen.'

Her heart leaps into her mouth. Gordon Allingham's all-too-familiar drawl jolts her into action. She presses forward, her hand firm on the gate, but before she can secure it he pushes against the wood with such force she is sent stumbling.

'It's rather rude to try and shut me out when I've only just arrived.'

'You have no right to be here. You're not welcome.'

'I want to see my son.'

Their shoulders collide as he shoves past her. She catches the sickly waft of spirits and knows he is drunk. He is moving quickly now, striding with purpose towards the farmhouse. She starts after him, calling his name, though she muffles her voice, conscious she does not want to wake Tom or attract any unwanted attention. She reaches for his arm, her fingers forming a vicelike grip as she yanks him round.

'Get out of here.'

'I want to see my son.' He looms over her. She is suddenly aware of the powerful pulse of his inebriated energy.

'He's not your son. Why won't you listen to me?'

'And why won't you do the right thing?' His voice blasts through the darkness. He staggers away from her, bitterness oozing from every pore. 'I told Helen she was wasting her time. She thought you'd see reason, she thought any mother would do what's best for their child when the realities were laid before them, but oh no! Not you!'

'He is my son and he is nothing to do with you.'

'*Lies.* Why are you insisting on spouting what we both know to be lies, Gwen? He is my son – that is an indisputable fact, and another indisputable fact is that the life I can give him far exceeds the one he would have with you.'

'He is my son. He will be loved and cherished and provided for and he will be free to pursue any dreams and ambitions he might have, and I hope he achieves them – through his own his efforts. Love and stability and support are the foundations a child needs to create a wonderful life, Gordon, and my son will have those in abundance.'

'You naïve fool. Can you really be so stupid as to think life is a fairy tale where good things fall into the lap of those who deserve them? Don't be so idiotic, Gwen . . . you're simply trying to excuse your own selfishness.'

'He's not yours, Gordon. I'm sorry I tried to mislead you all those years ago, but enough is enough. He is my husband's son.'

'Your husband?' He throws back his head and laughs. 'Your husband. This fantasy of yours has to end, Gwen, for all our sakes.'

'It seems to me, Mr Allingham, it is your misguided fantasy that needs to end.'

Jack saunters down the yard towards them with an air of nonchalance that Gwen can only envy. He stops next to her, his hands in his pockets, his focus on the man before him.

'We've met. Some years ago now, mind – I don't know if you'll remember. I'm Jack Ellison, Gwen's husband.' Withdrawing his hands, he opens his arms to present himself. 'As you can see, very much present and alive – not much of a fantasy, I would say.'

Though clearly taken aback, Gordon recovers with surprising speed. He snorts. 'Well, well, well. This is quite a conjuring trick, Gwen.'

'There's no trick, no conjuring required,' Jack assures him. 'I'm simply a soldier returned to his wife and son.'

'You were demobbed weeks ago.'

'I went to Newcastle to pay last respects to my mother. Gwen could have told you that if you'd bothered to ask. It seems to me you've been leaping to a lot of conclusions of late,

Mr Allingham – my apparent absence being just one of them. Gwen's told me all about your assumptions over Tom and I'm telling you in no uncertain terms, they need to stop. *Now*.'

'My assumptions? They're not my assumptions.' Gordon swaggers forward. Jack doesn't flinch, even when he leers into his face. 'I don't know for sure what the arrangement was between you two – I have my suspicions of course – but if what Gwen says is true, that you married her thinking she was carrying your child, well then, I'm sorry to break it to you but she's been taking you for a ride. You've been well and truly duped. Tom is mine, and I will have what belongs to me.'

'And now you listen to me.' Jack closes the gap between them, his voice softly menacing. 'Tom is *my* son. I haven't been duped or coerced or anything else you might wish to believe. I married Gwen of my own free will, knowing the bairn she carried was mine. And that is the end of the matter. You need to accept the facts . . . and then you need to walk away.'

Gordon suppresses a laugh. 'Are you trying to intimidate me?'

'No. I'm giving it to you straight. I've no reason to try and intimidate you, Mr Allingham, but you should know this – I will do anything to protect my family.'

'And I will do anything to get my son.' Gordon wheels around to face Gwen. 'I gave you a chance to do this the easy way, Gwen. But if it's a fight you want, it's a fight you've got, and I assure you now, it's a fight I'll win.' He starts walking away. 'You'll be hearing from my solicitor shortly.' He spins back to face them both. 'I'm not playing games here. You might want to think very carefully about your next move. I tried to do this the decent way, but now the gloves are well and truly off.'

CHAPTER FORTY-EIGHT

'A penny for them.'

Jack is startled by Nora's interruption. He is leaning against the gatepost watching the herd as they snort and huff past him on their way up the yard, the lamp in his hand warding off the pre-dawn darkness. Its light glistens on the Land Girl's lipstick as he briefly swings it towards her.

'You must have been up with the lark,' she persists when he fails to respond, but Jack refuses to be drawn. He has hardly slept and does not feel equipped to match her spirit this morning. Allingham's visit weighs heavily on his mind. But that is not all.

He had urged Gwen to return inside once Allingham's car had pulled away. The confrontation had left her quivering and she offered no objection. She ran back to the house with her arms wrapped around her middle, as if endeavouring to hold herself together. Seething, he had finished fastening the gate.

As he turned to go, the rasp of a struck match stopped him in his tracks. Ted had emerged from the shadow of the blackthorn hedge, his features thrown into relief by the flickering flame he brought up to light his cigarette. Neither of them spoke. Ted had batted out the match and then walked away, watched by Jack until he was swallowed by the darkness.

'You've gone again.' Nora's elbow digs into his arm, bringing him back to the present. 'Lost in those thoughts of yours.'

The last cow lumbers past, its hip joints undulating under its stretched hide, clouds of damp air emanating from its wet nostrils. Lamplight follows it as Jack pushes himself up to start his slow pursuit. Nora wastes no time in placing herself beside him.

'What time do you get up? I mean, I'm up early, God knows, but however early I get up, I never hear you leave.'

'I try not to wake anyone. It seems I'm succeeding.'

'But I never hear you at all. How on earth do you get across that landing – down those stairs – without setting off one creaking board? It's impossible.'

She is laughing, but he can detect the cunning behind her words. Suspicion. He stops, dazzling her with the paraffin lamp.

'I've just spent six years in the army, Nora. I wouldn't have lasted as long as I did if I didn't know how to move quietly.'

'Well, I must say, you're very good at it. It's like you're not even there.' She moves closer. 'I wouldn't mind some lessons, if you're up for it . . . I could do with perfecting my *sneaking around* skills.'

'I'm not sure I can help you there . . . I honed my skills in life-or-death situations. You pick things up pretty quick then, let me tell you.'

'I didn't say my needs weren't life or death.' She grins, cheeky and vibrant, inviting.

Jack lets out a sigh. 'I'd better get on with the milking.'

The conversation is over. For him at least.

*

Something wakes him. His eyes fly open. He is facing the outside wall of the darkened tack room with his back to the door, a position that renders him vulnerable. Instinctively he knows the threat is behind him, but he dares not betray himself with any movement. He seeks advantage from his weakness. He waits, silent, alert, his senses so acutely focused they seem to tingle. He knows he is not alone.

He detects a subtle shift of air. His heart is thudding against the wall of his chest as the tension in his muscles rachets. He forces himself to remember the war is over.

He turns, the coarse woollen blanket rough against his bare skin. The door to the tack room hangs open and leaning against its frame is Nora. The moonlight spilling through the gap in the mouldering curtains plays upon her satin nightdress, rendering it pearlescent and alluring in the darkness. She offers him a mischievous smile.

'I told you I needed to improve my sneaking skills. You clearly detected my presence too soon.' Jack's mouth is dry as she sidles through the doorway, the satin moving upon her like a tempting second skin. She runs her fingers over the shirt draped across the arched back of the Bentwood chair.

'I was right, then.'

He pushes himself upright in bed, the blanket slipping to his waist.

'What are you doing here, Nora?'

Light dances in her eyes. 'Testing my suspicions.' There is playful flirtation in her voice. 'She's kicked you out.'

'She hasn't done anything of the kind.'

'Then why are you out here rather than cosily tucked up with her? That's where I'd want you after six years of being apart. I'd want you as close to me as physically possible.'

'I have nightmares. I didn't want to disturb Gwen . . . I didn't want my shouting to frighten Tom.'

'Nightmares?' She breathes the word, filling it with a seductive appeal it should not possess. She moves nearer. Jack's retreat into the corner is subtle but she spots it all the same and smiles a slow, languorous smile as she continues her advance. 'If I heard you have a nightmare . . . I would want to comfort you.'

She is now so close he can smell the musky perfume radiating from her warm skin. He looks up into her eyes as she reaches out to skim her fingertips across the bristles on his cheek, filling the taut silence between them with a soft rasp. She appears intoxicated, but he is aware something far stronger than alcohol courses through her veins. The tips of her fingers fall from the cliff edge of his jaw onto the plane of his chest, where they continue to flow ever downwards. He draws in his breath. And places his hand upon hers to prevent its descent.

'Go back to bed, Nora.'

'Move over then.'

He smiles despite himself. It is impossible not to be impressed by her audacity. 'This isn't what you want . . .'

'I think it is . . .' She leans in so her breath teases his lips.

'Well, it's certainly not what I want. I'm a married man.'

She laughs, but the sound to him is like splintering glass. 'What sort of marriage do you have, Jack, when your own wife won't have you in her bed?'

His features tighten. He is weary now. Throwing back the blanket, he swings his legs out of the bed. He stands up, padding barefoot across the gritty floor to the chair where his trousers hang. Jim's hand-me-downs. He pulls them on.

'It's not your nightmares that keep you from her room, is

it, Jack? It's Gwen.' He refuses to react to her barb though it stings like a cat o' nine tails. 'I've been curious about the state of your marriage ever since I arrived here. She wears your ring, she raises your child, and yet there's just one token photograph of the two of you on the mantelpiece and that's it. You were nowhere to be found in that house . . . and you're still not. You've come home, but she denies your presence. She barely even wrote to you while you were away and when the war ended, she didn't seem particularly bothered to know your whereabouts. What type of wife treats her husband like that?'

'You know nothing about it, Nora.'

'Don't I? I know this much – I know I wouldn't push you away.'

He stiffens as he senses the space between them compress. Her hands explore his back, but he refuses to turn around.

'Let me show how glad *I* am that you've come back . . .'

He steps away and gives her a wide berth as he retreats to the window.

'The only person I care about being glad that I'm back is Gwen.'

'But she doesn't care, does she, Jack? What are you going to do? Wait forever for her to change her mind?' Nora's coy mask falls away. Being rebuffed has rankled her and now her temper simmers; it mars her beauty more than she will ever know.

'Perhaps you're too young, too impatient to realise this, Nora, but some things are worth waiting for.'

'She doesn't want you back, Jack. You might be waiting forever.'

'I'll take my chances.'

'I can't change your mind?'

He stifles a laugh and shakes his head. 'No. I'm flattered, like. But no.'

'You're a fool, Jack Ellison.'

374

'Aye, maybe. You're not the first to say so. I suspect you won't be the last.'

She smiles, convinced she can change his mind, but when he turns back to the window, lifting the edge of the curtain to admire the beauty of the moon, her confidence wavers and her smile gradually fades. He pays her no heed as she leaves.

She remains behind the closed door, listening, waiting, clearly expecting him to come after her, to plead for her return, but then the camp bed creaks and her rejection is complete. Her displeasure evident, she turns to leave and immediately draws in a terrified breath.

Gwen emerges from the shadows, spectral in her long cotton nightdress.

'God, you gave me a fright,' Nora hisses.

'Pack your bags. I want you gone in the morning.'

Gwen doesn't wait for her response. She turns on her heel and strides through the stable door back to the house, Jack's words ringing in her ears.

Nora challenges her directive the following morning. She gets up as usual to help with the milking, but Gwen is already in the kitchen waiting for her.

'You can't be serious?' Nora protests.

'I've turned a blind eye to your loose behaviour throughout the war, Nora. But I can't turn a blind eye to what happened last night.'

'Nothing happened last night.'

'No thanks to you.'

'If you're so concerned about your husband being tempted, maybe you should look at how you treat him.'

'Get out.'

Nora plants her palms on the table. 'What is it, Gwen? You don't want him, but you don't want anyone else to have him either?'

'You don't know what you're talking about.'

'Don't I?' the Land Girl snorts as she straightens up. 'You're the coldest fish I've ever encountered.'

'Well, that's better than being a whore like you.'

Nora barks with laughter. 'A whore? That's how you see me, is it? When it's convenient to do so? Not when you need the potatoes lifting, or the tractor driving or the harvest bringing in, or your precious son being looked after.'

'I'm grateful to you, Nora, for the help you've given me over the past few years. But I'll remind you, I've paid you for that work, *all of it*, including the rare times you've watched Tom for me. It's time for you to go. I cannot have you in this house any longer. Not behaving the way you did last night.'

'He said *no* . . . your darling Jack said *no* . . . Christ knows why. There's no chance of thawing you out.'

'Pack your things, Nora.'

'With pleasure.'

Gwen follows her as she stomps up the stairs, making enough noise to wake the dead – certainly enough to wake Tom. Ducking into his room, she finds him sitting up in bed, sleepily rubbing his eyes, wanting to know what the ruckus is about.

'Nora's leaving us, Tom. I always told you she would one day, and now the war's over she doesn't need to stay.'

'Now Daddy's back.'

'That's right.' She kisses his forehead. 'You stay in bed . . . it's early yet, too early for you to be up.'

'But if Nora's going, I want to say goodbye.'

'I'll tell her for you.' She tucks him back under the covers.

Nora storms downstairs with the single suitcase she arrived with. She retrieves her overcoat from the peg by the back door.

'This treatment of me is unforgiveable.'

'Your behaviour last night was unacceptable,' Gwen retorts, unfazed by her vitriol. 'You must have known there'd be consequences.'

They both jump as the back door bursts open. Muriel blusters in with a basket over her arm.

'Oh!' Her eyes dart quizzically between them, before settling on the case at Nora's feet. 'Oh,' she repeats, turning sober, but she passes no further comment as she deposits her basket on the table.

Nora picks up her suitcase. 'Well, I'd love to say it's been wonderful, but I'd be lying. Goodbye, Gwen, goodbye, Muriel.'

She slams the door behind her.

The breath Gwen has been holding hisses through her teeth like air from a punctured tyre. She rubs her face.

'Should I ask?' Muriel waits expectantly.

'I caught Nora propositioning Jack last night.' She hesitates. 'He didn't know I was there . . . that I was listening. I heard Nora creep out. I followed her.'

'What happened?'

'Nothing. He turned her down.'

'And you turned her out.' Muriel makes a dismissive sound as she pulls out the paraffin drawer on the range. 'Good riddance to bad rubbish, I say.'

'Don't you think it's strange . . . that he turned her away like that? She was offering herself on a plate.'

'A plate a good many have supped from if I know anything,' Muriel retorts sharply, but she relents when she sees Gwen's troubled expression. 'No,' she says at last, her voice softening. 'I don't think it's strange. I don't think it's strange at all.'

Jack is already milking when Gwen enters the parlour. He fails to hide his surprise as she collects her stool and pail.

'What?'

'I was expecting Nora, that's all.'

'Were you hoping for Nora?'

'No, just expecting her.'

'Nora's gone.' When he doesn't react, she presses the point. 'For good.'

She waits, but all he does is nod, his hands moving rhythmically under the cow's udder, the jets of warm milk splashing into the pail at his feet.

'Did you want Nora to help you this morning?' It is like a scab she can't leave alone. She is determined to pick it from the wound, however sore and exposed it might leave the flesh underneath. 'Did you? Did you want Nora to walk through that door?'

He stops milking. He shunts back the stool and stands, smoothing his hand over the cow's haunch, whispering soothing words as he retrieves the pail.

Gwen awaits his answer. He stops alongside her, their shoulders just inches apart.

'It was never Nora that I wanted.'

He continues to the hanging scales and proceeds to weigh his pail.

CHAPTER FORTY-NINE

The letter arrives three days later. Gwen is feeling horribly tired, her attention divided between the stack of post she is opening and Jack's recounting of the night's events that had so disturbed her sleep.

She had been rudely awoken in the early hours by hammering on the back door. Jack had bustled in when she had finally opened up, offering a harried explanation that a fox was prowling around the chicken coop. With no time to spare, he had retrieved the twelve-bore from the gun cupboard in the kitchen, loaded it with cartridges and disappeared back out into the night. She heard the blast of both barrels and was just pulling on her coat when he arrived back. The fox, he assured her, had been dispatched.

Parts of the shotgun are now spread across sheets of newspaper upon the kitchen table, and Jack is carefully cleaning each one as Tom perches next to him, agog at the drama he is relaying. Gwen smiles as Muriel asks when she might expect to have her table back.

It is then that she comes across the cream envelope, its thick nap and colour differentiating it from the flimsy brown ones that denote bills and statements. She stares at her typed name. The postal mark says Helvedon. A tiny dip appears between her brows.

'I'll be with you in a minute,' she murmurs.

A deep-seated instinct advises her to be alone and her withdrawal from the kitchen goes unnoticed. She strays into the office and pushes the door to, though not hard enough to close it completely. Laying the other letters on the desk, she turns the cream envelope over in her calloused hands and inserts her finger under the fold. Ripping paper tears the silence.

It is a single sheet. Her chest tightens as she sees the address of a local solicitors' office. She devours the words too quickly, before they have chance to sink in and before she can digest them. Her heart is hammering as she forces herself to slow down and return to the beginning with its innocuous pleasantry *Dear Mrs Ellison*. Yet even on a second reading, her mind swims with confusion.

'Gwen.'

Jack eases the door open. The letter quivers in her hand.

'Gwen?'

She senses his approach. Tom's voice drifts faintly from the kitchen; pans clang; in the yard the cockerel crows. She feels Jack's solid presence close behind her and part of her longs to sink against him, for him to scaffold her as he had all those years before. But those days, she knows, are long past, and she has no right to impose on him. Instead, she holds out the letter.

'I don't understand.' Her voice is like a breeze through a cracked pane of glass as she releases the letter to his custody.

'He wants blood samples?'

'Can he make us do that?'

'From this it's unclear whether it's a legal demand or a polite request.'

'What if he can?'

'I don't know enough about the law, lass, to say whether he can or not. I think it's time we sought some professional advice.'

'Oh God, Jack . . . what if he can take him?'

'I won't let that happen.' Setting the letter upon the desk, Jack grips the tops of her arms and peers into her anxious eyes. 'And I'm prepared to do whatever it takes to make sure it doesn't.'

Over the years, Gwen has come to know shame well. She has, at times, been intimately acquainted with it. She has borne its burn, nursed its pain, hidden its bruises. But in the elegant first-floor office of a converted Georgian townhouse on Helvedon high street, shame claims her anew, and she wonders if she has the strength to bear it.

She sits before the walnut desk of the senior partner of McVickers, Courtney and Cox. Giles Courtney is younger than she had expected, a man of middling years, cursed by a receding hairline but blessed with a cheerful demeanour. He had welcomed her and Jack into his office with a broad smile and firm handshakes, and now the two of them await his verdict with anxious anticipation. He scans the contents of the letter, having listened stony-faced to Gwen's faltering account of its background. Her cheeks had burned with humiliation as she stumbled over a selective version of events.

He finishes reading and pulls a face, then allows the letter to drop onto the inlaid leather top of his neatly arranged desk. Drawing in a deep breath, he unhooks his wire-framed glasses.

'Mr and Mrs Ellison, from what you've told me – and from what I see here – I think you have very little to fear. Very little indeed.'

'Are you sure?' Gwen pitches forward.

The solicitor releases a slow smile. 'Quite sure. Let us pare back this issue to the apparent facts. The child in question was born to you both within the sanctity of the marriage union. In the eyes of the law, he is therefore your legitimate offspring. If Mr Ellison does not question his paternity—'

'I do not,' Jack interjects gruffly. The solicitor suppresses a telling twitch of his lips.

'Then I don't think there is a judge in the land who would pay any heed whatsoever to Mr Allingham's claims. How old did you say the boy is, Mrs Ellison?'

'Five.' The number croaks free of Gwen's tight throat. 'He'll be six next March.'

'Even if Mr Allingham did have a legitimate claim of paternity over the boy, he has stood by for nearly six years and allowed him to be brought up at the expense of another man.' He glances at Jack. A shallow frown mars his forehead as Jack's eyes fall to his lap. 'By doing so he has, as far as the law is concerned, forsaken any rightful claim he might have upon the boy. Really, you have no need for concern.'

'But he said about blood tests . . .' Gwen shuffles forward in her chair, 'to prove paternity.'

'Ah . . . blood tests. Our Mr Allingham might think he's loaded up his Howitzer but I'm afraid he's fired a dud.' The solicitor observes her blank expression and chuckles to himself. 'Forgive me, I was Royal Artillery until very recently. You served, Mr Ellison?'

'I did. Infantry.'

'Good man.' He smiles. The letter regains his attention. He shakes his head as he scans its contents for a final time. 'I have to say, I'm very surprised at Mr Hodgkin for putting together such a missive – he'll be well aware that this is nothing more than a lot of hot air. But this Mr Allingham is an influential man, you say?'

'Wealthy, certainly,' Gwen replies in a drab voice.

'Well, I think Mr Hodgkin must have allowed his coffers to sway his judgement in this instance. I dare say he was loath to upset a valued client and has undoubtedly bowed to pressure. This letter, you see, strikes me as a rather misguided attempt to frighten you into acquiescence, given there are no legal grounds for its demands.' He pinches the bridge of his nose before replacing his glasses. 'Look, there is a precedent. Blood tests have indeed been used in some cases of disputed parentage, and if, in the *very* unlikely event, Mr Hodgkin was able to find a judge sympathetic to his client's cause, then that judge might support a request for the blood tests to be performed.'

'Surely they can't make us give them samples – they can't forcibly take our blood?' Jack protests.

'Goodness me no, Mr Ellison.' He sits back in his seat. 'Now our European neighbours are very fond of these tests and certainly in countries such as France and Germany – at least before the war, for what it's worth – one can indeed be legally compelled to provide a blood sample for the purpose of testing. Our laws contain no such provision, however. There was an Act tabled in 1939 to pass similar legislation here, but the war rather pushed it to the sidelines. So, certainly at present, you have every right to refuse to cooperate and you cannot be compelled to comply, but if that Bill I mentioned is ever revived – if the law changes in favour of permitting science to have its day – then there may indeed come a time when your right of refusal may no longer stand . . . and the truth . . . whatever it may or may not be . . . will out.'

'So his threats will always hang over us,' Gwen murmurs.

'My dear Mrs Ellison, I would ask you not to fret. It seems to me that now or in the future, Mr Allingham's case remains weak – he has shown *no previous interest* in the boy. He has never made any attempt to support him – financially or emotionally – or to care for him, or take any responsibility for him – indeed, to be any sort of father to him at all. In cases such as these, it is the wellbeing of the child that is of paramount importance and I can't see any judge removing Tom from what is clearly a loving, stable and supportive family to meet the whim of such a man as Gordon Allingham – however righteous his claim may or may not be.'

Sighing, he leans forward. 'Now, I suggest that we respond with a return salvo of our own. I will write to Mr Hodgkin and let him know, in no uncertain terms, that his client's position is untenable and that we have no intention of assisting him in the matter. Let me call his bluff. I'll offer a robust invitation for him to pursue it, if he wishes, through the proper legal channels. I suspect we shan't hear from him again. Mr Hodgkin is no fool; he might have been willing to placate a vociferous client by sending such a letter, but he will not be prepared to jeopardise his legal reputation with an ill-judged suit. Leave this with me and have no fear. Your son is quite safe and will remain where he is.'

He stands, giving Gwen and Jack their cue to leave. Moving

out from behind his desk, he escorts them to the door. Gwen thanks him for his reassurances and his time, before setting off down the corridor, eager to be gone. Jack offers him his hand, then gauchely expresses his own gratitude as he runs the rim of his cap through his fingers.

Mr Courtney draws himself up. He is not a statuesque figure by any means, but he has the deportment of an officer and Jack responds accordingly.

'I must say, Mr Ellison, I am not sure I could do what you have done.'

'Tom is my son, Mr Courtney.'

'Of course. Of course. And he is very lucky to have you.'

Jack lowers his head and attempts to leave.

'Mr Ellison.' Mr Courtney pauses as Jack turns back. 'You ought to be aware, should the situation change . . . the purpose of blood tests in cases such as these is not to *prove* paternity. I'm afraid the purpose of these tests is to *disprove* it. Beyond all question.'

CHAPTER FIFTY

Gwen is reattaching the potato spinner to the Fordson, ready to lift the second field of potatoes, when Ted comes walking up the yard. She checks the chain is secure and rubs her nose on the back of her hand as he raises his in greeting. He absently ruffles Kip's fur as the dog bounds over to him.

'Morning, Gwen.' He takes off his grubby tweed cap; its band has crimped his weathered forehead.

'Morning, Ted.'

'Lifting potatoes again?'

'Yes, I'm hoping to get them all up by the end of the day.'

'Good job if you can, the weather's turning. Hard frost tonight, they reckon.'

'Yes, so I hear.'

He studies the dreary sky as a rain-bloated nimbus drifts above them. 'I uh . . . I heard Nora's gone.'

'That's right.'

'Trouble?'

Gwen shrugs lightly. 'Well, she's not really needed anymore.'

'Not now Jack's back, I suppose.' He darts her a loaded

386

look which she refuses to entertain. 'She's not gone far,' he says, catching her curiosity, as he clearly intended to. 'She's shacked up with Dick Withers.'

Gwen snorts. One of Nora's younger conquests, a farm hand from down the valley with a tied cottage. 'I never doubted she'd land on her feet.'

'She was in the pub last night.'

The ironic smile Gwen is sporting quickly fades. Ted nods, responding to the change in her demeanour. 'You'd best be careful, Gwen,' his voice drops, 'she's not said anything outright, but . . . well, folks were asking what had happened.'

'And?'

'Let's just say she alluded to there being more to the set-up here than meets the eye.'

Gwen exhales sharply and braces herself on the wheel arch of the Fordson. 'I see.'

'I just thought you should know. She might set people talking.'

Pushing herself up, Gwen shakes her head, her fingers digging into her waist. 'Bloody girl. I should have known she wouldn't go quietly. Perhaps I was rash in giving her her marching orders.'

'Did she give you reason?'

'Yes, she gave me reason.' She doesn't mean to snap, but her voice is harsh and the words clipped. 'Next time you're in the pub you can let it be known that she was sent packing for propositioning my husband.'

She lays a restless hand back upon the wheel arch before whipping it away and dragging it through her hair. Ted uses the toe of his boot to unearth a stone protruding from the packed earth.

'That troubled you, clearly,' he says after some consideration, looking away. He releases a soft sigh. 'Look . . . I was only planning on doing some hedge planting today – what do you say I help with the potatoes? You don't want a frost getting into them.'

Gwen welcomes the distraction of his offer. 'Are you sure?'

'Ah, it's no bother. You know I'm always happy to help.' He manages some semblance of cheeriness, but it fails to alleviate the sadness that has drained the light from his eyes.

She repays him with a gentle smile, for the truth in the statement does not escape her. However cautious she has become around her neighbour – however suspicious of his evolving feelings – she knows without him she could not have survived the war and she certainly would not have kept her farm. 'I do. Thank you, Ted.'

He steps forward, and despite her generous thoughts her vigilance returns in an instant. As if detecting the change, he covers his advance by patting the tractor.

'You ready to go?'

'Yes.' She drops around to the back of the vehicle and climbs up into the seat. 'You can crank her up for me if you like?'

'I'll have a go.' He bends down to grip the starting handle. He whips it round to no avail, and then again. On the third time the engine splutters into life and he steps back.

Gwen shifts it into gear and eases forward. She applies the brake as she draws abreast of him.

'I forgot to ask,' she shouts over the thrum of the engine. 'How did your hospital appointment go?'

'Oh fine, fine . . . nothing to worry about, just as I said.' His indifference is reassuring.

They are both distracted by Jack approaching with Bobby and the wagon. Tom is straddled across the gentle giant's back, his small hands gripping the horse's collar, his little legs barely clearing its shoulders. Jack holds the bridle, carefully keeping the pace slow and steady.

'Well, look at you riding high,' Ted calls to the boy, who grins in response.

'Right then, we'd better get to it,' Gwen shouts, and shifting the gear lever she rolls the tractor forward and leads them from the yard.

The day stays dry, though great lilac clouds pillow the sky and the wind remains insistent. Gwen drives the tractor over the soft ground, the spikes of the spinner churning through the soil, pulling up the plants and throwing out potatoes in their wake.

Tom slipped from Bobby's back into Jack's welcoming arms as soon as the wagon had cleared the margin. The horse and cart now stand at the field's edge, a layer of dirt-encrusted potatoes spread across the cart's floor.

Ted walks behind the whirling spinner, sweeping aside the bushy stalks with his pitchfork, while Jack and Tom stoop to gather the potatoes into their wicker baskets. Tom is soon staggering under the weight of his load and begs Jack to help him – he is too small to unload the basket into the wagon alone. Jack makes him wait until his own basket is laden, then together they pick their way across the field to the cart.

Jack upends his basket first. The potatoes pound against the wagon's wooden floor, rolling off each other until they settle, like water finding its natural level. He lifts the boy up and Tom copies him, grunting with effort as his pickings tumble onto the rest. If either of them are aware of Ted's steady regard as he pauses for a moment, they show no sign of it. By the time they have returned to the furrows, the farmer is on the move again, sweeping the prongs of his pitchfork through the uprooted plants.

They walk back to the house for lunch, Tom squatting to pick yellow hawksbit flowers from the verge before racing to catch them up. When Jack swings him up into a piggyback, he kicks his feet as if riding a horse, steering him nearer to Gwen, and when he is close enough he leans over to tuck a flower behind her ear, jiggling on Jack's back with glee. Gwen laughs, her grubby fingers straying to the delicate petals, though she is careful not to dislodge the bloom, and there is humour in Jack's voice as he tells her it looks very fetching. Ted smiles despite himself as he watches the unfolding scene, but he is unable to hold the expression for long and his focus soon returns to the undulating lane before him.

They finish lifting the crop just before milking time, and Gwen is pleased with the bountiful harvest. She drives the tractor back to the farm, while Tom, Ted and Jack climb up onto the wagon, heavy now with potatoes. Jack flicks the reins and Bobby walks on, dragging the cart from the field and out into the lane. Tom is tired from the day's labours. Sandwiched between the two men, his head sags towards Ted. The farmer lifts his arm so the boy can better rest against him, before tenderly draping it back around his narrow shoulders.

Gwen has already left to bring in the cattle by the time they reach the yard. Jack guides Bobby up to the barn. He ties off the reins and climbs down while Ted gently rouses Tom. The boy yawns and rubs his eyes, before scooting across the bench seat to throw himself into Jack's upstretched arms.

'Go in now, see Muriel,' he instructs and, without issue, the boy races off.

Jack unfastens the wagon's backboard as Ted climbs down. He has already set up the riddle in the barn, ready for sorting and bagging up the potatoes. Between them, he and Ted guide Bobby backwards through the cavernous doorway, so that they can unload onto the freshly swept floor. They work together methodically, with little need for communication and when at last the crop is piled ready, Jack clips up the backboard and he and Ted set about freeing Bobby from the shafts. When they are done, Jack offers his thanks and begins to lead the great horse towards the door.

'I was wondering why you came back.'

He stops at Ted's words. Bobby shakes his head, tired and irritable. Jack runs his hand down his neck to settle him.

'I always suspected back then,' Ted continues, 'before the war, that you had feelings for her. I saw the way you looked at her. So, I wasn't surprised to hear you'd asked her to marry you – it was the fact she'd said yes that took me aback. For years after I had a hard time trying to make sense of it all until, that is, Jim told me the truth of it. I was hurt, I'm not going to lie. I thought I'd missed my chance, but then he went on to say that Gwen had assured him you had no intention of coming back, and I allowed myself a bit of foolish hope that perhaps all wasn't lost just yet.

'But then you did what no one expected and back you came, and I wondered *why*, but I knew soon enough. You couldn't stay away, could you? And I suppose what with this Allingham business it's a good thing you've turned up like a bad penny. She needs you here, I accept that. And I told myself it wasn't going to be forever, just for now . . . even though I could still see you looking at her the way you always have. But I had never seen her look at you that way. Until today.'

His words hang heavy in the air. He lets out a deep sigh of resignation and then he pulls himself up and walks out into the yard. In the distance, Jack hears the cows lowing. He stands in the echo of the farmer's words, his heart pulsing, and for the second time in his life, he dares to hope.

CHAPTER FIFTY-ONE

They hear the traction engine before they see it. They are in the kitchen finishing breakfast when its mighty throb vibrates through the house. Tom is out of his chair in an instant, running towards the door, bubbling with excitement, but Gwen cautions him as she rises from the table. Helping him on with his coat and wellies, she warns of the intrinsic dangers of the machinery visiting the farm that day.

Jack drains the last of his tea and takes his plate to the sink, thanking Muriel, who is already in the midst of washing up. He has never seen a threshing machine before and is unsure what to expect, but he is aware that today is an important day and Gwen has been looking forward to it. They had spent the previous afternoon removing the thatch from the towering ricks, with Gwen studying the sky, anxiously looking for signs of rain. But it has held dry and pale autumn sunshine now bathes the butter-coloured stacks of straw standing in the rickyard.

The three of them leave through the back door and hurry down the garden path as an enormous wooden monster rolls past them up the yard, pulled by the steam engine. To Jack it vaguely resembles a ship on wheels. A circular drum protrudes from the flat deck above them like a squat funnel, while its hull bears wheels connected by belts. Behind it comes another piece of equipment, which Gwen identifies as the baler.

They follow the machinery up into the rickyard and when it finally comes to a stop, a team of men clamber down – two from the engine, while five others scurry down the sides of the thresher like rats off a ship. Gwen greets each in turn, familiar faces all of them, her smile broad and welcoming.

Tom races forward to study the engine. Resplendent in bottle green it gleams in the sunlight. Gwen shouts a word of caution and Jack jogs to catch him up, hoisting him up onto his shoulders so he can better see its incessant pistons and the flickering needles in its gauges.

'Tom, I want you to go inside now to Muriel. I need you to stay out of the way today, the thresher and engine are very dangerous for little boys,' Gwen calls.

'But I want to stay and watch.'

'No, Tom. Daddy and I will be busy helping, we can't keep an eye on you at the same time. I'll ask Muriel to bring you out in a bit and you can stay and watch then. You'll soon get bored of it – I can guarantee that.'

'I won't.'

'Come on now, Tom, do as your mam asks. You'll get your chance in a little while.' Jack crouches down before him. He chucks the boy's chin. 'And what about I see if there's any chance you can stand up in the engine at some point – would you like that? And I wonder if there's a whistle to be blown . . .' He glances at Gwen unsure if he is promising too much, but her twitching lips reassure him. He grins. 'I bet you can make that whistle scream like no one else can. So, what do you say? Go in now, while your mam and I get sorted, and we'll make sure you have a proper chance to explore it all later.'

Appeased, Tom nods. Jack musses his hair and pushes himself back up, warmed by the appreciation in Gwen's eyes.

'We need the ladder and the pitchforks from the shed,' she says.

'I'll help you. Come on, Tom, let's get you inside.'

They watch Tom run up the steps, waiting until he has disappeared through the back door before they carry on to the implement shed.

'You seem to know this lot well,' Jack says, tipping his head towards the team of men.

'They've been coming here for years,' she says, entering the shade of the building. 'Since I was a little girl. They do all the farms around here. They'll be going on to Ted next. He'll probably pop over later to see how we're getting on.' She heads straight for the long ladder, hanging horizontally across the back wall.

'Let me,' Jack says, and reaching past her he lifts the ladder clear of its hooks. She falls back as their bodies brush, colour rising in her cheeks.

'I'll bring the pitchforks,' she says. She seems grateful for an excuse to move away.

Back in the rickyard, three men are busy connecting the thresher's belts to the engine's flywheel, while two others are hanging hessian sacks from the chutes on the thresher's end, ready to catch the grain shaken free of the straw. While the machine is prepared, Gwen and Jack harness Bobby to the wagon and ready it to be loaded with sacks of corn.

The foreman shouts to Gwen that they are nearly done. She props the ladder against the nearest rick and gestures for Jack to lead the way. He climbs swiftly, one hand on the ladder, the other gripping the heavy pitchfork. Once on the top rungs, he throws it onto the stack then scrabbles up after it. He relieves Gwen of her pitchfork when she appears, then offers her his hand. He sees her cautious hesitation, but after a second's deliberation she reaches out to take it and he pulls her up. She staggers slightly and his arm darts out to steady her. Their eyes snag as she finds her footing.

The men on top of the thresher unfold a narrow wooden platform which bridges the twelve-yard drop between the machine and the rick. The foreman below calls up to her, channelling his voice with his hands, and Gwen leans over the rick's side to signal that she is ready.

'What do I do?' Jack shouts to be heard above the noise of the shuddering machine, as the belts spin the wheels on its sides and the pistons underneath race back and forth.

'Just pitch the sheaf to the men on the deck. They'll cut the binding and feed the corn into the drum on top there,' she hollers back, pointing to the funnel he had seen earlier.

Gwen snatches up a sheaf on the prongs of her pitchfork and, with one foot on the wooden drawbridge, she whips it over to the first man on the deck. He slices the binding with his knife and passes it to the next man, who separates the straw and feeds it into the gaping mouth of the drum. Below, a couple of men loiter by the chutes, ready to replace the bags when they are full, while, at the back of the machine, straw falling in dribs and drabs lands on the baler's conveyor belt and slides slowly down into the bale chamber. Two more men, armed with sturdy straight-pronged forks, wait for the wire-bound straw blocks to appear, ready to stack them to the side. The team work in perfect synchronicity, as well-oiled as the machine they serve.

Soon dust billows about them, stinging their eyes and scratching their throats. By the time Ted ambles into the rickyard just before lunch, their faces are coated in a film of dirt and their hair is covered by a dry crust, but there is no time to dwell on their discomfort. There is still much work to be done.

Gwen pays little heed to Muriel when she first spots her, hurrying down the path into the yard. She continues to pitch sheaves to the men on the thresher, the muscles in her shoulders and back aching. It is not until she sees Muriel twisting left to right, her mouth wide, calling, her words drowned by the thresher's deafening digestion, that she feels the first stir of unease. Even as her body moves like an automaton, forking and pitching, her eyes trace back to the housekeeper. Her mechanical movements finally falter when Muriel runs towards them. Gwen's stomach grips. Muriel looks afraid.

Gwen watches as Ted breaks off his conversation with the foreman to listen to the old woman's rapid words, his brows dipping as he does so. She realises the interplay must also have caught Jack's eye, for he too is now monitoring their hasty approach.

Gwen drops her pitchfork and scrambles over the rick's edge, lowering herself down to the ground below, brushing away the strands of straw sticking to her legs as she goes to meet them.

'What is it?'

'Is Tom with you?'

'Tom? No of course not, he was with you.'

Muriel lets out a whimper, her hands knotting in her apron. 'He's been so eager to come out, but I said he'd have to wait until I'd got the lunch ready. Then I saw the back door was open and I thought he'd just gone into the garden, but I've checked and he's not there. I can't find him, Gwen – he's not in the house and he's not in the garden.'

'Where can he be?' Gwen spins round, dread crawling up her spine. She hollers Tom's name at the top of her voice, over and over, moving away from the chuntering machinery to improve her chances of being heard.

'He can't have got far,' Jack says. 'I'll go and look in the stables and milking parlour.'

'I'll check the barn,' Ted offers.

'Gwen, you take the implement shed,' Jack suggests, his fingers closing around her arms to steady her. 'Muriel, can you make sure he hasn't slipped out to the paddock? And where's Kip? There's a good chance he'd stick with Tom.'

His voice drifts off as the dog comes running through the gateway from the lane. Jack starts towards it, walking at first, but quickly picking up his pace. The thresher falls silent, the steam engine easing with a hiss behind them, as the men detect the rising emergency and begin to gather.

Kip dances between Jack and the gate, agitated and anxious. Gwen follows Jack as he continues forward, with Ted and some of the threshing team falling in behind her. She wonders what instinct is driving Kip as he continues to whine, dashing back and forth, leading them ever closer to the lane. But as they reach the gate all becomes clear, and Kip's instinct, Gwen realises, is sound.

CHAPTER FIFTY-TWO

Jack recognises Gordon Allingham at once. He is sitting astride a motorbike, cruising up the lane at walking pace. Sprawled in front of him, his stomach flattened against the petrol can so he can reach the handlebars, is Tom, his head covered in a leather aviator cap, its ear flaps hanging down the sides of his face. Allingham is laughing and Tom giggles in reply as the bike creeps along, purring seductively.

'What the hell do you think you're doing?' Jack shouts. He is certain Allingham has heard him over the restrained putter of the motorbike's engine and yet he gives no sign of it.

Jack breaks into a sprint. As Allingham reaches the bend in the lane, he slowly skims the bike back around. Tom lets out a yelp as he slips precariously, unseated by the slanting motion. Gordon's hand drops from the clutch to steady him, but the shock has rattled Tom. He now appears apprehensive, like someone who has merrily boarded a big wheel, only to realise as the ground drops away that a fright might be in store.

'Tom wanted to see my new motorbike, didn't you, Tom?'

Allingham's eyes trail from Jack to Gwen. 'Since his *parents* are too busy labouring to keep him entertained . . .'

'Tom, time to get off bike, lad.'

'We haven't finished yet,' Gordon drawls.

'Oh yes you have.'

'I promised the boy a ride and a ride he shall have!' Gordon shouts as he revs the engine. The motorbike roars like a tormented beast.

'Tom!' Gwen pushes past Jack. 'Gordon, let him off, now!' But as she comes closer, the bike leaps forward. Tom cries out as he slips again over the curve of the petrol can.

'Mummy!'

'For God's sake, Allingham, let the boy off!' Jack starts forward, but in a perverse game of cat-and-mouse Gordon twists the throttle and the bike surges past them before skidding to a stop. He laughs as Gwen and Jack give chase.

'This is fun, isn't it, Tom?'

'I want to get off! My arms are hurting.' Tom begins to cry. He is stretched taut gripping the handlebars he is now terrified to release.

'Let him off the bike, Gordon! He doesn't want to be on it!' A sob catches in Gwen's throat. She gets close enough to lay her fingers on Tom's arm, before Gordon sends the bike flying forwards again. Tom screams.

'For God's sake!' Jack races after them. Gordon is laughing now. Each time Jack makes it within touching distance, he jumps the bike on.

'Daddy!'

'Hold on tight, Tom, I'm coming!'

Allingham's expression darkens at the touching interchange.

His eyes deaden as he turns his focus to the stretch of lane before him.

'Gordon, *please* – he's frightened!' Gwen cries, but as soon as she is alongside he tightens his fist against the clutch.

'I promised him a ride!'

The motorbike roars forward but this time Gordon doesn't stop, instead he wrings the throttle and pushes through the gears with his foot.

'He's going to kill him!' Gwen screams, but Jack is already running after them, his arms pumping by his sides.

Ted has been waiting anxiously by the gate. As the bike tears towards him he steps out into the lane, spreading his arms wide, as if it is a charging horse he is attempting to stop and not a speeding vehicle.

Jack's pursuit abates as he realises with utter dismay that Gordon is showing no signs of slowing down. His heart falters in his chest.

'Jesus, he's not going to stop . . .'

Ted doesn't move. Grim-faced, he stands fast, blockading the road. There is not enough room for Gordon to safely skirt around him and yet the motorbike roars closer.

In Jack's mind, it takes minutes. He watches in abject horror as at the last second – just as Ted flinches, preparing for the impact that must surely come – Gordon hauls the motorbike away. The machine skids across the road, toppling sideways as its front wheel smashes into the hedge. Tom flies into the air like a rag doll. Gwen screams his name.

Jack's chest explodes as he races to the boy, curled up on the verge amongst the hedge garlic, knapweed, and nettles.

'Tom! Tom!' He collapses to his knees, feeling more fear

than he thought possible. With infinite care he lays his hands on the child who has come to mean more to him than he dares confess. When Tom whimpers, he chokes on his tears. 'Tom?'

'Daddy.'

Unfurling like a blossoming flower, Tom rolls over into Jack's waiting embrace. He is too dazed to cry; he simply wraps his arms around Jack's neck and clings on so fearfully that Jack can hardly breathe.

'I've got you,' he whispers. 'Do you hurt anywhere, lad? Your head, your legs, your back?'

Tom's face crumples as he nods. Jack takes off the aviator cap and throws it into the brambles. Gently easing the boy away from him, he clasps his grazed face in his hands, checking him for damage.

'Tom!' Gwen crashes down beside him. 'What hurts, darling?'

'I'm sore, Mummy, and the nettles have stung me.' He starts to cry, but to their relief he shows no sign of serious injury as he crawls into his mother's arms, sobbing against her chest as she rocks him. Gwen's own tears form runnels through the dust that coats her face. Jack pushes himself up and helps Gwen to her feet. She brings Tom with her, his legs wrapped around her hips, his arms looped around her shoulders, his head buried in her neck.

'Get him inside,' Jack says softly.

She nods and starts to make her way across the lane. The shocked men from the thresher fall back, clearing a path for her.

In the verge, the motorbike's wheels continue to spin, willow-herb and cocksfoot tangling amongst their spokes. Petrol fumes sully the air. Allingham, partially pinned, groans and curses as he tries to push the machine clear of his body. Ted crosses to him without hurry, his expression dark as night. His great paws grasp the upturned handlebar and the freshly crumpled fender.

'Keep still,' he growls as he pulls the bike up onto its tyres. He has only just rolled it clear when Jack throws himself upon its stricken rider. Grabbing the sheepskin lapels of Allingham's flying jacket, he hauls him from the verge.

'What the hell did you think you were doing?' He shakes Allingham with the ferocity of a terrier dispatching vermin. 'You could have killed him.'

The atmosphere has warped into something beyond fear. Clearly sensing the danger, Gwen hastens her retreat, her palm pressed to the back of Tom's head as if she is afraid to expose him to the anger writhing across Jack's face. Muriel gathers them up and shepherds them towards the house. Gwen casts an anxious look behind her.

'Get the hell off me!' Allingham cries, struggling to free himself, but Jack is taller and stronger and driven by a primeval fury that renders him invincible. Allingham has no choice but to accept defeat. A slow smile twists his lips. 'What are you going to do? Beat me to a pulp? Please do. I'll report it to the police, of course. And I'll let my solicitor know. It'll strengthen my case.'

'You have no case.' Jack battles the itch to pummel the man. Instead he crushes the sheepskin in his fists. 'Your solicitor has probably already told you that.'

'I haven't finished, Ellison. There are other solicitors, other opinions . . . amenable judges – a few of them family friends. I will not rest, it's *you* that's facing the losing battle.' He juts out his chin until it is so close to Jack's they almost touch. Dropping his voice to a whisper, he stares straight into Jack's eyes. 'I will have my son.'

With a furious bellow, Jack swings him round and smashes him into the brick pillar of the gatepost. Allingham gasps in pain. Undaunted, Jack hefts him up and rams him against the hard bricks again and as Gordon slumps against his hold, he brings back his fist and drives it into the man's stomach. Gordon wheezes, doubling over from the blow. Jack brings back his fist again, impervious to his shocked audience, but Ted intercedes.

'Easy, Jack,' he says, laying a firm hand on his arm.

Jack clenches his jaw. Lava flows through his veins as his fist flexes. He fights for his self-control and in the end he wins. He yanks Gordon up to his full height so that they are face to face.

'If you don't drop this, if you go anywhere near my family again, so help me I will kill you.'

He slams him into the bricks a final time, then with another furious cry, he hauls him round and hurls him to the ground. Allingham collapses prostrate in the dirt.

'Now, get out of here . . .' Jack snarls, 'because next time I'll make sure there's no one around to intervene.'

He kicks dirt into Gordon's face. The stunned threshing team warily part to let him pass. He doesn't look back.

He is vaguely aware of the motorbike throbbing into life and the furious rip of its engine as it speeds away down the lane. Ted jogs to catch him up, slowing his pace as he draws alongside, struggling to catch his breath, a hand to his chest.

'I want to check on Gwen and Tom,' Ted insists as they reach the steps. Jack keeps his head down and mounts them first. He looks back when Ted fails to follow.

The farmer remains in the yard. He pulls off his flat cap and absently runs the brim through his fingers.

'Ted?'

He pulls his cap back on. 'You go in and see they're all right, Jack. I'll go and help the men with the rick.'

'Come on, Ted . . .' Jack tips his head towards the house. 'Come and see her.' His voice is gentle.

Some emotion that Jack can't define crosses Ted's face. 'If you're sure. Thank you,' he manages, his voice hoarse as his feet scuff the steps.

Jack pushes open the back door to find Gwen sitting at the kitchen table. She lifts her head from her hands; her tear tracks form a braided stream down her dusty cheeks.

'Where's Tom?' Jack asks.

'Muriel is reading to him in his room.'

While Jack comes further in, Ted remains in the doorway.

'Is Tom all right?' he asks.

Gwen nods. She bites her lip. Her chest rises and falls. 'He's never going to stop, is he? He's never going to leave us alone. We'll never be safe. We will never be free of him.'

The two men watch helplessly as she buries her face in her hands, her shoulders quaking from sobs she is powerless to contain.

CHAPTER FIFTY-THREE

Gwen eventually rallies and returns to the ricks, though she is grateful when the time comes to collect the cows for milking, giving her an excuse to slip away. She is conscious of the threshing team's weighted stares as she passes by, and she wonders what deductions they have made from the morning's entertainment.

The lane is thankfully quiet and only serenading blackbirds and a wren that flitters amongst the entwined branches of the hawthorn attempt to keep her company.

She has walked so far without seeing anyone that when she does, she is startled. A pedal bike lies discarded on the grassy trapeze before a field gate. Its owner – a young woman – is leaning over the gate itself, the wind fluttering her headscarf and coyly lifting the hem of her tweed skirt. She shies away when she hears Gwen, shielding her face. Her stiff embarrassment hints at tears, so Gwen keeps her head down and lengthens her stride to afford the girl some privacy.

'Oh, it's you.'

Gwen stops in surprise as the young woman addresses her. She could have allowed Gwen to pass by without comment, but instead she catches her before she disappears around the bend. Now that she boldly reveals herself, Gwen sees it is none other than Helen Allingham.

'Is your little boy all right?'

'Yes – no thanks to your husband.'

'I'm sorry about what happened. You'll be pleased to know we got into a frightful row about it.'

It is clear without need for careful examination that she has indeed been crying, but there is more damning evidence on Helen Allingham's face than silken tear tracks. Her lip is split at the edge and a stark red blemish mars her porcelain complexion. Gwen looks upon her, appalled. Helen Allingham's fingers instinctively rise to the damage. She averts her gaze to the field beside her.

'So, it turns out your husband came back after all.' Her tone is sharp but it contains an intriguing undernote that prevents Gwen from walking away, as instinct tells her to.

'You didn't think he would?'

'Gordon was so sure.'

'And you thought I was lying?'

'You still could be. Just because your husband came back doesn't mean he's Tom's father.' Her bruised face takes on a sly look. 'Perhaps he has come back because he loves you . . . and because of that, he is prepared to love Tom too – just as I am willing to do, if Tom is Gordon's.'

'Well, he's not.'

Helen shrugs, as if the debate fails to interest her now. 'All I wanted was a child . . .' she says quietly.

'You can't have mine.'

'I can't have any now.' She is curdled by bitterness and makes no attempt to conceal the fact.

'You could adopt,' Gwen says, coming forward. 'Plenty of children need homes.'

'I told you before, I couldn't take in a stranger. I could have accepted Tom.' Helen glances back at her, before returning her gaze to the field. 'You should have let me have him, you know, regardless. Do you know the kind of life I could have given him? The royal family are often guests of my parents. I myself have shot grouse beside the Duke of Windsor.'

'Tom doesn't need that type of life. Connections don't enrich anyone . . . love does.'

'Love,' Helen snorts.

'Yes, love . . . don't you love Gordon?'

'I was charmed by him. We were a good match, that was the important thing.'

'What? You with your five thousand acres and him with his ten?'

'Eight,' she corrects sharply. 'And yes, things like that do matter and they can make all the difference.'

'Money can't buy you everything, though, can it?'

'It can't buy me a natural child of my own, if that's what you're getting at. You like rubbing my nose in it, don't you?'

'Did you ever love him, Gordon?'

'I did . . . perhaps I still do. Love is a strange thing. It can burn so brightly one minute and be gone the next.'

'Like fireworks.'

'Yes, just like that. Something so intense and beautiful, so full of promise . . . reduced to a disappointing wisp of smoke. All my hopes gone. And now I'm trapped with a husband who is increasingly not the man I thought he was and I have no way out.'

'You could leave him.'

She laughs. 'Just like that.'

'You have money, means . . .'

'Are you suggesting divorce? And be treated like a pariah? No, I think not.'

'Well, you should . . .' Gwen nods towards her face, thinking of the whispered gossip Muriel has shared with her over the years; the pitying shakes of her head as she speaks of some poor woman whose husband is quick with his temper and even quicker with his fists, and how no one steps in to stop it. She finds herself sharing the housekeeper's stark warning. '*If he's done it once, he'll do it again.*' She sees fear flicker across Helen's face and feels a desire to press her point. 'When a dog mauls a sheep, you have to put it down, because it won't stop – they get a taste for it, you see, a taste for blood. You should watch yourself. Gordon may well be the same.'

Helen winces, as if reliving her husband's hand landing its brutal blow. Her expression hardens.

'*Put him down . . .*' she echoes thoughtfully. 'He was drunk.'

'That's no excuse.'

'I didn't say it was.'

'He'll be drunk again . . . and then what?'

Helen regards her with detached curiosity. 'And can you honestly say that your husband – drunk or otherwise – would never lift a finger to you?'

'No, he wouldn't,' says Gwen, her voice hitching with surprise at how obvious her answer is, and how resolute. She thinks back to the unfettered fury Jack admitted unleashing upon Gordon earlier, and then to the time he interceded with her father. 'My husband would never hurt me. But I do know this . . . he'd kill any man who tried.'

CHAPTER FIFTY-FOUR

Gwen is not sure how she makes it through the rest of the day but somehow she does. She milks the herd alone, while Jack continues to work with Ted at depleting the ricks. The thresher rumbles deep into the evening, until they labour under an apricot sky. When it finally falls silent, they sweep up the carpet of chaff and loose straw and the scattering of lost grain, and lug the full sacks into the barn, where the bales have been stacked to the rafters.

She is so tired as she writes the team's cheque that the pen almost slips from her fingers. When the foreman tucks it into the breast pocket of his filthy work shirt, he seems less amiable than before, as if the incident in the lane has corrupted his previously good opinion of her. As she stands to wave them off, the traction engine thundering down the yard, the threshing box and baler rolling behind, she notices only one of the men raises his hand in farewell.

Ted departs soon after. He adjusts his cap as he mumbles his goodbyes and modestly waves away her sincerely expressed gratitude. His gaze strays to Jack who continues to tidy the yard and when he looks back at Gwen she notices a change about him.

'Try not to worry, Gwen.' He lays a dusty hand on her arm. 'If Allingham means you or Tom harm, it'll be over my dead body, you have my word on that.'

Tears sting her eyes, but she does not allow them leverage. She has cried too much already today.

'You have always been a pillar of support for me, Ted.'

He doesn't quite manage a smile. When he speaks, barely suppressed emotion throttles his words. 'It's always been my pleasure, Gwen.'

As he clears his throat, he catches sight of Jack emptying his yard shovel into the wheelbarrow.

'An honest hard worker, that one. Always has been.' He summons a mournful smile. 'Goodnight, Gwen.'

'Goodnight, Ted . . . thank you.'

She watches him as he strolls down the yard, fumbling in his pockets for his cigarettes as he goes. He pauses in the gateway just long enough to light one, flicking the extinguished match to the ground as he turns towards home.

Gwen sinks her face into her hands, then releases a long sigh, ready to face the world again.

Muriel appears at the top step. She has stayed late to look after Tom. She matches Gwen's worn smile.

'I've had the copper on a good while. If you take shallow baths, there should be enough for both you and Jack to get yourselves cleaned up.'

Gwen lets out a moan of delight. Her skin itches under its film of sharp dust and she can barely rake her fingers through her brittle hair.

'I can't think of anything I'd rather do right now than have a bath.'

'Well, I'll pour yours. Give me five minutes,' Muriel says. 'How's Tom?'

'In his pyjamas, but he refuses to go to sleep until he's seen you . . . and Jack,' she adds quietly.

Gwen looks up the yard again to Jack, still labouring away. She thinks back on the day's events, his swift response to the danger facing Tom, his tenderness as he rescued him from the verge. Her heart blossoms with the significance of it all.

'I'll be in . . . let me just tell Jack.'

She walks slowly towards him. Jack carries on sweeping, pushing the last remaining evidence of the day's endeavours into a neat pile beside the laden wheelbarrow. He looks up as Gwen draws near.

'Thank you for doing this,' she says.

'You don't need to thank me.'

Her eyes fill again, but this time she loses the battle and a tear bursts through her defences. She laughs brokenly as she dashes it from her cheek.

'What a day! I just keep crying.'

Jack does not respond; his focus does not waver.

'I came to say that Muriel has heated water for a bath. I'll grab a quick wash, then if you want to come in, we'll get the tub filled for you.'

'Thank you.'

Gwen starts to walk away. She hesitates. 'And then perhaps you might want to read a bedtime story to Tom? I think he'd like that.'

He answers with a smile, a shy lift of his mouth as the light fades around him. 'I'd like that too,' he admits. 'Very much.'

Gwen bathes quickly in the scant amount of hot water Muriel has tipped into the tin bath, positioned for privacy in the pantry. Her exposed skin is icy cold and, as she runs her lathered hands over her shoulders and arms, gooseflesh rises to greet them. Muriel has left out two jugs of lukewarm water for her to wash her hair, which wears its layer of dust like the crackle coating of a toffee apple.

She bends into her drawn-up knees, gasping as she empties the first jug over her bowed head. She lathers up her hair the best she can, then rinses and wrings it out so that it hangs like a rat's tail. Gripping the edge of the tub, she stands up through the surface scum, wincing as she steps out onto the freezing flags. She wraps a small towel around her head and dries herself with a larger one, before slipping into her scratchy plaid dressing gown. She knots the rope about her waist and tiptoes to the door.

Muriel is finishing some folding at the kitchen table as she emerges, the paraffin lamp burning bright before her, creating a circle of light that provides solace against the encroaching darkness.

'I'll get the tub emptied and refilled for Jack,' she says, 'and then I'd best be on my way.'

'Thank you for staying late.' Gwen squeezes her hand.

'I wasn't going anywhere after . . .' There is no need for her to finish. She folds the last piece of clothing into the basket on the table. 'Right, best get to it.'

'Can you manage all right? If you give me a minute, I'll race up and get dressed.'

'Oh, it's no bother, love. I'll soon get it emptied and filled – and I'll let Jack know it's ready as I head off.'

Gwen wishes her housekeeper, confidante and friend good-night, then heads upstairs, careful to keep her tread light as Tom is already in bed. It is late, and she hopes he has drifted off of his own accord, but as she inches his door ajar he squirms from under the bed covers and sits up to greet her.

'You should have been asleep ages ago,' she says, urging him to lie back down. The glow from the lamp on his bedside table catches his face. She sits down beside him.

'I want Daddy to read me another chapter of my book.'

'All right, but he's got to get washed-up first; threshing is very mucky work. He'll be up in a little while.'

'I'm staying awake for him,' he says, breaking into a yawn before the sentence is complete.

Gwen brushes the hair from his forehead. 'He won't be long.'

'Mummy . . . the man today . . . Mr Allingham. I didn't really want to have a ride on his bike, but he said I ought to and that you wouldn't mind.'

Gwen grits her teeth. She cups Tom's warm cheek. 'I don't want you talking to that man ever again, Tom, do you understand?'

'But if he speaks to me and I don't say anything back, won't that be rude?'

'Not in this instance, Tom. Not with him. You stay away from him and if he ever tries to talk to you again you come and tell me . . . or Daddy,' she adds, the unfamiliar word strangely comforting on her lips.

Tom yawns again, his eyelids drooping. 'How long will Daddy be?'

'Let me go and see.' She leans forward, pressing her lips to his cheek, close to his graze. 'I'll go and hurry him up, shall I?'

Jack emerges from the pantry just as she reaches the kitchen. His wet hair glistens in the lamplight.

'Tom's waiting . . .'

'Right,' he starts to tuck his shirt into the waistband of his trousers, 'I'll just empty the tub . . .'

'Don't worry about that . . . do it after, I don't think he'll last much longer.'

'Aye . . . all right.' They share a smile. 'Right . . .' he says softly.

Gwen gathers herself with a surprised 'Oh!' and steps from the door to make way, catching a drift of lye soap as he passes her. The staircase creaks under his weight. She slips into the hall and when she hears his muted greeting to Tom, tender and teasing, her hand finds its way to the newel post. She knows the stairs intimately – knows which treads are looser than others, where to place her weight to conceal her presence. She makes a slow and stealthy ascent, and when she reaches the top step she swivels round and sits, her ear cocked to the open door.

Jack begins to read. It is one of her old books, retrieved from the bookcase in the dining room a few days before – Tom's choice. She has only vague recollections of the story but, as Jack reads on, more escape from the confines of her memory. She rests her temple against the smooth wood of the stair pillar, closing her eyes. The gentle timbre of Jack's voice erases the unpleasant events of the day, until at last she feels the tension leach from her muscles and her eyelids grow heavy.

'That's enough for tonight, little one.'

Her eyes flare open. She hears the book clap shut. Tom's water glass clinks against his alarm clock as space is made on the bedside table. She is quick to her feet and deftly descends, silent as a mouse, as Jack says his goodnights and turns out the lamp. She dives into the sitting room, her father's chair welcoming her into its sagging embrace as she snatches up her knitting from the bag beside it. She sits, the needles poised in her hands, listening as the stairs declare Jack's approach. She is breathless as she waits, a delicious tremor of trepidation stirring deep inside. She hears him pause beyond the door. When he walks on past, she is crushed with disappointment.

But then she remembers the unemptied tub and, sure enough, she hears the faint swoosh of water sluicing down the kitchen drain, and the dull ring of cast iron. She tries to be patient, sliding her needles through loops of wool, endeavouring to keep an even strain, but they soon fall idle as she tries to predict how much longer he will be.

She hears his muffled footsteps on the hall runner. Her needles burst into action, their *click-clickety-click* forming a Morse code: *come join me, come join me . . .*

He clears his throat to catch her attention. She looks up, contriving surprise. He stands in the doorway, his shirt sleeves rolled to his elbow, his hair nearly dry.

'I've emptied the tub and hung it back up.'

'Thank you.'

He shifts his weight. 'Well, I'll head on out now . . . See you in the morning.'

'You don't have to.' The words spring from her without warning. Like fingers clawing at his shoulder, they stop him mid-turn. 'You're very welcome to join me.'

He does not respond to her offer immediately. She feels a humiliating crawl of colour up her cheeks, but then his expression becomes so wistful, her embarrassment seeps away and unexpected tenderness takes its place.

'I'd best . . .' he gestures vaguely outwards, 'I'll go back to the tack room . . . I have plenty to be getting on with, like.'

'Do you?'

His eyes spark with amusement. 'Do you not believe me?'

'I just thought . . . well, now Nora's gone, there's no need for such careful pretence . . .'

'It's not pretence. I am working on something.'

'You are?'

'Aye.'

'What?' Even she detects the hint of petulance in her voice; it provokes a twitch of his lips. He taps the side of his nose with his forefinger.

'Like I said before, it's a surprise.' And suddenly, without apparent reason, the merriment drains from his eyes, and the pained wistfulness returns. 'Goodnight, Gwen.'

Her needles remain idle long after he has gone.

She is unsure how long she sits there, the fire dying from neglect. Rousing herself, she finally abandons all pretence and sets down her knitting.

She checks on Tom and finds him sleeping deeply, his lips parted, his right arm flung above his head. She draws the covers over his shoulders and satisfied he is fast out she pads back down the stairs to the kitchen. She pulls on her gumboots and takes the lantern from the table to light her way as she shuts up the farm.

Kip rises from his bed in the implement shed as she descends the steps into the yard and she is grateful for his company as she skirts the shadowed buildings to reach the paddock. She shuts up the hens, pleased that for once few have remained outside the coop. Bobby snickers and trudges towards her, nibbling her outstretched palm with his soft lips. She strokes his blaze and pats his neck. He starts to follow her but breaks off to slurp from the water trough.

Her hand lingers on the gate's catch. For no clear reason, she experiences a sense of unease. She stands stock still, listening, but hears nothing out of the ordinary, just the soughing breeze through the shedding beech trees and the bark of a deer from the copse beyond. She shakes her head at her own foolishness and, holding the lantern at her side, she starts back towards the buildings. And yet her peculiar jitteriness remains and twice she gasps and whirls around, holding the lamp aloft, but she catches nothing in its wan beam except a fluttering moth.

As she walks down the side of the stable block, her steps slow and her thoughts turn to Jack. She rounds the corner and though she does not mean to look, she finds she cannot resist.

She is surprised – confused even – to see the tack room window reflecting the darkness back at her. She had anticipated a hint of light, for it is not late enough for Jack to have turned in and yet there is nothing to indicate that he is awake – or that he is even within. She remembers the moth-eaten velvet and presumes that the curtains are concealing light, but as her steps drift in she sees the curtains are undrawn and that the glass reveals only a black void.

She is tempted closer. She longs to peer through the grimy glass with its net of cobwebs and spy on him – if only to find he is on his camp bed, sleeping. Her feet shuffle towards the window with its flaking sill and vacant stare, but at the last minute she pulls away. She hurries past temptation, vaguely aware she is teetering on a line she must not cross.

She sends Kip back to his bed and mounts the steps to the house. She stops at the top. The breeze has dropped. The night is silent – it crosses her mind unnaturally so, as if nature is holding its breath.

She starts at a distant boom. A shotgun, she thinks immediately, recognising the dull report carried from some point beyond the farm, though she is unable to pinpoint from where. Poachers, she guesses. Over the years the meat ration has driven many into the woods at night in pursuit of a rabbit or a pheasant – even a deer. She has become accustomed to the practice, but tonight the sound makes her shudder and she draws her cardigan around her.

She does not tarry. Her desire to be safely inside is unusually pronounced.

CHAPTER FIFTY-FIVE

Jack and Gwen are almost knocked down by two speeding cars as they walk to Ted's the following morning. They throw themselves against the hedge as the lead car's horn blasts an impatient warning, while the pursuing vehicle leaves grit skittering across the lane.

The threshing team have already set up by the time they arrive. Ted strides out to meet them and to Jack's surprise he holds out his hand in greeting. His grip is firm and there is an intensity to him that leads Jack to ask if anything is wrong.

'What? Oh no, no . . .' Ted rubs the back of his head distractedly.

'You look done in,' Gwen observes.

'Ah, well . . . bad night . . .' he mumbles as they walk abreast towards the rickyard and the rumbling machinery.

They work solidly through the morning, pitching Ted's barley crop, blinking the dust and grit from their eyes, coughing up phlegm when too much rubbish clogs their throats. They break for lunch at one.

While the threshing team loll on bales eating their sandwiches,

Ted brings Jack and Gwen into the house. Jack is surprised to find it as neat as a pin. He had expected a man of Ted's age, living alone, to have let the place go. As their host busies himself filling the kettle, Jack whispers to Gwen, asking if there is a housekeeper, but she shakes her head.

The kitchen is small, with the table wedged up against the wall, three chairs set around it. He takes a seat while Gwen helps with the sandwiches, retrieving a loaf from the wooden bread bin and butter and cheese from the larder. Jack's eyes explore the room, taking in the row of Toby jugs on the mantel above the range and the amateur paintings of local landscapes on the walls, until at last they settle on a sepia photograph inside an oak frame: a smiling woman and a small boy. For the first time, he fully appreciates all the farmer has lost and his chest tightens as he looks away.

After lunch, with Ted having refused Gwen's request to wash-up, they don their dusty boots and head back outside.

They are prevented from reaching the rickyard by the frantic tingling of a bicycle bell. Muriel whisks through the gate, pedalling furiously, her cheeks streaked red from the rake of the bitter wind. Tom balances before her, squealing at their thrilling speed.

Muriel puts her sturdy lace-ups to the ground bringing the bike to a stop. Tom starts to jabber excitedly, but she cuts over the top of him.

'Have you heard?'

'Heard what?'

'About Gordon Allingham?'

Gwen looks at her blankly. From their position on the bales, the threshing team detect a hint of gossip and angle their heads towards it, like flowers seeking sunshine.

Muriel lifts Tom down. 'Go and play on the lawn for a minute, Tom, while I have a quick word with Mummy and then I'll take you home.'

'We bought buns from the bakery,' he announces as Muriel gently pushes him away.

'They sound lovely, save one for me.' Gwen's smile vanishes as soon as he is out of earshot. 'What on earth's happened?'

'He's dead.'

'What?' Ted and Gwen exclaim in shocked unison. Jack's face darkens, his brow furrowing.

'What do you mean, he's dead?' Gwen stares at her in bewilderment.

'They found him this morning in the lane, just beyond the Hall's gates.' Muriel pitches forward, her voice dropping. 'He's been shot.'

'Oh God.' Gwen's hand flies to her mouth. To her utter shame, her greatest emotion is relief.

'I heard from Mrs Grimsby – her brother-in-law is the lodge keeper – that he'd gone off on that new bike of his last night and hadn't come back. No one seemed particularly bothered until this morning, when one of the groundsmen headed out to do some maintenance on the park wall and found him there – bike on its side, skewed off the road, him underneath it. At first, he thought he'd had an accident, come off it like, but when he went running over, he saw . . .' She taps her chest. 'Hell of a mess, apparently.'

'I can't believe it. Oh God, I can't believe it.'

'You're trembling,' Jack says quietly, laying his hand on Gwen's back.

'I'm all right, honestly I am . . . I just feel . . . numb . . . and God forgive me, but I feel relieved.' Her voice breaks over her confession.

'That's a rum set of affairs,' Ted growls. Gwen is struck by how pale he has gone. He looks even wearier than before.

'The police are up there now apparently, crawling all over the place. I suppose it's hardly surprising – his family will be demanding answers sharpish.'

'It's definitely not an accident . . . I mean, he hasn't done it to himself?' Gwen asks cautiously.

Muriel blows a dismissive gust through her teeth. 'No . . . he's been murdered, without a shadow of a doubt.' The reality of the information drains her own colour. She stutters then falls silent, her swollen knuckles clenching the handlebars of the bicycle. 'Who could have done such a thing?'

'Well, there's nothing can be done about it now,' Ted says, taking a cigarette between his lips. His hand shakes as he brings up the match to light it.

'I can't say it's not for the best.' Jack studies the middle distance.

'He hit his wife.' Gwen's voice sounds strangled. 'I told her he'd do it again. I said he'd be like a dog that's tasted blood . . . that they always have to be put down . . .' She thinks of Helen Allingham's crystallising resolve. 'Oh God, you don't think I . . .'

But Jack quietens her with hushed reassurances. 'Whatever has happened is not your fault, lass. You must never think that.'

Before she can reply, a navy Austin Twelve comes crawling along the lane. Tom, busy climbing a tree at the edge of the front lawn, pauses to watch it. When it turns in through the gate, he grabs the branch above him and dangles before allowing himself to drop, tumbling to his knees. Picking himself up, he swipes the grass stains from the heels of his hands and races to Gwen. He clings to her legs, his focus fixed on the approaching vehicle.

They wait warily for the car to come to a stop. Both front doors fly open at the same time, like the shell of a beetle preparing for flight. Two men emerge, both sombrely dressed and wearing nearly identical raincoats.

'Afternoon, folks.' The taller of the two reaches them first in an unhurried gait. He does not offer his hand, but tips the brim of his Derby, his perfunctory smile exposing crooked yellow teeth. Reaching into his inner pocket, he pulls out a small leather wallet and flicks it open, though they are too far away to read the identity card it contains. 'Detective Inspector Alan Gibson. This is Detective Constable Davies.' He sees at once his arrival is of no surprise. 'You've heard then, have you?'

'You're here about Allingham?' Ted deduces.

'Mr Gordon Allingham was found shot dead this morning.'

'That's what we've heard.'

'We're just canvassing neighbours – people in the vicinity – who might have heard or seen something to help our enquiries, Mr—?'

'Ted Marsh, this is my farm.'

The Detective Constable scratches in his notebook as the Inspector elicits details from each of them in turn. He chuckles as Tom, never to be left out, chirps up his own name at the end. Gwen tells him to go and play. He skulks off reluctantly but is soon back climbing the tree.

'Did you all know Mr Allingham?'

'Not well,' Ted ventures first. 'Certainly not to speak to . . . though I go to the village events at the Hall, of course. I have contact with the farm manager mostly.'

The Inspector looks to Jack and Gwen.

'Knew him by sight,' Jack says.

The Inspector smiles when he catches ear of his accent. 'A Geordie in the Home Counties?'

'Aye, something like that.'

'How long have you been down here?'

'I was taken on as a farm labourer by Gwen's father just before the war. I joined up in 'thirty-nine, got back just a few weeks ago.'

'Very good,' the Inspector says. 'So, Mrs Ellison, you're the local?'

'Yes, yes that's right.'

'And did you know Mr Allingham at all?'

Gwen offers a disingenuous shake of her head. 'Not really. I used to ride with the Hunt, so I knew him a little from there.' Heat crackles up her cheeks. 'We're not really from the same circles.'

She wonders suddenly what Helen Allingham has said to the police and whether, in the circumstances, she might expose Gwen for the liar she is – or whether she will choose to protect her husband's memory and let his philandering secrets accompany him to his grave. The unwelcome thought crosses her mind that she might have had a hand in putting him there.

'I see . . . and can I ask all of you – did you by any chance happen to notice anything out of the ordinary last night?'

'What time do you think . . .'

'We know Mr Allingham left around eight o'clock. Unfortunately, we don't know where he was going or if he was intending to meet anyone, but it appears he was killed around that time.'

'I heard a gunshot,' Gwen blurts out. 'A twelve-bore, I'd say.' She hears Ted's sharp intake of breath and, from the corner of her eye, she catches Jack's rapid appraisal. 'Last night . . . as I was shutting up the farm.'

'What time would that be, Mrs Ellison?'

'I think I went out just before eight. It wasn't long after.'

'And you're sure it was a gunshot you heard? Specifically, a twelve-bore – that's quite detailed . . .'

'I know what a shotgun sounds like, inspector. I thought it was poachers in the woods and it might well have been.'

'Did you hear it, Mr Ellison?' The Inspector shifts his focus to Jack.

'Can't say I did . . . but then I was inside working at the time. I didn't hear a thing.'

The hairs on the back of Gwen's neck lift. She thinks back to the blank window of the tack room, with no hint of light within.

'Very well . . .' The Inspector glances at his constable, who concludes his note-taking with an almost imperceptible nod. 'Well, thank you, folks. If you do remember anything, feel free to contact me at Helvedon Police Station.'

'Should we be worried?' Gwen looks over to Tom.

He puffs out his cheeks. 'I don't think members of the public need to be concerned at this point, Mrs Ellison. Most murderers are known to the victim . . . but there's no harm in keeping an eye out for each other for a few days, maybe locking your doors at night. There's certainly no need to panic.'

'Thank you, that's . . . that's most reassuring.'

'They your workmen up there, Mr Marsh?' He nods towards the threshing box, where the team are starting to prepare for the afternoon shift.

'No, contractors . . . they work the local farms this time of year.'

'Right . . . right . . . you don't mind if I have a word . . .'

'No, no, you help yourself.'

They stand in awkward silence waiting for the police to finish up.

'We'll be in touch,' the Inspector promises when he finally returns to the car, the flaps of his mackintosh lifting on the breeze. Gwen hopes it is only her imagination that his narrow gaze lingers on Jack as he yanks open his car door.

The car whines as it reverses from the yard, gingerly backing around the gatepost into the lane before motoring out of sight.

'I'd best get Tom back home,' Muriel says at last, looking older than she had just a short time before.

'I'll be back to do the milking,' Gwen assures her, calling Tom to come. He races over, deliberately crashing into Jack's legs. Jack mock staggers, before hoisting him into his arms and tipping him upside down over his shoulder as he carries him to Muriel's bicycle. Tom squeals with delight.

Gwen's heart pangs as she watches their tomfoolery. She wants to laugh, but instead tears sting her eyes.

'I can't believe Gordon Allingham is dead,' she murmurs. 'Who would do that?'

Muriel swallows hard. She too is watching Jack. 'I don't know.'

'We'd best get back to the threshing,' Ted says. 'And I wouldn't cry any tears over Gordon Allingham.' He pulls his cigarettes from his pocket. 'If anyone had it coming to them . . . it was him.'

CHAPTER FIFTY-SIX

A rare engagement means Muriel must set off as soon as Gwen finishes the milking. Leaving Tom listening to the wireless, Gwen accompanies her to her bicycle, propped against the side wall of the house.

'Muriel . . .'

'Yes, love?'

'You don't think . . .' Gwen gropes for words as she summons the courage to voice her fears.

'What?'

'You don't think Jack could have done it, do you?'

'Done what?'

'He wouldn't have done anything to . . . to stop Gordon.'

'Dear God, Gwen . . .' Muriel spins to face her, sporting a look of horror. She drops her voice. 'You mustn't even think such things let alone say them out loud.'

'I know . . . I just . . . but what if he did?'

'Gwen, why are you saying this?'

'He said he was inside, but he wasn't. He wasn't in the tack room when I was shutting up, I'm sure of it.'

'Perhaps he was in one of the other buildings. The privy even!' But the housekeeper begins to chew her lip, and Gwen wonders if the same suspicion has already crossed her mind. Muriel takes her hand. 'You mustn't think things like that. Jack Ellison is a good man.'

'I know,' Gwen whispers. She has come to realise just how good he is.

'Don't think on it, love. It can't have been Jack.'

She watches as Muriel pedals from the house. She returns to the kitchen, her mind restless and fearful. She is about to check on Tom when the gun cupboard above the hall door catches her eye. For several seconds she stands staring at it. Are the doors as snugly shut as she left them? Is it her imagination or are they not quite flush?

She pulls herself together and crosses the room, determined not to encourage her fanciful thoughts, but as she reaches the hall she darts back to the kitchen table and lifts a chair clear. She slams it down on the flags underneath the cupboard and steadying herself on the dresser, she climbs up to pull apart the double doors.

The twelve-bore lies upon its shelf. She brings it down, breaks it open, sniffs the chamber for signs of recent use, but she can't be sure. Frustrated, she returns it to the cupboard and as she does so, she sees the cardboard box of cartridges, its lid up. Did she leave it that way? Was she the last one to use the gun? When had Jack gone after the fox? She reaches for the cartridges, wishing she could recall how many were left.

'Gwen?'

She jumps out of her skin. The chair wobbles and she grabs the cupboard shelf to brace herself. Jack is standing at the back door, his face black with dust, his clothes embedded with grime.

'What are you doing?'

'I just . . . I was just . . . checking . . .' She slams the cupboard doors. She is unable to look at him as she gets down from the chair. Without comment, she returns it to the table.

'You'll be wanting a bath,' she says.

'Aye . . . if there's any chance of one.'

'Yes . . . the copper's on, I got washed earlier . . . There should be water for you.'

He follows her as she crosses into the pantry to lift down the tub.

'Here, lass, I'll do it . . .'

She shrinks back against the shelves of jam and tinned produce as he stretches past her, wafting barley dust and sweat. Gwen turns away.

'I'm sorry,' he says gauchely. 'I'm probably in dire need of soap and water.'

'No, no . . . it's . . .' She cannot stem a sudden flow of tears. Her shoulders begin to quake.

'Oh I'm sorry Gwen,' he says, his eyes cast down. 'I should have thought . . . you must be upset about Gordon. Despite everything, you loved him once, I suppose.'

'I'm not crying for Gordon. I haven't cared about Gordon for years.' She tries to catch her breath but without success. 'Looking back, I'm not sure I ever loved him . . . I was just . . . just charmed by him . . . besotted, I suppose. If anything, I feel guilty for feeling so relieved . . . relieved that he can't take Tom anymore . . .'

'Then why are you crying?' Jack asks, his voice soft.

'Because I'm afraid . . .'

'Afraid of what? You're safe now, at least, you and Tom. He

has no hold over you . . . no one has anymore, Gwen. What have you possibly got to be afraid of?'

'Tell me . . .' It takes all her courage to face him. 'Tell me it wasn't you.'

Her gaze drops to the flaking mortar between the flagstones beneath her feet. A sudden wash of cold covers her skin as she waits for his answer.

'Is that what you think?'

'I don't know what to think.'

'Because you think I've done it before? Lost my temper, killed a man. Oh, Gwen . . .'

'You said you were inside . . .' She cuts him off, unable to bear any longer the knowledge that has been gnawing away at her since she heard the news – and heard his lie. ' . . . but I couldn't see any light in the tack room. I couldn't see any sign of you . . .'

'Were you looking for me, then?' His eyes glitter, the edge of his mouth tucking into his cheek, but the levity is fleeting. He studies the shelf above her head, crammed with cake tins and baking trays and the jelly moulds used only for birthdays and Christmas. 'I was in the tack room. I had the candle on my worktable at the back. You wouldn't have seen it, I doubt. It casts hardly a thimbleful of light, but it's enough for me to work by.'

He sets the tub on the floor and reaches down a large saucepan to ferry water from the copper.

'You'll have to make up your own mind what kind of man I am, Gwen.' He starts for the door and stops. 'Do you trust me with Tom?'

The hurt in his voice cuts deeper than she thought possible. 'Yes,' she whispers.

431

'Do you think I could ever hurt him?'

'No.'

'Do you think I would ever hurt you?'

'No,' she says, stronger this time, defiantly so, and it causes him to lift his head. 'You would never hurt me, Jack . . . I know that.'

He nods. His eyes shimmer. She cannot tell if it is rising emotion or simply the catch of the fading light.

'Then all I ask, is that you hold onto that knowledge. And I beg you this: whatever happens . . . never let it go.'

And before she can say anything more, he heads out into the kitchen, leaving her alone in the pantry, wreathed in shadows.

CHAPTER FIFTY-SEVEN

The navy Austin Twelve pulls into the yard just as Jack is leading a tacked-up Bobby over to the implement shed, where Gwen is busy replacing a blade on the scuffle in preparation for weeding carrots. The wrench stills in her hand as she hears the drone of the car engine and Kip's frantic barking. As the vehicle jogs her memory, her stomach sinks. She straightens up as Jack reaches the shed. The horse snorts, its tail swishing around its hindquarters. Jack's expression is guarded.

Kip prances around the car growling and threatening until Jack calls him to heel. Only then do the car doors clunk open. Detective Constable Davies emerges first, warily, as if he has been sent out to assess the danger. Satisfied all is safe, the Inspector climbs out next, raising his hat in greeting. Gwen is surprised to see a uniformed constable emerge from the rear. He pauses to put on his helmet, its strap cutting into the loose flesh behind his chin. The presence of the three men puts her ill-at-ease. She drifts closer to Jack.

'Mr and Mrs Ellison, good morning to you.' The Inspector hangs back, giving Gwen the impression he is uncomfortable around the animals. 'As I'm sure you're aware, we've been continuing our enquiries into the murder of Mr Allingham.'

'Yes.' Her mouth is dry. Muriel has proven tireless in conveying gossip from the village: the police are exhausting resources to solve the crime; Lord Allingham is ailing – he wants to see his son's killer swing before he dies.

'Mr Ellison . . . I was hoping you wouldn't mind having a bit of a chat with us down at the station.' His manner is amiable enough, but Gwen detects a wolfishness to his smile.

'Can't you question me here?' Jack asks, his voice even. 'As you can see, we've work to be getting on with.'

'I'd rather you came down to the station.'

'Are you arresting me?'

The Inspector chuckles disarmingly. 'Not unless you want me to.'

There is a frisson in the air. Gwen feels like she has a fist lodged in her chest. Her fingers are suddenly too weak to hold the wrench.

'All right,' Jack says at last.

'Why? Why do you want to speak to Jack?' Gwen blurts out, unable to stop herself. 'Gordon's death has nothing to do with him.'

'I'm sure it doesn't, Mrs Ellison, which is why, at this stage, it's important to eliminate him from our enquiries.'

'But why's he even in your enquiries?'

'Gwen . . .' Jack's hand rests lightly on her arm. 'It's all right.' He passes her Bobby's reins and somehow in the transfer their fingers tangle. When his rough skin finally slides from hers, tears spring to her eyes.

'Thank you, Mr Ellison. If you'd just go with my colleague.'

Gwen perceives a slump in Jack's shoulders as he follows the Detective Constable back to the car, the uniformed officer falling in beside him.

'I don't understand why . . .' Gwen's voice breaks before her words are complete. She leaves the shelter of the implement shed, the reins slipping from her slack fingers. 'Jack!'

He twists back, his face full of compassion. 'It's all right, Gwen. Everything will be all right.' The policeman pulls the car door open.

'You can't just take him like this, not without reason!'

'Perhaps we do have reason, Mrs Ellison,' the Inspector responds quietly.

Dread seeps through Gwen's body. She bites her lip as Jack ducks into the back seat of the Austin. The policeman pauses to remove his helmet then gets in beside him. He reaches out to yank the door to. The Detective Constable waits at the driver's side.

'I'll make my own way,' the Inspector calls, holding up a hand in farewell.

The constable gets in and slams his door shut. The engine splutters into life and Gwen watches helplessly as the car reverses down the yard. She struggles to see Jack in the back seat, hidden behind the driver. A breath shudders from her as the car reaches the lane. The Inspector calls her name twice before it registers. She turns around, dazed.

'I wonder if I might ask you a few questions?'

She desperately wants to object, but with Jack gone she is aware of her vulnerability, as if her defences have been drained. She acquiesces with a nod, wondering how she will find her voice when it seems to have deserted her. She loops Bobby's reins around the handle of the scuffle and absently smooths her palm down his neck.

'You mentioned the other day . . .' The Inspector pulls out his notebook and makes a show of flicking through the pages, but it fails to dispel the impression he remembers precisely what she said. '. . . Hearing a gunshot?' When she does not contest the evidence he smiles, his lips barely pulling clear of his nicotine-stained teeth. 'Could you show me where you were when you heard it?'

'At the top of the steps there . . .'

The Inspector nods.

'Do you mind?' His bushy grey eyebrows crawl up like caterpillars. He strides across the yard and, having little choice, Gwen follows behind. Kip springs up to trot alongside her; she appreciates his devotion. With a flair for the dramatic, the Inspector leaps up the steps two at a time, landing firmly on the path. 'So here? And roughly in what direction do you think the sound came from?'

'It's hard to tell,' Gwen says, resentful of his presence. 'It was dark, it was windy, sounds get distorted at night.'

'But roughly, if you had to say?'

She shrugs, her mouth thin with petulance. 'That way, I sup-pose.' She gestures vaguely before her, towards the woods that wrap round the swell of the valley. The woods, she realises, that ring the Allingham estate.

The Inspector scribbles in his notepad. 'You don't mind? Locking up the farm alone . . . at night . . . in the dark?'

'I've been locking up this farm on my own for years. My husband has been away fighting for his country for the last six.' She bites back the urge to ask him how *he* spent the war.

'Of course,' he smiles. 'And as you pointed out, you know the sound of a shotgun. I presume you own one yourself, Mrs Ellison?'

'I do.'

'Might I just take a look, do you think?'

'At my shotgun?'

'If you've no objection?'

It crosses her mind she should refuse, but she doesn't know her rights – and she doesn't know whether such a refusal might convey some guilt. All the same, she worries about the implications for Jack.

'Do I have to? I mean . . . legally?' she asks at last.

'It's probably easier for everyone in the long run, Mrs Ellison, if you cooperate voluntarily – saves us all so much paperwork and stress – and if you've nothing to hide . . . why wouldn't you?'

'Yes . . . of course.' He steps back from the path to let her pass. The kitchen window is ajar and she can hear Muriel talking to Tom. She pushes open the door but uses her body to keep the Inspector out of sight.

'Oh, there you are . . .' Muriel starts, but her voice fails as she sees the fear in Gwen's eyes.

'Can you take Tom upstairs for a minute?'

'Mummy!' Tom looks up from his drawing. His crayons lie scattered across the table.

'I'll be with you in a minute, Tom. I have a visitor I need to speak to. I want you to go upstairs to your room with Muriel, please.' Her tone is strict, warning him she will brook no nonsense, and for once he complies without complaint.

'Come on, Tom,' Muriel hastily dries her hands on a tea

towel and ushers him from the room. Only when they have gone, does Gwen open the door further and permit the Inspector entry.

He waits expectantly as she draws out a kitchen chair to open the gun cupboard. She removes the twelve-bore.

'Is that another rifle there, Mrs Ellison?'

'A .22. It's the shotgun you're after, isn't it?'

'It is indeed,' he says, pulling on a pair of leather gloves taken from his coat pocket.

Her hand trembles as she offers him the gun. She is horribly aware its evidence might put Jack's head in a noose.

'I'd like to keep it for a while, if you don't mind,' he says, taking it from her.

'I need it . . . for the farm. Foxes.'

'I'll get it back to you as soon as I can. At least you have another rifle to use in the meantime.'

Her stomach heaves as she closes the cupboard door and climbs down from the chair.

'Your husband mentioned he was busy inside when you heard the shot.'

'Yes.'

'Late to be working, isn't it, eight o'clock?'

'There's always a lot to be done. We farmers don't have the luxury of keeping civilised hours.'

'Of course. What was your husband doing exactly?'

'He was . . .' Gwen swallows. 'He's . . . working on something.'

Again, that wolfish smile – as if he is leading her towards a trip wire, distracting her, so he can have the pleasure of seeing her fall. 'What would that be?'

'It's a surprise,' she replies faintly.

'Well, I don't want to spoil anything . . . but, perhaps you wouldn't mind showing me where he was that evening?'

Gwen grips the back of the chair. She thinks of the tack room, the camp bed and the blackened window. Her mind races, as she wonders whether it is too late to construct a lie to help save Jack. But then she remembers how adamant he was about working on something these past few weeks. Praying fervently, she leads the Inspector from the house.

It has started to spit with rain, but she hardly registers it pricking her face or dampening her clothes, though the detective uses his free hand to hold both sides of his mackintosh together, while still carrying the shotgun.

Her heart is thumping wildly as she dips into the dimly lit stable block. She pauses before the tack room door as she wonders again if there is any way to avoid this, but the Inspector is close behind her.

'Mrs Ellison?' he prompts.

She lifts the latch and the hinges creak as she pushes the door wide. The camp bed is neatly made. Jack's spare clothes hang over the back of the Bentwood chair. On the upturned apple crate is the saucer with his candle – little more than a stub now, trickles of molten wax solidified down its side. The room resonates with his presence. She cannot bring herself to intrude.

The Inspector, however, shows no such reticence as he passes her to stand inside.

'Mrs Ellison . . . I think it only fair to say, I have heard some rumours about the possible state of your marriage.' He has sufficient tact to look sheepish. 'I know a lot of couples have experienced difficulties as a result of the war . . . the lengthy separation and so on. I have been led to understand you and your husband . . . might be living separately in some regards.' His eyes flick meaningfully towards the bed.

Gwen stiffens. *Nora*. She is willing to lay money on the source of the detective's rumours.

'My husband suffers nightmares due to his experiences, inspector. He sleeps out here by choice . . . he does not want to scare me and more importantly he does not want to scare Tom. If your rumours should emanate from a certain Nora Williams you should know that while she was working here as a Land Girl she propositioned my husband and was sent packing as a result.'

'I see.'

'I would think very carefully when it comes to listening to tittle-tattle.'

'Quite so. But what is not rumour, Mrs Ellison, is that your husband threatened Mr Allingham on the very day he was murdered. Threatened to kill him, indeed. That threat was witnessed – and has been reported to us – by several people.'

Gwen swallows a lump in her throat. 'Mr Allingham had behaved very foolishly by giving Tom a ride on his motorbike without our knowledge or permission. Tom fell off and Jack was quite rightly furious and so was I. Tom was very lucky not to have been seriously hurt. As I'm sure you're aware, things get said in the heat of the moment that shouldn't be taken literally.' She pauses to catch her breath. 'Is that why you've taken him in? On little more than gossip and misrepresentation?'

'And an eyewitness who recalls seeing someone matching your husband's general description in the vicinity of the Hall that night. Someone who appeared to be carrying something – something that could very well have been a shotgun.'

Gwen turns away so he can't see the colour drain from her face. She suddenly feels icy cold. 'It couldn't have been Jack,' she says, hoping her voice sounds steadier to the Inspector than it does to her. 'Because he was here, working.'

'So he claims. Did you actually see him in here, Mrs Ellison?'

'He doesn't like me coming in . . . he doesn't want me to see what he's working on . . . it's a surprise . . .'

'A surprise. So you keep saying.' He tuts to himself. 'Well, though I'm loath to do so, I might need to spoil that surprise to confirm Mr Ellison's story. So, let us see what exactly he might have been up to in here, shall we?'

The Inspector has already spotted the covered workbench. Taking a corner, he lifts the blanket clear. Gwen gasps.

'Goodness me, that's certainly rather impressive.'

He appears as stunned as she is. Laying the shotgun on the bed he carefully picks up part of Jack's creation – a beautifully carved Flying Scotsman, hand-painted in apple green and glazed so it shines. Enrapt, he moves the tiny wheels at its base. He sets it back down upon the lovingly constructed track, half-painted in black lacquer, and whistles in admiration.

'It's a train set,' Gwen whispers. 'He's making a train set.' A broken laugh escapes her, causing the Inspector to look round. Bittersweet joy cracks her heart. 'Tom's wish for Christmas . . . Jack's making it come true.'

CHAPTER FIFTY-EIGHT

She tries but she cannot settle. Worry is her constant companion and it casts a long shadow. Muriel's attempts to reassure her fall on deaf ears, and when Tom asks where his daddy has gone, she is too choked to answer.

She decides to keep herself busy by fulfilling the chores already allotted to the day. She returns to the scuffle and attaches it to the patiently waiting Bobby. She is comforted by the familiarity of the broad leather reins in her hands and welcomes the occupation of the task ahead.

But Bobby strides down the furrows with such instinctive precision that the labour does not provide the longed-for distraction. As the blades of the scuffle slice through groundsel and charlock, her mind wanders back to Jack and her thoughts churn so rapidly she becomes dizzy and sick.

She tortures herself by imagining him in a police cell, or being interviewed in some dank basement room. But worse, she wonders how long it might take for the police to connect him to the murder in Newcastle. The breathtaking selfishness of her actions drives a knife into her heart. Her dogged pursuit of her own self-interests has built Jack's gallows. He has risked his life by staying to help her and she has thanked him by tying his noose. Her shame runs deep and fear chills her to the bone.

'Gwen!'

She quickly wipes her cheeks. Ted is hurrying through the gateway. His boots sink into the damp soil as he crosses the field to reach her. He looks surprisingly haggard and his cheeks sink even further as he takes a final draw on the cigarette burning between his yellowed fingers.

'I've just come from the village. Iris said the police have taken Jack in?'

He is out of breath, his chest wheezing. She loops the reins around the handles of the scuffle and nods.

He swears and snatches off his grubby cap. His hand rests on the back of his neck. 'Why? Why have they taken Jack? He can't have had anything to do with it, can he?'

The darkened tack room window plays again in her mind's eye, but she also thinks of the train set. Could she have missed a flicker of light inside?

'His name has come up . . .'

'Bloody threshing team.' Ted takes out his frustration on a clod of soil, kicking it across the field. 'Someone must have said about that fight.'

'And Nora's been talking. That detective didn't have to tell me who it was, I knew from what he said. If anyone works out the connection between Tom and Gordon . . .' She turns, doubling over as a wave of nausea hits her.

Ted rests his hand awkwardly on her back. She pulls away – not to hurt him, she just can't bear being touched – but seeing the pain her perceived rejection causes, she mutters an apology.

She releases a ragged breath and looks up the field. Three crows skim the ground in low flight.

'When will he back?' Ted asks at last.

She shrugs and shakes her head. 'I don't know.' Her throat aches. 'I knew I'd go mad, sitting at home waiting . . . I thought it was best to keep busy.'

'I'm sure it'll be all right.'

'That's what Jack said to me. But I'm not so sure.'

'Is there anything I can do?'

'I just want him back.'

Her confession escapes as a whisper and this time it is Ted who looks away. He studies the solitary oak tree that stands guard over the field. It has cast off its autumnal shawl, leaving a tracery of branches silhouetted against the pale sky.

'I see.'

He says the words so softly they are almost lost on the rise and fall of the breeze that brushes their faces.

He pulls out his handkerchief and wipes his mouth. 'Well . . . I'd best be getting on.'

She nods, unable to shift her misery even to raise a farewell.

He starts to walk away, but stops, staring at the horizon. He turns back to her.

'It will be all right, Gwen. I promise you that.' He scuffs the soil with the sole of his boot, searching for the right words. 'He's a good man, Jack. I've come to see that. A good man.'

'He is,' she manages.

He looks at her intently for a moment, then summons a wistful smile.

'Goodbye, Gwen.'

She watches him go, his shoulders hunched, his head hanging

low, and suddenly she feels neglectful of him and realises that she has taken him too much for granted.

'Come over for dinner tonight? I'd appreciate your company,' she calls, wanting desperately to make amends – a gesture of gratitude long overdue.

He fails to acknowledge the offer. Fearing he hasn't heard she starts to go after him, but as he reaches the gate he raises his hand to accept. Without looking back, he walks out into the lane.

She is sluicing out the parlour, cleaning up from the afternoon milking, when Jack appears. Sweeping the murky water out into the yard, she looks up to see him at the gate. Her broom crashes to the ground and she is running.

Jack's arms wrap around her as she collides against him.

'Thank God,' she whispers.

He holds her tight, her cheek pressed against his collarbone, his chin resting on her head. He does not speak.

Eventually she pushes herself free. 'What happened? What did they say? You weren't arrested?'

'No . . . no . . . I was just "helping with enquiries", but they made it clear they've not finished with me yet.'

'Ted thinks one of the threshing team said something.'

'Aye, I reckon they did. He wanted to know everything about that day – what had led up to me saying what I did.'

'What did you tell them?'

'That he nearly killed Tom, riding that bloody bike of his, and I was justified in losing my rag. I did wonder whether Ted had said anything.'

'I'm sure he would never say anything to get you into trouble.

He was as shocked as I was that they'd taken you in. He's eating with us tonight . . . I didn't know if you'd be back and I couldn't face worrying alone.'

She stares at her boots, suddenly gauche.

'I'm here now, lass,' he murmurs, laying a light hand on her arm.

She summons a smile. 'Yes . . . yes you are.' She turns away quickly to hide the telling build of her emotion. 'And in perfect time for dinner.'

'Aye, I'm starving,' he says, his tone lightening to match her own, and as she lifts her eyes to his, he offers her a tentative smile. He tips his head towards the house. 'Let's go in,' he says, his voice suddenly thick with emotion. Gwen nods, blinking back her tears.

Muriel greets his arrival with similar relief. She lets out a cry and dashes across the kitchen to hug him.

'You look worn out, love.'

'Aye, it's been a long day, somehow.'

'You're home now, that's all that matters,' she says firmly.

'Daddy!'

Tom barrels into his legs from the hall door. Jack throws him up into his arms, cupping the boy's head as Tom clings to him like a monkey. Gwen is forced to turn away as Jack's eyes close and his weary expression eases into one of contentment. Claiming to have a splinter in her finger she scurries upstairs on the pretence of its removal. Shutting her door, she sinks onto her bed, as she tries to decipher the unfamiliar feelings that now consume her. She stays there until she hears Muriel's insistent cry that dinner is ready.

She is surprised to discover that Ted has yet to arrive.

'He definitely said he was coming?' Muriel asks, glancing at the clock.

'Yes . . . I'm sure of it.'

'Well, I can't wait much longer, it'll spoil. I'll make up a plate for him and leave it in the oven to keep warm.'

But an hour later the dinner is still in the oven, dried out and ruined.

There is no sign of Ted.

CHAPTER FIFTY-NINE

Jack tries to reassure Gwen that there will be a rational explanation for Ted's absence, but his comforting words fail to relieve her concern.

'If you're that worried I'll go over and see him, check everything's all right,' he offers, coming up behind her as she stands on the path, watching the lane.

'I'll come with you,' she says quickly. 'I'll ask Muriel to hang on with Tom. We shouldn't be long.'

They walk side by side, at times so close their fingers almost touch. The silence between them is comfortable and yet there is an underlying tension that neither of them attempts to address.

Ted's farm is quiet when they arrive. The yard is deserted and at the house blank windows are framed by curtains that have yet to be drawn, even though the day's light has drained away. The back of Jack's neck prickles. It is a sensation he is all too familiar with. But not in this setting.

Gwen knocks on the back door. Receiving no answer, she hammers again. Her face is pinched with concern as she cups her eyes to peer through the glass. Finding the door unlocked, she lets herself in, calling out Ted's name. The kitchen is as neat as the day they had taken lunch. There is a revealing stillness to the air and as they move together through the house, the silence that greets them is deafening.

'Where on earth is he?' Gwen asks.

'I'll go and take a look outside. Why don't you see if you can find any clues in here as to where he might have gone?' Jack suggests, picking up a torch sitting on the kitchen sideboard. The bulb glows when he tests it.

'It's too late for him to be walking the farm.' Gwen chews anxiously at a fingernail.

Jack knows they share the same instinct that something is terribly wrong.

'Let me have a quick scoot around, I'll be right back.'

Outside, he hollers for Ted. He swings the torch beam across the yard, assessing the different buildings: a rundown pig sty; a stable block with a flight of steps running up its side to the storeroom above. And then he sees the barn, with its red-brick footings and creosoted wooden walls. He walks slowly towards it.

The smell hits him as soon as he pushes open the small side door. His stomach knots and his pulse picks up, fuelled by a surge of adrenaline. He calls Ted's name in the same gentle tone one might use to wake a sleeping child. But he knows Ted is not sleeping.

He is careful to fasten the door behind him. He does not want Gwen following him in. The torchlight pools at his feet; he is in no rush – he knows what awaits him. He has seen too many sights like it over the past six years. He thought he was done with all that.

He advances carefully, his eyes scanning for what he cannot yet see. He does not look up at the rafters. He knows enough not to. The torch beam catches the side of the bale stack, tucked into the far corner. They have been arranged in decreasing steps, and Ted is slumped on the bottom row. The sawn-off shotgun has fallen from his hands. The bale his head rests against is slickly scarlet. Jack draws in a deep breath.

'Oh, Ted.'

He forces himself forward. The metallic smell sticks at the back of his throat as he crouches down beside the farmer's body. On the bale next to him is a brown envelope with TO WHOM IT MAY CONCERN written across its front. Jack drags his hand across his face. As it slides away, he notices a folded piece of white paper caught in the curled palm of Ted's left hand. His own name is written on the front.

Ted's fingers, cold but not yet stiff, yield easily as he gently removes it. He pauses for a moment, then opens the note.

Look after her.

He looks up at the rafters, swallowing hard to keep at bay the sudden swell of emotion that threatens to undo him.

'I will,' he promises in a roughened voice.

Tucking the paper into his trouser pocket, he pushes himself up to standing. He hears Gwen calling him from outside.

'Thank you, Ted,' he whispers.

Hearing Gwen's shouts coming closer, he runs out to intercept her.

*

They wait before the barn, Jack's jacket draped around Gwen's shoulders. He has tried to persuade her to return to the house, but she insists on remaining outside. It is fully dark now, and cold. The ambulance stands in the yard, the navy Austin Twelve beside it. Gwen buries her head into Jack's shoulder as the barn door opens and the first stretcher bearer appears. He holds her close, his expression grim, as Ted's body, covered with a red woollen blanket, is carried out. Neither of them can bear to look as the ambulance doors close behind him.

Detective Inspector Gibson is the last to leave the barn. He ducks through the doorway and heads straight for them, the brown envelope Jack wisely left undisturbed clutched in his hand. As he comes closer, they see it has been ripped open.

'Sad business,' the Inspector says by way of greeting. He pauses as the ambulance putters into life, its headlights beaming through the darkness as it manoeuvres out of the yard and into the lane.

'You've read the note?' Jack asks.

Gwen unfurls from his side. 'What does it say? Why did he do it?'

'The note . . . is a confession, Mrs Ellison.'

'A confession? A confession of what?'

'Murder.'

'What?'

'Mr Marsh confesses, in his note, to the murder of Gordon Allingham.' He allows the revelation to sink in before he continues. 'Apparently, he'd clipped a fox with his shotgun that night and had set off in pursuit to put it out of its misery. He was walking back along the lane when he saw Gordon Allingham approaching – he recognised the motorbike and his clothing, the flight jacket and aviator cap. I understand he'd witnessed the earlier altercation, Mr Ellison?'

'Yes. Yes, that's right,' Jack confirms quietly.

'He must have been very fond of your son. He writes that he was still furious with Mr Allingham for the danger he'd put Tom in that day – he was keen to teach him a lesson. He claims he was aiming for the bike, but the shot went high. He had only intended it to be a warning, by his account – he never meant to kill him.' Gwen refrains from commenting. Ted was an expert shot, even better than her father. She had never known him to miss his mark. 'It seems his sense of guilt was so overwhelming that, coupled with his cancer diagnosis . . .'

'Cancer?' Gwen exclaims.

'I'm sorry, Mrs Ellison, I presumed with you being so close, you already knew? I'm afraid, it appears that Mr Marsh had recently been diagnosed with lung cancer.'

'Oh God . . . Ted . . .' Gwen smothers her cry. Jack's fingers press into her shoulder.

'He never said anything to us,' he explains for the detective's benefit.

'I'm so sorry, I thought it likely he'd have told you. Anyway, it appears the prospect of the inevitable suffering ahead held little attraction for him. That was another factor that contributed to his decision to . . . take his own life.' He pauses, watching Jack closely. 'I suppose it must have been Mr Marsh my witness saw the other night with the shotgun, Mr Ellison . . . though I would have said you cut a much taller figure myself.'

'Mistakes are easily made, especially when it's dark,' Jack replies evenly.

'Indeed. Well, I have my confession and I think Mr

Allingham's family will be satisfied – they wanted the matter resolved as quickly as possible. I don't doubt they will be grateful to know exactly what happened . . . and why.'

'Ted loved Tom very much,' Gwen says softly. 'His own son died . . . I sometimes think Tom almost became a substitute for the boy he'd lost. He would have done anything for him . . . done anything to protect him. I know he was very angry that Gordon had behaved so recklessly that day. I just hadn't realised how angry.'

'Well . . . a man who has nothing left to lose is often prepared to do all manner of things he might not otherwise have considered, Mrs Ellison.'

'Yes . . . yes, I suppose you're right.'

'So, is that an end to it then?' Jack asks.

'Yes, Mr Ellison, I believe so. I would appreciate it if you kept tonight's events to yourselves for now. I'd rather the Allinghams heard the details from me. I'll speak to them first thing.'

'We won't say a word,' Jack assures him.

'Very well. I suggest you return home and get some sleep.'

Gwen calls out to him before he reaches his car.

'Despite all this Ted Marsh was a good man, inspector. One of nature's kind souls. Please don't forget that.'

'I'll keep it in mind, Mrs Ellison. You have my word on that.'

He turns to go, but Gwen calls to him again. Pulling away from Jack she hurries forward.

'Who was the witness?'

'I'm sorry?'

'The witness, the one who reported seeing someone with a shotgun. Who was it?'

The Inspector looks away, puffing out his cheeks as he

considers whether to divulge the information. Having reflected, he clearly sees no harm in it.

'Lady Helen, as it happens.'

'Lady Helen . . .' Gwen's pulse grows sluggish.

'It seems she was returning from running an errand – I didn't quite catch it but I'm sure she said it was something to do with grouse. I thought we were in the wrong part of the country for all that.' He snorts and rolls his eyes. 'How the other half live, eh? Goodnight, Mrs Ellison. Try and get some rest.'

Numbed, Gwen watches him drive from the yard. The car's engine grows faint. The unnerving screech of a barn owl carries on the breeze. Jack's steps crunch towards her.

'Let's go home, lass,' he says.

Taking his hand, she lets him lead the way.

CHAPTER SIXTY

Ted is laid to rest without great pomp or ceremony – just a quiet gathering of close friends and neighbours too shocked to speak much, and when they do it is in muted tones, in whispers that are not meant to carry. And yet, the nature of his demise and the reasons for it soon spread around the village, despite Gwen and Jack's best efforts. Gossip in a small place is like oil in water – it always rises to the surface; it is impossible to suppress.

In sharp contrast, Gordon Allingham is laid to rest in splendour, interred in his family vault, along with their hopes and dreams of progeniture. His funeral cortege is formed of a glass-sided hearse pulled by four plumed black stallions, with two sombre limousines crawling respectfully behind.

Most of the village turn out, lining the route from the Hall to the church out of curiosity if not respect. Gwen, though, does not. She and Jack treat it as a normal day of labour, though they happen to be in the lane brushing the Mere Field hedge when the cortege passes by.

Jack is tugging out a freshly hacked bramble when they

hear the *clip-clop* of high-stepping horses. He retreats further onto the verge as they appear, tossing their heads, their plumes shivering on the wind. Gwen's billhook hangs impotently by her side as she watches the hearse roll by – her son's father taking his final leave.

She pays scant attention to the first limousine as it inches past – until, that is, she sees its passenger. Lady Helen's face is turned to the window, as if she has no wish to be sitting beside her dead husband's grieving mother. Her drawn expression expands with surprise as she sees Gwen and for the briefest moment, their eyes meet. A sly curve appears upon her lips, as her black-gloved fingers stray to her cheek which benefits from a discreet covering of make-up. She lifts a single brow and dips her chin as the car slides past. Gwen watches her go, her heart beating faster, fuelled by the suspicion that Helen Allingham has just delivered a most terrible admission.

Gwen suggests they all visit Ted's grave that evening. They do not encounter a single soul as they make their way through the village and by the time they cross under the covered lychgate into the churchyard the sun is sinking low on the horizon.

They pay no attention to the raised stone mausoleum, freshly covered with a multitude of wreaths in colours that jar with the fading season. Gwen grips Tom's hand a little tighter as they pass by. She is reassured by the light touch of Jack's fingers on the small of her back.

Ted's grave is located to the side of the church. The headstone is not new; it already bears the names of his wife and son, their chiselled edges weathered, while Ted's is starkly defined. The flowers from the simple funeral service have begun to shed their petals, so Gwen and Muriel clear them away, carrying them in silence to the compost heap under the yew tree, while Jack and Tom lay a bunch of late-flowering phlox picked from the garden in their place. Tom leans against Jack's leg, his little face solemn. Gwen smooths his blond hair as she returns and rests her hand on his shoulder. She looks again at the layered names on the gravestone and takes comfort from her conviction that the family has been reunited in death.

By the time they walk Muriel home, the night sky has revealed itself. A splinter of moon pierces the thin cloud and rests in a circle of its own light, like a giant cat's eye spying upon them. They watch Muriel safely in, then carry on through the village, taking advantage of the streetlights, until at last it lies behind them and they are in the lane, dimly lit.

Tom walks between them. He tilts his head back to study the inky sky. Its smattering of stars, glittering like diamonds against a jeweller's velvet roll, captures his fascination.

'They're as bright as fireworks,' he says, his chin thrust upwards, his little mouth slack with awe.

'They're better than fireworks, Tom,' Jack says, lifting the boy into his arms. 'Fireworks are fleeting – there one minute and gone the next.'

'But stars are everlasting . . . they don't disappear in the blink of an eye,' Gwen adds with a gentle smile.

'And even when you can't see them . . .' Jack continues quietly, 'you can take comfort from the fact they're still there . . . burning bright.' He looks at Gwen. 'Burning as bright as they ever have.'

Gwen kisses Tom goodnight and leaves Jack to read him another chapter of his book. She hovers on the landing listening, smiling as his voice changes to reflect the characters, grinning broadly as she hears Tom giggle.

She does not retreat to the sitting room but waits for him in the kitchen. She intends to leave nothing to chance this time. Taking a small pan from the shelf in the pantry, she brings down the cocoa tin from the cupboard, then listens out for Jack's careful descent, readying herself for his entrance.

'I'm making cocoa – will you join me for a cup?' She keeps her voice light and the offer casual as she pours the milk into the pan.

'Aye . . . that'd be nice.' He crosses his arms and leans against the doorframe. His eyes never leave her as she moves about the kitchen, placing the saucepan on the hotplate before retrieving mugs from the dresser.

She is acutely conscious of his presence as she spoons the powder into the mugs. She snatches back the pan as the milk begins to froth. Only the sound of it rushing into the mugs and the catch of the stirring teaspoon breaks the silence.

He steps down into the kitchen to take his mug from her, their fingers brushing. Her skin continues to tingle long after the exchange has been made.

They stand, Gwen resting against the drainer, Jack against the dresser, nursing their mugs, sipping periodically. The silent tension provokes a strange hysteria in Gwen and she cannot keep her smile at bay.

'What?' Jack's own lips tweak in response. 'What's so funny?'

'Nothing. Really.' She tries to master her foolish nerves but, before she succeeds, her memory tugs. 'Oh! I forgot the bloody chickens!'

Jack puts down his mug. 'Come on, I'll help you get them in.'

They pull on their boots, choosing to brave the bite of the night air rather than waste time with jackets. The wind is whipping up and the stars are smothered now by bulky grey clouds. The moon teases them with its flirtatious appearances as it dips coyly in and out of cover.

The flickering flame of their paraffin lamp barely dents the darkness. Jack darts out his hand to steady Gwen as she stumbles. It remains on her arm for longer than necessary.

In the paddock, they begin to round up the stray chickens hunkered down among the hassocks, their feathers ruffled by the strengthening wind. Spits of rain strike Gwen's cheeks as she carries them into the hen house and as they close the door, thunder rumbles.

'I'd better get Bobby in,' she shouts over the wind, grabbing the halter and lead rope from the fence post.

With the thunder comes the rain. Without warning it lashes down, stinging their faces as they jog across the uneven ground to where the Clydesdale whinnies, unsettled by the growing tumult. Jack takes the halter from Gwen and eases it over the horse's broad face, delivering soothing words into its swivelling ears as another crack splits the air.

The driving rain and bracing wind slice through them with bladelike precision. Gwen's hair hangs sodden against her back and her clothes are wet through. Jack, she sees, is faring no better, as he pushes his slickened hair off his forehead, rain streaming down his face. He catches sight of her and grins.

Bobby's hooves slip on the wet cobbles at the stable door. Jack leads him straight into his loosebox, the straw bed rustling as they trample it down.

'I'll sort him out,' he offers. 'You'd best get inside and get dried off.'

'I'll check on Tom.'

Gwen is shivering as she runs back to the house. A gust of wind snatches the back door from her hand. She dives inside, slamming it shut behind her. Rainwater puddles onto the flags as she prises off her boots. She dashes upstairs and gently eases Tom's door ajar, but he is fast asleep, undisturbed by the hullabaloo of the storm.

Her teeth chattering, she returns to her room and quickly strips off her wet things, yanking open her drawers for fresh underwear and clothing. Once dressed, she dries her hair with a towel. A little warmth begins to seep back into her frozen body.

She pads out onto the landing and opens the linen press. As she stretches up to retrieve a cardigan from the top shelf she spots some of Jack's clothes, neatly ironed, on the shelf below. She hesitates for a second, then scoops them up into her arms and hurries downstairs. Setting them upon the kitchen table, she pulls on her jacket, then pushes her dry feet into damp boots. Shielding the clothes with her coat, she heads back outside.

Bobby is secure in his loosebox, munching on hay, as she dashes into the stables. Jack is no longer with him, but the tack room door hangs open and a faint glow of candlelight entices her in.

He stands with his back to her, his wet shirt hanging over the chair, dripping onto the cobbled floor as he towel-dries his hair. She is unable to find her voice. Only when he discards the towel does he notice her standing in the doorway.

'I thought you might need some dry things.' Her cheeks flush with embarrassment. 'I'll just leave them on the bed and then they're there if you need them.' Her feet feel heavy as she advances into the room. She places the stack of clothes upon the bed and turns to leave, but she stops as her eyes fall upon a bundle of letters lying on the apple crate. She has seen them before, buried in his kitbag. Her fingertips trace her name across the first envelope.

'I wrote to you every day.' Jack's voice is gruff. 'I just never had the courage to send them. I thought it better that I didn't.'

Gwen faces him slowly and as she does so, she notices for the first time the network of scars that bear testimony to his six years of service, his six years of survival. She is seized by a morbid fascination as the stitched white scars and puckered skin exert an irresistible draw. Her eyes stray from one to the next: the straight scar on his lower arm; the circular blemish in his shoulder; the line that tracks around his side; a silvered patch on his chest.

'Dear God, Jack . . . what happened to you?'

'It doesn't matter what happened to me . . . what matters is they never stopped me.'

'How did you get that one?' She gestures to what she presumes is a bullet hole in his shoulder.

'Dunkirk.'

'And that one?' she asks, braving a step forward as she points to his arm.

'Shrapnel, Gazala, 'forty-two.'

'And that one?' she whispers, drifting closer. Her fingers brush the stitched line at his side.

'Primosole . . . 'forty-three.' His eyes bore into her, but she does not meet them. 'Each time I thought I'd drawn my last breath I thought of you, Gwen . . . and another breath would come.' He swallows hard. 'All I wanted was to see you. To come home. To have a chance, Gwen . . . the chance of having you love me . . .'

'And that one?' Her fingertips slowly trace the puckered patch on his chest; it rises and falls under her touch. She lifts her gaze. Their eyes lock.

'Don't, Gwen,' he whispers huskily. 'If you don't mean it, don't come any closer. I beg you.'

Gwen's hand drops, but her gaze remains. She takes a single step forward.

He pulls her to him, his lips finding hers with an urgency that mirrors her own. Her fingers curl around his shoulders before sliding across his back and tunnelling through his hair, drawing him ever closer – for her need, her desire is every bit as great as his.

She abruptly pulls away. His hands fall from her waist.

'Gwen I—'

'You cannot stay, Jack.'

The light fades from his eyes. 'I suppose now Gordon's no longer a threat you've no need of me . . .'

'It's not that – don't you see? I can't let you take the risk. Your coming back was never part of the plan, Jack. If you survived the war you were supposed to get as far away as you could . . . to be safe.' She does not want to let him go, not when she has just found him, discovered him in a way she never thought possible. But he has sacrificed so much for her, letting him go is the greatest kindness she can do for him now, regardless of what it might cost her. The time has come for him to safeguard himself, not her. 'What if they find you, Jack? What if the Helvedon police have already shared your details and right now detectives are on their way down from Newcastle to—'

'Gwen—'

'I can't let you risk everything for us, Jack. If anything happened to you, I would never forgive myself.'

'Why?'

'What?'

'Why do you care what happens to me?'

'Because . . .' She closes her eyes. The truth of it all finally dawns on her. 'Because I love you.'

He does not answer at once. She stands before him, her heart exposed, and yet she does not feel vulnerable. She feels only regret that it has taken her until now to truly know herself. It is knowledge that has come too late.

'Gwen . . . There is something I've been wanting to tell you, but somehow I could never find the right moment.' Jack cups her face and Gwen cannot stop herself from leaning into his palm. He smiles, his thumb gently caressing her cheek. The touch feels magical. 'Now is that moment . . .'

French coast, 6th June 1944

Jack stood at the ship's rail in the early morning light, contemplating what the new day would bring. He was just one of hundreds wearing full battledress crammed upon the deck of the troop carrier. The time had come. The churning sea was crowded with vessels – minesweepers, frigates, battleships and destroyers, ships of all shapes and sizes as far as the eye could see – all destined for the golden beaches of Normandy looming ominously before them.

Craning his neck he could just make out the plumes of smoke rising beyond the silver barrage balloons that hovered over the ships ahead. The men ducked as an aircraft screamed over them. The cry of 'One of ours, boys!' was met with a muted cheer and a collective sigh of relief.

A few soldiers crouched together playing cards, while others stared out to the horizon, green-gilled and pale, their bleached lips moving in silent prayer. The man next to him nudged Jack with his elbow. He offered an open cigarette packet. Jack shook his head.

'Might be your last chance of a fag for a while, mate.'

'I don't smoke.'

'Jesus. Take it from me – now's a good time to start.'

Ignoring him, Jack undid the button of his breast pocket and pulled out the photograph. Its glaze was creased and broken now, threads of white marring the image, but its shabby condition did not lessen the comfort it gave him. He drew his thumb over Gwen's smiling features.

'Won't be long now, sergeant.' The men around him shuffled aside to make room for the lieutenant to squeeze in beside him. 'We'll get Jerry on the run and see if we can't get you home, shall we? Back to that lovely young family of yours. Get us all bloody home, if we can,' he muttered, flicking open his cigarette case. 'We'll be loading onto the landing craft soon. I'll leave you to get the men ready.'

'Yes, sir.'

'Good luck, sergeant.'

'And you, sir.'

The lieutenant moved on, struggling past men huddled like sheep on market day. Jack studied the photograph for a final time, then tucked it back into his pocket.

They'd be better off with him gone.

'Make way . . . come on, let me through . . . make way . . .'

The familiar cadence of an accent from home did not attract his attention anymore. He checked his watch. Thunderous booms sounded in the distance. One of the neighbouring ships let loose with its big guns. Great flashes of light erupted from barrels immediately engulfed by billowing smoke. Some of the men pushed their way to the railing to get a better view. A shell exploded in the sea beside them. The eruption of water provoked shouts of alarm but Jack paid it little heed. His mind was on other things.

They'd be better off with him gone.

'Come on, you bastards, make way . . .'

A sailor was battling through the thronged soldiers. He ignored the ill-tempered swearing and coarse remarks that greeted him as he threaded himself through the crush.

'All right, man, take it easy,' Jack grumbled as the man pushed past him.

'Jesus! Jack? Jack Ellison as I live and breathe, is that really you?'

The sailor gripped his shoulders. Jack gaped in disbelief as he found himself looking into a face he had consigned to the past. He let out a roar of delight as they pulled each other into a sturdy embrace, with backslapping and good-natured cursing.

'Ben? What the hell are you doing here?'

'I had the good sense to join the navy – what's your excuse?' Their laughter appeared carefree, but both knew this unexpected reunion was a precious gift; neither might survive the coming onslaught.

There was little time to catch up. Above them, RAF Typhoons droned like hornets protecting a threatened nest. Tipping his head back, Jack watched them fly over and swore softly under his breath.

'Aye, it's going to be some party, all right,' Ben said. 'Have you had any news from home?'

Jack snorted. 'No. I left all that behind me when I ran.' He saw something flicker in Ben's expression. 'Why? What should I know?'

'Your mam, Jack,' Ben proceeded carefully. 'You've heard surely . . .'

His insides tightened. 'Heard what?'

'I'm sorry, lad. Your mam died.'

Jack exhaled through clenched teeth. He wanted to feel something, and he did: guilt that he didn't feel more. He experienced no blow to his gut, no sadness, no pain in his chest. He had closed his heart to his mother years before – her own behaviour had made certain of that. He saw her in his mind's eye, wedged into the corner of his sister's room, the bloody towel in her stained hands: 'A week of Jenny's wages she cost me.'

'How?' he asked at last, through curiosity more than anything else.

'Accident. She was drunk, they say . . . walked in front of a tram.'

'Aye . . . that's about right,' Jack muttered, remembering how she would stagger out of the pub blind drunk, loud and uncaring, without the wits to keep herself safe.

'I'm sorry.'

'So am I,' he said, though his voice revealed little emotion. 'But I don't feel any sorrow.'

'I always thought you'd come back, you know,' Ben said quietly.

'I couldn't risk it, you know that. I've spent every day of the past five years waiting for my punishment. Jerry's bullet or the hangman's noose. I tell you now, I'd rather take the bullet, die like a man.'

Confusion crawled across Ben's face, but it quickly gave way to shock. 'My God, you don't know, do you?'

'Know what?'

'About Mickey . . . Mickey Jones.' Seeing Jack's wary expression, Ben swore, the colour draining from his cheeks. 'Is that why you stayed away?'

'You know why I stayed away, Ben . . .'

'He's not dead, Jack!'

Ben's words rang in Jack's ears. He began to sway, but it was not the undulating motion of the ship that sent him reeling. Ben grabbed his arm.

'My God, Jack . . . Mickey Jones is parading around Newcastle saying you did him a favour. He's all right, like, but the effects of his injuries were enough to have him deemed medically unfit for service. You gave him a pass out of all this and my God he's grateful for it. He's got involved in the black market at home – he's making a packet and acting like the smuggest man in Tyneside right now.'

'He's not dead . . .' Somehow the words escaped from the fuddle of Jack's thoughts and made it to his lips. 'He's not dead?' As the magnitude of it all finally hit him, he seized Ben's arms. 'Are you telling me that I didn't kill him?'

'No, Jack . . . Mickey was in a right bad way when they found him, mind. Spent weeks in hospital, it was touch and go . . . but he pulled through.'

'And the coppers . . .'

'Were looking for you, aye, but that was years ago, man. You'd disappeared, and then what with Mickey doing so well out of it, I doubt he'd be in a mind to press charges now. He'd be too afraid of exposing his own dodgy operation to scrutiny. He won't risk it.'

'I didn't kill him.' The revelation left Jack dazed. The photograph in his breast pocket seemed to burn through to his chest. 'I've done nothing wrong.'

Ben held Jack's shoulders. 'No, man, you've done nothing wrong at all.' He gave him a shake, then released him. 'Jack, I've got to go . . . good luck out there.'

'Aye . . . you be careful, Ben.'

'Aye, you too, you soppy sod. And when this is over, you owe me a pint.'

They clapped each other's backs, the gesture awkward with affection, and then Ben was gone, swallowed by the crowded soldiers. Jack almost convinced himself their reunion was nothing more than a figment of his wishful imagination, but then he spotted Ben's retreating figure clambering up a metal ladder to the top deck, and he knew it was not.

'Sergeant Ellison! Ready the men!'

His lieutenant's hollered order brought him back to the present. He pushed away thoughts of home and in a heartbeat was a platoon sergeant once more. He gathered his men at the side of the ship. Waves surged against the hull, rocking it back and forth. From the beaches came the rapid rat-tat-tat of gunfire, punctuated by the deafening blasts of exploding mines. The ships around them retorted with the shuddering booms of their guns.

Jack yelled himself hoarse as he urged the men over the metal railings and onto the scramble net cloaking the ship's side. He followed them down, his boots slipping on the wet rope as he descended towards the landing craft waiting on the tossing sea. When he was close enough he leapt onto the vessel's deck and jostled for space with the men stood shoulder to shoulder around him. The landing craft powered forward, lifting and pitching as it crashed through the waves that reared up to greet it.

'Jesus.'

He could see the beaches clearly now. Sand jetted skywards in volcanic eruptions. German machine guns raked the shallows. Men stumbled and fell. Some rose to press on past the Czech hedgehogs scattered across the shore like giant jacks; some screamed for medics and mothers, while others fell forever silent. And through it all, tanks rolled off their transporters and rumbled forwards through the surf, steadily advancing towards the carnage. To Jack, the sight before him was the definition of chaos; it was the embodiment of hell.

The landing craft shuddered to a stop, but the waves lapping the beach seemed too distant to Jack's eye.

'This isn't the bloody beach!' his lieutenant bellowed.

'It is! We've hit land,' the coxswain yelled back, wild-eyed and afraid.

'You've hit a fucking sand bank! We can't get off here, we're too far out!'

'I can't get her any closer, sir! Lower the ramp,' the coxswain ordered. 'Get your men off now!'

The lieutenant cursed, slamming his hand against the vessel's armoured wall. Jack shared his officer's frustration, but they both knew it was pointless to argue. Their voices collided as they shouted orders to the men. As the ramp cranked down, the *whole craft slewed to the side, battered by the rough sea. The young private next to Jack doubled over, his vomit splattering the deck.*

Ashen-faced, tin hats low on their brows, the men spilled down the ramp, burdened by their bulky packs, their rifles clasped before them. Jack watched in horror as they disappeared under the waves.

'Too fucking far out!' his lieutenant raged.

A few of the soldiers burst through the surface, spluttering, their arms flailing. Others did not.

'God help us,' the lieutenant muttered.

They exchanged a sideways glance, then together they charged down the steel ramp as bullets zipped around them. They plunged off the end.

Jack gasped as freezing water enveloped him. He dragged in a final lungful of air as the waves closed over his head.

His leaden pack dragged him downwards. His rifle dropped from his hands as he fought against the sea that had swallowed him whole. Through the grey gloom, bullets darted past him like lightning bolts, while blood feathered the water. Bodies drifted by, limbs suspended, their bleached faces inhabited by vacant eyes. His lungs were ready to explode. Jack knew he was going to die. Stars shimmered in his vision as air bubbled from his nostrils. He could not last much longer. He closed his eyes against the horror around him.

Mickey Jones is not dead.

His eyes flew open.

Gwen.

His numb fingers battled with the straps of his pack and, as soon as he had freed himself of its deadly load, his legs struck out. Kicking wildly, he propelled himself upwards, fighting the hungry pull of the sea with gathering might. He burst through the surface, deafened to the rat-tat-tat of gunfire, the boom of shells and the harrowing screams of men, by the memory of Gwen's voice.

As he drew air into his strained lungs, his heart powered precious life through his sodden veins. A wave crashed over him, but he forced himself through it, wheezing and thrashing, then he rolled onto his front and began to swim towards the tumult, knocking aside the bodies that drifted into his path. His feet finally hit shingle; the frothing waves shoved him up the beach.

Free of the sea, he crawled on his stomach to the bloodied body of a lifeless soldier, as German machine gun bullets kicked up the sand around him. He wrestled the rifle from the dead man's hands then pushed himself to his feet. He had to get off the beach, he had to escape the killing zone. He began to run, dropping to his knee to return fire.

His mind was sharp, his focus unwavering.

Mickey Jones is alive.

He would not accept death. Not now – not when he had been granted the chance to win Gwen's love.

As he made his determined charge, he knew this would not be his greatest battle. His greatest battle awaited him at home. It was a battle he was determined to fight. It was a battle he had to win.

He would break his promise

He would return.

ACKNOWLEDGEMENTS

As ever, I offer huge thanks to my agent David Headley and to my editor Kate Mills, who showed remarkable faith in me when I first provided them with very sketchy details of this project and who have shown great belief in it ever since. Thank you also to my wonderful HQ team – Becky Heeley, Joe Thomas, Melissa Kelly, Dawn Burnett and Janet Aspey – for continuing to take such good care of me, and to the sterling Emily Glenister at DHH Literary Agency.

There are so many people who have worked tirelessly behind the scenes to bring this book to fruition and who have paved its way into bookshops and the hands of readers everywhere, and I offer each and every one of them my heartfelt gratitude. I also want to offer my sincere thanks to the reviewers, book-bloggers and booksellers who take the time to share their book love. I, for one, appreciate all you do and am enormously grateful for your support.

There are several people who deserve individual thanks for the help they have given me with *The Return*.

Firstly, my dear dad, Michael Frank, a farmer born and bred, who has patiently shared with me his knowledge of farming and his personal reminiscences of driving Fordson tractors and working reaper-binders, potato riddles and threshing machines. His help has been invaluable, and any mistakes that remain are very much my own.

Thank you also to Mike Ellison for sharing with me his Newcastle knowledge – and his name! He has helped me with various regional predicaments, and I claim dramatic licence for any inaccuracies that now exist.

I am also indebted to Carolyn O'Brien, who directed me to information on the historical legalities of paternity which proved both crucial and inspirational.

My thanks also go out to the Robinson family at Strickley for their wonderful Twitter account @1940atStrickley, which offers daily tweets of date-appropriate entries taken from the family's farming diaries written in the 1930s and 1940s. This resource proved most useful when I was deciding what tasks to give my characters, and it also inspired the scene where Gwen re-reads her father's diaries. If you have an interest in country life and the farming practices of bygone days, this charming account is well worth following.

I was very lucky to have some brilliant first readers – my thanks to Rebecca Netley, Kate Galley, Corin Burnside and Anita Matthews. As always, a special shout out to the fabulous (and totally bananas) #VWG, surely the most supportive writing group there is and certainly the best writing buddies a girl could ever hope to have.

I must save a special thanks for my friends and family – especially for Rod, Isabel, Molly and Jack – for all the love and support they have given me, without which I would be lost. And, of course, to my Welsh Springer Bonnie, who provides no help whatsoever with the plot problems I share with her at great length on our dog walks, though the walks themselves are exceedingly useful for unravelling those tangled plot points.

And last but by no means least, I must thank *you* for choosing to read *The Return*. I really hope you enjoyed it and, if you did, I would be beyond grateful if you would consider taking a moment to leave a brief review somewhere – they really do make the world of difference to us authors. And if you are on social media, I can be found on Twitter at @Ajes74 and on Instagram @anitafrankauthor – I'd love it if you popped by to say hello.

Because after all, where would I be without you?